Dedicated in memory of my son-in-law Rob Waibel
He was my Hero and Ironman in many of my stories
September 14, 1965 - March 26, 2020

I0650277

CALL of the COLUMBIA
River of Redemption

Brian D. Ratty

Sunset Lake
Publishing

Brian D. Ratty

Sunset Lake Publishing LLC
89637 Lakeside Ct.
Warrenton, OR 97146
503.717.1125

First Edition published in September 2020 - final edits Jan. 2021
ISBN-13: 978-0-578-71213-0 (Sunset Lake Publishing LLC)
Printed in the USA

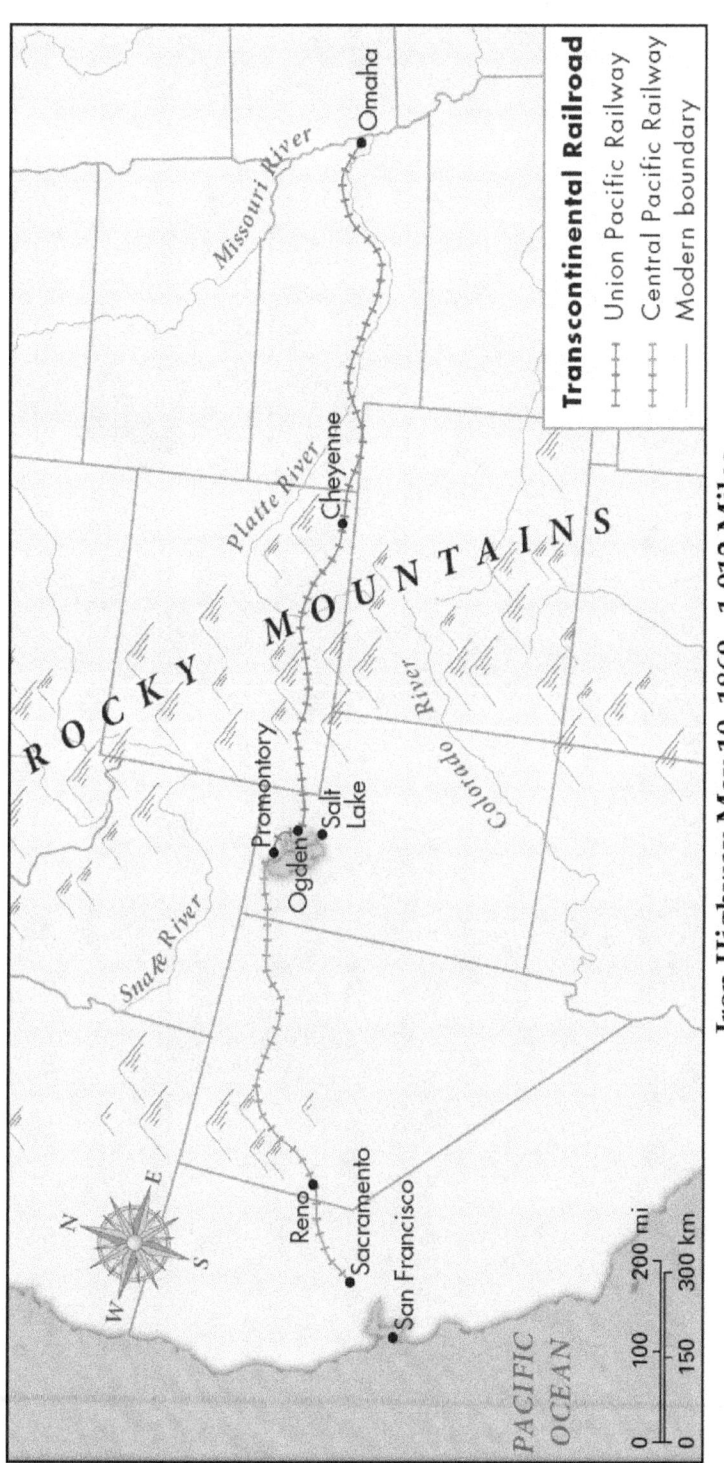

Iron Highway May 10, 1869 - 1,912 Miles

Brian D. Ratty

Prologue

There is a very special place where I like to walk. It is a narrow, windswept spit of beach with the mighty Columbia River on one side and the roaring Pacific Ocean on the other. It's a strip of land where seagulls fly backwards, the sun seldom shines, and the salt air is filled with the thundering sounds of the sea. Today, this place is called Point Adams, or the South Jetty, where the Columbia and the Pacific become one. It is here, if the time and tides are right, that I can hear the whispering sands in the shallows. This rhythm of the waves and wind tell a story of long ago in the far North Country where, in the summer, the sun never sets and in the winter, darkness prevails. It was here, eons ago, that the first people from Beringia arrived from their arduous land-and-maritime migration to the New World. Twenty thousand years ago this land, like most of Siberia and Northern China, was not yet glaciated and had a temperate climate. The landscape was mostly steppe grassland with rocky rugged shores and minimal sea levels. These ever-changing conditions also revealed numerous land bridges that stretched for hundreds of miles into the North American Continent, on either side of the Pacific. During the glacial epoch these land bridges were the migration routes east for people, animals, and plants from Beringia.

These Argonauts came from different regions, traveling with family, clans and tribes, in large groups and small. Some followed the animals across the bridges, while others just followed their instincts. All were seeking a better way of life. Each of these explorers had their own reasons for undertaking such a treacherous journey, their own hierarchy, culture and beliefs. Some were war-like, others peaceable. Some worshiped the moon, others fish.

None developed a written language, but over the generations some learned artisan traits such as canoe making, wood carving, weaving, pottery and more. Without the written word, their tribal history was verbal, recounted thousands of times around the campfires. These Beringians were a hardy bunch, as different from one another as the evening stars. Over the years, they developed strange names, such as Sioux, Cheyenne, Pawnee, Chinook, and many, many more. Their journey across these mostly frozen land bridges took years of travel, and many died along the way. But it is human nature to seek new places, just as it is God's way to provide for all of his creatures, two-legged and four, fish or fowl.

When these Indians finally arrived, some planted roots and built villages, while others turned south and continued their march of migration. Many generations later, descendants from the people of Beringia roamed the lands of America from coast to coast, and north to south. These were the true Native Americans, our forefathers in spirit, curiosity and determination. But all of that changed, like footprints in wet sand, when the steps of their moccasins were replaced with the boot prints of foreign sailors. Once that happened, the people of Beringia were doomed.

Within a few generations of their first contact with the white man, nearly all of the Indians were either tamed or dead. Many of the warlike tribes were hated and feared: as brutal as a bear. Those people would die by the white man's hand, but the vast majority of them would perish not from malice and violence, but from the many unforeseen European diseases.

Today, the descendants of the people of Beringia are mostly admired and respected. Their culture has reached full maturation, with many Americans having Indian blood flowing within their own DNA. Therefore, when I walk Point Adams and watch my footprints disappear, I remind myself of the Clatsop Indian village that once thrived on this very shore only 150 years ago. Our *we* and *our* culture destine for the same fate?

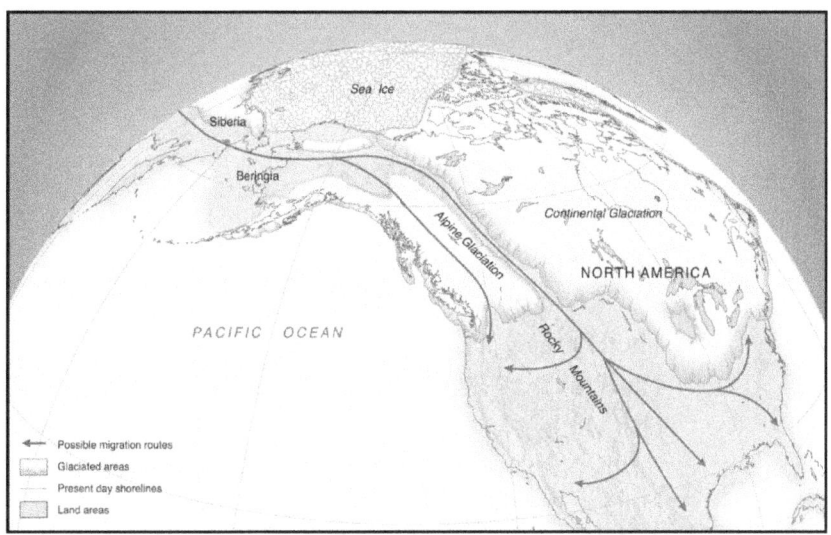

Beringia is defined today as the land and maritime area bound on the west by the Lena River in Russia; on the east by the Mackenzie River in Canada; on the north by 72 degrees north latitude in the Chukchi Sea; and on the south by the tip of the Kamchatka Peninsula.

Call of the COLUMBIA

Swept on forever, to be lost in the stormy sea,
I can still hear this roaring river calling out to me
Roll on mighty river, roll on through the day
Neither winds nor rain will sway my way

Above the swirling winds, I can hear your siren song
welcoming me to where I now belong
Roll on, mighty river, roll on, with all your awesome power
I've built my home where the timbers still tower

I'm grateful to those who were here long ago
They were the keepers of this place that I have come to know
Roar on, mighty river roar on, you cannot frighten me
for I truly know how powerful you can be
Brian Ratty

CONTENTS

Interview 1: *Searchers*

Astoria, Oregon - October 1899

With a loud caw, a seagull came to rest on the railing of the widows walk of a stately hilltop home. The weather was gray and windy, with light rain and a blanket of gloom shrouding the town and river below. The gull puffed up its breast and waddled around with wings outstretched, shaking himself from the dampness.

With glass rattling from the wind, the door of the beacon opened, and a woman with a long dark coat pulled up over her head rushed out with binoculars in hand. As she put the glasses to her eyes, she pulled the coat farther over the lens. Slowly, she scanned the sprawling town and moorage below, and then turned her view downriver, trying to find any approaching ships. To her chagrin, she saw none.

"Missy, what are you doing out there?" a matronly lady shouted, filling the open doorway.

"I'll be right in," Missy called back, her binoculars still pointed downriver. "I can't see to Ilwaco, this morning. The bar is lost in the fog, without a ship in sight."

"The telegram wasn't sure which day he would arrive," the older lady answered. "Please get in out of the rain."

Missy nodded reluctantly and turned for the open door, just as the seagull cawed another mocking call. She stopped in her tracks and shooed the bird away with the wave of her hand. "Go away," she yelled. "You are bad luck today."

Once inside the lady removed Missy's wet coat, revealing a slim figure wearing an elegant pink morning dress. And then shook the rain off the coat and hung it on a hook next to the closed glass doors. Norma, the older lady and housekeeper, was dressed in a black skirt with a white ruffled blouse. She had been in service to Missy and her family for almost twenty years. But she was much more than just the housekeeper; she was a confidant and a dear friend. Norma loved her mistress and family, warts, secrets and all.

"Stand over by the fire," she fussed fondly. "I'll help you fix your hair. It's a mess."

The observation room, with its cast-iron coal stove, was one of the warmest retreats in the three-story, five-bedroom, wood-framed house. The walls were covered with teak paneling and oak shelves that held hundreds of volumes of books. The space was also filled with nautical knickknacks, numerous paintings, and a large ornate reading desk where Missy spent most of her time.

Standing by the stove, with a small mirror in hand, Missy watched as Norma used a brush to restyle her blown hair. Norma was a distinguished-looking matron with graying hair, a friendly face, and eyes that twinkled when she smiled.

"Don't keep fretting about the Major," Norma counseled. "He'll be here when he's here."

Missy frowned. "I know you're right. But it seems like I'm always waiting for him."

Norma soon finished with the younger woman's pompadour and turned Missy around for one final look-over. For a woman in her forties, Missy still looked beautiful with her wavy auburn hair, flawless honey complexion, and deep-set green eyes. Mrs. Mitchel did not look like the widow she was.

With a perfunctory knock on one of the outer doors, an older gentleman in a butler's uniform walked in. "Sorry to disturb you, ma'am. The reporters are here. I've put them in the parlor."

"What are they like?" Missy asked, curiosity on her face.

"That's hard to say, ma'am," the butler answered. "One is older and pudgy, the other young and skinny. They seem very taken with the house."

"Are you sure you want to tell strangers your secrets?" Norma asked.

Missy nodded soberly. "Yes. With the Major's return, the accusations, lies, and half-truths will start flying again. I have to set the record straight. I owe that to him."

With a white wool shawl draped around the shoulders of her morning dress, Missy slid the double wood doors to the parlor open and walked into the room. The two reporters sat next to each other on the Queen Anne couch, in front of the ornate wood-burning fireplace. The older, pug-faced reporter stood as she came into the room. He was a large man with graying temples and wire-framed glasses, dressed in a wrinkled seersucker suit. In hand, he had a spiral notebook, which he waved at the other man as a signal for him to stand, which he belatedly did. Wide-eyed, and with his mouth open, the second reporter seemed as young as a new fawn. He wore an oversized brown frockcoat, with baggy pants and white button-up spats. He was skinny as a rail and as fresh as wet paint.

"Good morning, gentlemen. Folks call me Mrs. Mitchel or Missy. Sorry to keep you waiting," she said warmly.

The men introduced themselves. The older man was Hank Hawks, a seasoned reporter, representing the Oregonian paper out of Portland. The younger man was Jimmy Adams from the Morning Astorians Newspaper.

Missy invited them to take their seats again as she came to rest in a stuffed armchair across from them. "Thank you for coming out on this cold, wet, blustery day."

Jimmy glanced around the room. "You have a beautiful home, ma'am. What style would you call it?"

Missy smiled at him. "Victorian. It seems to be all the rage, these days."

"There are some who say you are the richest woman in Oregon," Jimmy continued. "Is that true?"

Missy frowned. "I came to the river with nothing and will leave it the same way. Money has never been important to me, so I don't count it and I don't care."

"Some say you're the original daughter of the Columbia, while other people say you made your money swindling folks out of their timberland Government Grants," Hank ventured, with a raised eyebrow. "Is that true?"

"People say a lot of things," Missy answered. "Not all of it is true."

In hope of changing the subject, she rang a small silver bell on the table next her. Almost instantly, Norma slid open the parlor door. "Yes, ma'am?"

"How about some coffee for our guests?"

"Yes, ma'am," she answered, and closed the door.

Hank's smile was bemused. "I don't get it. For years I've tried to interview you, and you've always turned me away. Why now and why here?"

Missy adjusted her shawl and then said nonchalantly, "The Northwest Brigade is coming home today or tomorrow, and I want to set the record straight."

The fact that the Militia was coming home was big news. Hank brightened visibly.

"How do you know that?" Jimmy asked.

"Colonel Roosevelt sent me a telegram from San Francisco, last week. A troopship is on its way here with the men. They will drop off the locals in Astoria and then sail for Portland, where trains will be waiting to take the men home all across the northwest. The Spanish–American War is over."

Both men were busy writing when Norma returned to the room with the silver service. She put the tray on the coffee table in front of the reporters and poured three cups of coffee. She winked at Missy as she departed the room.

Hank looked at Missy over the top of his wire-rimmed spectacles. "Is the Major coming home with his men?"

"Yes. That's why I invited you here, this morning. It's time to stop all the gossip with the truth."

Hank asked boldly, "If that's so, is it true the Major was wanted for murder when he first came to Astoria?"

"Yes," she replied. "But I can explain all that."

"You have my attention, ma'am," Hank answered sternly. "Tell me your story."

Missy picked up the white porcelain cup of coffee and took a sip. "That's the difficulty. I don't know where to start."

"From the beginning," the older reporter said pencil in hand.

Astoria Oregon 1870

Chapter 1 – Rock Springs

The Hunt
March 1869

The shrill cry of a lone red tailed hawk broke the silence of the afternoon. Circling high in the bitter cold winds, blowing off the distant snowcapped mountains, this hunter was just another predator living on the scraps in the high prairie of southwestern Wyoming. Below dark threatening clouds, his flight across a rocky wasteland was littered with bleached buffalo bones, sagebrush and scrub grass. This wilderness was on the razors edge of civilization, where only rattlesnakes, jack rabbits and kangaroo rats could survive. The land offered no mercy and provided no quarter. All that ventured into it, did so at their own peril. As the hawk soared even higher, he cried out a warning of the approaching cavalcade of invaders that would disturb his hunt.

Through the dusty whirlwinds appeared a squad of cavalrymen, riding single file, across the barren landscape, heading due west. Their march was straight and their gait a slow trot. Above the sounds of the whirling winds, only hooves against the rocky terrain, rubbing saddle leather and the whicker of the horses could be heard. In the wispy dust cloud eleven riders could be seen. Leading the troop was a black-eye patched officer wearing a forage cap with Captain's bars, soiled blue overcoat, white scarf, and yellow striped blue canvas trousers with knee-high boots. The rider sat squarely on his mount watching the hawk with a mariners spyglass pressed to his one good eye. He was young, lean and clean shaven, riding a tall ten-year-old chestnut gelding. Captain Gus Savage was in command of the First Platoon of the 7th Regiment, Kansas Volunteer Cavalry. He was hated and feared by the local Indians, who called him 'Night-eye,' but well respected by his troop. The Captain was a decorated veteran of the Civil War and had lost his left eye and two fingers of his right hand at the Battle of Honey Springs '63. He had been mustered out of the

Cavalry at wars end, but called back to duty in '67. He knew his business and for the last two days that business had been searching out a band of Cheyenne Indians for revenge and retribution.

"Lightfoot is coming in," the Sergeant behind the Captain shouted.

Gus twisted the telescope from the hawk to the horizon in front of him. There, about a mile out, he saw his Scout Lightfoot maneuvering down a rocky ridge filled with tall boulders and scrub. His approach was not rushed.

"He's not in a hurry," the Captain replied. "I hope he found their camp. It will be dark soon and we need to get out of this damn wind."

"Yes sir," the Sergeant replied. At thirty five years old, Sergeant Nathan Pike was the 'old-man' of the troop. He was stocky, with a large head, a broad open face, and a bull neck. He and his mount, a gray sorrel, were covered with trail dust and like the rest of the squad Nathan had a yellow bandana over his face. He too was a veteran of the Civil War and had volunteered for this duty.

Behind the Sergeant was Corporal Nelson. He rode as guidon for the troop, flying a small flag on a lance denoting the first platoon as the 7th Regiment. Nelson was a tall, lean, trooper of twenty who had earned his Corporal stripes, during the last two years, the hard way…fighting Indians. He had sharp green eyes and keen instincts when it came to doing battle with the enemy. His only weakness was his Christian humanity when it came time to kill them.

Behind the Corporal were eight other riders, ranging in age from nineteen to twenty three, all volunteers for this hard and lonely life. Back in camp, some forty miles away, were thirty more troopers just like them. Why all these young men had joined the Regiment was a mystery to most. Many of them had missed the Civil War and were now seeking the lost glory of battle or maybe just the notion of ridding the red menace from the land. All were getting bonus pay, which made the duty more palatable. Some of the soldiers were slackers, others ruffians, and some plow-boys looking to escape the farm. Each trooper had his own story and had spent the last two years surviving on the high desert flatlands escorting and protecting the Union Pacific Railroad workers as they were building the Transcontinental Railroad across the Great Plains.

Captain Savage slowed the march of his troop to a walk as Lightfoot approached. His Scout was a breed; a Comanchero. Half Mexican and half Kiowa Indian, with the Christian name of Clint Roe. He was dressed in fringed buckskin trousers, a tattered red wool serape and a gray confederate forage cap. Around his waist he wore a black sash and his gun belt with a large ornate silver belt buckle. His mount was a tall, fast golden appaloosa with a black mane and a white spotted rump.

Lightfoot was a remarkable Scout in many ways. Although he was mostly illiterate, he could read almost any map and track almost anything, across almost any terrain. He also had a knack with all the different tribal tongues and could communicate with them using Indian words and sign. His only weaknesses was his fiery temper, whiskey and his lust for the ladies; red, black or white.

In a cloud of dust his Scout pulled his horse to a stop, "Whoa Loco."

The scout had a bronzed pocked face with deep set brown eyes and a dark shaggy mustache.

"Did you find them?" the Captain asked.

"Yes sir," he replied brushing off the dust from his serape. "They are camped about three miles from here, in a shallow ravine. I counted five teepees. They look to be a small bunch with no more than a few braves and their squaws."

"Did you see our horses?"

"Yes, they are tethered just downstream from camp."

"Good, you lead the way. We need to get out of this weather before dark," his Captain replied.

Lightfoot nodded and turned Loco due west and dug-in his heels. Captain Savage twisted to his Sergeant, "Let's pick up the pace Nathan or that appaloosa will leave us behind."

Two nights before, a band of Cheyenne had raided the railroad livestock pens, killing, scalping and mutilating three wranglers. In the process they rustled nine horses and two mules. It had been the typical gruesome raid by the red menace and was now the business at hand. The railroad demanded the return of their horses and retribution for the deaths of their employees. The Union Pacific Railroad owned the right-a-way for almost a hundred miles on each side of their tracks and considered all Indians trespassers. This was one of the many duties that Captain Savage and his first platoon had been carrying out for the last two years. They were both the protectors and the terminators.

As the squad approached the gully they could see smoke from a campfire drifting up into the swirling winds of the darkening sky. Lightfoot had already arrived and dismounted. He silently motioned to where the troop and their mounts should take shelter out of the wind. Captain Savage and his Sergeant dismounted and joined their scout moving up a small hill with a good view down on the Indian encampment. In the fading light, they removed their hats and crawled out to a rocky perch looking down on their prey.

The ravine was shallow with a creek flowing from the north and meandering around a large lazy bend before continuing west. On the opposite shore there were some small groves of cottonwood trees. On the waters-edge of the large bend in the creek the Indians had set-up their five buffalo hide teepees. Behind the camp was a few scrub trees with a thick underbrush.

"The horses are just downstream behind the trees," Lightfoot whispered.

Gus put the spyglass to his eye and Nathan did the same with his field glasses. They took a few moments, carefully studying the terrain. Both could see horses tethered behind the trees, while in front of the teepees they watched two squaws and a young girl butchering and cooking one of the stolen mules. Squatting just behind the cooks was an old man with four braves drinking from a jug of whiskey. The men were so close to the camp they could smell their cooking and hear the faint chatter of the Indians. Just then, an old squaw appeared from one of the teepees with a young boy and started screaming at the men drinking. She seemed as mad as a hornet.

Gus turned his glass back up stream and whispered to Nathan, "See that swell in the gully about four hundred yards up? You can get the troop across the creek there. Have them bed down in the cover of the cottonwoods. Cold camp, stay quiet and no smoking.

I'll take Lightfoot and Corporal Nelson downstream and the do the same. Tomorrow at first light, we'll stampede the livestock. When you hear our ruckus, charge the troop in from upstream while we close the backdoor to anyone trying to escape."

Nathan nodded his understanding and the three men crawled back down the hill to their waiting troop. The Captain convoked his men and explained his plan again. He emphasized the dangers of setting-up a cross fire, "Make sure you have a target before you pull the trigger. I only want to see dead Indians." The trooper's only comment was grumbling about another cold camp.

Savage finished up with his standard spiel, "Remember our skirmish decree; everything of value belongs to the UP. No exceptions! And no scalping the dead or looting the village."

With an earnest face one trooper asked, "What about arrow-heads Captain?"

Savage frowned shaking his head, "Who the hell would want to save those damn things?"

"I send them to my mother sir. She thinks I'm ferocious Indian fighter."

The troop snickered. "Alright," Gus answered, "but nothing else."

With snowflakes in the air, Lightfoot found a game trail about a hundred yards behind the Indian encampment. The three men walked their mounts down to the bottom of the ravine and quietly crossed the arroyos. It was twilight by the time the men found some proper cover in a thicket. With the snow increasing the men hobbled the horses and removed their gear to their cold camp. Dropping the saddles on the ground they rolled out their rain slickers and blankets. At dusk, Gus sent Corporal Nelson out to stand the first night watch. He and Lightfoot then sat back on their saddles and whispered to each other in the coming darkness.

"I hope this damn snow stops," Gus said chewing some buffalo jerky. "I'm getting tired of living on the crumbs of this god-forsaken place. I need a soft bed and long rest."

Lightfoot searched his saddlebags and uncorked a bottle of whiskey, "So what are you going to do after the link-up with Southern Pacific?"

"Don't know. I'm thinking about the goldfields of California.

A man could get rich out there."

"Yea, sure" Lightfoot answered. "You're still thinking about going after Colonel McKay." This had become a nightly conversation in the last few years and Lightfoot wanted to change the subject. So he continued, "I sure hope Mrs. Orr and her girls have moved up to the railhead when we get back. I need a soft bed as well."

Gus glared at him in the fading light, "Clint, one of these days you're going to get a bad case of crotch rot from one of those girls. And you won't like it."

Lightfoot chuckled, "Remember back in Missouri Gus? I had you all setup with a real beauty. And you walked away... guess you just don't like girls?"

No trooper or scout in the Calvary would ever talk to Captain Gus Savage in such familiar terms, it just wasn't done. But with Lightfoot, when they were alone, it was different. They were personal friends. Gus had even wrangled him the job as Chief Scout for the railroad. They had met after the war, when Gus had gone looking for answers about a raiding party of Quantrill's Bushwhackers that had raided his home in Lawrence Kansas in August of '63. The rebel Colonel McKay was in command of these Confederate partisans that had killed his folks and burnt down the family farm. Over their graves, Gus had sworn retribution and had traveled to Missouri in search of the Colonel. He planned to kill the bastard on sight.

"Have a snort," Clint said handing the bottle to Gus. "It will take the chill off."

Savage had met Clint Roe in a bar in Springfield, where Gus had gone to look up some war records. They hit it off right away, two veterans arguing about the war from two different points of view. Clint had ridden with Quantrill, but not on any of the Kansas raids. His job had been organizing the Indians against the Union, which he had done very well. But he had friends who had been on the Kansas forays and he introduced them to Gus. The gray-coats had vivid memories of the raids and remembered all the commanders. The leader of the bunch that had killed Gus's family was a Colonel William McKay. He was from Alabama with a thick southern accent, red hair, about thirty years old, and with a jagged ruby scar over his right eye. He was remembered as one of the most brutal commanders to ride with Quantrill. After the war, one of the gray-coats recalled hearing that McKay, and a few of his men, had lit-out for the California goldfields.

The Captain took a drink of whiskey. He was indebted to Lightfoot for helping him find out about McKay. He still planned to kill the Colonel, if their trails ever crossed.

Gus handed back the bottle, "That girl in Missouri was ugly as sin and I don't have any proclivities for working girls."

"*Proclivities*, what kind of six-bit word is that?"

"It means desire. She just wasn't right for me,"

Lightfoot grinned and took a swig of whiskey, "I'll remember that."

Gus pulled up a blanket and rested back on his saddle. "I'll take the late watch, wake me up at two."

At first light the next day, under clear blue skies and with the snow threat melted, Gus rousted his compadres with a nudge from his boot while saying, "It's time to kill some Indians boys."

After saddling up, the three men quietly walked their horses to where the Cheyenne herd was tethered. There was no guard.

Whispering to Corporal Nelson he said, "After we stampede the nags you run with them so they don't scatter." Turning to Lightfoot he continued, "You take the last teepee on the right and I'll take the last on the left. Load and lock, let's mount up."

Each rider was armed with a Spencer repeating carbine and a Colt pistol, while Captain Savage had a new lever action Winchester rifle, Remington revolver and a knife with a quick release sheath on his gun belt. Because of the loss of his last two fingers on his right hand, Gus would cradle his rifle with his left hand, while cocking the lever and firing the weapon with the stump of his hand and the three fingers that remained. It was an awkward motion, but it worked for him.

With the morning sun spilling over the eastern horizon, Lightfoot bent down and cut the rope tethering the livestock while the Captain and the Corporal started yelling and firing their guns into the air. In a blink of the eye the morning quiet was broken with yapping dogs, thundering hooves and gunfire from the troop charging in from upstream. With a loud roar the livestock started running with Corporal Nelson right behind. Gus and Lightfoot turned their mounts and came galloping into the Indian camp from the rear. With the wind in his face, Gus noticed the gray-haired warrior stumbling out of his teepee flap with a gun in his hands. Savage shot him in the chest, which blossomed crimson red and he fell back half in and out of the lodge. From inside the tent the old squaw rushed to him. Savage shot her as well and she fell on top of the old brave. Next he turned his rifle on a barking dog and a wounded squaw.

The skirmish lasted only a few minutes and then the troop linked up. When the dust settled, the camp looked like a tornado had blown through. Three of the teepees had toppled over, the soot of the cook fire filled the air with Indian bodies and dog carcasses sprawled all about the sandbar. The Plains Indians were on their heels and this small apocalypse of death and destruction was all too common a landscape for Captain Gus Savage and his troopers.

Gus pulled up his horse Buck in a cloud of dust and dismounted with his rifle still in hand. Sergeant Pike stopped his gray sorrel as well, but stayed in the saddle.

"Anyone get away Nathan?" Gus asked looking up at him.

"I don't think so sir," he replied.

Lightfoot overheard his answer and pulled up his appaloosa next to them. "I saw a squaw and the young boy run across the stream and scurry up the other side of the ravine. Do you want me to go after them sir?"

Gus thought a moment then shook his head, "No, let them tell their story around the Cheyenne council fires. Maybe they'll mend their ways. Sound the recall Sergeant."

With the bugle blowing the troop gathered around their Captain atop their horses. As the horn continued blasting, Sergeant Pike turned to the bugler and shouted, "Stop that damn racket or I'll put that horn up your ass. Everyone is accounted for."

The young bugler stopped blowing with a sheepish look. The troopers snickered at him.

"Anyone hurt?" Captain Savage asked his men.

"Only the dead Indians," one trooper shouted back with a big smile on his face.

Gus nodded, "Good job men. Now let's clean up. Sergeant, send a couple of troopers to help Corporal Nelson with the herd. The rest of you, search the camp for anything of value, build a travois for the loot and layout the dead bodies for the count. I want to be out of this gully within the hour."

As the men went to work, Gus walked over to where he had shot the two old Indians. Their bodies were still sprawled half-out of their lodge. He was curious about the pistol the old man still held in his hand. It was an old flintlock, not even primed. He couldn't have fired even one shot. The fool had died for nothing. Then he noticed the look on both their faces. Their dead eyes were open as if they were looking at each other. The old squaw had one of her bloody hands grasping hold of one of the old man's hands. It was like they were content to have died together. The sight of the old couple reminded Gus of what his parents must have looked like when they had been killed by Colonel McKay. They too had died together and very much in love. Was Gus like that bastard McKay, just another butcher? Had he become only a killing machine with no feelings or emotions? "God no!" he mumbled to himself as he turned and walked back to his mount.

The Prey

"Captain... Captain," Lightfoot yelled from the inside of the only other teepee still standing. "You need to see this."

When Gus walked through the open lodge flap he found Clint holding onto the young Indian girl they had seen the day before. She was short, skinny and had greasy black hair. She looked to be nine or ten years old and was squirming in a blood stained buckskin frock. Around her waist was a beaded belt with an empty knife sheath. She didn't say a word while fighting off Lightfoot's powerful grasp.

"She's a damn hellcat," Clint blurted. "I found her under some buffalo robes and she came at me with her knife. I damn near shot her until I saw her eyes." He twisted her head towards the Captain with one hand while holding her wrists with the other. "Take a look at them."

"Has she said anything?" Gus asked approaching them.

"No, I tried Cheyenne and English with no response. She could be deaf and dumb."

The Captain looked at her frightened eyes. Clint was right, they weren't brown... they were green. Then he lifted up the front of her frock showing her legs. They were creamy white and scared with red welts.

"What's with all those scars?"

Lightfoot shook his head sadly, "More than likely from repeated beating from the other squaws. She is a white he'eo'o as the Cheyenne's would say. And white captive girls are beat into submission. It's a brutal tradition."

"How did they get her to look so much like an Indian?"

"It's an old Comanche trick, they rub her with buffalo fat and fire soot and do the same to her hair. From a distance she looks just like a damn Indian."

Gus touched her grimy face…she flinched. "Why all the bother?"

"White captive girls are highly prized for the young bucks of the tribe. They don't want anyone to steal them back until after the braves can spoil them."

"Spoil them in which way…raping them?"

"Ya, but this one is too young even for the amusement of a Cheyenne warrior. But she's already been spoiled in the Indian way of life, survival and struggle. She'll never fit-in again in white society."

Gus looked around inside the teepee; it was littered with buffalo robes, cooking utensils and raw meat hanging from the lodge poles. "What *is* that stink?"

"It's the buffalo fat on the girl."

"We should throw her in the stream."

Lightfoot grinned, "It will take a lot more than water to get this one cleaned up. What do we do with her Captain? Should I let her runoff to join up the squaw and boy that got away?"

Savage had no idea of how to answer Clint's question. But as a Jayhawker he hated slavery and knew that this girl had lived with the Cheyenne's as a slave. "No," he finally answered. "We'll take her back with us. She's something of value that now belongs to the Union Pacific Railroad."

Clint released the girl and raised both palms. She ran towards the open flap but Gus caught her before she was outside.

"That's a mistake Gus; she's as dangerous as a bobcat. The railroad will never take her."

Squirming and kicking, the little girl looked up at Captain Savage with fear in her wild green eyes. "We'll have her tamed before we reach the railhead," he replied.

Lightfoot chuckled, "Sure we will."

Outside the lodge, Gus tied the girl atop his horse with some rawhide and had a trooper hold Bucks reins so she wouldn't ride away. She had calmed down some, but her face was still frightened as she watched the men cleaning up the camp and dragging the bodies around.

Corporal Nelson had returned with the herd and Sergeant Pike had finished the livestock inventory. He then watched as the travois was loaded making notes on paper of each item recovered. There wasn't much; some buffalo hides and robes, a few trade blankets and a few belts of ammunition with a few old guns and knives. The last thing Nathan did was to count the dead. Then the trooper's drug all the bodies into the old couple's teepee, threw in all the lances, bows and arrows and set it on fire. For a long moment, the squad stood around watching the lodge burn. It was if they were saying a silent goodbye to the spirits of the Cheyenne's that had died that morning.

Finally the troopers threw all the other teepees on top of the burning lodge. The flames shot skyward over hundred feet with the smoke and soot filling the ravine.

"Nathan, have the troop mount up," Captain Savage shouted. He hated the smell of burning flesh, "Let's get out of here."

Under clear cool skies, the squad was soon out of the gully and heading south, southwest for the railhead. Lightfoot was a mile out on point, with the troop following and the herd was riding drag. The landscape was brown, flat, bleak and seemed to stretch from horizon to horizon. There wasn't a cloud or bird in the sky. This trail would be long and slow, with the livestock and sled, but if the weather held, Gus hoped to back in camp by the late afternoon.

Lightfoot had wanted to rawhide the girl to the travois, but

Gus had secured her riding double with him. Her hands tied around his waist and then to the saddle horn. She still had not said a word. So as they rode slowly across the prairie Savage tried to have a conversation with her.

"I don't know if you can hear me, or if you can talk. But you should know that you are safe now. There is nothing to fear," he said slowly with a calm voice and his face twisted over his shoulder. "Maybe my black eye patch frightens you, but it shouldn't. I'm just a soldier doing my job."

He could feel the girl's body against his. But she didn't react to anything he said, so he continued. "My name is Augustus Savage, my friends call me Gus and so can you. I'm from Lawrence Kansas and I took my first breath in 1840. My father was a Quaker preacher and a farmer. He hated anything to do with violence and killing. My mother raised us kids, and taught us how to read and write. She was a good teacher. I was studying mechanical engineering when the war started. I love anything to do with machinery. Anyhow, I quit school and joined the Calvary. My father was disappointed with me, but I had to fight. When I went off to war, it was the last time we talked together. I had a younger brother named Nick and a younger sister Martha. She was much like you, quiet and determined. They were all killed during the war. So I'm all alone just like you." Still no reaction from the girl, "If you understand anything I'm saying squeeze me." He waited a moment and was just about to start talking again, when the girl gave him a timid squeeze around his waist. He smiled, "Alright, you know the word squeeze. Now we are getting somewhere. I'll do all the talking, but you can speak up anytime."

Gus did just that for the next hour. He told the girl how he had lost his eye and his two fingers and showed her his mangled hand. He talked about his family again, especially his sister, "Martha was just a little older then you and I loved her very much." He even talked about the remorse he was feeling for killing the old Indians back in the gully. "They didn't do me any harm. I should have let them live." The Captain rambled on and on, with some of his troopers watching from afar with inquisitive faces.

Finally he pulled Buck up in front of a small thicket of scrub brush. He untied the girl from his saddle and lifted her down to the ground. He unhorsed as well.

Pointing to bushes, he said, "Pee."

She looked at him with a blank stare. Gus squatted and mimicked a girl lifting her smock and peeing. She caught on and with a slight nod walked into the tall weeds.

As Savage waited for her, he removed some jerky from his saddlebags and took a drink of water from his canteen. He was taking a gamble, the girl could runoff and he would have to go after her. But a few moments later she returned. He gave her some jerky and a drink as well. Then he handed her the reins for Buck.

"It's my turn. Hold on to my horse, I'll be back."

She looked at him with defiant eyes and shyly nodded yes.

Standing in the weeds, Gus knew he had doubled down on the gamble. More than likely she'd run off with his horse and the troop would have to catch her again. He should have tied her up before going into bushes. Trusting this she-wolf was a big mistake. He hurried his business.

When he walked out of the thicket he was pleasantly surprised to see the girl still waiting. She handed back the reins and he mounted Buck and then reached down and helped her aboard without tying her up. Her hands went around his waist and he felt her small body against his. If he had eyes in the back of his head, he would have also noticed a slight gleam of contentment in her eyes.

"I'll be damned," he mumbled to himself, "I just *might* have you tamed by the time we reach the railhead."

It was mid-afternoon when the troop arrived at the top of a ridge. They found Lightfoot standing next to his horse rolling a cigarette.

"Well Captain, I see you still have the damsel. That's a surprise," he said sarcastically. "Look yonder, that damn railhead has moved almost ten miles in last three days. Now, that's as much of a wonder as you and the girl."

Gus frowned at Lightfoot and looked out across the Rock Springs Valley. Glistening in the sun was the grand iron highway that had started in Omaha Nebraska six years before and was now crawling its way towards the Mormon State. When finished, the Pacific Railroad would be over nineteen-hundred miles long. This construction project was the biggest enterprise ever attempted by mankind. The newspapers called it the Eighth Wonder of the World. Looking down from the ridge, it was an incredible sight to behold.

At the railhead, the main track was filled with the working train. It stretched a half mile long with flatcars and boxcars containing the rails, spikes, ties, fishplates and other needed supplies. On each side of the main track were temporary spurs with other railcars. One side had the gray working cars with all the tool bins, freight, finance, accounting, personal, and commissary departments. At the very end of this line, looking out at the work being done was the black luxurious private car for the UP's Chief Engineer and Construction Supervisor. Grenville Dodge, a former Union Army General, was the judge, jury and executioner for all things owned or controlled by the UP Railroad. He was the most powerful person in camp and Captain Savage reported directly to him.

The other spur had a long line of brown sleeping, dining and kitchen cars. This was where the workers slept and ate. Each car could sleep seventy five men and the first platoon shared a car with the camp's hunters and scouts. At the very end of this line, also looking out at the work was the medical car with the camp doctor and his staff.

"As you can see," Lightfoot said lighting his cigarette, "I got my wish. The 'hell-on-wheels' town caught-up with us. There will be a hot time in the old town tonight."

Gus glanced back across the valley. Next to the sleeping cars he could see the ragged roofs of the tent city that had popped up again while they had been gone. *"Why not,"* he thought. *"It's Saturday and the men would get paid. 'Hell-on-wheels' would be the perfect place to be if you're looking for saloons, cheap liquor, card-sharks and prostitutes."*

Gus shook his head and looked back at Lightfoot, "Good luck with that thought. Half of these poor boys will be broke by tomorrow morning."

Lightfoot remounted his horse and took a drag from his

cigarette, "Yep they'll be broke again. But they'll have some sweet fond memories."

As the herd approached the ridge line, Gus gave Nathan his orders. "Lightfoot and I will report to General Dodge. Give me your inventory list. You and the troop take the herd to the livestock pins and drop off the loot at the freight car. Then get the men cleaned up for chow. Well see you in camp."

Sergeant Pike handed his paperwork to the Captain, "Can I give the men passes for town tonight sir?"

Gus nodded sadly, "Yes, but curfew is midnight. No exceptions."

He smiled and nodded back, "yes sir."

"How did you do with the girl? Did you get use to her stink?" Lightfoot asked as they turned their mounts towards the rail camp.

"No," Gus replied, with girl still grasping his waist. "But I think she understands some of what I'm saying."

"The UP will never take her Gus, nor will the Army. You're going to be stuck with her Captain, and that's that."

Gus glared at his friend fearing he could be right. Then he changed the subject. "Can't believe how fast the tracks are being laid. Soon we might be out of a job."

Over distant hills, some forty or fifty miles in front of the railhead were the surveyors. These men laid out the road with lines and flags, selecting the best western route with the fewest bridges and trestles. The surveyors slept on the open prairie and foraged for themselves. They were a wild bunch, much like the mountain men of fifty years before.

Behind the surveyors were hundreds of graders working on building the road bed. This work was all done by hand, with shovels and spades, carts and mules, dynamite and sweat. They slept in open bunkers and were fed by chow wagons set out from the main camp.

The railhead was crawling with other workers; some positioned the ties, laid the iron rails and spiked in the fishplates. While others, built the water towers, constructed the repair facilities, boarding terminals and the hotels. There were also crews that strung the telegraphic wire and planned and plotted new towns. Most of the time there were over a thousand workers laboring with sledge hammers, crowbars, picks and shovels. These young workers were mostly Irish, with hundreds of Civil War veterans, gray coat and blue, and many freed slaves working with a few Indians from peaceful tribes. It was a massive work force that General Dodge managed like an army.

When they arrived at camp, they turned directly for the superintendent's car in the front of the line.

"We should have cleaned up before we reported," Lightfoot said.

"No," Savage replied. "I want Dodge to see us grubby, so he knows we've been working."

At the shiny black car with gold leaf lettering, they dismounted and tied their mounts to a railing. The girl was big eyed looking around at the jobsite. She couldn't savvy anything she was seeing, hearing or smelling. As Gus helped her up the stairs to the railcar, she pulled back with fear in her face.

"It's alright, no one is going to hurt you," he said coaxing her up the steps.

Once on the platform, the trio walked down a narrow passageway with windows on one side until they came to a frosted glass door. On the floor, next to the door, was a big woven mat with a small sign, 'Clean Boots.' Gus and Lightfoot used the boot scraper and wiped their feet with the girl watching their strange dance with great curiosity. The Captain knocked on the glass until he heard Mr. Dodge call out "Enter."

Inside the plush wood paneled compartment the girl's wonderment grew even more as she twisted her head looking at the brass chandeliers, overstuffed chairs, blue velour drapes and the white marbled floor. She had absolutely no idea what was before her. It was as if she had stepped onto the moon.

General Dodge was standing with one of his construction foreman next to a long narrow table, stacked with maps and plans. In the center of the room was a brass plated, coal fired, pot belly stove. At the very end of the car, was the supervisor's massive mahogany desk, behind which, was a clear glass door leading out to an observation platform. It had been said that this specially constructed railcar was the most opulent carriage ever built.

"I've come to report," Captain Savage said.

Mr. Dodge looked up from his work. He was a big Scotsman in his forties, with salt and pepper hair and round rimless glasses covering his neatly trimmed bearded face. He wore a business suit, each and every day, even while out making inspection tours. He was a fair and firm man and not use to being trifled with.

"Did you bring back my horses?"

Gus approached and handed him Nathan's inventory. "Yes sir, we lost nine horses and two mules and came back with fourteen nags and one mule."

"And the Indians?" he asked glancing at the paper.

"All the braves are dead. The count is on the list sir."

"What's with the Indian girl?" Mr. Dodge asked still looking at the list.

Gus motioned to Lightfoot and he stepped forward with her, "I found her this morning under some buffalo robes. I almost killed her before I noticed her eyes. They are green sir, she's was a white captive of the Cheyenne."

"Why did you bring her here?" he asked looking up from the inventory.

"She's something of value and that's our skirmish decree," Captain Savage answered smartly.

With his remarks, General Dodge did something very few people had ever seen before, he smiled. "No Captain. Nice try. The UP doesn't traffic in human flesh. That would be illegal. Slavery is dead."

Gus frowned at the superintendent, "Reckon we killed off what family she had and now she has no place to go. The Calvary can't take care of her sir."

"That's your problem Captain," Dodge answered glaring at the girl. "She smells and I'm busy. Is there anything else?"

Gus was mad as hell, but he knew better then to cross swords with General Dodge. "Were there any problems while I was gone sir?"

"No, your Sergeant Major had things well in hand."

"Do you know the link-up date with Southern Pacific sir?" Lightfoot asked with a curious face.

"Yes, May 7th. That will be all gentleman."

31

The Moth

"What are you going to do now?" Lightfoot asked when they remounted their horses.

Gus pulled the girl up and put her behind him. "I'm going to take her over to Mrs. Orrs and pay one of the ladies to clean her up."

Lightfoot chuckled, "There's no ladies over there Gus. Are you sure you know what the hell you're doing?"

A few months before, Captain Savage had traveled to an officer's retreat at Fort Laramie. When he boarded the crowded train to return to the rails end, he sat next to an attractive young woman who had introduced herself as Laura Reed from Chicago Illinois. She seemed as sweet as candy and smelt like spring flowers. She had asked him about all the medals on his dress uniform and about his exciting life in the Cavalry. He had been taken by Laura with her curly blonde hair, hazel eyes, petite figure and Sunday go to meeting clothes. She talked a lot about her family, her schooling and her dreams of coming out west. She seemed to be the picture of virtue. Enjoying the conversation, Gus had asked her which of the three remaining rail stops was hers. She answered nonchalantly, "The railhead."

Gus was confused; he could count on one hand the number of ladies living in the camp.

"Are you visiting someone?"

"No," she had answered. "I have a new job working for Mrs. Orr at her hospitality house."

Captain Savage was shocked. This sweet young girl was as naive as house cat.

"How do you know Mrs. Orr?" He stammered with a concerned face.

"She and my mother are old friends. Mommy use to work for her in New Orleans, that's where my mother met my father. I hope to do the same"

Gus sadly shook his head, "Do you know what really goes on there?"

"Oh yes the hospitality part. Mommy says it pays really good. I hope you will come and see me sometime."

He smiled at her. It was none of his business! But now he needed her help.

Savage pulled up Buck in front of the Hospitality Saloon. It was still early, just before five, and the 'hell-on-wheels' town was near deserted. He helped the girl down and dismounted. Tying his horse to a hitching post, they walked into a large canvas room, with wooden floors, about the size of a circus tent. Behind a long bar, made of sawhorses and wood planks, were two men preparing for the evening trade and Mrs. Orr. Captain Savage had met her twice before. Both times it had been when his troopers had been called in to break up barroom brawls. They didn't like each other much.

"What's the problem now Captain?" She snarled from behind the bar.

"No problem ma'am. I would just like to talk to Laura Reed. Is she around?"

Mrs. Orr was one big woman with every part of her adipose body oozing out of her red velour dress. Her painted face was overdone with thin bright red lips, rosy cheeks and bleached hair with a large yellow bow. She looked ghastly to Gus.

"She's not taking gentlemen callers tonight Captain."

Gus glared at her, "I'm not here for that kind of business. I'm here to talk with her about other matters."

Mrs. Orr shrugged her shoulders, "Fine. She's out back in her crib, third tent on the right, the one with the red flag."

The madam hadn't even mentioned the young Indian standing next to Gus. Freakish sights like a filthy Indian girl must have been all too common in this despicable town.

They found the right tent and Miss Reed called out that they could come in. When they entered they found her dressed in white ruffled bloomers, a pink blouse and sitting in front of a mirror putting on makeup.

She looked at them in the reflection, "Captain I'm surprised to see you here. But I'm sorry I'm not taking any callers for the next few days. Didn't you see my red flag?"

Gus glanced around the tent. It was neat and tidy with a large feathered bed with silk pillows and old whiskey bottles as candlestick holders on the nightstand. With his imagination running wild, the meaning of the red flag finally hit Gus like a locomotive.

"Oh," he blurted red faced, "I'm not here for that. I need your help with this girl."

She twisted from her makeup table and looked directly at them. "What kind of help?"

Gus told her the story of finding the girl and that she had been a white captive of the Cheyenne Indians. "She needs to be cleaned up and scrubbed up. Get the buffalo grease off of her and find her something decent to wear."

"How old is she?"

"I'm guessing nine or ten. She can't talk, but she understands a few of my words. She's going to be hand-full so I'll pay you for your services. This is something that I just can't do."

Laura looked carefully at the girl, "Captain, bring her over here by my mirror."

Gus did and he pointed to her in the reflection. She was wide-eyed again, not sure what she was seeing. She kept touching herself and wriggling around. "Well Miss Reed will you help me?"

Laura nodded with a smile, "Why not. I'm not busy right now and I love a good challenge. Give me a couple hours and I'll bring her back to your tent when I'm done."

"And the cost?" Gus asked.

Looking at the girl in the mirror Laura grinned, "I get $2 a poke and she looks to be worth about three pokes."

Before leaving 'hell-on-wheels,' Gus stopped off at Mr. Chans Baths and for two bits enjoyed a hot soapy tub. And for another two bits, one of the Chinaman's daughters shampooed his hair and gave him a shave. These baths were one of the only luxuries Gus enjoyed in town.

Returning to camp, he pulled Buck up in front of two identical Army tents built upon wooden platforms. Each contained two hard fabric cots, a small desk, two chairs and a small, coal fired, frost stove to keep the chill off. For convenience, these walled canvas shelters were positioned next to the platoon's brown sleeping car. One of the tents was his bivouac. The other was for his second in command.

"Sergeant Major are you in there?" He called from his saddle.

"Yes sir," answered a bellowing voice from a man who quickly showed himself in the open flap. Sergeant Major Albert Hook was a short fireplug of a man, with arms as thick as his thighs and a booming voice with a British accent. His weathered face was round and filled with mutton chops and full sideburns. The Sergeant was a veteran of the American Civil War and had reenlisted after the death of his wife. Captain Savage had promoted him to Sergeant Major, and second in command, after Lieutenant Hollings had been killed in an Indian skirmish the year before. Sergeant Hook was a no-nonsense soldier who went by the book.

"Where's the men Albert," Gus asked looking down the long line of deserted sleeping railcars.

"They just marched off for chow sir. I was waiting for you to make my report."

"You go get chow. I'll take Buck down to the corrals and get him fed and rubbed down."

"I can get a trooper do that sir."

Gus untied his bedroll and saddle bags and handed them to Albert. "No I'll do it Sergeant. We need some time together. It's been a long three days."

"Can I bring you back a plate of food sir?"

"Yes, thanks. I'll see you after chow."

Captain Gus Savage didn't own much and his most prized possession, other than his new Winchester rifle and burnt out farm back in Kansas, was his horse Buck. Three years ago, he had purchased the seven year old chestnut gelding from a breeder in Missouri for fifty dollars. At the time, that was a large amount to pay for horse flesh, but over the years the horse and rider had become one. Gus enjoyed tending his animal and talking to him, as if he understood.

After getting Buck squared away, Savage walked the mile back to camp in the twilight. It was a clear cool night, and in the far off distance, he could hear the shrill of train whistles working up the line. Those lonely sounds reminded him of his past, and how his life might have been different if he had remained in school. By now, he could have been a mechanical engineer, designing and building powerful locomotives. It would have been a life of wealth and fame, not of guns and bullets. He could have built things of value and beauty, not destroying them out of anger. Gus was concerned about his future and the girl's as well. He was tired of living on crumbs and bones for twenty-five dollars a month. He had strong opinions about the failed Indian strategy, the UP's greed and life living on the frontier. With a head full of remorse he knew he had to find redemption while making a better future for himself. That's when he recalled and old Quaker saying his father had taught him: *The world can only be changed by example, not opinions.*

"It's your life son, and only you can change it," his father had said when he had ridden off to war. *Oh, to have those moments back again!*

It was dusk by the time Gus returned to his tent. He got a fire going in the stove and lit a couple of oil lamps and sat down at his desk to write a letter. He was working on the third draft when the Sergeant Major returned with the tinplate heaped with food and bread.

"The hunters got lucky sir," Albert said placing the plate on Gus's desk. "They killed some buffalo, so we are having bison stew. It even has a few vegetables. It's quite tasty sir."

As Captain Savage ate his dinner, the Sergeant Major stood braced and made his usual detailed report. There really wasn't anything of importance to it. One squad was up in the forest, fifty miles away, protecting some lumberjacks making the rail ties, while another squad was doing the same at graders camp. These were all normal deployments.

"What about the town patrol tonight?"

"Two sets of two, sir. I'll check on them shortly. Hope we can get through the weekend without any more killings."

"Did you hear about my patrol?"

"Yes sir, Lightfoot told me about it and the girl. Where is she?"

Gus checked his pocket watch; it was just after eight o'clock. "She's getting cleaned up. Hopefully she'll be here soon."

The Sergeant grinned, "Yes, I heard. Where will she sleep sir?"

"Here with me, in the spare cot."

Is that wise sir?"

Savage scowled, "Well, I can't put her in with the men. She'll be safe with me. But keep an eye on her. I don't want her to run off."

"Yes sir," the Sergeant Major answered. "Is that all sir?"

When Sergeant Hook departed the tent, Lightfoot entered carrying a half full bottle of Tequila. His cheeks were flush and his steps unsure.

"Is she back yet?" He slurred looking around.

"No, she should be here anytime now." Gus answered reaching for his water glass. "Pour me a shot of that cactus juice. I think I'm going to need it."

A few moments later, Laura called out from outside the tent, "Captain, can we come in?"

Gus responded, "Come on in, Miss Reed."

With both Captain Savage and Lightfoot seated at the desk, they turned their attention to the closed flap of the tent. As the canvas was peeled back, Laura and the girl stepped into the shadows of the lamp-light. Gus blinked his one good eye and stood holding the desk lamp high. The girl was wearing a blue, floor-length gingham dress with a white high collared blouse. Her face was concealed by the wide brim of an oversized summer straw hat. Gus moved closer to them with the lamp.

Laura stood next to her in a brown jacket and skirt with a proud face. "Captain you brought me a moth," she said with great zeal reaching for the girl's hat and removing it. "And I bring you back a butterfly."

For a fleeting moment the room went silent and Captain Savage's jaw dropped. Standing before him, with shimmering shoulder-length auburn hair, big round green eyes and a creamy bronze complexion was the girl they had rescued that very morning. Gus glanced over to Lightfoot at the desk; he was speechless staring at her.

As the girl squirmed and pulled at her collar, Laura asked, "Well Captain what do you think?"

"I can't believe my eye," Gus answered. "She's a real beauty. How did you do this?"

"It wasn't easy. You told me she didn't talk. Well she sure knows the word NO. She screamed it loud and clear when I striped off her deerskin rags and dragged her into the first hot water turf. It took two more tubs before I got all the buffalo grease off her. She was a real hell-cat, kicking and screaming Indians words I've never heard.

Captain you thought she was eight or nine. That's wrong sir, she's already developing, so I guess she's around twelve. She isn't in season yet, but that's coming soon. What are all those red welts on her body?"

Lightfoot broke his silence, "She was beaten by the other squaws. It's the Cheyenne way."

Laura frowned and shook her head, "Horrifying beyond belief. Some of those welts will turn into a lifetime of scars, which will always remind her of her life in captivity."

"Did she see her reflection in the mirror when you were done?" Gus asked.

"Yes," Laura replied with a big smile. "She couldn't take her eyes off herself. She kept touching her face and arms. I think that grease and soot had been on her for a long time." Laura put a hand in her skirt pocket and removed a long strand of rawhide with a small pewter medallion attached. She handed it to Gus, "I found this around her neck when I got her frock off."

He looked at the necklace in the lamp light. The front had a prairie schooner engraved on it. He flipped it over and found her name etched on the other side. This was a typical trinket purchased by many pioneers traveling the Oregon Trail. He smiled and pointed to her, "You Lucy Fisher," and then pointed to himself, "Me Gus."

She answered with a nod, "Lu...cy."

The Captain slipped the necklace back over her head and put her hand into his. He gently pulled her towards the spare cot. She pulled back with a frightened face, still fussing with her collar.

Gus unbuttoned her choker and tried again. She still resisted.

Lightfoot shouted out some stern Cheyenne words and Lucy finally complied with Gus. He pointed to the cot and then using hand signs said, "Lucy sleep here." She nodded, "Yes." Then she sat down on the made-up bed.

"Did you feed her anything?" Gus asked looking at her.

"No," Laura answered. "I tried, she would have none of it."

Gus reached for his cold dinner plate. "Lightfoot, tell her its buffalo meat."

He did, and Gus showed her the plate of scraps. She looked at him defiantly. He took a piece with his fingers and ate it. "Good." She glared back at him for a moment and then did the same.

"I'll be damned," Lightfoot blurted. "She can talk, eat and is as pretty as a button… I found her!"

"And I rescued her," Gus replied as she continued to devour the food.

Laura moved to the bed. "I washed her deerskin frock. Most of the stains came out," She said, placing the folded dress on the cot. "One of the other girls at Mrs. Orr's gave me the outfit she is wearing. It's a little big for her but she'll grow into it. Also I gave her a spare brush and comb. She's going need more clothes, lots more clothes."

Captain Savage reached into his pocket and gave Laura a ten dollar Gold Eagle. "You did a marvelous job Miss Reed. It's much more than I expected. Thank you."

"Thank you Captain!" she replied looking at the gold piece. "You'll have a credit with me if you ever come and see me," she flirted back.

Lightfoot chuckled, "Sorry missy you're not part of the Captain's proclivities."

"That's enough Clint," Savage barked back at his friend. "Butt out. Lucy and I are tired and we are going to get some sleep."

After Laura departed, Lightfoot remained to argue with his friend. Clint had strong misgivings about the Captains safety, sleeping alone with Lucy. "She's still just a savage inside," He kept saying. Lightfoot suggested they rawhide her to her cot or allow Clint to sleep at the desk to help him keep an eye on her. Gus would have none of it, and finally ordered his friend to leave.

At first light the next morning, after a troubled night of fearing Lightfoot might be right, Gus sat at his desk and finished the letter he had started the night before. As he worked, he kept glancing at Lucy sleeping peacefully on the cot. She was the true image of virtue. *What was he going to do with her? What was he going to do with himself? Which way was the future?"*

He finished the letter and then read it one final time.

Colonel Frank Rollins
Commanding Officer 7th Regiment
Kansas Volunteer Cavalry
Fort Leavenworth, Kansas

March 14, 1869
Re: Letter of resignation

Dear Colonel Rollins,

After much reflection, I have decided to forgo my life of a Cavalryman and seek new opportunities following the sun. Therefore, it is with great regrets that I tender my resignation as Commander of the first platoon, 7th Regiment, Kansas Volunteer Cavalry, effective May 7th of this year. It has been my pleasure to serve with you and the other fine men of the Kansas Seventh.

If the platoon continues its mission of working with the Union Pacific Railroad, I strongly recommend you consider promoting Sergeant Major Albert Hook to First Lieutenant and placing him in command of the first platoon.

With much admiration
Captain Gus Savage

Chapter 2 - Railhead

Butterfly

The United States Government, which financed the construction of the Pacific Railroad, viewed the Iron Highway project as the greatest national enterprise ever undertaken. The politicians saw the railroad as the opening of the west for settlements and commerce. The Army viewed the line as a way of transporting large numbers of troops and supplies from coast to coast within days, not months or years. But the Sioux, Cheyenne, and Arapaho Indians had differing views. They saw the coming of the iron-horse as an invasion onto their sacred lands, and decreed that *all* of the Great Plains was their domain. These conflicting beliefs soon found Indians chasing trains across the prairie, shooting wooden arrows at the steel-plated locomotives. After many deaths of passengers and rail workers, the US Government finally responded with a perplexing strategy: "The Indians must die or submit to our dictation." Therefore, as the road was being constructed, the military provided protection along the route with a string of wilderness forts. These far-flung military posts provided well over five thousand troops for the protection of the road, but that protection could take days or weeks to arrive. So the railroad and the Generals devised a plan to provide smaller units, such as the First Platoon of the 7th Regiment, as quick-response units for local protection. Additionally, the UP provided rifles and ammunition for all of its workers on the road. These two precautions gave their young workforce confidence in the safety of the line.

≈

Lucy moaned loudly in her sleep, mouthing Cheyenne words, Gus couldn't understand. He went to her bedside in the early morning light just as she yelled, "No *kok'-shut*, No *kok'-shut*." He gently shook her, and she opened her eyes with a snap.

He put his hand gently on her cheek, "Just a bad dream. You're safe."

She blinked at him with a look of serenity and closed her eyes again. Gus watched her fall back into slumber. She looked as peaceful as a spring brook. But sadly, he reminded himself, she wasn't his. When she was in a deep sleep again, he quietly slipped out of the tent with his letter to post. His intention was to have the Sergeant Major watch after the girl while he went off to get them breakfast. But once outside, the Captain found Lightfoot fast asleep, crouched on the ground with his back resting against the platoon flagpole. He looked pathetic, with a thin gray blanket around his shoulders, and his head and hat resting on his knees. On the ground next to him was the empty Tequila bottle.

Gus approached his friend and nudged him with his boot. "What the hell are you doing here?" he demanded.

Lightfoot moved and groaned, then slowly lifted his head. "What time is it?" he whispered, looking up with blood-shot eyes.

"Just sun-up. What are you doing?"

Clint slowly got to his feet. "How's Lucy? See you made it through the night. Good."

"She's still sleeping. I'm going to have Sergeant Hook watch over her while I get us some chow."

"I'll watch her," Lightfoot answered, brushing off his clothes.

"No, I'll get the Sergeant. You go get some sleep."

Clint frowned at him, shaking his head. "I watched over the two of you all night, Gus. She got up once and looked down at you sleeping. I had my knife out and was prepared to leap through the canvas, but she just stared at you for the longest time. Then she turned and peed in the corner of your tent and went back to bed. We've got to teach this girl about bed-pans and living in the white world. You need me, Captain. I speak her language."

Gus glared at his friend. "How could you see into my tent?"

"There are a few bullet holes in the back canvas panel."

Gus smirked. "I have no idea why I tolerate you so!"

"I do. It's because I always have your blind side. Get me some chow, too, sir. We can start by showing her how to eat properly. I'll get the coffee going."

The work day on the railhead was from sunup to sundown, with Sunday the only day of rest. There were seven dining cars, supported by three kitchen carriages located just behind the long line of sleeping cars. The most forward carriage was the executive dining car. Feeding the UP workforce was a major operation supported by dozens of chefs, bakers and a platoon of helpers. Each employee at the railhead, other than the executives, paid $2.00 per week for their room and board while, depending upon their specific jobs, each man earned anywhere from $1.50 to $4.00 per day. The executives paid no such fees and drew salaries twenty to thirty times greater than the average worker. At $25.00 dollars a month, Gus made about the same salary as the lowest level employee but, being a Captain in the Cavalry, he had access to the executive dining room. Rank had some privileges.

As Gus stepped up to the carriage platform, he noticed how deserted the workers dining cars were. Most of the men were still in bed, nursing hangovers or crying in their beers about all the money they had gambled away. This was all too common an occurrence. The 'hell-on-wheels' town preyed on the young workers and while the railroad could have outlawed the town, they didn't. It was rumored that some of the top executives were pocketing a piece of the action, but no one could prove it. The UP liked their men broke; that way they came back on Monday morning, ready to work and do it all over again.

Entering the carriage, Gus found a mostly empty car. On Sunday mornings, there were no white-shirt porters, and breakfast was served as a chow line. He approached the front of the food line and dropped off his tin plate from the night before. Taking two sets of utensils, wrapped with a cloth napkin, he put them in his pocket. Then he picked up two white porcelain plates and started moving down the line. He heaped on scrambled eggs, grits, peaches from a can, pork sausage and on top of each plate, two biscuits with strawberry preserves.

When he finally finished and looked up, he found General Dodge right behind him, watching his every move. "Are you eating for two, Captain?" he asked with a smirk.

"No, sir," Gus answered. "I have my Scout on duty, back at my bivouac. One plate is for him."

The General glared at the two heaping plates, "And the Indian girl?"

"She's at my bivouac as well, sir. She's all cleaned up, as pretty as a button."

"The UP isn't in the business of feeding vagabonds or half-breeds, Captain."

Now there were more curious executives watching and waiting in the food line.

"She isn't a breed, sir. She's a hundred percent white," Savage snapped back. "Her name is Lucy Fisher, and she was taken by the Indians while she and her family were crossing the Oregon Trail. She's just like us, sir, looking for a way home."

All eyes shifted to General Dodge as he snarled at Gus for a long moment. Then he snapped, "Bring her by my office on Tuesday afternoon, after I've returned from Laramie. I'll have another look at her and see if she's worth a plate of grits."

"Yes, sir!" Captain Savage replied with a nod, and headed for the door.

Back at his tent, Gus found Lucy awake and sitting on her bed. Across from her was Lightfoot, on a chair, holding a white porcelain bedpan. Her eyes brightened as he entered through the open flap. In the morning light, she was as pretty as a sunrise but, to his dismay, she was wearing her buckskin frock again.

She pointed at Gus as he came in. "Night-Eye." Then she pointed at the bedpan. "Coomo."

He smiled and nodded at her. "Why isn't she in her dress?" Gus asked, placing the food on the table.

"That's the way I found her when I came in," Clint answered. "I taught her those words, and she seems to understand the commode. She's smarter than we think."

Gus shook his head. "Alright, let's see if we can teach her how to eat."

They spent the better part of the next two hours showing Lucy how to use the knife, spoon and fork. With Lightfoot giving her instructions in Cheyenne words and hand signs, she slowly overcame her instinct to use her fingers. As Lucy sampled the food without saying a word, only her facial expressions told them if she liked or disliked the different tastes. She curled up her nose at the grits, didn't care much for the scrambled eggs, and devoured the peaches and pork sausage. But her favorite taste was the biscuits with the strawberry jam. Lucy had a sweet tooth, and consumed both biscuits on her plate.

As she ate, Gus and Clint shared the other plate of food and made plans for what to do next. The girl had no shoes, no nightclothes, no coat, and only the dress she had slept in. She needed more. Then there was the matter of an outhouse for her to use. Gus couldn't allow her use of the platoon's latrine. That wouldn't do.

"So what are you going to do about her, long term, Gus," Clint asked, finishing his coffee.

"Find her a home with a good, God-fearing family."

"Good luck with that," Clint chuckled. "She doesn't know but a few English words. She's still a savage inside. No family will take her like that."

"Then I'll teach her," Gus replied. "Let's start with more clothes, and maybe a book with pictures. Laura Reed said there was a dry-goods wagon in town."

"I can help, too. I know both her words and ours."

"Yeah," Savage answered with a frown. "Barracks words. I don't want that."

On their way to go shopping, they stopped off at the Sergeant Major's tent, and Gus introduced Lucy to Sergeant Hook. She was immediately fascinated with Albert's hairy face, and kept peering at him with a look of wonderment. He noticed her stare and good-naturedly offered her a feel of his mutton-chopped face. With a wink and a nod, Lightfoot said a few Cheyenne words, and she approached him cautiously.

Rubbing his chin, Albert kept saying, "Come on, sweetie. Feel my chops."

With great courage and curiosity, Lucy moved closer and

placed her hand on his face. Then, ever so slowly and with great glee, she felt his soft whiskers.

Turning to Lightfoot with a smile, she said, "Indians no fur."

The men chuckled. "What did you say to her?" Gus asked.

"Something about as soft as a cloud, I think," Clint answered. "My Cheyenne is a little rusty, sir."

The Sergeant Major melted at her touch. "Never had no children of my own. She's a real peach, Captain."

"Pleased you like her, Sergeant Major. She needs a latrine behind my tent. Just a one holer with a canvas pavilion and a sign, 'Captain Savage Only.'"

"Yes sir," the Sergeant Major answered, still fondly eyeing Lucy.

It was mid-morning by the time they found the dry-goods wagon. The town was just waking up with a massive hangover, and few people in the streets. The store wasn't much, just a rickety old prairie schooner with open canvas tarps on both sides. Out front, there was a large Confederate flag flopping in the morning breeze. On both sides of the wagon was a hand painted, all-too-familiar sign that read: *No niggers, no breeds, no Indians.* Inside the prairie schooner were wooden crates and gunnysacks filled with used clothing, shoes, and other sundries. Most of it looked like junk. The proprietors were an older couple with stern faces and sad eyes. The man, dressed in an aging Confederate jacket, was small, with a slender face, and spectacles resting on a large, bony nose. He had an ear trumpet dangling from his neck. The woman was big, with a hard face and mousy brown hair. Neither of them offered any help.

"I'm looking for girls shoes. Do you have any?" Gus asked.

"Reckon we might," the lady answered with a distant glare.

Gus and Lightfoot rummaged around the wagon and came up with a crate of shoes marked at *25¢ a pair*. Inside the box, they found some old slippers that looked like they might fit. Gus told Lucy they were 'white-mans' moccasins,' but she put up a big fuss when he tried to put them on her feet. Lightfoot had to spew out a string of harsh Cheyenne words before Lucy finally let him put them on.

In doing so, Gus noticed the bottom of her feet. They were

calloused, and as hard as a rock. Lightfoot looked at them as well, shaking his head. "Bet she never had moccasins, the whole time she lived with the Indians."

The woman overheard the Cheyenne words and what Lightfoot said. She turned to her nearby husband and yelled, "The breed is talking Indian to the girl. She is some kind of a squaw."

He rushed over to the wagon with the trumpet in his ear. "What you say? She's a dangerous Indian?"

The lady repeated herself even louder, with fear in her eyes.

Gus yelled back, "NO! She is no Indian squaw." Loudly, he went on to tell them the story of Lucy's capture and rescue. "You have nothing to fear. She's as gentle as a butterfly."

After hearing Lucy's sad story, and seeing the bottom of her feet, the old couple suddenly became overly helpful in searching out what she needed. They soon found a wool coat, two pair of shoes, some mismatched socks, a flannel nightshirt, a pair of faded blue overalls, another pair of bloomers, and a yellow gingham shift, all fairly clean but well used. These clothes would have to do until they came to a real town.

"Do you have any picture books?" Gus asked, sorting through more items in the wagon.

"Yes, Captain," the lady answered, reaching into a box. "It's an animal picture book, in real good condition."

Gus bought the book and a trade blanket. His final selections were two traveling bags, one made of leather with rawhide straps, the other made out of colorful carpet material.

"Why two bags?" Lightfoot asked as they were finishing up.

"I'll tell you later," Gus answered, and paid the couple $3.85 for all of the used merchandise he'd chosen. Their prices were highway robbery, but he had no other place to go.

With their goods packed away in the bags, the trio started back for camp. The weather looked promising, and the streets started filling with early drinkers. Each tent or wagon they passed had something to sell. Most proprietors paid a huckster to stand out front, yelling encouragement for customers to come in and enjoy the offerings. Booze, tattooing, peep shows, and prostitutes were the favorites for the young men building the line. The 'hell-on-wheels' town was a true den of indecency.

They walked by one large tent, with open flaps and a sign over the entrance proclaiming 'Reverend Thomson's Temple of Temperance, all welcome.' There was a young woman standing in front, passing out pamphlets, and yelling about the sins of drink.

"What time is the next sermon?" Gus asked.

The young girl handed him a pamphlet. "In a half hour, sir."

"Let's go in for the message. It would be good for Lucy," Gus said to Clint.

He frowned. "She won't understand a word. No poppycock for me. I'm getting a beer."

"All right. We'll see you back at camp."

"Wait a minute, Captain. Why the two traveling bags?" Clint asked, his expression serious.

"I've resigned my commission, effective May 7th. I'm out of the Calvery and a civilian again."

"Why didn't you tell me?" Lightfoot fumed.

"I just did. You're the only one that knows."

"Where will you go?"

"Maybe home to Kansas. Or back east to find some of her kin. Or maybe go west to Sacramento or further up the coast to the Pacific Northwest. I want to find her a decent family. Don't really know. I just feel responsible for her."

Clint shook his head with a smirk and turned to leave. "I told you we should have let her go back in the gully."

When the sermon started, there were only a few people sitting on the wooden pews. An older woman came out from behind the stage and introduced herself and her family. The family looked beleaguered and bored. A hymn was sung, and then she introduced her husband, Reverend Thomson. He appeared at the pulpit in a wrinkled black and white suit. He was a tall man, thin as a spider, with a high-pitched, squeaky voice. He started his tirade by chastising all of the sinners in the town. Then he talked at length about the evils of the flesh, and how alcohol was the tool of the devil. His voice was monotone and nerve-wracking. He was unsteady at the pulpit, swaying back and forth, with bright pink cheeks and slurred words, and Gus realized that the good Reverend was as drunk as a sailor. He was, like most people in the town, a false prophet. Gus shook his head sadly, recalling all the wonderful sermons his father had preached on this very same subject. His father had been a gifted preacher, not like this charlatan drunk. Gus was only glad that Lucy hadn't understood a word. They exited the tent before the Reverend finished the message. Gus Savage hated hypocrites, even if he was one himself when it came to drink and cards.

That night, back at camp, Gus stretched a rope inside his tent and hung the trade blanket on it. Now he and Lucy could have some privacy. After she dressed in her flannel nightshirt, they sat at the table and opened the picture book. Lucys look of bewilderment returned as Gus showed her the animals and told her the right names for each. With her green eyes dancing in the lamplight, she laughed and giggled at all of the funny names. She kept touching the book pages, trying to understand how these creatures could appear to be so real. When they finished and Gus closed the book, he turned to Lucy, using English words and hand signs, asking her how many winters she had spent living with the Cheyenne. He slowly put up three fingers, and then four, and then five fingers. She nodded yes with five winters. She had been taken when she was seven years old. That helped explained her understanding of some English words.

Later that night Lucy asked from the other side of the hanging blanket, "Night-Eye, where is your woman?"

Gus turned down his lamp and replied, "I have no woman."

"No squaw, why?"

Smiling he pulled off his boots with a thud, "I not find the right squaw."

"Why blue coats kill Indians?"

Gus shook his head sadly, "They were thieves that kill railroad men."

Lucy thought for a moment, "What word thieves?"

Shaking his head, "Lightfoot will tell you tomorrow. Good night."

The next morning, Captain Savage and the Sergeant Major made out the platoons weekly duty roster, leaving Gus in camp for the next two days. He wanted to spend that time preparing Lucy for the meeting with General Dodge. He hoped to teach her how to greet him with a few English words and a small curtsy. That would impress the General.

As Gus finished up with Sergeant Hook, he received a written note from one of the ladies in camp. It was an invitation for Lucy and Captain Savage to have afternoon tea with one of the executive wives.

There were only four women in the camp. Three of them were bakers, and shared compartments on an old sleeping carriage. The other woman was Mrs. Wilkins. Her husband was the Chief Surveyor for the railroad. They had three young adopted children, and lived in a specially made railroad car for executive families. Mrs. Wilkins was a delightful Christian lady, and well respected at the railhead.

Gus and Lucy paid her a visit at three o'clock that afternoon. Mrs. Wilkins had heard the story of her rescue, and was very pleased to meet Lucy. Lucy, in turn, practiced her curtsy, along with a few words like 'thank you' and 'yes, ma'am.' Mrs. Wilkins and her children were very polite, and everyone had tea. Lucy had no idea about tea cups and pots, so the other children showed her the proper way. Lucy did best at devouring the cakes, but curled up her nose at the taste of the tea. During the conversation, Mrs. Wilkins offered to watch over Lucy when the Captain was away on duty. It was a very generous offer which Gus gladly accepted.

On Tuesday afternoon, when Lucy and Gus entered the black private car again, they found General Dodge at his mahogany desk, studying blueprints. He glanced up from his work as they walked the length of the carriage. He had a stoic look on his face. Lucy wore her yellow gingham dress, with her hair neatly brushed and adorned with a red ribbon. She looked like the picture of innocence.

They stopped a few feet in front of his desk. "General Dodge," Gus said with a formal tone, "I wish to present Miss Lucy Fisher." Turning to Lucy, he continued, "Miss Fisher, I would like to introduce General Grenville Dodge, the Chief Engineer and Construction Supervisor for the Union Pacific Railroad Company."

Gus nodded at Lucy with an encouraging glance. She curtsied with a smile, just like Gus had taught her. "Nice meeting you, big chief sir," she said in a clear voice.

The General's expression turned to a grin. "Big chief. I like that. You've unwrapped a pretty package here, Captain. That raven hair is stunning. How old is she?"

"I'm guessing twelve, but I don't have any particulars, sir."

Dodge got up from his chair and approached Lucy. "I've got a ten-year-old at home, just like this one. I miss her dearly."

Lucy looked up at the General with mischievous eyes, then quickly reached out and pulled on his neatly trimmed beard.

Gus was stunned. "I'm sorry, sir. I didn't see that coming. She has a fascination with beards."

The General laughed. "My daughter does the same thing. Can I spoil her, Captain?"

"Yes, of course, sir. What did you have in mind?"

"How about something she might recall from her childhood? Ice cream."

Gus nodded his approval with a grin. General Dodge reached for a small brass bell on his desk and rang it.

The sound startled Lucy.

Almost instantly one of his white-shirted porters entered the car. "Yes, sir?"

"Three bowls of ice cream, with some strawberry preserves on top."

"Yes, sir," the porter answered.

The General gestured for his visitors to have a seat in two overstuffed leather club chairs, and returned to his desk. Lucy's gaze started drifting around the room, and curiosity filled her face again. As they waited, General Dodge proudly told Gus some news. The railhead would be in Utah the next day, and Brigham Young was sending five hundred additional workers to help get the line to Ogden. That alone was great news, but he had saved the best for last. The 'hell-on-wheels' town was packing up for good. The Mormons would not tolerate such a town. "They'll move up the road but stay close to the state line so the Jack Mormons will have a place to spend their weekends," the General confided.

"That's great news, sir!" Gus said with a broad smile.

The General opened a desk drawer and brought out a fancy quart glass bottle and handed it across the desk.

"What's this?" Gus asked.

"I learned this morning, from Colonel Rollins at Fort Laramie, that you have resigned your commission. I'm sorry we are going to lose you. This bottle of brandy is our way of saying thank you for your service."

Gus was moved by his gift. With the new telegraph, news traveled fast up and down the line. Just as he was thanking the General, the porter returned with the ice cream.

Savage showed Lucy how to hold the cold bowl, and how to eat the treat with the spoon. She was timid at first, but after a good taste she devoured it with great joy.

As the strawberry stain around her mouth grew, both men watched intently, with big grins. "Well, General, is she worth a plate of grits?" Gus asked.

He nodded. "Yes, and much more. She will be my unofficial guest. Bring her by the executive dining car so the other men can get to know her. With that raven hair, she will become the belle of the camp. Is she why you resigned?"

"No, sir," Gus answered. "The Cavalry taught me how to kill. Now I want to learn how to live."

The Line

The American Continent is vast and at the turn of the 18th Century, was difficult to traverse. When the Lewis and Clark Expedition first crossed the continent, they did so by foot, pole, paddle, sail, and on horseback. It took the explorers years to travel from the Atlantic to the Pacific and return again. There were no roads or highways, just game trails, Indian paths, rivers and lakes. Travel was long, arduous, and dangerous. After Lewis and Clark, only a few hearty mountain men followed in their footsteps.

The invention of the steam engine in 1781 by James Watt led to the development of steamships and railroad locomotives. With the advent of steam power, travel times started shrinking, and the dreamers started scheming about a railroad that could link the Eastern seaboard with the Pacific. There were many fathers of the Transcontinental Railroad, dating back to the 1840s when young Greenville Dodge revealed his planned route for the line to a youthful railroad lawyer named Abraham Lincoln. These two men agreed that the Pacific Railroad would be the harbinger for

America's future prosperity.

In California, a young surveyor named Theodore Judah found a route over and through the High Sierra Mountains which led to the development of the Central Pacific Railroad. This line was started by four local businessmen willing to take high risks for potentially high profits.

In the east, another company was formed, the Union Pacific Railroad. The idea was simple: somewhere in the middle of the continent, the Central Pacific and the Union Pacific would link up and jointly own the Transcontinental Railroad. But, because of the magnitude of such a construction project, only the Federal Government had the resources to pay for the line.

Prior to the Civil War, the US had only about 9,000 miles of rail tracks, most of which were short-line railroads, mainly concentrated in the northeast. The government and the politicians planned four potential routes for the Transcontinental Railroad: a northern, a central, and two southern corridors. Unfortunately, because of the issue of slavery, the north and south could not agree on the routes, and the plan for the railroad was shelved.

America was only one hundred years old when the Civil War was won and slavery abolished. With the end of the war, the dreamers and schemers returned to Washington DC with new plans and routes for the Pacific Railroad. With the strong support of President Abraham Lincoln and General Ulysses S. Grant, Congress finally approved the line. The first tracks for the Union Pacific Railroad were laid at Omaha, Nebraska, in July of 1863.

≈

Crossing into Utah proved beneficial for the Union Pacific Railroad. With the additional Mormon workers, railhead track production increased to four or five miles per day. These new volunteers filled all the camps, and Grenville Dodge managed this increased track production like the Commanding General he was.

The next few weeks for Captain Savage and his platoon were just routine. Two squads were always on patrol, with one squad staying in camp to protect the railhead. But Utah proved to be a lot safer then Wyoming, as the Mormons had eradicated almost all of the local Indian tribes.

When Captain Savage was in camp, Lucy stayed with him in his tent. When Gus was on patrol, she stayed with Mrs. Wilkins and her three children. On his first patrol, Gus had fussed for three long days about whether Lucy was doing good with the Wilkins family. Upon his return to camp, he was relieved to hear that she had done very well, and that Mrs. Wilkins had enjoyed her stay.

"I've got her started with her A, B, C's. She's a smart girl, Captain, and my children like her very much," Mrs. Wilkins had told him.

But, upon his return from his second patrol, the report wasn't as encouraging. Mrs. Wilkins told him what happened: "The children were outside playing when Lucy spotted a jackrabbit hiding under a boxcar. She picked up a nearby rock and threw it. On her first throw, she killed the rabbit. Then Lucy crawled under the car and brought the dead bunny out for the other kids to see. With the children watching, she searched out a sharp obsidian rock from the rail ballast and proceeded to gut and skin the rabbit. The other children, horrified by all the blood and guts, ran home to their mother. Lucy finished her work and nonchalantly took the carcass to Mrs. Wilkins, saying simply, "Cookpot."

"I know we live in a wilderness, Captain," Mrs. Wilkins said with a frown. "But our children have not yet been exposed to killing and hunting, and we want to keep it that way. Please have a talk with her. No more hunting."

Gus agreed, but deep down he respected Lucy's moxie. She knew how to survive on the prairie.

The railhead moved forward by leaps and bounds. And, with every passing mile, Lucy's vocabulary and curiosity grew. She had become a celebrity in camp, and many of the men knew her by name. Lightfoot was like her shadow, as was Sergeant Hook and the entire platoon. Every man watched out for her. Lucy was totally safe in camp.

Mrs. Wilkins had given her a McGuffey's First Reader, and she always had that book in hand. Gus and Sergeant Hook read to her, every chance they had, while Lightfoot taught her more practical matters, like how to find her way around a sprawling railroad camp. Ever so slowly, Lucy started blossoming into the beautiful young child she was.

One night, in the men's dining car, Lucy asked, "Why so few squaws here?"

Lightfoot chuckled. "Yes, Captain. Tell us why so few squaws."

Gus thought a moment, "This place only for warriors."

"Why so few children? They sick?"

"No," Gus answered. "They are at Indian camp with the squaws."

"Why no ice cream every night?"

This was typical Lucy, firing questions like a Gatling gun – so many questions that she made Gus think about thoughts he didn't know he had.

As the line approached Ogden, Gus learned that the link-up date had been changed to May 10th at a place called Promontory Summit, a strip of desert thirty miles west of town. He also received a telegraph from Regimental Headquarters, requesting hotel rooms in Ogden for Colonel Rollins and a Pay Officer for May 8th through the 10th.

Both Gus and Lightfoot saw these new developments as an excuse to visit Ogden for a couple of nights in the biggest town they had seen in two years. They would take Lucy along, for some clothes shopping and with an eye towards finding a good Mormon family that might take her in.

It was a pleasant six-hour horseback ride from the railhead to town. The journey was easy. All they had to do was follow the graded roadbed. As they traveled down the road, they passed many crews building timbered train trestles and bridges. When they returned in three days, the railhead would be a good twelve miles closer. That's how fast the line was moving.

With Lucy and Gus riding double on Buck, and Lightfoot on Loco, the trio was astounded at how quickly the topography started changing, blending from sage and burnt brown desert to rich fertile land. On the north, there were tall, snow-clad mountains, with foothills of green trees and high chaparral. The rock formations were tall and bold, with jagged cliffs, waterfalls and streams all rushing towards the Great Salt Lake on the south. The boulders that lined the roadbed looked like granite sentinels protecting the entrance to Ogden. As they got closer to the lake, Gus noticed unfamiliar birds circling high over the water. Soon the trio stopped and dismounted.

"Being from the Midwest, bet you've never seen a Seagull before," Lightfoot said, using his binoculars

"Nope, nor a blue inland sea," Gus answered, using his spyglass.

Gus showed Lucy how to use the telescope. Soon, that look of wonderment returned to her freckled face. "So near," she said with glee. Gus turned the spyglass backwards and let her look again. "Now so far," he answered. She looked again. "Where bird go?" He smiled at her and turned the tube back again. "Bird return." She became so fascinated with the spyglass that she continued using it all the way to town.

Ogden was a quaint mountain village of a few thousand souls, nestled in a large valley. It was destined to become much bigger with the coming of the railroad. When the trio rode into town, they found UP Surveyors laying out the large rail yard, and another group doing the same for the train terminal.

Gus recognized most of the surveyors, and yelled out from his saddle, "Where's the livery stable, boys?"

One man pointed down the road and shouted back, "Three more blocks on the left, Captain."

Gus tipped his forage cap and moved on.

Inside the livery, the trio met a tall, lanky stable boy called Hector. He was dressed in blue overalls, skinny as a string bean and as slow as mud. As he took in the nags for a two-night stay, he kept talking proudly about the new rail line and terminal that Joseph Smith was building. "He's a great man of vision," Hector kept saying.

Finally, Gus had to correct him. "Didn't see any Mormons laying out the yard when we rode in. They were all UP men."

Hector smirked and kept jabbering on about Joseph Smith. Then he turned his attention to Lucy, eyeing her with lust on his face.

"What's the best hotel in town?" Gus asked, with a raised eyebrow.

"Depends. You folks Mormons?"

"No. Why do you ask?" Lightfoot replied.

"The Joseph Smith Hotel is for the Mormons, while the Ogden Hotel is for the non-believers."

"What's the difference?" Gus asked.

"There is no open drinking, gambling or prostitution allowed in town. The Joseph Smith Hotel abides by those rules. Some others don't."

Lightfoot smiled. "So, if we stay at the Ogden, we can drink and play cards?"

"Yep, as long as you're a registered hotel guest."

"Hmm." Lightfoot grinned. "Where do we find this palace of sin?"

"Wait a minute," Gus responded. "I want to meet some good Mormon folks who might consider taking this girl into their family."

Hector nodded, with his gaze still on Lucy. "Oh, if it's adoption you're after, you should take it up with Bishop Johnson. He's the church man to see."

"Where would I find him?" Gus asked.

The stable boy smirked again. "Over at the Ogden Hotel. He owns the place."

"Your church Bishop owns the non-believers hotel?" Gus asked in surprise.

"Yep, he's one smart businessman."

"Where's this hotel?" Lightfoot asked.

"Just across the street from where the new terminal will be. It's the only four-story building in town."

As they walked to the hotel, Lightfoot shook his head. "These Mormons are a strange bunch. Don't rightly know if I understand them, Captain."

"Nor me. We'll see what this Bishop has to say."

"What word adoption?" Lucy asked, looking up at Gus.

"I'll tell you later," he answered.

Once inside the four-story, wood-framed hotel, they approached a lady working behind the front desk. She was a pleasant middle-aged woman with blue eyes, a trim figure, and brown hair with a hint of gray.

"We will need two rooms for two nights," Gus said.

"Sure hope this hotel has feather beds," Lightfoot added.

"We do," she answered proudly. "And we have a bathroom on every floor."

Gus filled out the registration book for Lightfoot and himself, putting Lucy's name under his own. "We will need a single room for my Scout and a double with two beds for me," Gus said, turning the book back to the clerk.

She read the names on the ledger. "Is this pretty young girl your daughter, Captain Savage?"

"No, ma'am. She is my ward."

When Gus went on to explain Lucy's plight and his need to talk to Bishop Johnson, the woman behind the counter told them that she was the Bishop's wife, and that he was in Salt Lake City on business.

"But I'll be pleased to make some local inquiries on the girls behalf," Mrs. Johnson volunteered.

She seemed quite sympathetic to Lucy's story, and encouraging that she might find a Mormon family that would take her in.

The lady gave them two rooms on the second-floor front, overlooking where the train terminal would soon be. They were wonderful rooms with soft beds, overstuff chairs, cool window breezes, kerosene lanterns, and indoor plumbing just down the hall. All of these were new experiences for Lucy, prompting numerous questions that she started rattling off, mostly having to do with the bathrooms.

After washing the trail dust off, the trio went downstairs and walked around Ogden. It was a nice little village with a few cobblestone streets, friendly shops, and well-dressed citizens eager to help strangers. They made a few purchases, bought a few trinkets, and then, with the evening shadows growing longer, returned to the hotel for dinner.

The dining room was just off the hotel lobby, with large bay windows that fronted the main street. There were upholstered booths on one side of the room, with numerous square, white-clothed tables and bentwood chairs in the center. The red-flocked walls were covered with western paintings and stuffed animal heads such as bobcat, elk, bear, and buffalo.

When they entered the half-filled room, a young lady showed them to a booth. After she departed, Lucy jumped up and walked around, looking with open curiosity at all of the stuffed animal heads. When she returned to the table, wide-eyed, her questions started flowing in both Cheyenne and English words. Were these animals dead or just sleeping? What happened to their bodies? What magic put them on the wall? Could they come alive again? Gus and Lightfoot did their best to explain taxidermy, but Lucy had a hard time understanding why white people would do such a thing to animals.

When the waitress returned with menus, Gus and Lightfoot ordered beef steaks, beans and biscuits, while Lucy just wanted biscuits and the pork sausage.

"Do you have any vegetables?" Gus asked the server.

"Yes sir. We have stewed tomatoes with green peppers."

Gus nodded at Lucy. "Bring her a bowl and a glass of milk."

"And I'll have some Tequila," Lightfoot added.

The waitress frowned. "I'm sorry, we can't sell alcohol openly. If you're a hotel guest, you can buy it by the glass in the Bamboo Room, and bring it back to your table."

"Where is this room?" Gus asked.

She pointed to a door at the back of the dining room. "There is a small bar and a few poker tables back there. Just show your room key to the bartender."

Lightfoot slipped out of the booth. "What do you want, Captain?"

"Beer."

The meal was outstanding, even Lucy liked the tomatoes, which she called "blood apples", and her glass of milk. After the meal, Clint made an announcement that Captain Savage was shocked to hear: he had resigned his position as Chief Scout for the railroad, effective on the date of the linkup. "I would like to join you and Lucy, either back to Kansas or out west. I too, feel responsible for her sir."

Gus tried to talk him out of it. It was the best money he had ever made and with all the spur lines to be built, he would have a good job for many years. But Clint was stubborn, reminding Gus that he would always have his blind side. "I've always been a rambler," he said with a serious face. "It's time for me to think about planting roots, somewhere. Our futures should be together, sir, if you'll have me."

In the end, out of friendship, Gus shrugged his shoulders. "Sure, Clint. Why not? You're welcome to join us. But Lucy might soon be gone."

"Where me go?" Lucy asked with an inquisitive face.

After finishing dinner, they visited the Bamboo Room. It wasn't much, just a nook with a small bar, no windows, a few tables and chairs, and three round, green-felt poker tables. Above the bar was a sign: '*Hotel Guests Only.*' The bartender was a big, surly fellow with a perpetual scowl and gray eyes.

The trio sat at one of the small tables and waited. All the eyes in the room drifted their way, which was only normal, given Gus's black eye patch and his Cavalry uniform.

The bartender soon approached. "Did you see our sign, Captain?" he asked, pointing to another sign behind the bar. "It says no colored, no breeds, no Indians."

Lightfoot's face turned angry, "I ain't no breed. I'm a Comanchero."

"Never heard of them," the bartender barked back.

Gus looked up at the surly barkeep. "Now look here, my good man. Comancheros are direct descendants of the Spanish Conquistadors. They live in the New Mexico Territory and are considered Americans Citizens by act of Congress. Anyhow, he is my guide and under my command. We would like to have a drink."

The bartender thought a moment, and then reluctantly replied, "Can I see your room keys?"

Gus and Lightfoot showed him their keys.

"We don't have drinks for children, Captain," he added, glaring at Lucy.

"She'll have a glass of wine, and we'll have two whiskeys." Gus answered, staring back at him.

Lightfoot hated being called a breed, and fumed in his chair as the bartender turned to get their drinks. "I'll cut his damn ear off if he ever calls me a breed again."

Gus chuckled. "They will soon have to add Chinamen to their list, once the SP gets here."

Lucy had understood the word 'whiskey,' having heard it many times around the Cheyenne camps. So when her glass of wine came, she pointed at it and asked, "Whiskey?" Lightfoot told her with Cheyenne words that it was firewater for squaws. She tried it with a curled-up nose. She didn't much like it, but she had questions about the wine, the whiskey, and what the other men at the green tables were doing. As Clint answered her, Gus got up and walked over to the poker tables.

Before losing his eye, Gus had fancied himself to be a good poker player. Because of his engineering background, he had a mind for numbers, and playing poker was all about numbers. He wondered if, with only one eye, he could still play the game. Soon, he sat down at one of the tables and played a few hands. He was amazed that he could count the cards faster with one eye then two. And, for some reason he could focus on his opponents better. A half-hour later, with Lucy hovering over him asking questions, he cashed in his chips. He had made a profit of twenty-five dollars. While he wasn't any card-shark, he had enjoyed playing cards again.

That night in the room, with the lamps out, Lucy asked from her bed, "Gus, what word adoption?"

Gus frowned in the dark, then did his best to sugar coat his answer. "It's when a young Indian has no kin and another tribe takes them in."

"You sell me for horses?"

"No, never! Go to sleep."

The next day, the Bishop's wife arranged two meetings with Mormon families interested in taking Lucy into their homes. These encounters took place in the hotel lobby, with Mrs. Johnson providing the introductions.

The first was with a fat man with a bull-frog neck, black pants, and a white shirt with wide red suspenders. He was accompanied by his plain-looking wife and two poorly dressed teenaged children. He did all the talking, and professed to be a successful pig farmer. He and his wife had four more children back on the farm. Captain Savage explained how they had found Lucy, and the deplorable conditions in which she had been living.

"She is a very bright girl," Gus said. "Do your children go to school?"

"No time for that," the farmer answered. "They have hogs to raise. My wife teaches them what she knows, which isn't much. But the farm keeps them out of trouble."

At one point, the farmer approached Lucy, who was sitting on the round settee, and felt her upper arm. "She's skinny and will need some fattening up."

Lucy pulled away from the man's touch with fire in her eyes. "No touch."

The farmer glared back at her. "She's a little wild, huh? How much is her dowry?"

"There's no dowry," Captain Savage snapped back. "She needs a good Christian family to show her the way through life."

The farmer shrugged, "Well then, she ain't for us. It takes money to fatten them up and get a good days work out of them."

Gus fumed under his breath; *this hog farmer was a pig himself!*

The second family meeting was stranger than the first. It was with a wealthy, gray-haired gentleman who owned a local freight company. He was accompanied by an older, nice-looking lady who he introduced as his wife, and a pretty, much younger gal that Gus assumed was his daughter. But, as it turned out, the younger woman was also his wife! Gus had forgotten that many Mormons practiced Polygamy.

The older man asked how old Lucy was, and Gus lied to him, answering that she was only ten. The gray-haired gentleman appeared disappointed, "sorry that just won't do." He was looking for a young girl, in season, to become his third wife. Neither of his two wives spoke during the entire conversation but, when they turned to leave, Gus noticed the look of satisfaction on their faces.

After everyone was gone, Lucy approached Gus and looked him straight in the eye. "No damn good," she said with a snarl.

"Why you want leave me?"

The next morning, when they checked out of the hotel, they made arrangements for Colonel Rollins and the Pay Officer. They also made reservations for their return trip, to witness the link-up ceremonies.

The Spike

Gus had learned much from his trip to Ogden. He had enjoyed the feather beds, and being in a society with women again. He had missed that life of comfort more than he realized. And then there was the poker; he had enjoyed that challenge, and found that he was better at it with one eye than two. Gus had also learned that his Quaker upbringing would not allow him to place Lucy with a Mormon family. He just couldn't do that to her. Somehow, he would find her a safe Christian home. And now there was Clint to deal with. The man had saved his life more than once, and he owed him a great deal. Gus recalled something his father had said many times, *"Thou is a rich man that has friends"* So Lightfoot was now part of his future.

Two weeks after returning to camp, the railhead arrived at Ogden, and all of the supporting railcars were moved onto the tracks of the sprawling new yard. What remained to be built was just thirty more miles to Promontory Summit. The linkup was on schedule.

On May 7, 1869, Gus gave his last official order to the First Platoon: with Sergeant Major Hook in command, all three squads were ordered to set up a protective perimeter around Promontory Summit. The UP feared an Indian attack and the negative publicity it would bring. The troop would leave for patrol right after pay call, the next morning, and remain on patrol until the ceremonies were completed and both trains were safely back in the Ogden Yards.

Gus and Lightfoot knew that, one way or the other, the only way out of the Utah desert was going to be by rail, so they reluctantly decided to sell their beloved horses to a local rancher.

Buck and his traps brought seventy-five dollars, while Loco and his saddle sold for sixty dollars. It was a hard decision for the men to make but, after the link-up, they wanted to travel light and fast.

With the coming of the railroad, Ogden quickly started filling with dignitaries, politicians, and the press. The Union Pacific and the Southern Pacific were sending out special trains for the link-up. These two trains would meet up at the summit, early on the morning of May 10th. After a few speeches, the ceremonial golden spikes would be driven into the last rails linking the east and west. Then the official photograph would be taken. That historic picture of the two trains joined was by invitation only, with the companies hand-selecting personnel they wanted included in the photo. None of the First Platoon was on that list, but Gus was, with special instructions to wear only civilian clothes. After the ceremonies, the Union Pacific train would back up the thirty miles to Ogden, with the Southern Pacific train following. Once both trains were safely in the yards, the railroads would continue celebrating with a gala party for all.

Late in the afternoon on May 8th, Colonel Rollins and his Pay Officer arrived from Omaha. Gus met them at the depot and saw them across the street to their hotel. After checking in, the Colonel asked Gus to join him in his room for a drink.

His room was on the top floor front, with an unobstructed view of the new yards which sprawled out ten tracks wide like strands of spaghetti. The room was considered the best in the house.

"Why are you out of uniform, Captain?" the Colonel asked, removing a bottle of whiskey from his valise.

"My resignation was effective May 7th, sir."

Colonel Rollins poured the whiskey into two glasses and handed one to Gus. "We've been on that damn train for almost three days. It's a long ride across this god-forsaken wilderness." He raised his glass. "Here's to you, Captain Savage, and your First Platoon. Have a seat and let's talk."

Colonel Rollins looked tired as he did his best to talk Gus out of resigning from the Cavalry. "Your resignation is still on my desk. I can tear it up and forget about it. You're too good an Indian fighter to lose. General Mackenzie is in Washington, raising a new regiment of Indian fighters. They are going to Texas and wipe out the Comanches. This is a great opportunity for you, Gus. You'll have a Majors gold leaf on your collar before the campaign is over."

Gus smiled politely at the Colonel. "Sir, the only gold I'm thinking about is in the fields of California. Anyhow, I've never seen a one-eyed Major in the US military. It's just not for me, sir. "

Colonel Rollins wiped his face with a handkerchief. "Alright, Captain. I wish you well. I only hope you have a good-sized grubstake, because I understand going after gold is an expensive proposition."

"Thank you, sir. What about Lucy Fisher? Is the government willing to take responsibility for her?"

The Colonel shook his head sadly. "You don't want that, Gus. There are over a dozen white female captives living at Fort Laramie. Most of them are crazy, and they live in squalor. They will never blend into white society again."

"Lucy is smart, sir. She will blend in again." Gus finished his drink. "What do I do with her, sir?"

"That's up to you, Captain. You found her. She's yours to deal with."

Over a second drink, they talked about the First Platoon. The Sergeant Major had gotten his promotion to First Lieutenant. He would be the new Platoon Commander. But the entire troop was being rotated back to Kansas to join General Mackenzie's new regiment. They were being replaced by a platoon of Negro Buffalo Soldiers. The government was making another, all-out effort to wipe the red menace from the Great Plains

Early the next morning, using Captain Savage's former bivouac tent, the troop had its final pay call at the railhead. Each trooper, dressed in a clean, fresh uniform, marched into the tent, one at a time, and saluted the Pay Officer, while smartly stating his name, rank, and serial number. The Pay Officer then found the man's name on his roster, paid him off with gold and silver coin, and had him sign or make his mark on the pay ledger. All of this was done under the watchful eye of Colonel Rollins, who supervised the proceedings.

As pay was underway, Captain Savage, Lightfoot and Lucy waited outside, talking with the troopers in line. It was a time to say goodbye and to talk about the many changes for the platoon. All seemed happy with Sergeant Majors promotion, and most were happy about the troop returning to Kansas, but a few were apprehensive about joining General Mackenzie's new regiment.

As usual, Captain Savage was the last to be called into the pay tent. As the officer paid Gus, Colonel Rollins explained the different amounts. One stack of coins was for repayment of platoon expenses, another was for two months pay, and the final stack was his bonus for serving two years in the field. It was a considerable amount, just over four hundred dollars – more money than Gus had ever had before.

When done, the Colonel shook his hand and offered a friendly smile. "I'm sure this money is your grubstake Gus. I hope it is enough. Good luck to you and to Lucy. She is indeed a bright young girl."

A few moments later, with a bugle call, the entire First Platoon rode by the pay tent. Leading the three mounted columns was Lieutenant Hook. Colonel Rollins, Gus, and Lightfoot stood outside, saluting the men as they passed by, starting their last patrol. Lucy stood next to them, waving goodbye to the troopers. In many ways, it was a sad sight. But in other ways, it was liberating.

After the troop was gone, Gus walked Lucy to Mrs. Wilkins railcar, carrying her carpet bag and bedroll. "We'll be back to get you, tomorrow evening. Then we'll go on a long train ride. It will be fun."

"Why can't I come with you now?" Lucy asked, holding his hand.

"Lightfoot and I have things to do. Tomorrow morning, we will be far out in the desert at a big council meeting. It will be a very boring powwow."

Lucy suddenly stopped, looking up at him with defiance in her eyes. "You not leave me here?"

"No. We'll be back tomorrow to get you. I promise."

That afternoon, the special train from Omaha arrived, packed with more dignitaries and press. It was a long, freshly painted iron snake, with six day cars, two sleeping cars, a dining car, baggage car, and a brand-new red caboose. Gus and Clint walked across the street from their hotel to have a look at the new carriages.

As they were poking around the newly finished terminal, Lightfoot ran into an old friend who was a crew member on the special train. Clint introduced him as the Brakeman, Red Reed. He was a large man with straggly brown hair peppered with gray, and a weathered face marked with deep lines and wrinkles. He and Lightfoot had fought off an Indian attack a few months before. Red invited them into the caboose and proudly showed them around the new working carriage.

"I owe you," he said to Lightfoot. "You saved my life that day. If you're going up to the Summit tomorrow, ride in here with me. It's a much better ride."

That was exactly what they did, early the very next morning. And Mr. Reed was right: the view from the caboose was the best.

Promontory Summit was just a barren piece of wasteland. But it was here that the two roads came together. The UP pulled its locomotive No.119 to the very end of their tracks while the SP nudged its locomotive Jupiter into position just in front of it. Here, under a warm desert sun, the speeches started in front of a crowd of a few hundred people. The words were elegant and the themes the same: the many benefits of the Overland Route. Finally, with cheering workers looking on, the golden spikes were driven home. Then the two Superintendents, General Dodge and Lewis Clement, called for the photographer A.J. Russell to take the official photograph.

With Mr. Russell yelling out orders, Gus moved into position right behind the two supervisors. Other men moved in and out of the picture as the invitation list was checked and double checked. When the composition was about finished, Gus saw Lightfoot sneak into the picture with a group of surveyors. He also noted the absence of any ethnic workers. There were no Chinese, Negroes, or Indians in the picture. He frowned, just as the picture was taken.

≈

The promise of the Transcontinental Railroad was quite simple: the iron road would replace the slower and more dangerous wagon trains, Pony Express, and stagecoach lines that crossed the country by land, and the equally difficult sea journey around the southern tip of South America.

After the golden spike ceremonies, it would take twenty more years before the Canadian Pacific railroad spanned the northern part of the continent, and twenty-five years more before the Russians completed the Trans-Siberian Railroad, using two hundred thousand Chinese and two hundred thousand convicts to build the line.

At a time when travel was limited to horseback, buggy, raft or boat, and with the help of many people such as Surveyor Theodore Judah, Road Builder Greenville Dodge and Railroad Lawyer Abraham Lincoln, the Transcontinental Railroad was the greatest building project of the Nineteenth century. This marvelous engineering feat, constructed by an all-volunteer labor force, would not be overshadowed until the completion of the Panama Canal in 1914. The new iron highway beckoned the beginning of America's Gilded Age.

≈

The ten-mile-an-hour backup ride to Ogden was long and slow. Lightfoot and Gus were put to work standing on the rear platform of the caboose, watching for any obstructions on the tracks. They would call out any problems to Mr. Reed, who was perched in his rooftop lookout, signaling the engineer with flags. Green flag, go. One red flag, slow to half speed. Two red flags, stop. It was the only way the engineer and fireman could be sure that the tracks were clear.

"Which way are we going tonight?" Lightfoot asked, standing on the rear platform.

Gus stared out on the ribbon of rails and the telegraph poles passing him by. "I say Sacramento. Lucy can't recall anything about her family. What do you think?"

"That's fine with me, Captain. I just want to get the hell out of this desert. Do we buy tickets or ride with Red, if he'll have us?"

"Let's see if he'll have us. It would be more fun for Lucy."

It took a little over three hours for the 119 to back into the Ogden depot. Before Gus and Lightfoot got off the train, Red agreed to let them ride to Sacramento in the caboose. "The Conductor won't like it, but he never comes back here. It's a two-day ride, so bring some extra grub. We depart at 1900 hours from Station Platform One. Listen for the whistle, two long, one short. Don't be late."

Red was a great guy, and they thanked him for his consideration.

When they stepped down to the station platform, they found the terminal filled with party goers and tables full of food and drink. There was even a Mariachi band strolling through the crowds. With the festivities in full swing, Gus and Lightfoot hurried across the street to their hotel. There, they both bathed, shaved, and packed for the long train ride to the coast.

Clint finished first and volunteered to pick up some food for the trip, while Gus checked out and went to pick up Lucy. They would meet up again at the party. The last thing Gus did in his room was roll up his pistol and holster, and pack them away in his leather traveling bag. On top of the bag, he strapped down his bedroll and Winchester rifle in its saddle boot. Almost everything he owned was in that valise, and his future was before him.

The Wilkins railcar was parked on the farthest siding from the terminal. To get there, in the waning afternoon light, Gus had to cross the rails of both main lines and the tracks of seven other sidings. When he got to the car, he found Lucy waiting at the door with her bag and bedroll, anxious to go. Gus thanked Mrs. Wilkins, she hugged Lucy and murmured some words of encouragement. "You're a smart young girl and I hope we meet again. Just keep reading your books sweetie."

As Gus and Lucy turned and started walking for the terminal, all three of the Wilkins children rushed to the door, waving goodbye. The oldest boy yelled, "Next time, Lucy, you'll have to show me how to skin a rabbit."

Lucy had a sad face and a tear in her eye. It was hard saying farewell to good friends.

Holding hands, she and Gus walked together through a maze

of railcars, with the sounds of gaiety and Mariachi music floating in the air. The party grew louder with every track they crossed.

Just a few rails from the mainline, they turned down a long row of empty boxcars with all their freight doors open. As they continued down this line, they heard a loud cry for help coming from the other side of the boxcars. Gus stopped, put his ear to the breeze and heard the cry again. They picked up their pace, Gus pulling Lucy along, while he looked through each cars open doors. As they rushed past the next car, Gus caught a glimpse of a big man in the shadows between two cars, holding a woman against the end of a boxcar. She was struggling and trying to fight him off.

Gus yelled at the man through the open door to stop, but he didn't.

They hurried to the end of the car and ducked under the coupler, coming out on the other side. When Gus looked down the line, he saw the man with one of his hands up the girl's dress, and his forearm pressed across her throat.

Gus dropped his bag and turned to Lucy. "Run for the terminal. It's just on the other side of these cars. Get Lightfoot."

She nodded, dropped her bag, and scurried across the row and under the next coupling.

After making sure she had crossed safely, Gus turned and rushed down to where the big guy was holding the girl. Like a monkey, he jumped onto the man's back and pulled him off the woman, throwing him to the ground. The man landed in the rock ballast with a surprised look on his face which instantly turned to anger.

"Get the hell out of here!" Gus yelled at the woman, who was gasping for air. She stumbled out of the shadows, sobbing and rearranging her clothes. She turned and headed down the line of cars at a staggering run. "Thank you, thank you," she called back as she stumbled forward.

The big man, in a brown waistcoat and ruffled shirt, got to his feet with fire in his eyes. "Do you know who hell I am?"

Gus recognized him. "Yep. You're the bigoted bartender from the Bamboo Room."

"Yeah, and you're the Cavalry prick who told me your breed friend was a descendant of the Conquistadors. You made me look like a fool, believing that bull shit."

Gus glared back at him. "All Mexicans are direct descendants, dummy."

"Well, Captain, it's payback time. Now your one eye will be joined with only one ear." He reached under his coat and pulled out a ten-inch, bone-handled knife. He reeked of alcohol and his face was red and puffy.

"I don't want any trouble fatso," Gus snarled. "Just move along and sleep it off."

The big man took a knife fighter's crouch, tossing the knife from one palm to the other. "Your ass is mine."

Gus was tempted to reach for his knife, but he didn't. "I'm not fighting you. I'm out of the killing business."

The big man slowly stepped away from the railcar, still tossing his knife from hand to hand. "You've got a blade on your belt. Fill your hands, you little prick," he said, moving closer to Gus.

The Captain's anger welled up inside of him. "I don't need a knife to take down a tub of lard like you. I'll show you how the Indians fight."

With a red face, the man lunged at him, yelling curse words. Gus pirouetted and ducked out of the way, but hit him with a hard right-cross to the jaw.

He stumbled past Gus and turned around, holding his chin. "You little twerp! Stay in one place."

Gus crouched into a wrestler's hunch, with both fists closed, as they started circling each other, between the rows of cars.

From the other side of the boxcar, Gus heard someone yell, "Fight!"

The fat man, angrier than ever, lunged at Gus two or three more times. Each time, because of the Captain's agility, he missed. Out of the corner of his eye, Gus noticed people rushing down the line of cars.

The big man lunged again, but stumbled on the rocks and fell heavily against Gus, causing both men to tumble to the ground, where they rolled around on top of each other in the ballast.

The bartender was big and heavy, and he was doing his best to stab Savage. With a lucky jab, Gus finally got loose from the other mans grip and jumped back to his feet. Glancing up the line, he saw Lucy and Lightfoot running his way. With a quick hand signal, he told Lightfoot to stay out of the fight.

The fat man was on his feet again coming after Gus, who slowly back-tracked to the boxcar, where its wooden walls stopped his retreat. The fat man rushed him, knife held high over his head. With his one good eye, Gus picked just the right split second to twist away from the powerful stab. The knife blade missed and plunged deep into the wooden planks with a thud.

It was stuck, and the big man couldn't get it out.

Gus turned to him and kneed him hard in the groin.

The bartender grabbed himself and crumpled to the ground. Doubled up, he lay groaning on the rocks. He was finished, with his knife still stuck in the wood.

Gus looked down at him. "That's how Indians fight." Turning away, Gus walked towards Lightfoot and Lucy who were standing in the crowd.

But Clint's expression suddenly turned to fear. "Gun," he yelled.

Before Gus could react, he heard the muffled report of a gun, and felt the hot sting of lead in his upper right arm. Twisting back to face the fat man, Gus saw him holding a double-barreled Derringer, about to pull the second trigger. It misfired.

Gus filled his hand with his knife and flipped it underhand at the shooter, aiming for his chest. In the approaching darkness, he missed his mark, and the blade lodged deep in the man's throat, cutting his main artery. Blood squirted from his larynx. With big eyes, making gurgling sounds, he grabbed his neck.

Gus rushed to him, shouting, "No, you son-of-a-bitch! This isn't what I wanted."

The man glanced up at the Captain, rolled his eyes and in just a few more heartbeats, slumped over dead.

Lightfoot hurried to Gus. "Let me see your arm, Captain."

Gus just stood there, stiff as a cigar-store Indian, staring down at the dead man. With his adrenaline pumping, he couldn't even feel his bullet wound. Clint got his jacket off and looked closely at the injury. "In and out," he said, tying a bandana around it. "I'll need to stitch it up."

The crowd moved around the dead man, and one of the onlookers shouted, "Do you know who that man is?"

Gus looked up at the gawkers. "The bartender from the Bamboo Room."

Another man shouted, "That's Martín Brown, the younger brother of Bill Brown, our County Sheriff. He's one mean SOB. He'll have you hanged in a heartbeat."

"It was self-defense," Gus protested. "You all saw it."

"It won't matter to Sheriff Brown. He makes his own laws," another man yelled.

"I'd get out of here, if I were you," a woman's voice shouted.

Just then, they heard a train whistle from the other side of the tracks: two long and one short. Lightfoot turned to Gus and said loudly, "She's right, Captain. That's the Jupiter about to leave for Omaha. Let's get on it."

Gus moved to the dead man and calmly removed the knife from his throat. Wiping it on his coat, he turned to the crowd. "Bear no false witness here, tonight. If you do, the wrath of God will be upon you."

The trio hurried across the main tracks with their bags. Once on the other side, they climbed up to the station level and rushed down Platform One. They jumped onto the rear of the caboose just as the 119 was pulling away.

Once on the observation deck, Gus turned to Lightfoot. "Why in the hell did you say we were taking the Jupiter to Omaha?" Lightfoot grinned. "If we're going to run from the law, let's start with them running the wrong way."

Official 'Golden Spike' photo by photographer A.J. Russell, May 10th 1869.
The coal burning UP locomotive No. 119 on the right, and the SP wood burning locomotive Jupiter on the left. Note the lack of any ethnic diversity in the picture.

Chapter 3 – The Pacific

Caboose

The carriage was empty when they entered the last little red car of the train. As the locomotive picked up speed and turned onto the main tracks, the carriage bounced from one side of the rails to the other. Lucy, new to trains, stood in the center aisle, swaying back and forth, looking for something to hold on to.

"Iron horse buck," she said finally, holding a post.

Lightfoot helped Gus sit down on the bench next to the stove. "Take off your jacket and shirt. I'll get some water hot and find the first aid kit."

"Where's Red?" Gus asked, struggling to slip off his blood-stained jacket.

Lucy swayed over to him and helped him remove his coat.

"He's up front, getting the other passengers settled in," Lightfoot answered, pumping water into a large pot.

When Gus got his coat off, he looked at the sleeve with the bullet hole. "That son-of-a- bitch ruined my new fleece jacket."

Clint put the water on the stove. "It will clean up, Captain. I'll sew it up when we're done."

The caboose was tiny, less than half the length of a day carriage. The rear of the car had a three-bench settee and a small nook for a coal stove, with a metal table for food prep. Near the center of the carriage were two tall seats so Mr. Reed could look out his windowed cupola. In front of those seats was a little sleeping compartment, toilet room, and storage bins. The caboose was a working car, and the interior wood walls were all whitewashed and void of any fancy decorations.

Lucy helped Gus off with his shirt, just as Lightfoot returned with the first aid kit. The yellow bandana tied around his upper arm was still damp with blood.

"The kit has some iodine, bandages, and sutures. This is going to hurt. Where's that bottle of brandy the railroad gave you?" Lightfoot asked.

Gus nodded to his traveling bag, and Clint opened it and removed the bottle. Pulling the cork with his teeth, he took a big swig for himself and handed the bottle to Gus. "The water's not hot enough yet. Take a few hits of this. It will take the sting off."

Gus took a couple of big gulps, examining his new shirt. "That son-of-a-bitch also ruined my blouse."

Lucy took the shirt from his hand. "I clean and sew."

"You sew?" Lightfoot asked, wide eyed.

"Yes, Mommy showed me. She good with needle," Lucy answered shyly.

Gus took another gulp of brandy. "Now she remembers her mother."

Lightfoot removed the bandana from Gus's arm, and Lucy washed it out in cold water. Clint got a lantern and held it close to his wound while carefully wiping away the blood with a warm, wet handkerchief.

"Just a deep nick," he said, handing the light to Lucy. "I'll put some iodine on it, three or four stitches, and bandage it up. You'll be as good as new."

As Lightfoot went to work on his arm, Lucy studied his actions with wonderment. Indians knew nothing about iodine and bandages. They used animal fats, pitch, and leaves. But Lucy knew Gus was in pain, because he moaned and groaned while gulping more brandy.

"Bring the light closer," Clint growled as he started sewing up the wound.

Gus did his best to hold back the pain, watching his friend carefully suture up his arm. Clint, with all of his faults, was the one person Gus could depend on. He was lucky to have such a friend. But in the end, Gus's one good eye filled with tears that ran down his cheek. When Lightfoot was done, Lucy wiped his face with the wet bandana and said with an inquisitive look, "Why you fight big man?"

"He was beating a woman."

"She bad squaw?"

"No. He bad warrior."

"She your squaw?"

"No. White men shouldn't hit women."

Lucy thought a moment. She didn't understand why he cared about a squaw that wasn't his. "White man strange."

When Mr. Reed came into the car, he found a shirtless Gus still on the bench, with Lucy helping him look for another shirt from his valise.

"What goes on here, Captain?" he asked, staring at his bandaged arm.

"I had a little trouble back in the yard, Red. A big fellow came at me with a Derringer. Just a nick, Lightfoot sewed it up."

"What's the other fellow look like?" he asked.

"He's dead," Lightfoot answered nonchalantly. "The big fella shot the Captain when his back was turned."

Red nodded. "Alright, boys, I just hope you're not bringing me any trouble."

"No, sir, we wouldn't do that," Lightfoot replied. "This is the young girl we told you about." He turned to her and continued. "Lucy Fisher, this is my good friend, Mr. Reed."

Lucy got up from the bench and curtsied to him with a smile, something she did every time her full name was mentioned. Red's expression turned to a broad smile as he approached her with a slight bow. "What a sweetheart," he said. "I'll get some coffee going."

As they waited for the coffee to brew, Clint unpacked the extra food he had purchased: three pounds of beef jerky, a dozen corndodgers, two cans of peaches, and four tins of sardines. "This will hold us until we get to Sacramento," he said proudly.

"Looks like we are going on another patrol," Gus frowned. "I think I'll have another brandy."

As they drank their coffee, Red explained that the train was full, and he hoped the conductor was too busy to come back to the caboose. "But if he does, just explain that you jumped on the train late, and offer to buy the tickets from him. He won't like it, but he won't kick you off."

He also told them that it was two hundred sixty miles to the next stop, Elko, Nevada. "It will take us about ten hours, so I'm going to get some sleep. You'll find blankets and pillows under the bench seats. When we get to Elko, you can buy some real food from the local vendors," he grinned.

"I like sardines," Lightfoot answered.

Before turning in, Red showed Lucy where the sewing kit was.

"Thank you," she said. "The Indians say I like a butterfly, but sting like a bee. Why you called Red? Hair not red."

He smiled at her, "A long time ago I had red hair. Now it's just my nickname."

"What is nickname?"

"I'll tell you later. Good night, butterfly."

With half the bottle of brandy gone, and the swaying of the rails, Gus and Lightfoot were soon sprawled out on settees with blankets and pillows, snoring like locomotives. Lucy with needle and thread in hand, sat on the bench next to the stove, with the kerosene lamp close. She had washed away the blood from Gus's garments as best she could, and was now stitching up the bullet holes. As her little fingers worked, pushing the needle through the fabric and pulling it tight, her head filled with old family memories. The most vivid was of a beautiful young woman with brilliant red hair and creamy skin, also sewing by lantern light. "Keep your stitches tight and your rows straight," she said in a loving voice. Lucy recognized her as her mother. She was at the table in their cabin, mending a shirt for Father. He sat next to her, sharpening an axe with a pumice stone and oil cloth. He was tall and muscular, with an olive complexion. She recalled him only as Father, with his dark hair and neatly trimmed beard that she loved to pull. He was a lumberjack, and they lived in a forest. That was why they were going to Oregon. "The forests out there are tall and deep, and we'll build a new cabin twice the size of this one." Mother said Daddy was a dreamer. In her reverie, Lucy could see her older brother Leon sitting next to her at the table. She smiled, pleased to finally remember his name. He had Mommy's red hair and a fair complexion. Leon was always whittling a stick into a gun, and playing cowboys and Indians in the forest.

They had been on the trail for months when their wagon broke down in the middle of the Great Plains. Horrified, Lucy had watched her mother and father killed, scalped, and mutilated by the Cheyenne, and she was taken. But she couldn't recall seeing her brother, that day. She loved Leon because he always protected her.

Why was he gone?

With the sounds of the wheels and the swaying of the car, she finally finished the garments and looked up from her work. With sleepy eyes, she gazed across the car to where the two men were sleeping. Now they protected her. Were they her new brothers? What had happened to Leon?

As usual, Gus woke at first light, but on this morning he smelled fresh coffee brewing, and heard muffled words coming from Red's lookout. His sore arm stung as he sat up on the bench. Gus moved the arm around slowly, getting the blood circulating. Lightfoot was still sleeping but Lucy was gone from her bed. In the faint morning light, he pulled on his boots, got up, and poured himself a mug of coffee. It tasted good. He was hungry and his arm was on fire. Then he noticed his mended shirt and jacket.

He examined them. She had done a marvelous job, and he was proud of her. He put the shirt on and moved down the car to the observation chairs. Looking up, he found Red in one and Lucy in the other.

"Thank you for fixing my shirt," he said to Lucy.

"I ride in crows nest," she answered with excitement in her voice.

"We're watching the desert sunrise," Red added.

"Why is sky blood red?" Lucy asked.

"Because the sun is angry when it wakes up," Gus answered. "How far to Elko?"

"About twenty miles," Red said. "We'll take on water and coal there. The layover will be about half an hour. If you get off the train, stay clear of the Conductor. We don't need him snooping around."

Lucy looked down at the Captain. "You come up here with me, Night-Eye. I sit on your lap. I have powerful dream, last night. I remember my brother's name."

The layover in Elko was uneventful. When Red got off the train to secure the brakes, Gus slipped out the rear of the caboose. Quickly, he snuck inside the new depot and purchased a local newspaper, some hard-boiled eggs, three apples, and a bottle of milk before returning to the caboose. A few minutes later, the 119 pulled out of the station, heading for the next stop, Winnemucca, Nevada.

When Red returned from his brakeman's duties, he and Lucy climbed back to the cupola with breakfast in hand, to keep an eye out for any hot boxes. While they were in the cupola, Gus and Lightfoot ate their breakfast, and Gus read the paper. There was no mention of any killing back in Ogden, and he breathed a sigh of relief. He told Lightfoot the good news. "I'm sure the Sheriff thinks we're on our way to Omaha," he answered with confidence.

Reading the paper, Gus was close enough to the lookout to overhear the conversation between Red and Lucy. She was peppering him with questions.

"What is hot box?"

"Smoke or fire coming from the wheels. It's caused by friction."

"No understand friction. What caboose mean?"

"It's from the Dutch word Kabuis. It means little room or hut."

"What is Dutch?"

"They are people who live across the sea."

"They are Indian tribe?"

"No, they are just people like us, with a different language."

"Why caboose red?"

Lucy was a precocious little gal, with a mind like a sponge and with a curiosity like a beaver. These questions went on for hours.

When they got to Winnemucca, only Red got off to set the train's brakes. As he went to work, the trio sat in the crows nest, watching the activities on the platform. There was a large crowd of people and a brass band waiting, with an overhead banner that read, 'Welcome UP Railroad.' As passengers disembarked, the companions could hear the music and the applause coming from the waiting crowd. Soon, dignitaries were making speeches while new passengers boarded the train. In the midst of all this confusion, Lightfoot slipped off the back of the caboose and went into the new terminal. When he returned, he had another local newspaper, more beef jerky, some hard candy, and a bottle of Tequila.

As Clint gave the candy to Lucy, Gus opened the paper to a headline that read 'Town Welcomes Rail Service.' He read the story. The railroads had built Winnemucca as a major repair facility, with spur lines going north and south, adding the town to the transcontinental line. Winnemucca was destined to be one of the major rail hubs of the west. That explained the welcoming committee.

He continued reading the paper. On the last page, he found what he feared, a small headline that read, 'Man Killed in Ogden Yard.' The story said that County Sheriff Bill Brown was searching for a one-eyed man with a black patch over his left eye. The Sheriff called the man a 'cold-blooded killer.' He claimed he had witnesses that saw the one-eyed man kill Martín Brown by stabbing him in the back. Gus shook his head sadly and read the story to Lightfoot. They decided to hide the paper from Red.

That afternoon, Gus and Lucy rode in the cupola with Mr. Reed, and they talked about the bleak and barren landscape of northern Nevada. Red seemed to know every mile post, curve, and trestle they crossed. It was as if he had traveled this way before.

"How do you know this road so well?" Gus finally asked.

"Last month, the 119 crew was sent to the UP railhead when it was still in Wyoming. From there, we traveled by stagecoach to the SP railhead in Nevada. Then we rode an SP train all the way back to Sacramento. It was done so we could become familiarized with their line. From Winnemucca to Sacramento, I memorized it. Going over the Sierra Nevada's for the first time is something I'll never forget."

"I'm impressed," Gus answered. "Memorizing this terrain takes a special gift."

Red smiled. "I don't have many gifts, but I'm glad to have this one."

Seven hours later the train pulled into Reno. It was just getting dark, so Red lit one of his lanterns and walked the long line, setting the brakes on the railcars. He returned half an hour later with a stern expression, carrying a yellow slip of paper.

"The Conductor gave me this," he said, giving the paper to Gus.

It was a telegram addressed to the Conductor of Train 119 c/o Reno Station. Gus read it out loud. 'US Marshals searching for one

Captain Gus Savage US Calvary. He is recognizable by a black patch over his left eye. Wanted for murder and considered dangerous. Marshals will search train upon arrival in Sacramento.' Omaha rail dispatcher.

"I killed that man in self-defense," Gus said, handing back the telegram.

"I know that, Captain," Red answered, with a concerned look. "But you can't be on the train when we get to Sacramento. It could cost me my job."

"Does the Conductor know we're back here?" Gus asked.

"I don't think so," Red answered.

"Should we get off here in Reno?" Lightfoot asked, pouring himself some mescal.

Reed shook his head. "No, it's a long walk over the Sierra Nevada's to get to the goldfields from here. I've got a better idea. We are going to be delayed for a couple of hours of maintenance. We won't leave until about midnight. That puts us in Sacramento about nine in the morning. I know a place where the train slows for its last big grade. You could jump off the caboose safely there."

"How far would we be from Sacramento?" Gus asked.

"It's about fifteen miles east, but you'll only be about fifty miles from the goldfields."

Gus and Lightfoot agreed with Red's plan, although both were anxious about not having food or horses for the journey to the fields. It was going to be a long, slow walk.

At first light the next morning, the trio stood around the stove, drinking coffee and eating what remained of their food. With the light of the new day, they got their first good look at the Sierra Nevada's. They were breathtaking gray monoliths of granite peaks, white snowcapped mountains, and numerous tunnels hand-carved through the stone.

Red told them the story of thousands of Chinese workers, hired by the Central Pacific Railroad, who worked for many years to chisel out the line. "Everything was done by muscle power, in the hot summer sun and the cold, deep snowdrifts of winter. Many died. Some bodies are buried here, some have never been found. It was the skills of the white surveyors, the knowledge of the engineers, and the sweat of the Chinese that built this road."

The companions were impressed with Red's story, and marveled at the accomplishment of building such a road.

Under a bright, clear sky, the way through Donner Pass was quickly traveled. Then the train started its long descent into Sacramento.

"The final grade is coming up in a few miles," Red told them, looking out a window.

The last upgrade was long, straight, and steep, with tall mounds of rock rubble on each side of the tracks. The 119 slowed, working hard, its wheels spinning as it pulled the long snake of cars over the last hill. Finally, everyone inside the caboose moved to the rear platform, judging the trains speed and saying goodbye.

"We've only got a few minutes," Red said. "Do you see the American River through those trees down there?" He asked pointing to the forest line.

"Yes," Gus answered, with his bedroll and valise in hand.

"Once you get off the train, slide down the rubble to the tree line and walk to the river. If you go upstream, you're heading for the goldfields. Downstream is Sacramento and San Francisco."

Gus shook his hand. "Thanks, Red. Hope we didn't get you in any trouble."

He nodded at the trio with a smile. "Stay safe, folks. It's time to go."

As the train slowed to a crawl, Gus threw his bag and bedroll off the platform and jumped, with his feet running. Lightfoot threw Lucy's belongings off and then picked her up and handed her down to Gus, running alongside the train. Then Lightfoot jumped, running with his own traps in hand.

Red watched from the rear of the caboose to make sure they were good. Then, waving, he shouted, "Don't be showing your face in Sacramento, Captain. You'd stand out like a railroad flare."

Gus stopped running with Lucy in his arms and put her down gently, waving back to Red as the train pulled away. When he did, he noticed the Conductor, dressed in his black uniform, hanging out of the open doors of the baggage car, waving back at them.

"That son–of–a–bitch knew we were here all the time," Gus said to Lightfoot with a smile as they walked back to pick up their bags.

"Yep," Lightfoot replied. "You do stand out in a crowd, Captain."

They slipped and slid down the loose rock rubble on their butts. It was steep, and the rocks were sharp and hard. With dust flying, they finally came to the tree line as, with one final blast from the train whistle, the 119 disappeared over the hill.

They were on their own.

When they got to the American River, they found a well-used wagon road next to it. They stopped there to catch their breath and to dust off their clothes. Lightfoot sat down on a trail log and rolled a cigarette, while Lucy walked across the road to the water's edge to get a drink.

Gus paced up and down the dirt road, thinking. They had no horses, no food, not even a coffee pot. Would it be wise to walk all the way to the goldfields? Maybe San Francisco was better. Maybe they could find Lucy a home there, and then go to the fields.

With the morning sun still low, Gus finally made his decision and walked over to where Clint rested on the log. Just as he was about to announce his decision, he noticed a buckboard coming their way from upstream.

The driver pulled up his wagon in front of the men. "Good morning," he said as the dust settled. "It's a little early to find pilgrims on the road. Did your horses run off?"

He was a young man in dungarees, driving a two-up empty wagon. The lad had sandy hair, blue eyes, and a friendly face.

"Nope," Lightfoot replied, getting up from the log. "We were just kicked off that train. We were supposed to get off in Reno, but we slept through the stop. We didn't have any tickets for Sacramento so they threw us off."

"Heard the train go by," the lad answered. "Sorry they threw you off. The SP always seems so accommodating."

Gus approached the wagon, "We were just making up our minds which way we'd go, upstream to the goldfields or downstream to Sacramento."

The lad stared at Gus with his black eye patch. "You a member of the Grand Old Army of the Republic?"

"Yep," Gus answered. "And my friend here was a member of the Confederate Republic. But the war is over and we don't look back."

"That's smart," the young man answered. "Can't believe the SP would kick a veteran off its train. It just doesn't make any sense."

"What about the goldfields?" Lightfoot asked, trying to change the subject.

"I'm coming back from the fields," he answered. "If you're looking for work, I wouldn't look there. Most of the mines are played out by now. They are laying off men."

"What do you mean, played out?" Gus asked.

"The heyday of the California fields are gone, sir. No more gold, no more miners," he answered.

Just then, Lucy returned from the river and crossed the road in front of the wagon. Dressed in a pair of blue bib overalls and a yellow-flowered cotton blouse, somehow she looked older and more mature. As she approached, Lucy looked up at the young driver with a smile and winked at him.

"What do we have here?" he asked, smiling back at her. "Is this your daughter?" Before Gus could answer, Lucy said, "No, these are my Brothers. We are on our way to San Francisco."

Lightfoot and Gus glanced at each other, shrugging their shoulders. *Why not?*

"Where could we get a riverboat going that way?" Lucy continued, with an alluring smile.

Gus looked at her. Where in the hell did she learn this stuff?

The young man blushed a moment and introduced himself as Robert Hume. He and his two brothers lived on a river barge fifteen miles downstream. "Where we live is as far up the river as most paddleboats can go. It's too shallow to go any farther." He offered them a ride to his barge; moored in a place he called Turner's Cove. "Tomorrow, you can catch a boat for San Francisco."

It was an offer they couldn't pass up. Gus introduced himself and his friends, and they loaded their baggage and themselves into the empty wagon. Lightfoot and Lucy rode in the back, with Gus riding up front with Robert. As they moved down the road, Lucy started peppering the young man with questions. Robert was twenty years old and had come out to California just two years before. He and his brothers were all from Maine, where their family owned a fish cannery. Now the three brothers owned a similar business, canning salmon on their river barge. "My oldest brother invented a process for safely canning salmon, a few years ago," Robert said proudly. "They needed help, so I came out to lend a hand." His brothers sent Robert out to the goldfields twice a year with a thousand cans of salmon. He sold the fish directly to the miners for two bits a can. He would return downriver when he was sold out. Gus did some quick figuring and determined the lad had made five hundred dollars selling one-pound cans of fish. He was impressed.

Robert told them that the fish would stay fresh three to four years without spoiling. While still driving his team, he opened a can he had under his seat and passed it around as a sample. It was amazingly good. Even Lightfoot commented it was better than his sardines.

"I'd eat more if you had any more," Gus said, tasting the last morsel.

Robert smiled at him. "I happen to have more samples under my seat." He handed three more cans and a small, palm-sized can opener to Gus.

"I'll be glad to pay you," he answered, opening the first can for Lucy. The can opener fascinated Gus. "Who invented this?"

"One of my brothers," Robert answered. "No pay necessary, Captain. These sample cans are how I drum up new business."

Lucy looked at her can of fish with great curiosity. "How do big fish get in small can?"

Robert chuckled and told her in detail how they packed the fish.

As Gus ate more of the salmon, he asked, "If the goldfields of California are dried up, where did all the prospectors go?"

Hunched over, with the reins in his hands, Robert turned his young face to Gus and answered, "Some went east to the Truckee River in Nevada. Others headed north as far as Oregon. Who knows where the next gold rush will be? One old sourdough told me last week that he had heard they'd found gold dust in the black sands of a place called Coos Bay on the Oregon Coast. He said you could just rake up the gold from the sands." Robert snickered. "Once you're bit by the gold fever, you just keep moving on."

"How do you get to a place like Coos Bay from here?" Gus

asked with great interest.

"Ship, I guess," Robert answered. "Someone said that ships stop there all the time to take on coal."

Bob turned out to be a real chatterbox with a big heart and a wealth of information. The conversation made the time fly.

Paddlewheels

In the early afternoon, they arrived at the sun-drenched, tree-lined cove on the American River. It was a large, sparkling moorage with log floating docks that stretched from the shallows to the deep water. The ramps were wide enough to accommodate wagons that were transported by riverboats down to Sacramento and further south to San Francisco. The Hume Brother's river barge was moored next to the portage where paddlewheels loaded and unloaded.

Under a warm sun, they drove the wagon out onto the floating ramp, and Robert stopped next to his barge. "My brothers aren't here now. Our fishing boat is gone," he said, stepping down from the wagon. The square-bowed, fore and aft, wood-planked barge was about fifty feet long and thirty feet wide. There was a small deck at each end, with a flat-roofed cabin in the center. Robert explained that the brothers lived in half of the boat and did their canning business in the other half.

"Can we see where you work?" Lucy asked.

"Sure," he replied eagerly.

They went aboard and the lad showed them the factory. It wasn't much: a filleting table for the fish, a small scale for weighing the cutup fish, and stacks of empty tin cans and lids. The compartment smelled of fish and sweat. Robert showed them the tabletop machine that sealed the lids to the cans, and a deep metal barrel where the cans were steamed in hot water.

"The secret is canning the fish in all their natural oils, and slowly steaming the sealed cans in the hot water. This way, the fish will cook with a vacuum seal that won't let them spoil."

Holding an empty tin can, Lightfoot asked, "Do you make your own cans, as well?'

"No," he answered. "We buy empty cans from Bay Can Company in San Francisco."

"What's it cost to make a can of salmon?" Gus asked, looking around the factory.

Robert shrugged. "Only five cents if we catch the fish ourselves or ten cents if we have to buy the fish."

Good profit, Gus thought. He was impressed, not only with the process and the taste, but with the Hume Brothers, as well. They seemed to know instinctively that they were onto something.

"Show me how fish get in can," Lucy replied, holding an empty can.

Robert opened a wooden barrel full of fish in water, brought out a large, cleaned salmon, and placed it on a wooden cider board. Taking a long skinny knife, he filleted the fish on both sides with just a few quick swipes of the sharp blade. Cutting up the pieces, he weighed each portion, then rolled and tucked the red meat inside the empty cans. Draining the oils from the cutting board into the cans, he placed one of them into the table-top canning machine and hand cranked a tin lid on the top of the can.

"That's how we pack 'em in," he said to Lucy. "All we do next is slow steam them in their own natural juices."

Clint was mesmerized with Robert's skills with a knife. "Never seen such quick hands with a blade before," he complimented. "How about giving me a lesson?"

"Yes, please do," Lucy added.

As Robert gave him a lesson, using another fish, Gus studied the canning machine with its iron cranks, levers, wheels, and gears. It was an ingenious machine, simply designed. This was something he could have built, if he had just stayed in engineering school.

Before leaving the barge, Gus bought six more cans of salmon and put them in his valise. "We'll eat these on our riverboat ride. What time will it arrive here, tomorrow?"

"You'll hear it coming up the river about nine in the morning," Robert answered.

"Is there a general store nearby?" Clint asked.

Yes, just down the road half a mile."

They said farewell on the dock with handshakes and smiles. "I'd ask you to stay here on the boat," the lad said, "but when my brothers return we'll have fish to clean, and we'll be up all night, processing their catch."

"Not a problem," Gus answered. "Thanks for the ride and the

fish. We'll find a place to camp."

When Robert said goodbye to Lucy, he stammered, "I hope our trails will cross again, when you're older and I'm wiser. You're one pretty lassie."

With her green eyes dancing, Lucy blushed and turned away.

After stopping off at a country store for some basic supplies, the trio found a campsite on a sandy beach next to the teal-green river. It was a warm day, and so they washed their traveling clothes and hung them on tree limbs to dry. Then, with great glee, they gave themselves a bath in the cool, slow flow of the stream. With whippoorwills singing and frogs croaking, the tree-lined river sparkled in sunlight for as far as they could see. Every now and then, a fishing boat would row past the campsite. One of them held two young men who might have been the Hume Brothers. Lightfoot shouted out to them, "How's the fishing, gents?" One held up a gigantic salmon and yelled back, "Five more just like it."

The American River was a bountiful stretch of water filled with endless opportunities for those that had an eye to the future. Gus remembered a saying his father often said, *'Ask for it and it will be given, seek it and you will find it. Opportunity waits for no man.'*

With the sky crimson red, the friends rested on their bedrolls next to a small shore campfire, eating cheese, bread, and jerky while drinking wine. The evening was warm, and the beach sand was soft.

"I long for my horse Loco and his saddle as my pillow," Lightfoot complained, with his back against a log snare.

Gus handed him the open bottle of wine. "Use your jacket. It's so warm, you won't need it tonight."

"I like this California," Clint answered, taking a drink from the bottle. "The weather is warm, the trees are tall, and the fish are big."

"That reminds me," Gus answered. "Lucy, where did you learn about riverboats?"

Lucy was sitting on her bedroll with firelight dancing on her face. "Mrs. Wilkins tell us about fancy riverboat she took to a place called New Ol'lens. She say the river best way to travel."

Lightfoot handed the bottle back to Gus. "It's called New Orleans."

"And how do you know about San Francisco?"

"The Sergeant Major tell me. He say it is a golden city on bay."

"And who taught you to wink at boys?"

She glared across the fire to Clint. "I can't remember."

"I did," he said. "It's no big deal. I told her it was a friendly greeting, just like curtsying."

"Winking is not proper!" Gus replied firmly. "We have to teach her to be leery of men."

"What is leery?" Lucy asked.

"The Captain thinks you should be scared of men."

"Why? You are men. I'm not scared of you."

Gus stood and paced around the fire, thinking about how to answer. Finally, he looked down at her and replied, "We are men that respect you. But there are others, like the big man back in Ogden, who drink too much firewater and won't respect you."

"What would they to do to me?" Lucy asked, looking confused.

Gus shook his head. "You are too young to know. Someone will tell you, when you are older. From now on, no winking at men. It's just not proper. Do you understand?"

She frowned and took a drink from the bottle of wine. "I think so. What is lassie?"

With Lightfoot grumbling about no coffee, the trio broke camp early the next morning and walked upriver to Turner's Cove. When they arrived at the dock, they found half a dozen filled produce wagons waiting in line. There were also a few dozen people, waiting with suitcases in hand. In front of where the riverboat landed was a map of the river route to San Francisco, with four scheduled stops. Below the map was a sign with fare information: so much per stop, per person, per head of livestock, or per wagon load. Passengers paid by the deck they would ride on. The main deck with the wagons and livestock was the cheapest. The second deck was called the promenade and the third called the salon deck. The prices got higher with each level of deck.

Gus read the fare options to Lightfoot and Lucy. "I think we should just walk on to the main deck. It's the cheapest," he told them.

Lightfoot frowned, "Not a good idea, Captain. Let's get a compartment on the second deck so you can stay out of sight while we paddle through Sacramento."

"Is that really necessary?"

Both Clint and Lucy nodded. "Black patch, everyone see," Lucy added.

Gus nodded his approval. "You're right, everyone will notice my eye patch. So I'll just take it off." He turned his back on his friends and removed his hat and eye patch, then turned back to them.

Lucy and Lightfoot were shocked and silenced by how their friend looked, standing in the morning sun. His disfigure-eyeball bulged and was half closed by an eyelid and turned inward as if he was crossed eyed. His deep eye socket was covered with scars, and a jagged reddish gash replaced where his eyebrow had once been. It was a horrific and painful sight to behold.

Gus slipped his sweat-stained hat back on and turned down the front brim. "Everyone will still gawk at me, but they will only remember my deformed eye, not my black patch," Gus said to his stunned friends. "When the boat arrives, I'll put my hand on your shoulder, Lightfoot, and you can lead me as if I'm blind in both eyes."

"Can you see anything out of that eye?" Clint asked.

Gus shook his head. "Only some occasional bright light and a few shadows. My bad eye conflicts with my good, so I have trouble with my balance without the patch."

Lucy moved closer. "It hurt?"

"No," Gus answered. "Just get me to our cabin and I'll stay out of sight."

They heard the boat's whistle before they could see it on the river. When it came into view, the side-wheeler slowly turned into the cove and navigated docking, with everyone on shore watching its approach. As the boat got closer, the side wheels reversed, slowing it to a gentle thud against the floating log dock.

The name of the boat was *Chrysopolis*. It was long and wide, with a red hull, a white superstructure, and tall black smokestacks with colorful pennants flying. The steam whistle blasted again, with white fog and water dripping from brass cylinders as the boat was secured to the pier with thick ropes by the crew. She was a beautiful boat, just as pretty and complicated as a locomotive. They watched the arrival with great anticipation. None of them had ever been aboard such a ship before.

After a boarding ramp was placed on the dock, the boat's purser came ashore and stood by the fare sign, selling tickets. The companions got in line with the other passengers, with Gus keeping a hand on Lightfoot's shoulder. When their turn came to buy tickets, the purser's glare was frozen on Gus's mangled eye.

"Did that happen in the war?" he asked as Lightfoot paid for the tickets.

"No," Clint answered with a frown. "He was a powder monkey up in the goldfields."

"That's tough," the purser replied nonchalantly. "Your cabin number is 112, second deck. We'll be in San Francisco by eight o'clock tonight. "

Their tiny wood-paneled compartment was long and narrow, with bunk beds facing a settee. At the far end of the room was a wash bowl with a small table and at the other end was the cabin door, with a window next to it. It wasn't fancy, but it was private.

The first thing Lightfoot did was close the curtains of the window. "We can open this again after Sacramento. I'd like to walk around the ship. I've never seen a ship so big before."

Gus moved to the wash bowl and gazed at himself in the mirror, frowning at his reflection. "My dead eye is as ugly as sin. No wonder people stare."

Lucy moved to him and looked at him in the mirror. "Without patch, no one see warrior face."

Gus removed his hat, reached into his pocket, and put on his eye patch again. "That's better," he said after it was in place. With his sandy blond hair, sun-drenched copper complexion, and square jaw, the black eye patch made him more mysterious looking. He liked what he saw.

Lucy grabbed his arm and squeezed it. "Oh, Night-Eye, now you look like beautiful warrior you are," she said, winking at him in the mirror. "How you lose eye?"

Gus turned to her in frustration, about to say something about winking again, but Clint interrupted. "Yeah, Captain, how did you lose that eye?"

With time to spare, and Gus impatiently pacing the cabin deck, he started telling Lucy stories about the Civil War and the Battle of Honey Springs, where he had lost his eye.

"My doctor told me that my raised right hand and my sword grip saved my life when a rocket exploded. It cost me two fingers and an eye, but it was better than being dead."

"Will you ever see out of that eye again?" Clint asked.

"No. They wanted to put a glass eye in me but I didn't want any part of that."

"What is glass eye?" Lucy asked. As usual, she was like dry sand, soaking up every word.

After a short layover in Sacramento, and with the town in the boat's wake, Lightfoot opened the cabin curtains, and the friends explored the ship.

As they walked around the promenade, Gus noticed the city fashions of the other passengers. It was as if this was the Sabbath. He also marveled at the luxury of traveling by steamboat.

On the lower deck, they got a look at the engine room, where two large wood-fed boilers turned water into the steam that made the pistons turn the two thirty-foot-tall side paddles. It was a maze of machinery and noise, much like that of a locomotive. Gus tried to explain the principles of steam power to his friends, but they seemed more interested in the beauty of the boat and the colorful types of people walking the decks.

On the salon deck, they found a café that sold coffee and sandwiches. Here they had lunch and then strolled into an attached bar just behind the bistro. It was a small, fancy salon with an ornate wooden bar, and a bandstand on the back wall with a piano. In front of the piano were green-felt poker tables, with other chairs scattered about the cabin. The room looked of money and smelled of cigars.

Gus and Clint walked to the bar and ordered two whiskeys and a glass of wine. Lucy didn't join them right away, as she was walking around the room, looking at all of the risqué paintings that graced the saloon's red-flocked walls.

Lightfoot chuckled as they waited for their drinks. "She didn't understand all those animal heads back in Ogden. What do you think she'll say about all the naked ladies?"

Gus didn't reply. He was busy studying two of the poker tables and the men playing cards. They were dressed up in high-collared shirts, vests, and long frock coats. These weren't hayseed cowboys playing poker in a bunkhouse; they had an air of wealth and aristocracy.

"Well, what do you think she'll say?" Clint asked again.

The drinks came, and Gus turned back to the bar. "Don't know. You tell her. I'm going to have my drink and then change into my new black coat and play some poker."

Clint paid the barkeep and took a swig of his whiskey. "Those gentleman look like they know what they're doing. You sure you want to lock horns with them?"

"Why not? I won in Ogden and I'll win here."

Before Gus could finish his drink, Lucy stepped between them at the bar, her eyes wide. "Why do white squaws have no clothes?"

Clint shrugged his shoulder with a grin. "White man like to see their squaws without clothes."

Lucy smirked. "You want to see me without clothes?"

"No," Gus replied quickly. "Clint and *some* men like to see naked girls. I do not."

"Ah, yes, that's right," Clint said mockingly. "The Captain doesn't have that proclivity. He likes his women with clothes on."

Lucy frowned. "What is meaning of word?"

Gus finished his drink with one gulp and smiled at his friend. "Yes, Clint, explain the meaning of word 'proclivity' to Lucy, while I change my clothes and play some poker."

When Gus returned to the bar in his fancy frock, he found that Lightfoot and Lucy were gone. Of the five poker tables, only two were active. One was full with six players, and the other held just four. Watching the play for a few moments, he approached an empty chair at the four-player table.

"May I join you gentleman?" he asked.

All of the players gazed up at him inquisitively.

"Aye, we like new blood," one player finally answered, and the others nodded their approval.

Gus took a seat. "What's the buy-in?"

"We're playing a friendly game of stud poker. Hundred dollar buy-in with a dollar ante," the older man next to him answered. "Hope you won't be handicapped, with just one eye."

Gus chuckled. Reaching for his money, he placed Gold and Silver Eagles on the table. "I see better with one than most see with two. I like to bluff, but I don't cheat," he answered with a smile, tossing out his ante.

For the first few hands, Gus played conservatively with few raises, and folding most of his hands. He did this on purpose, to watch the other player's behavior and demeanor. He called this observation determining the 'tell.' Each of the gentlemen had a little habit or quirk, with good hands or bad. Some rolled their eyes; some fussed with their dealt cards or nervously tapped their fingers on the felt table. Everyone had a 'tell'; the trick was to find it and remember it.

The second part of his strategy was counting cards. All numbered cards were five, picture cards ten and aces twelve. As each player was dealt a new card up, Gus kept a running total of their tally in his number-friendly head. That way, he could compare his dealt hand with his opponents. This method of poker wasn't foolproof, but it gave him an edge.

As the cards were shuffled and dealt around the table, Gus got to know each of the other players. The table talk was mostly about the completion of the Iron Highway, so Gus told them of his two-year service to the road. He also told them about being in the 'golden spike' picture. They all seemed impressed, and asked questions about the construction of the line.

The distinguished-looking older gentleman next to Gus was called Mr. Prescott by the other players. He introduced himself as a banker. He was a quiet man with piercing blue eyes and a neatly trimmed gray beard that covered much of his aging face. The player on the other side of Gus was a young architect building a new building in downtown San Francisco. "It will be the tallest building in the city, built entirely of quarried stone," he said, scooping up his winnings from a small pot. The other two men across the table were surveyors, working on irrigation projects for the farming communities on the east side of the Bay. San Francisco was growing, and these men were some of the visionaries building the city. Gus enjoyed their chatter immensely.

The cards started out poorly for Gus, but as the table talk continued, the cards got better, and his system started paying dividends. A couple of hours later, his losses were gone, replaced by a modest profit of about forty dollars. Sadly, that's when the boat's whistle signaled a scheduled stop, and the two surveyors bid their farewell from the game. With only three players remaining, it was decided that the game was over.

"Can I buy you a drink, Captain?" Mr. Prescott asked, collecting his money from the felt.

Gus glanced over to the other poker table, hoping for an open chair, but there was none. "That would be nice," he answered to the banker.

The two men took stools at the bar and ordered their drinks. The banker asked for a brandy and coffee, and Gus had the same.

"What brings you to San Francisco, Captain?" He asked.

How did he know I was a Captain? Gus wondered. He hadn't told that to the table. "Came out for the goldfields," he finally answered, eyeing the old gentleman carefully.

"Got the gold fever, eh?" Mr. Prescott replied, and glared back at Gus. "I know who you are."

The drinks came, and the banker paid the bartender with a dollar tip. After the barkeep's departure, Mr. Prescott turned back to Gus. "Your secret is safe with me, son. I'm a Jayhawker like you."

Gus's body tensed up and his palms got sweaty. How in the hell did he know that? "I'm afraid you have the wrong man, sir," he answered, watching the old man's expression.

He shook his head. "No, I saw the Golden Spike picture in Sacramento yesterday. A Federal Marshal had the picture, with your face circled, and posted on the station's wall. That black eye patch stands out like a priest in a pleasure house. The Marshal told me you killed a Sheriff, back in Ogden. But my old friend, Colonel Rollins, told me the charges were trumped up. He had it on good authority that it was self-defense."

Gus was dumbfounded by the old gentleman's story. "How do you know the Colonel?"

The banker grinned and took a sip of his coffee, "Had lunch with him yesterday. He came out on the 119 from Ogden. We go way back to the war. I was once his Commanding Officer. We've remained friends ever since. He told me you were traveling with a young girl and one of your scouts. You should be safe in the city. I don't think the Marshal will be looking there."

Gus felt relieved by the news. "Colonel Rollins was my Commanding Officer. He's a fine officer. Would you be General Prescott, sir? Killing Joe Prescott?"

He frowned while shaking his head. "I hate that nickname. But yes, a long time ago I was that general. Colonel Rollins thinks the world of you, Gus. Why San Francisco?"

Just then, they heard some loud cursing from the active poker table. Both men turned their attention to the commotion, where one player was just scooping up his winnings from a fat pot.

"See that scoundrel in the pink ruffled shirt, the one collecting the money? That's Lucky Jake Collins, a steamboat shill. Never play cards with him. He's a cheat," General Prescott said, watching him closely.

"What's a steamboat shill?" Gus asked.

"They're professional gamblers that are partners with the boat owners. They ride for free, eat and drink the same, and split their winnings with the owners. Most are cheats, and Lucky Jake Collins is the best of the worst."

"Do the owners know they cheat?"

"Yes, most do. It's all about the money."

General Prescott and Gus continued talking through another round of drinks. Soon, the two men were bonded as comrades-in-arms. Gus told him the story of Lucy and his desire to find her a family in San Francisco. "That will be hard to do," the General said. "The blue bloods on Nob Hill won't take kindly to a white captive girl." Gus also told him that he hoped to find a ship that would take him to the goldfields of Coos Bay Oregon.

Prescott grinned, "That I can help you with. The bank owns the paper on lots of ships. I'll find one going your way. Where will you be staying?"

"Don't really know, sir. I thought we'd just find a hotel."

General Prescott removed two business cards from his pocket. "That's an easy fix." On the back of one card, he wrote out the address for the Seafarer Inn. "This hotel is just a couple of blocks west of where we'll dock, this evening. Give my card to Mrs.

Brown. She's the innkeeper of the hostel. She'll give you a good rate. The Seafarer is one of my clients, and a clean place to stay, with no rats, bedbugs, or fleas. I'll send you a message there, when I find a ship going your way."

Then the General gave Gus the second card. "Put this in your pocket. The Iron Highway is going to open up the west. If you ever need some banking, drop me a line."

Gus looked at the front of the card. Joseph Prescott was the Vice President of Wells Fargo & Company. What a friend to have!

The General pulled out his pocket watch and clicked it open. "I've got to leave now, Gus. My wife will be waiting. Good luck with the goldfields."

"May I ask one more question before you leave, sir?"

The General nodded his permission.

"During the war, you saw action on the western frontier. During that time, did you ever run across a rebel Colonel named William McKay? He was a Bushwhacker riding with Quantrill."

The General's blue eyes turned to fire, and he frowned. "I know that assassin. By the end of the war, I had him and his younger brother Jasper in custody and on their way to Fort Knox for hanging. Then they escaped and vanished into the wilderness. Some say they came to California, but I never heard of him again. Why do you ask?"

"The Colonel killed my family while I was away. Mutilated and burned them all."

"The McKay Brothers are truly the devil," the General answered with a scowl. "There's a Federal reward for them both, dead or alive. But be aware, the Colonel conceals a Derringer in his right boot. That's how he got away. If you see either of these bastards, kill them. Don't wait for the law, just kill them! They are the worst of the worst."

"All I know about the Colonel is he has red hair and a jagged scar over his right eye. Do you remember anything else about him?"

"Yes. He walks with a slight limp, favoring his right leg. If you see him, Gus, just kill him!"

"How about Jasper? Do you know anything about him?'

"Yes, he stutters and is deaf in one ear. I've got to go."

Gus stood with a long face and outstretched hand. "Thank

you, General. Given the chance, I'll kill them both." They shook hands firmly realizing that the Civil War was still not over.

As Gus finished his coffee, watching the General depart, he noticed a player leaving the active table. He was tempted to take his seat, 'steamboat shill' or not, but just then Lucy burst into the room and ran over to his bar stool.

"Night-Eye, you know what I've been doing?" she asked, with a grin from ear to ear.

Gus smiled back at her; she was such a bolt of sunshine. "No, tell me please."

"I've been watching a monkey, a real monkey, not like in the picture books! Edgar is so friendly! Would you like to meet him?"

Gus wrinkled his brow. "Where's Lightfoot?"

"He's down below, watching Edgar. Come with me and see."

Gus saw the excitement in Lucy's eyes, and gently put both of his hands on her face. "You go tell Clint that someone recognized me. I don't want to be seen in public again. Tell him I need to talk to him."

In an instant, Lucy's expression turned sour. "We leave ship now?"

"No, not now. You just get Lightfoot."

From the shadows of the bar, Gus watched Lucy exit the poker room as quickly as she had entered. On her way out, she passed an elegant-looking woman coming into the room. The lady was tall and slender, with a tiny waist, and dressed in a short blue gown that exposed her bare shoulders. Gus was smitten with her stylish looks, and had to turn back to the bar to keep from staring at her. She was the prettiest woman he had ever seen.

He ordered another coffee and lit a cigar, with his back to the tables. He reminded himself to keep his wits so he could tell Clint about General Prescott. When his drink came, he turned back to the tables and found the lady hovering over Lucky Jake Collins. They were whispering to each other, with smiles on their faces. The table was now filled with six players, and the pot looked considerable. Gus turned back to the bar to wait for Lightfoot; she was the cheating gambler's girl and he was disappointed.

A few moments later, the lady approached the bar and stood

close to Gus, ordering a drink for her boyfriend. She smelled of perfume, with her blond hair pulled up high into a bun with black sticks and a blue bow attached. Around her bare neck was a white choker, and she wore white linen gloves. Her youthful face, with deep-set eyes and high cheekbones, seemed as soft as a cloud.

Gus couldn't resist. All he needed now was courage. "Good afternoon. That's a beautiful dress."

She glared at him, saying nothing as she waited for her drink.

"Do you live in San Francisco?" he heard himself ask, his heart racing.

Her drink came and she took it in hand. Turning to leave, she stopped for a moment and glanced at Gus silently. Finally, with a frown, she said, "Your eye patch is intriguing, but it doesn't cover up that you're just another saddle tramp. Not what I'm looking for."

Gus about melted with her rebuke and stammered back, "Sorry, ma'am, just trying to make some conversation."

She shook her pretty head, with her hazel eyes on fire. "Start with a conversation about yourself – dirty fingernails, straggly hair, scuffed boots and Army trousers. Even your coat has a repaired bullet hole. No, you're not for me, soldier. See that man in the ruffled shirt, playing poker? He's *my* man. He knows how to take care of a lady like me. He's no saddle tramp!"

She turned and walked away, leaving Gus with his mouth open and his gaze sad. Her spiteful words were frozen in his mind.

As she departed, Lightfoot and Lucy approached him. "Did that lovely lady you were talking with live up to your proclivities?" Clint asked with a smirk.

"Don't start with me!" Gus snapped. "Where in the hell have you been?"

Lightfoot and Lucy were taken back by his anger. "There's an organ grinder and his monkey on the main deck, entertaining the passengers. We were watching the show and having fun," Clint answered. "What's going on? Why are you so mad?"

Lucy grabbed one of his arms and looked him in the face. "Did that lady know who you were?"

Gus nodded sadly. "Yes, I think she did."

Back in their cabin, they packed up their belongings while Gus told them the story of running into General Prescott, and the promises he'd made. As the conversation continued, Gus stared at himself in the mirror. He had been humiliated and he vowed it would never happen again.

"Why do you keep looking at yourself in that damn mirror?" Lightfoot finally asked.

Gus turned away from his reflection, straightening his black frock coat. "Tomorrow we are going clothes shopping. We must look respectable if we are going to find Lucy a new home. We are not saddle tramps."

San Francisco

With a breeze in their hair and the evening sun on their faces, the companions stood on the promenade deck, watching across the glistening water as San Francisco approached. This place was truly a magical-looking city. It was sprawling and beautiful, with its large waterfront of piers and docks, as well as tall buildings and elegant homes perched on hillsides overlooking the bay. They overheard another passenger say that the city, with its population of a hundred and fifty thousand people, was the tenth largest city in America. He continued, "This city was born before the American Revolution." Now San Francisco was the gateway to the Pacific and the trailhead for their futures. They were overwhelmed by the view.

Mrs. Brown and her husband, Louis, turned out to be a wonderful pair. She was big and tall, while he was short and skinny. This unlikely couple owned the five-story Seafarer Hotel, just a few blocks up from the waterfront. General Prescott's business card got them two-dollar rooms for a dollar each, and two meals a day for only four bits more. The rooms were clean, the mattresses soft, and the food excellent. Mrs. Brown even offered to help them find what they needed in the city. And what a city it was, with wide cobblestone boulevards, interesting architecture, and a cosmopolitan population that looked much like the pictures from a European city.

The next day, they all got haircuts and manicures, and bathed before they went shopping for clothes. Neither Clint nor Lucy had ever had their fingernails trimmed by another person, and protested loudly at the cutting of their nails. Gus reminded them that such grooming was a common practice in the society of San Francisco. "We are not vagabonds or saddle tramps," he kept reminding his friends.

After they had washed the trail dust off, Mrs. Brown gave them directions to a large emporium that sold clothes for every need. This four-story building turned out to be the biggest variety store any of them had ever seen. In addition to its large assortment of dry goods and agricultural supplies, they soon found one full floor of clothes just for men, with a large section just of Mexican wear. From sombreros to boots, Lightfoot was in heaven as he started perusing the tables and bins of the emporium's offerings.

While he shopped, Gus took Lucy to the ground floor, where they found a section dedicated to young girl's clothing.

As they browsed the bins, a lady sales clerk approached. "Would you be looking for something for your daughter, sir?"

"Yes," Gus warmly replied. "Something appropriate for her age."

"And how old would she be?"

Gus frowned, shaking his head. "Lucy is my ward and I'm not sure of her age. She was rescued from the Cheyenne Indians, a few months back. I think she's ten or eleven."

The lady sales clerk's smile turned to a frown. "Is she dangerous, like those other crazy white ladies that live with the savages?"

Gus wrinkled his brow and glared back at her with his one eye. "No, she is as sweet as cream and as smart as a whip. She understands our words, and all we need is a nice new dress."

The clerk nodded slowly, and turned to Lucy and then, with obvious hesitation, put both of her hands on Lucy's shoulders. "Let me take a look at you, honey, so I know your right size."

Lucy just stood there, glaring back at the lady, dressed in an old knee-length dress that Mrs. Wilkins had given her, back in Ogden. She looked like a poor, forgotten orphan.

The lady turned back to Gus. "I think you're wrong about her age, sir. She is twelve, maybe thirteen. Being that age, she should wear an ankle-length dress. I'll help her try some garments on, in the dressing room, and you can tell me which one you like."

By the time they finished, Lucy was wearing a new pair of black walking shoes, a blue ankle-length cotton skirt, and a white blouse, with a spring bonnet. Gus was astounded by her new look. Somehow, the simple finery had transformed her from a scrawny little urchin into a budding, delicate rose. He was stunned by her beauty.

As Gus paid the clerk, she whispered to him, "Lucy is about to be a young lady, sir. She is closer to thirteen than twelve."

"Thank you," he replied. "I'm looking for a good home for her. Would you be interested?"

No, sir," she answered firmly. "I value my scalp."

When Lucy and Gus returned to the men's floor, they found Clint all decked out in his new clothes. With a broad smile and a cheerful voice, he praised Lucy. "Look at our butterfly, how beautiful she is." Then he pranced around her, wearing his new duds of buckaroo boots, canvas vaquero pants with silver Concho buttons, and a black denim shirt with a colorful serape. The only thing marring the picture was that he still wore his old felt slouch hat.

"Why not buy a new Stetson?" Gus suggested. "That old hat's stained with sweat."

Lightfoot shrugged. "It's my sweat, and I like this old hat."

Gus grinned at his friend. "Have it your way. You look like you just stepped off the boat from Mexico."

As Clint looked over some silver belt buckles, Gus wandered over to the men's evening clothes and started looking at garments. With help from a skinny old sales clerk, Gus was soon wearing new ankle-high boots, a red frock coat, black wool trousers, and a pink ruffled silk shirt with a red bolo tie. As he admired himself in a full-length mirror, Lucy and Clint gathered around, shaking their heads. "Captain, that silly pink shirt makes you look like an eastern dude," Lightfoot snickered.

"I like it," Gus replied, looking again at his reflection. "I look like a gambler."

Lucy shook her head. "No, Night-Eye, you look like preacher in 'hell-on-wheels' town. No good color for you."

After a good-natured debate, Gus bought the outfit, but without the pink silk blouse. He replaced that item with a high-collared ruffled white shirt, and a felt Stetson hat that matched the color of his eye patch. Gazing at his reflection again, he finally convinced himself he looked respectable enough to sit in at any poker table.

With their old clothes rolled up under their arms, they walked back to their hotel in the late afternoon sun. With smiles all around, they finally blended in with the San Francisco crowd.

When they had first checked in to the Seafarer, Gus had told Mrs. Brown the story of Lucy, and his plight in trying to find her a new home. She'd seemed quite sympathetic to his mission but, just like General Prescott, she had expressed reservations about taking Lucy around to the wealthy residents of Nob Hill.

The next morning, after their shopping spree, Gus approached Mrs. Brown again, asking for directions to the wealthy neighborhood.

"I've thought much about your plight, Mr. Savage," she said with a serious look, standing behind the front desk. "It's obvious that you care deeply for the girl. But I don't believe Nob Hill is the answer. Those rich folks up there are not noted for their good hearts. They care more about money than family. And *if* Lucy was taken in, she would soon become only a domestic slave to the household. I know this is none of my affair, Mr. Savage, but I ask you to reconsider your plans."

Gus hated the word 'slave' and was surprised by her thoughtful comments. "Thank you for your candor, Mrs. Brown. But I'm desperate to find Lucy a good home. Clint and I are off to the goldfields soon, not a good place for bringing up a young girl like Lucy. She needs a good education with a Christian family that loves her."

"I agree," Mrs. Brown said, nodding. "But Nob Hill is not the place. Why don't you try St. Mary's? It's the biggest Catholic church in the city."

"What could they do?"

"I understand the nuns have a farm called Paradise, just south of the city. The good Sisters take in wayward girls. This would be a safe place where Lucy could get a good education."

Gus liked the idea. "Is this like an orphanage where a family might take her in?"

"That I do not know. But you can certainly go to the church and find out."

Later that morning, dressed in their new duds, the companions walked into the gothic St. Mary's Cathedral on California Street. Built in 1854, it was the most impressive church any of them had ever seen. After entering the cathedral, they were directed to the rectory, where Gus told one of the young priests that he was there to see whoever was in charge of the Paradise Farm. A few moments later, they were all seated in front of an ornate mahogany desk, in a well-appointed, plush, wood-paneled room. The office was almost as luxurious as General Dodges had been, back at the railhead. The room was large and as quiet as a tomb, with only the sounds of ticking clocks.

Finally, one of the outer doors opened and an older, plump, gray-eyed Padre entered the room, dressed in robes of black, with a starched white collar around his neck. The friends stood as he moved behind his desk, and Gus introduced himself and Clint. Lastly, he introduced Lucy Fisher, and she curtsied to the priest.

Stone-faced, staring at Gus's eye-patch, the Padre took his seat and motioned for them to take theirs.

"I am Father Riley. Is this the wayward girl in question?"

"I think so," Gus answered, "if your Paradise Farm is an orphanage."

"Which of you is this girl's father?"

"Neither of us," Lightfoot replied quickly. "Her father was killed many years ago on the Oregon Trail."

The priest frowned. "Where is the rest of her family?"

Gus shook his head. "She hasn't any, other than a brother who might have survived. But we're not sure, and she can't recall. We rescued her from a band of Cheyenne Indians, a few months ago. Now we are looking for a good home for her."

"What happened to her Cheyenne family?" the Padre asked in a condescending tone.

"We killed them," Clint answered matter-of-factly.

"That's a shame. You killed her only family. May God have mercy on your souls."

"We are not looking for mercy, Padre, only a good home for Lucy," Gus answered.

"The Indians killed and mutilated three wranglers that worked for the railroad, and it was our job to retaliate," Lightfoot added sharply.

"Revenge is mine, sayeth the Lord," the priest said in a loud voice. "Now you wish to dump the fruits of your sin on the church's steps?"

"That's a spiteful thought," Gus replied, trying to hold back his temper. "We have no intention of 'dumping' Lucy anywhere. We are only looking for a good Christian home for her. So I will ask you again, Father, is your Paradise Farm an orphanage?"

The old priest pondered Gus's reply and slowly nodded. "Yes, we have placed some of our girls in good homes. For an annual stipend, we can make such arrangements for Lucy."

"What is word stipend?" Lucy asked Clint. He responded in the Cheyenne language. She frowned and said something back in Cheyenne.

"How old are you, girl?" the Padre asked. "Did you fornicate with the bucks?"

Lucy looked confused by the question. Clint repeated it in Cheyenne.

"No, only young maiden," she answered. "Night-Eye say I am twelve seasons. Why you need ransom?"

"Yes, Padre, how much?" Gus added.

"One hundred dollars a year for her upkeep and education until she is seventeen," the priest answered, with a forced smile.

Gus glared at Clint, then winked at him. "That would be fine with us," he said to the Padre, returning the cool smile. "But we would like to see this farm before we make any commitments."

"Good," the old Padre answered. "I'll send a message to Sister Mary Ann, telling her that you'll be out to the farm next week. Will Monday be all right?"

"That will work for us," Gus replied, getting up to leave. "So, at Paradise the nuns would care for Lucy's needs?"

"Yes. They will nourish her, body and soul. And Jesus will always love her. So bring her belongings when you come out, next week."

No one said another word until the trio was standing outside the cathedral in the bright sunshine. Then Clint broke the silence.

"I didn't like that pompous priest. He only cared about the money."

"I no like him. Please don't put me in his home," Lucy added, her eyes pleading.

"Well then, let's go see his home," Gus answered, moving down the steps. "That way, we'll know for sure."

Once on California Street, he hailed a cab and asked the driver, "Do you know a place called Paradise Farm, south of the city?"

"Yes sir," the driver answered. "I've taken a few girls out there before; its twenty miles out and twenty miles back. The fare would be five dollars."

"That's a little rich," Gus answered.

The driver glared. "It's a long way, sir."

Gus handed him a two dollar and fifty cent gold coin "Let's go there. I'll pay you another Quarter Eagle when you bring us back."

The companions mounted the two-up open horse carriage and sat back to watch the city pass by.

"You told the priest Monday. Why are we going now?" Clint asked as the black buggy turned into the traffic.

"I learned long ago that the best inspections are snap inspections. So let's see what Sister Mary Ann has to say when we just drop in."

As they moved through the city the landscape slowly turned to open country, Gus sat back, his head full of thoughts about Lucy. Yes, the priest had been pompous and as cold as a winter day. But the idea of getting her a good education, with maybe an adoption into a Christian family, was far more important than one man's personality. Lucy needed stability and friends her own age. Gus could afford the first-year stipend, but what about the next? Would the goldfields pay-off? His thoughts rambling on as the cab wheels turned.

Out in the middle of farm country, the buggy finally pulled up to an old stone monastery surrounded by fruit trees and other outbuildings. The cloister had tall stone walls and a massive wooden front door above which the Spanish word *Paraíso* was etched into the rock.

Gus pulled the rope for the bell. A few moments later, the

door opened a crack, revealing a small, skinny nun dressed in a black habit, with a white headdress and veil.

"What do you want?" she asked, peering out at the friends.

"Good morning, Sister. We'd like to speak with Sister Mary Ann. Father Riley has invited us to see the farm."

The door opened wider and the little Sister showed them in. Standing just inside a beautiful courtyard, with a trickling water fountain, the nun asked them to wait while she fetched Sister Mary Ann.

As they waited, Lucy asked, "Why that woman look like penguin in book?"

Clint and Gus chuckled. "They are called nuns," Lightfoot answered. "They all dress in that same costume as part of their religious beliefs. You must be very respectful of nuns."

Lucy nodded, shrugging her shoulders, but she looked confused.

When Sister Mary Ann joined them, Gus was quite impressed with her. She was cordial and welcoming, even though she mentioned that she hadn't been given any notice by Father Riley. She was middle-aged, with bright brown eyes that twinkled, and a charming smile. Gus performed the introductions and Lucy curtsied to her. Then Clint told the story of Lucy's rescue and redemption. Sister Mary Ann seemed enthralled with Lucy right away.

She showed the companions around the monastery and explained that Paradise was originally built as a retreat for older padres and monks who had retired from their missionary work. Now the facility was used to house almost fifty wayward girls of all ages, from birth to seventeen. She showed them the classrooms, the kitchen, the dining hall and finally, two large dormitories that shared a white-tiled bathroom with indoor plumbing. Everything seemed neat and clean, but the only girls they saw were a few scrubbing and cleaning the floors.

"Where are all the girls?" Gus finally asked.

"They are all outside, enjoying the sunshine while working the soil," Sister Mary Ann answered. "We will go there next, so you can see our beautiful gardens."

As they walked outside, Gus excused himself to use the

lavatory. When he finished and exited his stall, he found a forlorn-looking girl kneeling and scrubbing the bathroom floor. She looked up at him with sad eyes. "Pardon me, sir. Are you thinking of leaving your daughter here at Paradise?"

She wore a dirty gray robe with a rope belt. She looked about Lucy's age, with big blue eyes and unkempt, straggly hair.

"Yes, we are thinking about it," Gus replied with a smile. "Do you like it here?"

She wiped her brow with the sleeve of her robe and looked around to see if they were alone. "I am Abigail, and have been here four years," she whispered. "No sir, I hate this place. It is Hell on Earth."

"How did you come to be here?" Gus asked, also looking around the lavatory.

"My father brought me, so he could go to the goldfields. Then he died, and I was stuck here. Do not do this to your daughter. She will never forgive you."

"What is wrong with this place? It seems so friendly and clean."

This started a short conversation that Gus would never forget. Abigail told a tale of slavery, discipline gone wild and watered-down porridge with stale bread. Yes, there a few adoptions, but only for the youngest girls. She said the gardens that Sister Mary Ann was so proud of, were where the girls toiled from sunup to sundown. And she added that, during the growing season, there was no classroom work, as everyone worked outside.

Gus felt sorry for her, but reminded himself that she could be just a malcontent with an overactive imagination. "Why aren't you working outside today?" he finally asked.

Abigail extended one leg, while still on the other knee, and pulled up the hem of her robe. "I sprained my ankle when I fell off the hayloft. The good Sisters gave me scrubbing duty for my carelessness."

Sure enough, her ankle was wrapped, but Gus also noticed bright red welts on her leg. "Where did those red marks come from?"

Abigail shook her head sadly. "From Sister Mary Ann's willow switch. She calls it God's rod of love."

Gus was stunned by what he saw. Those welts looked just like the ones he had seen on Lucy's legs in the Cheyenne teepee. Who were the savages now?

They heard another cleaning girl come into the outer dormitory, and Abigail quickly tucked her leg back under her robe, and then put a finger on her lips. Gus walked over to her and gave her a Quarter Eagle from his pocket. "Hide this until you are released," he whispered. "It might help in some small way."

She nodded up at him with tears in her eyes, and he turned to leave with her quiet words following him: "Thank you."

With Abigail's comments swirling in his head, Gus caught up with his friends and Sister Mary Ann, standing in the shade of a fruit tree by the gardens. Paradise had a half section of land, most of which was dedicated to growing grapes for wine and wheat for bread. The remaining acreage was a vegetable garden that Sister Mary Ann said was used exclusively for feeding the girls. "We raise cows for their milk and cheese, hogs for their fat and meat, and chickens for their eggs. Our girls have more than enough to be self-sufficient all year long."

As Gus looked out across the fields, watching the girls toil under the hot spring sun, he felt sorry for them. Clint asked a few more questions about what they grew, but Lucy didn't say a word. Soon Gus felt uncomfortable listening to the hollow words of Sister Mary Ann. Was Abigail right or was she wrong? Finally, he looked at his pocket watch and announced it was time to leave. He had seen and heard enough.

They said their farewells just outside the front door of the courtyard. Sister Mary Ann was as cordial as an old friend. "Lucy, I certainly hope you will join us soon," she said in a pleasant voice. "And, gentlemen, every Sunday is Visitors Day, so I hope you come to see Lucy often."

The men responded with a nod of their heads. "I will send Father Riley a message with our decision next week," Gus replied as the carriage pulled up to the front door. Gus and Clint mounted the buggy and sat in the back seat, while Lucy jumped into the front seat, with her back to the driver.

"Thank for your hospitality, Sister," Gus said, and waved as the carriage pulled away. Once out on the road, Gus called up to the driver, "You told us that you brought a few girls out here before. Have you ever taken any of them back to the city?"

The driver turned his head to Gus with a long face. "No, sir. I'm told that most of the girls end up in a convent."

Gus nodded at the driver and sat back. "Thank you."

As usual, Lucy's ears perked up. "What is convent?"

Clint explained the meaning to her, in both Cheyenne and English, while Gus sat quietly with a stone face. He hadn't liked what the driver said. The last thing he wanted to do was to make Lucy a slave for the Catholic Church.

"I don't want to be a penguin," Lucy said with her eyes on fire. "Lightfoot, you like that Paradise place?"

He shrugged his shoulders. "It was nice. Lots of sunshine, good food, and you would get a good education."

Lucy frowned and sat back in her seat with a solemn face. Not another word was spoken for the longest time, with each of them lost in their own thoughts.

Gus considered telling them what he had learned from the girl Abigail, but he decided against it. He had no real proof, one way or the other – just more questions and concerns.

By the time they approached the city, however, he had made his decision. The convent comment, and his own Quaker ways had tipped the scales.

Removing his new hat and wiping the brim, he looked over to Lucy, who still had a long face. "You're not going to become a penguin. Paradise is out. You're going to come with us to the goldfields. It's going to be hard and dangerous work, but I promise you this – somehow, somewhere, you're going to get a proper education. I got you into this mess and I'll get you of it."

"*We'll* get you out it!" Clint interrupted with a look of relief. "I promise what the Captain promises."

Lucy leaped across the carriage with both her arms out-stretched, her eyes filling with tears. Turning, she landed on the laps of both men, placing an arm around each of their necks. She hugged and kissed them on their cheeks. It was the first expression of affection either of them had ever seen from her. "You are my brothers, my family. We will always be one."

Gus and Clint were stunned, and gently hugged her back.

"Lightfoot, did you teach this girl to kiss?"

Clint shook his head with a grin. "No, Captain. First kiss I ever got from her."

Lucy giggled. "Maybe Indians teach me. They kiss, you know."

With all the commotion in the carriage, the driver turned to them with a raised eyebrow, and a silly expression made them all laugh.

When they returned to the hotel, they found Mrs. Brown still at her front desk. She was curious to hear what had happened at the church. Gus was very diplomatic in explaining the day's activities. He told her about the meeting with Father Riley, the drive out to Paradise, and Sister Mary Ann.

"The school looked very pleasant and the Sister is a nice lady, but we've decided it's just not right for Lucy. We are going to stay together, miner's camps and all. But thank you for the suggestion. It was very helpful."

Mrs. Brown frowned and turned to Lucy. "You stay close to your friends, sweetie. They are your protectors."

With a bright face, Lucy looked at her. "Yes, ma'am. They are my brothers."

Mrs. Brown turned away, reaching into a wooden cubby-hole behind her. "Mr. Savage, you have a message," she said formally, and handed over a small envelope. Obviously, she disagreed with their decision.

Up in their rooms, Gus opened the envelope and read the one-page message aloud to his companions.

Gus, I have found the ship you are looking for. You will find the steamship Enterprise moored at Pier 7 and ready to sail north at 10AM Monday next. Suggest you make arrangements with Captain Seymour and/or his wife Martha post haste. I have told them of your needs. Good sailing and good luck.

Joseph Prescott

When Gus finished reading the note, he looked up at his friends with a big smile. "This is our ticket to riches. Monday our next adventure begins."

Chapter 4 – Goldfields

Sea Legs

"Who is Jesus?" Lucy asked from her bed in the darkened room.

There was a long silence.

"Why do you ask?" Gus finally said from his bed.

"Penguin squaw say Jesus always love me. I not know Jesus."

"I will tell you His story," Gus replied. "There is a book called the Bible. We will read it together."

"Once a Preacher's son, always a Preacher's son. Poppycock," Lightfoot yelled from the adjoining room.

More silence.

"What is poppycock?" Lucy asked.

The next morning, Gus wrote two short messages. One was to Father Riley at St. Mary's Cathedral, informing him that Lucy would not be attending Paradise. The second note was to General Prescott, thanking him for his help in finding them the steamship *Enterprise*.

Then, after another tasty breakfast provided by Mrs. Brown, the trio dressed in their new finery and hailed a cab for Pier 7 to buy their passage north. Upon arriving at the wharf, they found the ocean-going steamboat tied to the dock and taking on freight. The timbered ship was long and sleek, with two decks and a wheelhouse above the main promenade, propelled by two paddlewheels amidships. The ship also had three tall sailing masts and a big iron smokestack painted black and red. The *Enterprise*, pulling at her lines and glistening in the sun, looked like a stallion ready for a race. She was by far the biggest and most beautiful ship any of the friends had ever seen.

Finding the gangplank, they went aboard. Once they reached the main deck, a sailor showed them forward to where they found Captain Seymour and his wife Martha, working in their sea cabin behind the wheelhouse.

The couple greeted them warmly. "Any friend of Mr. Prescott is a friend of ours," the lady said, inviting the trio into the cabin. Their compartment was small, with a desk, chart-table, bunk beds, and bins of rolled-up maps.

Gus did the introductions and Lucy offered her usual curtsy.

The Skipper's wife was impressed. "How sweet you are, young lady. We have a daughter at home about your age. She attends boarding school here in the city. I hope we will be friends, Lucy."

Gus and Clint shook hands with the Skipper; his grip was firm and calloused. Captain Seymour was an older man, with a neatly trimmed gray beard that covered most of his wrinkled, weathered face. He had a big wide nose, with deep-set brown eyes, and when he spoke it was with a slight Irish accent. "Mr. Prescott told us of ya needs. We be pleased to have ya aboard. It be three days and two nights to Coos Bay, if the weather holds."

His wife Martha was younger, approaching middle age. She still had a glow of fading beauty, with a sweet, caring personality. Her words were without any accent and were spoken in a pleasant voice. "My husband takes care of the ships needs, while I take care of my passengers needs. We have a nice second-deck stateroom for your trip and because you are friends with Mr. Prescott, your fare will only be that of steerage rates."

"And what would that be?" Gus asked.

"Two dollars a day, per person."

Gus reached into his pocket and handed Martha a Double Eagle. She placed the gold coin in a small rawhide pouch and wrote out a receipt, then handed back the paper and two silver dollars, along with a big smile. "Your cabin number is 204, second deck aft. And before I forget, here's a note from Mr. Prescott that arrived just this morning."

Gus glanced at the envelope and put it in his pocket, along with his change.

"We hope to stay in the good graces of Mr. Prescott," Martha said. "He is financing a new ship for us."

"The *Enterprise* is getting old like me," Captain Seymour said, then added, eyeing Gus's black patch, "Steel ships are the future. But they cost lots of money."

His comments started a conversation about the *Enterprise*. The ship had a crew of fifty sailors, half of whom helped sail the vessel, while the other half took care of the passengers, who numbered just over one hundred and fifty souls. The ship had four decks for passengers, as well as two cargo holds, one forward and one aft, for freight. The forward hold was the largest and carried dry goods, while the aft hold carried commodities such as coal, wood chips, and sawdust. There was also a third small bin of coal for the ships consumption. The 250-gross-ton *Enterprise* had been built in Boston in 1853, and had worked for many years as a packet ship designed for carrying domestic mail, passengers, and freight on the eastern shores. She had sailed around Cape Horn in 1865 with supplies for the Transcontinental Railroad, and the Seymour's had purchased her that same year. Now the vessel had a scheduled route, plying the waters of the west coast. Once a month, she sailed from San Francisco to Astoria and back again, with stops each way for coal and freight at Coos Bay, Oregon. The *Enterprise* was just one of many packet ships working with such a scheduled itinerary.

"Is there a place on your ship where a man can buy a drink?" Clint asked.

"Aye, we have a nice pub next to the dining hall," Captain Seymour answered. "It be for passengers only, as the crew is not allowed to imbibe during the voyage."

"How about poker? Is that allowed?" Gus wanted to know.

The Skipper smiled, "Yes, in me pub. But we don't allow shills or sharks on my ship. Friendly, honest games are all we tolerate."

"What about food? We bring our own?" Lucy asked.

Martha shook her head, smiling. "You can if you want, sweetie, but your fare includes two meals a day. We have a good cook who serves hearty dishes for crew and passengers alike."

Gus asked about the Coos goldfields, but was disappointed with what he learned. Captain Seymour had taken many passengers to Coos Bay, and had even taken some gold bullion back for the San Francisco mint, but he had no idea about the fields or where to go. "All I know about Coos Bay is the frightful Bar I have to cross to get into port. I've only been on the docks of Marshfield a few times, to supervise the unloading and loading of freight and coal."

"I've been to Marshfield," Martha said. "And I know this – everything in town is expensive. If you're going to the goldfields, buy your grubstake here in the city. You'll save a lot of money."

"We sail at noon on Monday, folks, so bring your sea legs with you," the Skipper added with a smile. "Come aboard a few hours early and we'll stow your traps in the forward hold."

Martha turned to Lucy as the trio was leaving. "I hope we can have tea during the voyage, I would love to learn more about your life with the savages."

Lucy nodded with a curious look on her face. "Oh yes, I like tea parties," she answered. "What is sea legs?"

Everyone chuckled. "When we get out onto the ocean, the ship will buck like a wild horse," Martha answered, her hands waving like the sea. "You will soon learn how to ride the waves with your sea legs."

Lucy frowned and turned to Gus. "It be like iron horse?"

Gus nodded with a grin. "Yes, just like the red caboose."

Once back on the dock, the trio watched the longshoremen manhandling the freight into the forward hold. It was an operation of brute force with cargo nets, steel cables, pulleys and ropes, as well as a lot of shouting of words that could make a bartender blush. The companions watched a while, and then Clint asked, "What does the General have to say?"

Gus opened the envelope. It was two pages, one a handwritten note and the other a flyer with his likeness printed on it. He read the message aloud. *"Gus, I was just interviewed by a Federal Marshal. Somehow, he got wind that we played poker together on the Chrysopolis. I told him very little and directed him to Colonel Rawlins, who has a list of witnesses of your brawl at the Ogden yards. He seemed interested in my information and gave me this copy of a poster that is being circulated. Thought you should know. Keep your head down and bon voyage, my friend. Joseph Prescott."*

He showed the poster to his friends. It was a crude line drawing of Gus, traced from the Golden Spike photo. The headline read: One thousand dollar reward, wanted dead or alive, for murder.

Gus smiled. "I'm worth more dead than alive." He folded up the pages, put them back in the envelope, and slid it into his pocket. "Let's keep our eyes on the goldfields," he said, shrugging. "There's nothing I can do about this."

With the weather warm and the docks bustling, the friends decided to stretch their legs and walk back to the hotel. As they strolled along, they talked about what their needs would be once they arrived in Coos country. Martha's advice was well taken; they would buy all of their supplies at the Emporium, to save money.

"We'll need tools, work clothes, and gold pans," Clint said. "And a tent, with all the trail gear."

Gus agreed. "And a book about gold mining, so we know what the hell we are doing."

"And I need a new Reader, with some paper and pencils," Lucy said, excitement in her voice.

All seemed upbeat, but deep inside Gus was worried. That damn poster was an invitation to all the bounty hunters looking for a quick dollar. He needed to disappear deep into the wilderness of the west.

The trio spent the afternoon making trips to the Emporium and a few other shops, to buy their long list of needs for the trip north. The last item they purchased was a new, metal-clad steamer trunk to hold their grubstake. In the end, Gus bought his book on gold mining and a beautiful gold-leafed copy of the Bible, while Lightfoot bought pouches of tobacco and six bottles of Tequila, and Lucy got a new McGuffey's Reader, with a pad and pencils to use.

They spent Sunday carefully packing away all their supplies. The last items added to the trunk were the rifles from their bed rolls. They would keep their hand guns but not their rifles, as they saw no reason for them on the ship. When the lid was finally secured and locked, the trunk weighed nearly eighty pounds, and the supplies had cost them almost a hundred dollars.

Back in their room, the money spent kept swirling in Gus's head, and he finally pulled out his purse and counted his coins. "Our poke is getting a little thin. I've got only a hundred and twenty-three dollars remaining," he said to his friends. "How about you, Lightfoot?

Clint checked his purse. "A little over sixty dollars, Captain. It's been a while since our last pay call."

Gus nodded. "Yep, and we've been spending money like greenhorns. I'll need to win at the tables on our voyage north."

That evening, the trio went out for dinner to say farewell to San Francisco. They found an open-air bistro that overlooked the bay. The city had been good to them, and they all talked about retuning someday. With drinks in hand, Gus made a simple toast. "Soon we will be sleeping in the weeds and sweating in the sun while panning for our future. Hopefully, we will all find our *own* golden city by a bay."

With bedrolls, valises, and the steamer trunk in hand, the trio arrived at Pier 7 early Monday morning. The dock and the decks were a beehive of activity, with people and baggage coming and going. Standing on the pier, the ships purser checked them in on a roster and gave them a receipt for their trunk. They watched as it and other baggage was lifted in a cargo net that then disappeared into the ship's forward hold. "Your luggage is safe," the purser said. "No one is allowed into the hold while we are underway." Next, a young steward arrived and showed them to their stateroom on Deck 2. It was a large cabin with white bead board walls and a small separate bedroom. The main salon was spacious, furnished with two settees that folded into berths. At the rear of the cabin was a small table and chairs, near a sink and coal-burning stove. There was even a small bathroom with another sink, to be shared by both rooms. The *Enterprise* was a much more luxurious ship than the *Chrysopolis,* and the friends were impressed with their accommodations.

Lucy took the small bedroom, while Gus and Clint settled into the main salon. After unpacking and getting organized, the friends exited their cabin and walked the decks, watching the preparations for getting underway. Sailors were in the shrouds, rigging the sails, while other crew members were dogging down the hatch covers and stoking the boilers. Just before noon, with black smoke filling the sky, two small tugboats came alongside and secured lines to the *Enterprise,* fore and aft. Then, with the shriek of the ship's steam whistle, the mooring lines were hauled in and the gangplank came aboard. As the tugboats gently pulled the ship away from the dock, the passengers stood at the rails, waving to family and friends still on shore. It was a traditional event for wishing the travelers bon voyage and safe-passage. Some passengers had long faces, with tears in their eyes, while others were celebratory, with smiles and shouted words of encouragement. Gus explained to Lucy the reasons for the conflicting emotions.

Once the ship was out on the bay, the tugs slowly turned the *Enterprise* with the outgoing tide, and her paddlewheels were engaged. As the ship vibrated and picked up speed, the tow lines to the tugs were removed, and the little work boats turned back to the docks. With the ship under her own power and churning up white water, most of the passengers removed themselves, to get in out of the weather.

With a stiff breeze in their hair, the trio moved to the main deck, determined not to miss a thing as the ship moved towards the sea. Just forward of the tall wheelhouse, they found a young, sandy-haired sailor curling up the tow lines. For a few moments, the friends watched quietly as San Francisco slipped by.

"I wonder how many people live in this town?" Gus asked to no one in particular.

The young sailor answered, "Before the Gold Rush of 48, only a few hundred, after the Rush, over three thousand."

"What island out there?" Lucy asked, pointing to the starboard side.

The young sailor straightened from his ropes and gazed at where she pointed. "That's Fort Alcatraz, Miss. During the big war, there were a hundred cannons out there to protect the bay from the Graycoats stealing our gold. Today, it's an Army prison for rebellious Indians and a few Confederates that never surrendered."

Clint pointed. "And what's that, over on the left?"

The sailor winked at Lucy and she blushed. "On the port side, sir, is the Presidio. In 1776, when we were fighting for our independence, the Presidio was Spains northern-most military outpost. We took it from the Spaniards in 1846. During the big war, it too had a hundred cannons protecting the bay. Today, it's a sprawling Army post."

"How long before we get to the sea?" Gus asked him.

The young sailor continued flirting with Lucy, and she started flirting back. "In about an hour, sir. Soon, we'll be in the Bonita Channel and then steam under Bonita Point. A few miles past the lighthouse, and beyond the shoals and reefs, we'll turn due north and raise the sails. That's when the green gills will come out."

"Mr. Henderson!" a loud voice shouted down from above. "We don't pay you as a tour guide. Get those lines aft on the double," the First Mate yelled from the wheelhouse window with a voice horn.

The young sailor looked up and shouted back, "Yes, sir!"

As he placed the curled-up lines on his back, he turned to Lucy with a sheepish look. "See you around the deck, Miss. My name is Randy."

As he walked away Lucy watched him. "He's a nice boy."

The men chuckled. "You're like honey to the bees," Lightfoot said.

They stayed on the open deck for the next hour, watching the sites go by. Bonita Point, where the bay turned into the ocean, was the most stunning seascape they had ever seen. With tall green trees and golden sea grass, the mountains on both sides of the opening stood like sentries guarding an invisible gate. It was as if their ship traveled upon an aqua-blue carpet from land to sea. With their eyes fully filled, the friends were lost in their own thoughts for the longest time.

A few miles past the Bonita lighthouse, the ship turned north, and bosons whistles called the sailors to the shrouds. Shortly thereafter, the sails were unfurled and filled with the wind. Now, with both steam and wind power, the ship picked up speed and heeled over a few degrees. With the hull tilted and the speed increasing, the ship started bucking the choppy sea swells, throwing the ocean over the bow.

The friends made a hasty retreat back up to the second deck and the comfort of their cabin. Once inside the room, Lucy said, with sea spray dripping from her pretty face, "Now I know meaning of sea legs."

Sadly, over the next few hours, Lucy also became familiar with the meaning of green gills. Her sea sickness started slowly enough. First, she became quiet and surly, trying to read her new book. When that didn't work, she became restless, pacing the deck with the boat still dancing about. Finally, she yawned a few times and excused herself to her bedroom. With her somber demeanor and no questions from her lips, both men sensed something was wrong.

Not long after her departure, she returned to the salon with a face as pale as paper. "I no feel well. Need air," she mumbled, stumbling towards the cabin door. Gus and Clint both jumped to their feet and helped her out onto the deck, where she rushed to the rail. Looking down, she saw other people below her. Turning back with sad eyes, she shook her head. "Go below, please."

Once on the main deck, she raced to the railing again and threw the top part of her body over it, vomiting. Gus and Clint quickly moved to stand on both sides of her, holding her tightly so she wouldn't fall overboard. As she continued throwing up, the men looked away, and saw that others passengers were similarly afflicted.

"What's happening here?" Lightfoot asked.

"This must be the green gills that the sailor talked about. These folks are all seasick."

Lucy stopped heaving for a moment and looked up at Gus with the saddest face he had ever seen. "Cloth, please," was all she said, turning her face to the sea again.

Randy, the sailor, appeared just then, carrying a wooden bucket of hot wet towels, which he passed out along the rail line of sick passengers. When he got to Gus and Lightfoot, he said sadly, handing them two towels, "Sorry it's your daughter, sir. She will need this."

"She is not my daughter," Gus answered, handing the towel to Lucy. "She's our sister."

The young man smiled. "After she's done, give her lots of water. What is her name, sir?"

"Lucy. How long will she be sick?"

"This happens every trip. She should be on her feet tomorrow.

Tell her I came by."

Clint tried to hand back one of the clean towels. "We won't need this."

The sailor shook his head. "You should keep it, sir. You don't look that good yourself."

Sure enough, after Randy moved on, Lightfoot joined Lucy in misery. Now Gus had two sick comrades, and he started questioning his own stomach. He had never been on the sea before. Would his sea legs hold up, or would he soon be joining them at the rail?

A few moments later, with nothing more to throw up but spit, both Lucy and Clint rested on the deck, waiting to see what might happen next. Lucy looked the worst, and had been there the longest, so Gus took her up in his arms. She seemed as light as a feather. "I'm taking her back to our cabin and putting her to bed. I'll be back for you," he said.

Clint, looking dazed, didn't respond.

By the time Gus got her to the stateroom, she was fast asleep in his arms. She had been a trooper at the rail, never complaining, just fighting off her sickness with determination and dignity. He was proud of her. Gently, he put her on her bed and removed her stained blouse and skirt. Before putting a blanket over her, he noticed the Oregon Trail medallion still hanging around her neck. He also noticed that, under her camisole, her breasts seemed larger than he had recalled. In the Indian culture, she would be considered a maiden by now. Gus scolded himself for thinking such thoughts.

Before going back to get Lightfoot, he made up his companions berth and put out a glass of water. Then, as the ship continued to buck, he locked the cabin door and returned to the main deck.

With the ocean still choppy, it was an hour before he got Clint on his feet. Helping him to walk was like leading a drunken sailor. As they stumbled up the stairs to the second deck, Lightfoot kept mumbling, "Why? I have iron stomach. This boat ride to hell."

Once inside the cabin, he sat Clint on his berth and helped him remove his scrape and denim shirt. Both were soiled and reeking. Before Gus had finished removing his boots, Clint's head hit his pillow, and he was asleep in a heartbeat. Lifting Clint's legs onto the bed and covering him with a blanket, Gus stood staring down at his friend. This was not what he had planned for the first night of their voyage.

With the stateroom cooling off in the late afternoon sun, and the smell of vomit in the air, Gus knew what had to be done. He opened the cabin windows and lit a fire in the coal stove. Then, with both sinks filled with hot water, and some bar soap in hand, he washed and rinsed the soiled clothing for both of his friends, and hung the garments around the room to dry.

When he was finished with the washing, he lit some incense he had bought in San Francisco and closed the windows. Looking around the cabin, he chuckled to himself. The stateroom looked and smelt like a Chinese laundry. What should he do next?

He was checking his pocket watch when a knock came at the door. Opening it, he found Martha Seymour standing on the outside deck with a basket of food in hand.

"Sorry to hear about your friends, Mr. Savage. Sea sickness is not fun. I have some chicken soup for them and some stew for you. May I come in?"

"Of course," Gus answered, opening the door all the way.

She put her basket on the table and removed two porcelain bowls with lids and some bread wrapped in a napkin, along with some utensils. "The soup is good, hot or cold and the beef stew is very tasty." She glanced around at the hanging clothes with a smile. "I like your décor."

From his berth, Lightfoot let out a loud moan, and Martha turned to him. "I'd like to check to see if he has a fever. Would that be all right?"

Gus nodded.

She felt Lightfoot's forehead and whispered, "He'll be fine tomorrow." She did the same for Lucy, but said she had a slight fever.

"Was she feeling alright when you came aboard?"

"Yes," Gus answered looking down at her on the bed.

"Nothing to worry about. It might be just her time. She'll bounce back by the morning."

At the door, she said softly, "The weather should improve tomorrow, but don't let your friends eat too much. Give them lots of liquids. The dining room opens at seven for breakfast.."

Gus was impressed with Marthas kindness, and he thanked her at the door. That's when he noticed that she had a wheel-cart on the deck, with more food baskets for other seasick passengers. Martha was a saint.

Gus wanted to go play poker, but that didn't seem right with both friends down. No, that would have to wait. He put the bowl of chicken soup on the stovetop to keep it warm. Then he sat down, devoured the beef stew, and ate half the bread.

Just as he finished, Lightfoot mumbled from his bed, "Is that food I smell?"

With a broad smile, Gus answered from the table, "We've got some hot chicken broth and bread. Do you want some?"

"You're damn right I do," Clint replied. Slowly, he swung his legs to the deck and looked around the room. "How's our Butterfly?"

"She's still sleeping. Martha came by and said she had a fever, but not to worry."

Lightfoot took a drink from the glass Gus had set out. His face turned cynical and he spat it out. "What the hell is this?"

"Water. Martha said you should have liquids."

"Mescal is a liquid. I'll get my own," he answered, trying to get up on his feet. Immediately, he fell back upon the bed, holding his stomach. "Holy Mother, my gut feels like a mule kicked me. Get me a shot of tequila, Captain."

Gus moved to his friend with the bottle in hand. "You drink the water and I'll replace it with mescal. Then we'll have some soup."

After a few drinks, Clint finally got to his feet and gingerly moved to the table. "Never been so sick before. I always thought I had an iron stomach," he said, drinking some hot soup. "What's with the laundry?"

"Your clothes reeked and needed cleaning. They'll be dry in the morning."

Lightfoot used some bread to sop-up the remains of Gus's stew. "You've been a busy beaver, Captain. Thanks for watching over us. Now, why don't you go play some poker? I'll keep an eye on Lucy."

Coos Country

"Three of clubs," the dealer announced to the table as he dealt Gus' final card face-up.

Gus fumed silently, careful not to show his tell. He needed a three, but not that one. A three of hearts would have filled out his straight flush. Now all he had was a baby straight, and two other players had the best of him on the table. Gus thought about bluffing but folded his hand again.

The top deck of the *Enterprise* was where the dining hall and galley were located. Forward from those cabins were the pub and the wheelhouse with the officers quarters. Outside on the deck there were rails, port and starboard, where canvas-covered lifeboats sat on blocks, at the ready.

The pub itself was small, just a dozen felted tables with bentwood chairs and a stand-up bar with a brass foot rail and two spittoons. Three of the tables were playing poker that night, with the remaining tables occupied with passengers playing other games.

For the last few hours, Gus had played low-stakes stud poker with five other gentlemen, three of whom were traveling to Astoria. The other two were disembarking at Coos Bay. One of the locals was a young lumberman, returning from San Francisco with a fat timber contract in his pocket. The other local told the table he worked for the government as an Indian Agent. He was returning to the reservation in Klamath Falls with a supply of farming implements for the Indians. He was a funny little guy who telegraphed more poker tells than Western Union. He had a squeaky voice, and a nervous twitch, and the bad habit of curling up his little fingers if he had a good hand. He introduced himself as Horace Bagbee from Sioux City, Iowa.

Poker wasn't just a game of chance to Gus; it was also an exercise in intelligence gathering. He had learned long ago to keep his one good eye open and his two ears listening for the truth. For some reason, playing poker was the closest thing to gossiping that any man could do, and if you had the talent of reading a player's tells, like Gus could, you'd know what and what not to believe.

That evening, no one had said a thing about his black patch, and he fit in with the table like a glove. But the cards weren't friendly and as midnight approached, Gus collected what remained of his coins. He had lost near twenty dollars but had learned much from the locals about Coos Bay. They had described the area as a large inland peninsula, surrounded on three sides by rivers, sloughs, and wetlands, with a narrow, deep-water opening to the Pacific Ocean. That Bar was protected by rocky shoals and the Cape Arago lighthouse on the south, and by a long, narrow spit of sand on the north. The crossing from the sea to the bay was one of the most treacherous passages on the Oregon Coast. There were two towns on the inland peninsula: the county seat and commercial center of Empire on the west side, and the workers town of Marshfield on the east side. Coos Bay had been named for the local Indians, who had been moved to a reservation a few years before. "After the Indian Wars, all the tribes had been put on reservations," the agent had said. "We still have a few renegades and breeds, but for the most part the Indians are all gone now."

Gus had asked both locals about the goldfields, but they knew very little. The lumberman only wanted to talk about the gigantic forests, and the agent only about the sad plight of the Indians.

After Gus excused himself from the table, he strolled out on deck to have a cigar and enjoy the view. It was a seascape like no other he had ever seen. The sea looked as calm as a pond, with moonlight glistening on the water. He had never seen an ocean before, and now he sailed upon the largest of them all, the Pacific. He was impressed with the view, but also concerned. Captain Seymour and now two locals knew nothing of the Coos Bay goldfields. How could that be? Maybe they were just tight lipped with strangers.

At dawn the next day, Gus was awakened not by the morning light but by the sounds of a flushing toilet. Shortly thereafter, he heard Lucy return to her bed in the next room. Moments after that, he thought he heard her weeping.

He sat up in his berth and looked around the cabin. Lightfoot was still sleeping, and the dried laundry was still in place. He moved his feet to the deck and pulled on his stockings. *Why is she crying?* He pulled on his pants and tucked in his nightshirt. Quietly getting out of bed, he moved to her door and went into her bedroom, where the morning light was just spilling into her compartment.

Gus moved to the side of her berth and found her all curled up, sobbing.

"What goes on here?" he whispered, peeling back a blanket.

She had tears in her eyes, and her face was puffy and red. "Go away," she mumbled.

"Are you still sick from the sea?"

She shook her head sadly. "No. Please go away."

"Then why are you crying?" Gus demanded, still whispering.

She stared at him with wet cheeks from her tears. "I'm dying."

"You are not dying. You are the bravest girl I know."

"I bleed no stop."

"Where are you bleeding?"

"Go away. Only tell old squaw."

Old squaw was the clue, and Gus reckoned her condition. "You bleed between your legs?"

"Go away," she replied with an angry glare.

Gus was relieved. His older sister had come into season when she was twelve. At that time, she had only wanted to talk to her mother. But what did a mother say to her daughter? Gus remembered what his father had told him about the animals coming into season.

"I know what's happening. My sister was just like you. I had a bitch puppy once, and it came into heat by bleeding between its legs. My father told me young girls do the same."

Lucy's eyes turned to fire. "You call me bitch dog?"

"No, I'm just saying this is normal. You will bleed when you come into heat."

Lucy started crying again. "I need squaw to tell me."

Red-faced, Gus realized that he had not helped at all. "Then you can tell Martha. She'll know what to do."

Gus fetched a napkin from the dinner tray and gave it to Lucy before they left for breakfast.

"What the hell is going on in here?" Lightfoot demanded from the doorway, rubbing the sleep from his eyes.

Lucy frowned at Gus, shaking her head. "No tell him."

"We were just talking about going to breakfast," Gus replied in a cheerful voice. "Are you going to join us?"

The dining hall was a large, open room with a dozen wooden tables and bench seats bolted to the deck. The food was served buffet style, just like Sunday mornings at the railroad camps. When the trio entered the room for their first time, they saw Martha talking with other passengers and the cooks. Soon they found a table, and Lightfoot made a beeline for the food, still not aware Lucy's problem. After his departure, Lucy asked, "I go see her now?" She had that defiant look on her face.

"All right, but whisper your problem to her. Don't blurt it out."

Gus sat and watched as Lucy, with great hesitation, approached Martha and whispered in her ear. At one point, Martha looked up and saw Gus watching. She smiled at him with a wink. Then she whispered something back to Lucy.

Just as Lightfoot returned to the table with a heaping tray of food, Lucy returned. Now her face was all bright with smiles.

"I could eat a horse," Clint said, sitting down.

"What did Martha say?" Gus asked.

"We have tea after breakfast. I no bitch dog."

With a spoon full of scrambled eggs, Lightfoot looked up from his tray and asked, with a startled expression, "What the hell are we talking about?"

The passengers got two meals a day included in their fare. These meals were breakfast at seven and a supper of soups, breads, and stews at five. If anyone got hungry during the day, the pub sold cold sandwiches and hard-boiled eggs for two bits more.

While Lucy was having tea, Gus explained to Lightfoot her coming of age saga. The men felt helpless giving her any advice about her condition. Both knew farm yard biology, but that was about it. They also talked about what other ways they could help her grow. She couldn't tell time yet and while she could count up to a hundred, she couldn't count or understand money. These things they could teach her.

When Lucy returned, the drama of the morning seemed long

forgotten. Martha had given her a little supply of cloth pouches but she didn't want talk about it. Both men agreed, and dropped the subject like a stick of dynamite.

With the trio feeling free of seasickness, they spent the day exploring the ship. When they first came on deck, the sailors were in the shrouds, furling up the sails, since the wind had dropped off to a dead calm and the sea was as flat as a pond. Now the ship was totally dependent on the paddlewheels.

As they walked the decks, they learned from listening to the crew that, without the sails, the ships speed had been reduced to only six knots an hour. The sailors were grousing about being late to port.

But, with the weather warm and the seas flat, the friends enjoyed their walk and even relaxed in the deck chairs, watching other passengers. The boat ride to hell had turned into a peaceful cruise for everyone.

That evening after supper, while Gus got dressed in his poker finery, Lucy read aloud to Lightfoot from her new Reader. Clint loved following along with the pictures and listening breathlessly to the story. These sessions reminded Gus of how his own mother had taught him the joy of reading, and what a special time that had been.

When Gus arrived at the pub to play poker, he found Mr. Bagbee, the Indian Agent, having a heated discussion with the Bar Steward. As Gus waited to order a drink, he eavesdropped on their conversation. Horace was demanding that his cargo of farm tools be offloaded first when they arrived at Empire. "I'm willing to pay extra," he insisted. The steward seemed frustrated by his demands, and told Bagbee he had nothing to do with offloading freight. Looking angry, Bagbee demanded to talk with whoever was in charge of the freight. The steward finally relented and agreed to have the Third Mate come to the pub. Fuming, the Indian Agent gave him a few coins as a tip and walked away.

Gus got his drink of whiskey without saying a word to the steward about what he had overheard. Why did farm implements need to be offloaded first? Horace was a strange little man, and Gus didn't like him much.

Steamship Enterprise

With passengers coming and going in the pub, Gus soon joined a table with three other players. The table stakes were low: just a two-bit ante with limited raises. While the action was small, the table chatter wasn't, and Gus enjoyed listening to their stories. One man owned a hardware store in Astoria and was returning from a buying trip in San Francisco. Another gentleman was a surveyor, hired to map out railroad right of ways from Astoria to Portland. The third player was a big older woman with a tongue as sharp as a knife and a voice like a foghorn. She introduced herself as Lilly, the owner of a saloon/boarding house in Astoria called The Uptown Pub. These folks were all cordial, and Gus regaled them with a few stories of his time on the Iron Highway.

"With three thousand young men working at the railhead, and only three women in camp," Lilly said with a chuckle, "Now that's my kind of odds."

The table was soon joined by two other players, and the game improved immensely. With the pots bigger, Gus system of card counting started paying dividends. An hour later, he was up almost fifty dollars. As he played his cards, Gus kept an eye on Mr. Bagbee, who had been waiting patiently to talk with the Third Mate. Finally the mate appeared, and the two men exited the pub for the promenade. With his curiosity up, Gus collected his money from the table and announced he was taking a latrine break.

"We'll watch over your winnings, honey," Lilly snickered.

Gus smiled at her, putting the coins in his pocket. "Thank you, ma'am. No need. I'm just taking your money for a walk."

When Gus exited to the deck, he was surprised to find the darkness shrouded in a swirling fog. Looking up and down the promenade, he could just make out the two men standing in the passageway next to the dining hall. Slowly, he moved down the deck, using the lifeboats to hide his approach. When he was within earshot of the men, he moved into the shadows and listened to their conversation.

"My cargo must be unloaded first. There will be a wagon waiting on the dock," Mr. Bagbee said in his squeaky voice. "Put my crates in your cargo net and drop them down to the wagon. My friends will load them on the buckboard and be on their way."

"How will I know which crates?" the third mate asked.

"Simple. All four are of the same size, about six feet long, and they're freshly painted dark gray, with the white stenciled words 'Farm Implements' on the top."

There was a long pause, "Uh, you said something about extra pay."

Mr. Bagbee chuckled. "Yep, that's right, mate. Here's a twenty-dollar Gold Eagle for your trouble, and another to share with your crew."

"You won't be mentioning this to the Skipper, will you?"

"No," Horace answered. "Just get my cargo safely down to the wagon."

With his head swirling with suspicions, Gus turned away and walked the deck in the opposite direction. *What the hell was all that about? Why would anyone pay a forty-dollar tip to get farms tools onto the dock first?*

Full of questions, Gus didn't return to the tables. Instead, he continued walking the decks, thinking about what he had just witnessed. Maybe it was common for shippers to pay tips to expedite their cargo. Being late spring, maybe the Indians needed the tools for their growing season. Gus couldn't go around making accusations about Horace or the third mate. He needed proof that something wasn't right. But what kind of proof?

The next morning at breakfast, Gus told his friends about his evening of poker and eavesdropping. "I don't know what to do. Should I tell my suspicions to Captain Seymour or just forget about it?"

"I know what I'd do," Clint answered. "Take a look inside those crates."

"How do we do that?" Gus remarked. "They told us no one was allowed in the forward hold while the ship was underway."

Lightfoot smiled. "Let's have Lucy ask Seaman Henderson for help. He's sweet on her."

"What kind help?" she asked with a confused look.

"Tell him you need a shawl from our sea trunk. Just flirt with him and he'll get us into the forward hold."

"How flirt?" Lucy answered.

"Wink at him. Flutter your eyelashes," Lightfoot said,

showing her how. "Let him know you're interested."

"Wait a minute," Gus inserted quickly. "She's precocious enough. She doesn't need more lessons from you."

"He is a cute boy. What is precocious?"

They found Randy in the noisy boiler room, shoveling coal. With his shirt off, the sweating muscles of his upper torso were on display, and Lucy stood transfixed, watching him. Lightfoot finally tapped him on the shoulder. When the boy turned around, he was clearly astonished to see Lucy in his coal bin. They all talked for a few moments, shouting their words over the sounds of the machinery. He agreed to come to their cabin after his watch was over at noon, Lucy winked at him as he returned to his shoveling.

"How are we going to open the crates?" Gus asked Clint as they waited for Randy.

"There's a claw hammer in the trunk. It's under our tent," Lightfoot replied.

"I don't have shawl in the trunk," Lucy said.

"It won't matter," Gus answered. "Randy will forgive you."

Just before noon, a freshly cleaned-up Seaman Henderson appeared at their door. He was invited in and Lightfoot poured himself and Randy a glass of tequila. At first, he was reluctant to take the drink but he relented when Lucy began to butter him up. "Your body hard like rock," she said. "You strong warrior." He blushed, his gaze locked on hers as she continued with more words of encouragement.

"Lucy needs your help," Gus interrupted. "Her wool shawl is locked away in our sea trunk and we need to get it for her. Will you take us to the forward hold?"

"We'll be in port by this afternoon. Can't it wait?" Randy answered.

"Please?" Lucy said, with a pathetic look.

The seaman stood there for a long moment, staring at the trio. Then he said, "Sure. Why not? I know where the key is hidden."

Randy led them down the gangways to the steerage deck, which was two decks below the main promenade. At the forward-most point of that narrow passageway was a timbered bulkhead with a thick, locked door. Reaching above the doorway, Randy searched for and found a key which he used to unlock the hatch.

Just inside the door was a rope locker, with kerosene lamps at the ready. He lit two and handed one to Gus.

"It's black as a coal inside the hull, so watch your step," he said, lighting a third lamp and giving it to Lightfoot.

Once inside the forward hold, they saw a gigantic room filled with freight crates, wooden barrels, and other cargo stacked almost to the ceiling. The gallery was cool and damp, and it smelled of rotten eggs.

"The passengers luggage is kept over here," Randy said, leading Lucy and Clint to a corner of the room. As they looked for their trunk, Gus held his lamp high over his head, looking for Mr. Bagbee's four gray crates. He didn't have to search long. The Third Mate had done his job, stacking the cases two high on a cargo net, ready for unloading.

"I found the crates over here," Gus called, noticing a fat rat scurrying across the deck.

Lightfoot found their trunk and opened it. With his lamp high, he put his hand inside and felt around the container. "And I found the hammer," he announced to Gus, pulling it out of the trunk.

"What h-hammer? What crates?" Randy stammered.

Clint moved towards Gus with the hammer in hand, and Lucy followed. "We just have to take a quick look at something," Lightfoot told the boy. "It will only take a minute."

"You didn't say anything about snooping around in other freight."

As everyone gathered around the crates, Gus used the hammer to pry open the first lid. As he worked, he said to Randy, "Sorry for the ruse, mate. See the markings on this box? It says farm implements. I sure hope that's true."

With some help from Clint, the crate cover was soon off, and Gus brushed away the wood shavings on top of the cargo.

Everyone stared.

Gus reached in and pulled an item out, shaking it free of the wood shavings. "This 'shovel' looks more like a Henry rifle to me. Now, how could that be? What would an Indian Agent be doing with an arsenal?" He handed the rifle to Seaman Henderson. "Is this ship smuggling guns to the Indians?"

"Absolutely not," Randy retorted, and pointed. "Look what it says under the lid."

Gus moved his lantern to the lid and read the words aloud: "Property of the Presidio and the US Army."

"These are stolen weapons," Randy said, shaking his head. "We have to report this to Captain Seymour." He hesitated. "But I'll get beached for bringing you down here."

"No, you won't. I'll take care of this," Gus promised. "Let's make an inventory of what we've found and then put it all back like we didn't find it."

The last thing Gus and Lightfoot did in the hold was to retrieve their rifles from their trunk. With rifles in hand, and the inventory list safely in their pockets, they secured the hold door and sent Randy and Lucy back to their cabin.

"Don't say a word to anyone about this," Gus told them sternly. "We'll go talk to Captain Seymour and see what he wants to do."

They had counted forty-eight Henry rifles and five thousand rounds of ammunition – more than enough fire power to cause an Indian uprising if those crates fell into the wrong hands.

With the sun low in the sky, they found the Skipper in the wheelhouse, talking with his helmsman and the navigator about their approach to Coos Bay. Captain Seymour wasn't pleased to see them in his Pilot House. "Why the guns, boys?"

"There's trouble afoot, Captain, and you need to know about it." Gus answered.

"We are busy here, Mr. Savage. Can't this wait?"

"No, sir. We need to talk to you now, privately."

Reluctantly, the Skipper agreed and showed them into his sea cabin. "We will be crossing the Bar to Coos Bay in a few hours, so please keep this short."

Gus told him everything about playing cards with Mr. Bagbee, the Third Mates involvement, and the discovery of the smuggled weapons. They showed the Captain the inventory and warned him about what could happen if the guns fell into the wrong hands.

Captain Seymour, stunned by the information, sat wide-eyed, listening to the men. "Did you figure this all out on your own, Mr. Savage?"

"Yes, sir, with the help of my friend Clint here."

"How in the hell did you men get into the forward hold?"

"The door was unlocked. We just walked in with our suspicions. What should we do now?"

Captain Seymour thought long and hard about that question. "We'll need to contact the Sheriff in Empire. He'll have the authority to confiscate the rifles. But how in the hell do I do that?"

"If the guns make it into the wagon, they'll be gone." Lightfoot replied.

"And if we try to stop the loading, there could be gun play." Gus added.

"Yes, you could be right," the Skipper answered, looking deeply troubled. "Let me get the ship across the Bar. When you see we are inside the bay, report back to me. By then, I'll have a plan. It will be dark in a few hours, so we'll have to move fast. You gentlemen get ready to disembark, and not a word to anyone about this!"

Back in their cabin, Gus told Randy that his name had not been mentioned to Captain Seymour, and that he had no need to worry about being beached. The boy, relieved, departed back to the forecastle for duty. Once he was gone, Gus and Clint told Lucy all that had happened, then packed-up their belongings and strapped on their gun belts.

They crossed the Bar late in the afternoon. The ship was five hours behind schedule, due to adverse weather conditions, and many of the passengers were complaining.

Once inside the bay, Gus and Clint went back to the wheelhouse to hear Captain Seymour's plan. It was detailed and well thought out: When the ship was within a few hundred yards of the Empire dock, it would drop anchor and run up the quarantine flag. As this was happening, Gus and Lightfoot would be rowed ashore from the ship to the docks. Once on the pier, one of them would search out the local Sheriff while the other kept an eye on the wagon and men who would be waiting for the smuggled arms. Once the Sheriff and his Deputies were in position, Gus was to signal the ship to come to the dock with a flare that the Captain gave him.

"I'll tell the passengers we are waiting for a doctor to come aboard. They won't like it, but it's the only way to buy us some time. Once I know that all is well on shore, we'll offload the rifles and the Sheriff can take over."

It sounded simple enough and the men agreed.

As luck would have it, Randy was one of the two sailors who rowed Gus and Clint to shore.

"What's with the quarantine flag?" he asked, pulling on his oar.

"You'll see soon enough," Gus answered.

He chuckled and turned to the other sailor rowing. "Never trust a one eyed man. They will tell you they are looking for a shawl, when they are really looking for trouble."

Lightfoot smiled at him. "That's all right, Randy. It only happened because you were thinking with your wrong head."

"Do you want to join us when we get up on the dock?" Gus asked.

Randy shook his head. "No way. They don't pay me enough to fight. I'll go back to the ship to console your sister."

"Be careful there, mate," Lightfoot said. "A few months back, she was a white captive living with Cheyenne Indians."

"She's a real she-wolf," Gus answered, pointing to his bad eye. "Maybe she'll scratch one of your eyes out, as well."

That got the young seaman's attention, and he soon seemed lost in thought.

When Gus and Clint reached the dock, the shadows were long and the sun was about to set. The pier itself was built out over the bay, with a row of wood-framed buildings on the shoreline. The wharf had a few people waiting for the ships arrival, and they also spotted a two-up buckboard waiting.

As they walked past the wagon, one of the teamsters asked, "What's the hold-up with the ship?"

Gus shrugged his shoulders. "Someone aboard has the sniffles and the Captain wants a doctor to give him clearance."

"Go figure," the other driver said, puffing on a hand rolled cigarette.

Gus and Clint walked over to the row of buildings behind the wagon and slipped into a dark alleyway. "Let's drop our gear here," Lightfoot said. "I'll keep an eye on the wagon while you go get the Sheriff."

Gus nodded, dropping his bag and removing his Winchester rifle. Then he turned and started to walk away.

"I've got your blind side, Captain," Lightfoot whispered from his vantage point.

Gus strode along the road in front of the buildings and turned the corner for town. Once out of sight of the pier, he picked up his pace until he found a man walking towards the bay. "Can you direct me to the Sheriff's Office?" he asked the stranger.

The man pointed up the street. "Two blocks up and turn left. County Courthouse on the right. Sheriff Moody's office is on the first floor."

Gus tipped his hat and moved on.

When he got to the office, he found the door locked. A hand-written note said, 'Across the street at Empire Café.' Gus went out and headed back down the steps. Sure enough, he saw the restaurant across the street. Hustling through the street door, he spoke to a waitress, who pointed out the Sheriff, who was eating alone at a table at the back of the café.

Gus approached him. "Would you be the Sheriff?"

"Yep, but I'm having my supper now. Come back later."

Sheriff Moody had curly black hair, a birds-nest beard, and a handlebar mustache. He wore a black frock coat with a high white collar, and had a bowl of chili and a schooner of beer in front of him. With no gun belt or tin star, he didn't look like a Sheriff

"Don't see any badge," Gus said, looking down at him.

Moody finally looked up at Gus and narrowed his brown eyes. "Don't need a badge to have a bowl of chili. You're a rough-looking hombre. What's on your mind son?"

"Do you know the ship *Enterprise* is anchored off your Pier, flying the quarantine flag?"

Sheriff Moody looked surprised. "No. You have my attention. What's going on?"

Gus rattled off the story of the stolen rifles and Captain Seymour's plan for the Sheriff's involvement. While Gus was telling the story, Moody calmly finished his dinner and wiped his mouth with a napkin. Then, reaching into his pocket, he brought out his badge and pinned it on his lapel. "My only Deputy is down at Marshfield," the Sheriff said, finishing his beer. "He won't be any help. Reckon it will be just you and me to confiscate them rifles."

"Not sure it's my fight."

The Sheriff chuckled. "Yes, it is, son. I can see it in your good eye." He got to his feet and put some money on the table. Moody was tall and lean. He put on his hat and strapped on his gun. "Don't like being interrupted when I eat. It's bad for the digestion. You any good with that rifle, son?"

"Sadly, yes. There's more than just us. My Scout is watching the wagon. We better get a move on before it gets dark."

As they walked briskly towards the dock, the Sheriff finally asked, "Who the hell is your scout, and why are you guys in Empire?"

Gus told him the short version of their time fighting Indians. "You won't see him, but he'll be there on my blind side, so you stay on my right side."

"Why are you in Coos Bay?"

"Came out for the goldfields."

The Sheriff chuckled. "You're twenty years too late. The only real color bein' taken now is over at Canyonville."

When they got to the pier, they stopped and moved into the shadows. "You wait here. Let the drivers load the crates before you approach," Gus told him.

"If there's going to be gun-play, I'd like to know your name," Moody said.

"Folks call me Gus, and my Scout is Lightfoot."

"Are the teamsters armed?" the Sheriff asked, looking in the direction of the wagon.

"The young guy has a pistol, the older man a shotgun. That's all I saw when I walked by." Gus reached into his pocket and gave the claw hammer to the Sheriff. "You'll need this to open the crates."

"One thing is for sure, son – you look mean as hell with that black patch," the Sheriff replied. "But I don't want to die over some obsolete rifles."

"Nor do I, Sheriff, so stay on my right side."

Moody nodded soberly. "I'll be ready."

Gus continued out onto the dock and moved to the waterline. There he lit the flare and waved it in the air. The ship answered the signal by lowering the quarantine flag and giving three loud blasts from its steam whistle.

He threw the burning flare out into the bay and watched it smoke and sink while the ship weighed anchor and moved towards the pier. Then he approached the wagon, with a friendly smile. "They got their clearance. They'll be docked in a few minutes."

The two drivers nodded and climbed up to their buckboard, moving the wagon closer to the water.

With twilight fast-approaching, the ship was soon secured to the dock and the gangway was pushed into place. As this was happening, other sailors undogged the forward hatch and prepared to start unloading.

Just as planned, the first shipment out of the hold consisted of the four crates of farm tools. Once the cargo net had the casket sized boxes on the dock, the teamsters started carrying them to the wagon and loading them aboard. As this was happening, some passengers started to disembark, and Gus gave Sheriff Moody a hand signal to move in.

The Sheriff stepped out of the shadows and approached the wagon, saying in a friendly tone, "Good evening, gents. I'm Sheriff Albert Moody, and I need to take a look at your farm tools."

"Why?" the older driver snarled.

"I got word there might be rifles in them boxes."

The younger driver moved his hand closer to his pistol. Gus called out, with his Winchester pointed at the man, "Keep your hands where I can see 'em."

The older man looked over to his scattergun, propped up next to the wagon seat. Then he looked back at the Sheriff. "We ain't got nothing to hide. We were just hired to pick up this shipment. So take a look."

Sheriff Moody used the claw hammer and started prying open one of the lids. This took a few moments, as tension built on the docks. Gus glanced at the ship and saw Captain Seymour watching from his wheelhouse.

Then, from his blind side, Gus heard the familiar 'click' of a rifle being cocked, and Lightfoot's voice boomed, "You, on the Mustang, touch that hog-leg and you'll be dead before you hit the ground."

Quickly, Gus looked to his left. In the remains of the day, he found Lightfoot standing out of the alley with his rifle pointed at the back of a dark-skinned Indian mounted on a chestnut horse. The mounted man held both of his hands out, away from his gun.

The Sheriff finally got the crate open and pulled out a rifle, which he held up high for all to see. "Drop your guns and put up your hands, gents. You're under arrest for smuggling firearms to the Indians."

The people on the dock and standing at the ships rails applauded the Sheriff's actions.

Turning to Gus, beaming, he said, "Do you know who that Indian is that your Scout has the drop on? Boston Charley, a Modoc renegade wanted by the Army. This will be big news around these parts. I think I like you, son."

With the smugglers disarmed, Captain Seymour and two husky sailors escorted Horace Bagbee off the ship. They had found him cowering in the boiler room. Instantly, he claimed he was innocent, as did all the others as they were marched off to jail. No one died that night and not a shot was fired. It was the end of another good patrol.

After the prisoners and the rifles were safely secured inside the Courthouse, Sheriff Moody told Gus and Lightfoot to come by early the next morning to sign an affidavit as witnesses to the arrest. They agreed and hurried back to the wharf, expecting to find Lucy waiting and the ship gone. Neither expectation proved true. Because of the darkness, and the lack of navigational aids on the bay, Captain Seymour had decided to remain in port until the morning. He and Martha had also invited the trio to stay aboard as their guests, to celebrate the capture of the smugglers. With free beers and corned beef sandwiches, it was a gala affair for the passengers, who wanted to hear all the details of the arrest repeated again and again. Gus and Lightfoot regaled them, but soon, with too many whiskeys under their belts, the heroes had to be helped by Lucy and Seaman Henderson back to their cabin to sleep it off.

Early the next morning, standing on the gangway with their heads throbbing, Gus and Lightfoot said farewell to Captain Seymour and Martha. Lucy did the same with tears in her eyes, hugging Martha and whispering a secret in her ear. It had been a memorable voyage, and the friends now had a soft spot in their hearts for the Seymours and their ship, *Enterprise*.

Chasing Rainbows

With dew dampening the wet timbers of the dock, Gus held a handle of their steamer trunk with one hand and his valise, bedroll, and rifle with the other. Lightfoot did the same. Lucy walked with them, carrying her own carpet bag. With a cool mist on their faces, the men were quiet and surly from their hangovers, and had long faces and cotton mouths.

"Remember Red's crows nest on Iron Horse?" Lucy asked cheerfully as they moved up the dock. "Ship has crows nest too. Randy show me, last night. We climb up rope ladder to see stars in sky. It fun."

"What else did he show you?" Clint grumbled.

"I don't want to know," Gus answered firmly.

"He ask kiss me. I say no. Only kiss brothers. He nice boy."

"Enough, please," Gus said. "My head is throbbing and I don't want to know."

Lucy looked at them with a big smile. "Too much cactus juice."

They turned into the Empire Café to have breakfast and to wait for the Courthouse to open. With their trappings stacked up just inside the entry, they took a table, and the men drank coffee while Lucy devoured a plate of bacon, eggs, and cottage fries. "Where we go now to find gold?" she asked, as the men turned away from the smell of her food.

With a wry grin, Gus asked their waitress that same question. She chuckled and told them about a place called Whiskey Creek, but another customer said that the area was all played-out. Other patrons joined in with more ideas. Everyone seemed helpful but, in the end, there were many answers to his question but no real notion of where the actual goldfields were.

Leaving their luggage at the café, the trio walked to the Courthouse at the appointed hour, where they found Sheriff Moody in his office. He greeted them warmly and invited them to take a seat while eyeing Lucy as the friends sat down in front of his desk.

"What do we have here?" he asked, looking at her.

"We call her 'Butterfly'. She's my ward," Gus answered. "We rescued her from some Cheyenne Indians, a few months back."

"Would she have a Christian name?" Moody asked.

Gus smiled at Lucy while nudging her under the desk. "Not that we know of."

She looked confused by his answer, but luckily the Sheriff moved on. "This won't take long. I just need you to sign this affidavit about last night's arrest." He handed the legal-looking handwritten paper to Gus, who read it with the eyebrow above his one good eye raised.

"Says here you got the drop on Boston Charley, seems to me that was Lightfoot. You are also taking credit for the recovery of the rifles. What's up with this story?

"It all happened so fast. This is just how I remembered it," Moody answered.

Gus handed back the document. "Is this an election year?"

The Sheriff smiled at him, "You're a bright kid. You know how small towns work. Next year is the election. All I need now is your full names for the affidavit."

Gus heard danger in his words. He didn't want the Sheriff to know his true identity. Glancing at Clint, he shrugged his shoulders, "I'm Augustus Roe."

Lucy looked as if she might say something, so Gus nudged her again. "My Scouts only Christian name is Lightfoot. He's a Comanchero."

The Sheriff glared at the trio for the longest moment. Then he wrote in their names and handed the document back for the men to sign. "I was born in the morning, but not yesterday morning," he said, his fingers dancing on his desk top. "There's something here that I'm not getting...but I don't care. I owe you for last night."

Gus signed the document, using Clint's last name, and Lightfoot made his mark. "If you owe us," Gus replied, handing back the affidavit, "tell us how we can get to the goldfields."

Moody nodded and without hesitation, advised them to look up an old gold hound named Sourdough Sam who lived in a town called Marshfield, some twenty miles southeast of Empire. "In the afternoons, you'll find him at the Ship Ahoy Tavern. If he's not there, he'll be out on his steam scow, ferrying folks around the bay."

"Does he know where the gold is?" Lightfoot asked.

The Sheriff told them that old Sam had been panning for gold in the rivers, streams and creeks of southern Oregon over twenty years. "He never hit the mother lode but always brought back enough color to go searching for more. He's a real colorful character. Just don't tell him I sent you. He doesn't like me much."

"How will we find his boat?" Gus asked.

Moody chuckled. "You'll fit right in. It's the only scow flying the Jolly Roger."

"Would there be a cab here in Empire to take us down to Marshfield?" Lightfoot asked.

"Nope. We float, ride, or walk around here. It's a good stretch of the legs to Marshfield, so you might want to buy yourself a mule. That's the animal of choice for most folks that live around here."

The last thing that Sheriff Moody did was give them a map of the county and direct them to the local stable where they could haggle for a mule. As the trio departed Moody's office, he said, "If you ever give up chasing gold, I know a fellow who is always looking for some good coal miners."

Gus stopped at the door and glanced back at the Sheriff with a smile. "We're after gold, not coal."

With the wagon ruts deep, it was late morning by the time the friends started walking down the Marshfield road. They had in tow an ornery brown mule called Harriet. She had cost them thirty-five dollars for the animal and a packsaddle, and now she carried their luggage and the steamer trunk. Harriet didn't like her heavy burden and had serenaded the trio with her loud fussing all the way down the trail. A mule lacks the proud whinny of a horse; instead making a hee-haw sound much like an old lady cackling. The mule was driving them crazy.

"Don't ever ask me to ride a mule," Clint said with a grumpy face. "I'm a horseman, not a pig farmer. Mules are God's mistakes."

"Better than you and I carrying that damn trunk," Gus replied.

Lucy patted Harriet's neck. "She is good animal. I ride her. Brother, why you tell man with badge, I no have name?"

"And why did you let him steal our thunder?" Clint added sharply.

"We didn't do it for thunder. We did it because it was right. And the Sheriff had no business knowing our names. We don't need bounty hunters looking for me in the goldfields."

"What do we tell this Sourdough Sam, if we catch up with him?" Clint asked.

"First names will do just fine. I have a feeling this is going to be a long stretch of the legs."

The wagon road east was a pleasant walk, with many gullies and draws under a gray sky, with a warm breeze on their faces. They passed many farmhouses, wood-framed and logged, with fenced, rolling green pastures. Timbered bridges crossed many streams and sloughs, and much of the land was still wild, with tall forests ready for clearing. From the sparkling waters of the bay to the hills and dells of the fertile prairie, Coos Bay looked like an endless land of promise.

A few hours later, with the sun peeking through the clouds, the bay came back into view as it arched around the northern point of the inland peninsula. Here the road turned south-southeast, and the trio stopped to share the last two cans of salmon they had purchased back on the American River. The men were starved, with only coffee in their bellies. "Can't believe how good this fish is," Clint said, using his fingers to feed his face. "We need to buy some more for the goldfields."

Gus agreed. "Hopefully, Sourdough Sam will tell us what we'll need. In any event, I guess we'll be doing a lot of huntin'."

"Where we sleep tonight?" Lucy asked, also eating from a can.

Gus used his knife to stab a last morsel of salmon. "Wherever the trail takes us."

It was late afternoon by the time the road dropped down to the shoreline and Marshfield came into view. As the buildings and homes got closer together, they soon came upon the Ship Ahoy Tavern, overlooking a cove of floating docks and timbered wharfs.

The tavern wasn't much of a wood-framed building, just two stories high, with weathered clapboards in need of paint. They tied Harriet to the hitching post and went inside through swinging saloon doors. Immediately Gus felt the prying eyes of the few patrons in the bar. The tavern was long and narrow, with a standup counter on one side and wooden booths on the other. They approached the bartender and asked if Sourdough Sam was in the saloon.

He glared at the strangers, and then yelled out into the room, "Sam, you've got some visitors up here."

A high-pitched voice yelled back from a booth at the rear of the tavern. "I'm not here, unless they have drinks. Send them away."

The bartender smiled. "Sorry, folks. Sam ain't takin' no visitors today."

"What's he drink?" Lightfoot asked.

"Schooner of beer," the barman answered.

"Pour us a bucket and we'll take it back to him."

The bartender nodded and poured.

Gus paid him and grabbed three empty glasses. With bar eyes watching, the trio marched to the back booth with the bucket in hand.

Sam's eyes widened as the trio slipped into the booth with the beer. He was a short, funny-looking older man, with a scalp of thinning gray hair, and deep-set blue eyes. "Sam likes his brew," he stated in his high-pitched voice, while staring at Gus's face. "And Sam has a fancy for pirates. Would you be one?"

"No, sir. We're just looking for the goldfields," Gus answered, pouring beer into his glass. "Could you tell us how to find them?"

The old man glanced at Lucy with a smirk and narrowed his eyes. "Sam wants to know who the girl is."

"She's our sister, Lucy," Lightfoot said. "Can you guide us to the gold?"

The old man took a long drink from his schooner. "Why these people here?" he mumbled to himself. "Sam ain't a gold hound anymore, so don't waste his time."

Sourdough Sam was indeed a character; he talked to himself, and about himself, always in the third person. It was as if he was thinking out loud.

Gus did the introductions while filling up the glasses. "We would like to hire Sam to take us to the goldfields and give us some pointers about finding gold."

Sam just smiled, shaking his head. "Sam's not in that business anymore."

"What kind of business are you in now?" Lightfoot asked.

"He now owns the paddlewheel scow *Marianne*. She's a big, flat-bottom barge working these waters."

"We'll hire Sam and the *Marianne* to take us to the fields. What would be his fare?" Gus asked.

Sam took another long drink from his schooner, still shaking his head and carefully eyeing Gus. "He can't go anywhere now. His boat broke down. You're just wasting his time."

In many ways, Sam turned out to be like an open book. With a little patience and a few more beers, he told them about the current gold conditions in Coos County. It wasn't encouraging. He also talked, in his third-party way, about the Coast Range Mountains, and how a few sourdoughs were still finding color up there. "Sam knows there's gold up there somewhere, but when he bought his scow, he promised his wife to give up the hunt."

Now his beloved *Marianne* was in dry-dock and he wasn't making any money.

With a few more questions, Gus learned that Sam had ordered the parts needed to fix his engine from Crowley's Hardware Store in Marshfield. The parts had come in, but old man Crowley wouldn't extend credit to Sam, so he had been beached for the last few weeks.

"How much are the parts?" Gus asked.

"Sam says the parts would be twenty-four dollars and some change. So, right now, he's broke and on the beach. "

That opened the negotiation doors, and soon Gus and Sam had a deal. The trio would buy all the supplies for the expedition, and buy the needed parts, and help him get the steam engine working again. He, in turn, would guide them on a two-month search for gold up into the coastal mountains.

"Sam wants to know how the gold will be split up."

"Four ways," Gus answered.

The old man frowned. "Sam thinks gold camps no good for a girl. She's not strong enough."

Gus glared back at the old man. "Lucy is as smart as a beaver and as strong as a bear. She gets her share or no deal."

Sam mumbled to himself again. "Girl in camp bad luck...but Sam agrees,"

That evening, when they went to where Sam's scow was moored, they were surprised to find his wife waiting. She was a big, bow-legged, copper-skinned Indian squaw who spoke mostly the Coos language. Her name was Marianne, just like his boat. The couple lived in the forward compartment of a square-hulled barge of about sixty feet. Behind their cabin, and amidships, were the boiler and the steam engine for a portside paddlewheel. The rear of the scow was a big open deck for carrying cargo and livestock. In addition to the Jolly Rogers flag on the masthead, Sam had a small swivel gun mounted on the rail next to the helm. Sourdough Sam fancied himself as a real pirate.

The boat *Marianne* looked about as seaworthy as a river raft, while the wife Marianne looked as mad as a hornet. She and Sam had some heated discussions in her native tongue before she served up a meal of boiled fish and stale bread. Sam might call himself the Skipper of the *Marianne* but, at least while in port, it was obvious his wife was the boss.

In the fading light after dinner, the trio set up camp in the cove on the soft sands of the shoreline. That night, from their bedrolls Lightfoot said, "That Sam is one crazy loon. He gets on my nerves."

"I hope he's crazy like a fox," Gus answered in the dark. "He's our only hope of finding gold."

"Cheyenne believe crazy people have big powers," Lucy replied. "I hope they right."

The trio spent the next few days getting the engine fixed and making preparations for their trek into the wilderness. But there had been a few setbacks. When they went to Crowley's Hardware Store for the parts, old man Crowley would only agree to sell them the items if Sam's entire account was paid in full. That added another Double Eagle to the cost. Sam's only remorse about this oversight had been, "Just take it out of Sam's share of the gold."

Then there was his mule. He owned an old one also named Marianne, just like his wife and the boat. It, too, needed money for its release from a local stable.

As a matter of fact, Sam was full of costly surprises, including his long list of food and supplies needed for their journey: sacks of coffee, flour, sugar, beans, and six slabs of bacon. Then there were the tools, the whiskey, the rain gear, and other camp supplies. So much was being packed in that a third mule was rented to help carry the burden. This all cost far more money than Gus had counted on. Chasing the gold rainbow was an expensive gamble!

On the first day of summer, the boat *Marianne* finally slipped her lines and headed east across the bay, with the wife Marianne at the helm. It was a beautiful morning, with hardly a ripple on the water, and the rear deck filled with their animals and supplies. As the paddlewheel churned up the calm waters, the friends stood in the sun with Sourdough Sam.

"Do you know where we are going?" Gus asked him.

"Sam knows," he replied in his high-pitched voice. "Many years ago, he found a high meadow he calls Elk Valley. There are many rocky streams up there flowing from a high granite cliff that he's never panned. The last time he was up there hunting an elk, he got chased away by a winter storm."

"How far is it from here?" Lightfoot asked, gazing across the glistening waters.

"Thirty miles by boat and fifty on foot, Sam says three hard days."

Lucy looked at him; she stood as tall as he did. "Why you call everything Marianne?"

He smiled. "Marianne was Sam's mother, so he calls all he loves the same, even his wife."

Gus chuckled. "Good. With our empty purse, I sure hope we find a lot of Marianne's up in Elk Valley."

The boat crossed the bay and turned east on the Coos River. An hour later, it turned northeast into a large slough which twisted and turned for many miles before running aground in the shallow waters. Here the boat stopped and was unloaded. With the weight off the boat, everyone used poles and ropes to free the *Marianne* from the muddy bottom and turn her with the tide for the journey back across the bay.

As the trio packed up the mules on shore, Sam went back aboard his boat to say farewell to his wife. They had another heated discussion, using words only they seemed to understand. Then Sam returned ashore with an angry face. His wife put the boat in gear and with the paddle wheels just starting to turn, she rushed out onto the empty rear deck and yelled back in English, "Tell Sam he's my man. No look at pretty girl."

Sam yelled back to her, "He no look. Don't be jealous! See you in two months from today. Sam only loves you."

Under the hot mid-day sun, and without another word, they watched from the shore as the barge returned to the labyrinth of the slough.

Once it was out of sight, Sam turned with his mule's rope in hand and started across the green, marshy prairie of sea-grass. Lightfoot, with the rented mule, was just behind him, with Lucy, Harriet, and Gus bringing up the rear.

"What jealous mean?" Lucy asked, with Harriet's lead in hand.

Gus nodded with a smile. "It's a word you should know. Many will be jealous of you."

They walked all afternoon and into the evening before they arrived at the foothills of the coastal mountains. There they made camp and in a nearby creek, Sam gave them their first lesson in panning for gold. He started by explaining that gold was heavier than the pebbles and sand of the creek beds, so any gold they might find would always be at the bottom of their pans. The trick was to carefully wash away the rubble, leaving only the gold.

This required swirling and shaking the water to wash away the pebbles and sand. For a demonstration, he used two small iron ball bearings, which were also heavier than the creek silt. If the panning technique was right, the ball bearings and/or gold would always be at the bottom of the pan. "We will practice each evening," Sam told them, "until it is second nature and we find color." It was a slow process that took much patience and a gentle touch. They found no color that night, but Sam had more to teach them when they set up their first camp.

The trio pitched their tent on soft, level ground close to the creek, but Sam wanted nothing to do with the tent. Instead, he found two trees and hung a hammock between them. Inside his swinging bed, he placed his bedroll and covered it with a canvas tarp. "Sam not sleep on ground with snakes and other vermin," he said, placing his shotgun inside his cocoon. "Sam says we have cold camp while we travel. Sunrise, we leave for long walk."

After the camp was set up, everyone sat on a long log snag, eating Johnny cakes and drinking whiskey while watching the sky turn crimson.

"Why wife jealous of me?" Lucy asked Sam while eating her corn dodger.

"Sam will tell you story," he replied in the growing darkness. "Coos Indians are a hard tribe to understand. Long ago, to stop inter-clan unions, only the chiefs could allow marriages. But then one young couple from the same clan made the mistake of copulation. They were soon discovered and taken before the chiefs. Their punishment was death, and they had the couple stripped naked and hog-tied, facing each other, to log pilings placed in the bay at low tide. Then, with all the tribes watching, they were slowly drowned in the incoming tide. Their bodies remained in the water for the next two days to remind other lovers that only the chiefs could allow copulation. My wife, Marianne, was the younger sister of the drowned maiden. With their wild screams for help echoing off the water, she watched it all. Now she is jealous of all women. She is fearful that I might leave her, and she would be returned to the Reservation to be drowned by the chiefs, as we never asked for their permission."

There was a long silence after Sam's tale. He was quite a storyteller.

"I know word love. What is cop-ulation?" Lucy finally asked.

Gus finished his tin cup of whiskey with a surly face. "That's a word for another time."

The next two days, and two cold camps, were a trek almost straight up. They crossed many streams, climbed many steep inclines, and battled their way through the thick brushwood. There were no roads, no paths, only a few game trails that always seemed to twist and turn in the wrong direction. The march with the stubborn mules was exhausting, difficult, and dangerous.

But, as promised, by the end of the third day they stood on a ridgeline looking down on a large forest-lined meadow with a few scrub trees, the place that Sam called Elk Valley. The backdrop of that picturesque view was a tall granite mountain with green-treed slopes and numerous waterfalls all rushing down to the valley floor. At the base of those cliffs, the waters pooled up and then drained into many brooks and streams that flowed across the grassy meadows and continued down the gentle slopes toward the sea. Elk Valley looked like the Garden of Eden. *Here is our future*, Gus said to himself with great anticipation.

They made camp that night close to the waterfalls, on nearly level ground, where they pitched their tent and unpacked the animals. Then, with gold pans in hand, like children in a candy store, they rushed to the streams in the fading light. It didn't take long; Sam soon found some color in his pan of silt. It wasn't much, just a few flakes and two small nuggets about the size of pinheads But it was gold, and everyone rejoiced.

Sam dropped the nuggets into an empty pint mason jar and used a glass tube to suck up the flakes. "May this vial be full when we leave this valley," he said, with his eyes bright and his smile wide. "We are on the gold, and now the hunt begins."

They worked the valley in teams. Gus and Lightfoot took one stream while Sam and Lucy took another. They started a few hundred yards downstream and slowly worked their way up towards the waterfalls. From sunrise to sunset, in the hot sun and cold rains, it was damn hard work. Crouching, kneeling, and resting on their haunches with a tin pan in hand, they washed away the creeks sand and silt, looking for gold. When color was discovered, Sam came over and made detailed notes of how much gold and where it was found. Ever so slowly, his jar of nuggets and the smaller glass vial for flakes and dust started filling up with color. Sam seemed pleasantly surprised that his Elk Valley was so bountiful.

The work soon became a routine. At first light each morning, Sam was up first to put the coffee on and wake either Gus or Lightfoot for their morning hunt. Their game was mostly squirrels or rabbits, with a sprinkling of a few porcupines and game birds. They never did see an elk, bear, or deer in Elk Valley. But then, they were high up in the mountains, and those animals had likely moved to the lower elevations for the summer.

Back in camp, Sam always made breakfast, and the menu never changed. In an iron skillet, he fried up thick strips of bacon while mixing a bowl of flour and warm water into dough. When his mixture was ready, he removed the bacon and placed the dough in the drippings. Covering the pan, he removed it from the direct fire and let it cook until it was done. That was their morning meal: coffee as thick as molasses, bacon as chewy as leather, and bread with a crust as oily as axle grease.

Lucy cooked the evening meals. Mostly it was an Indian stew of boiled greens and whatever game the men had killed. If there was no game, dinner would be just a plate of beans with a corn dodger. The food wasn't fancy or tasty, but it kept them going while the gold grew in their jars.

Half–a-day on Sunday was their only day off. They used this time to wash themselves and their clothes in the waterfalls, and to explore the valley for wild game and berries. It was a time of back-breaking work, tempered with the excitement of being on the gold. Sam often told the trio that when they returned to the valley next, he would pack-in the wood needed to build a proper sluice box, which would double or triple their output. "First, we'll file a claim for this valley, and then squeeze it dry of its gold. This will be our El Dorado."

Around the campfire each night, they enjoyed a single cup of whiskey while playing poker, using matchsticks as money. It was a great game that helped Lucy with her numbers and taught her the value of counting cards and managing her bets. As they played, Sam would usually regale them with a story. Little did anyone know at the time that one of his tales would change their lives forever.

Sam was talking about his journey crossing the continent on the Oregon Trail in 1856. His wagon train had started in Missouri and ended in Oregon City, where he signed a special book kept by a man call Doctor John McLoughlin.

"What kind of book?" Lucy interrupted.

Sam shrugged. "It was a kind of ledger that had all the names of the Immigrants that crossed on the Oregon Trail. Why do you ask?"

Lucy's expression turned hopeful in the flickering campfire. "Maybe my brother Leon has his name in that book. If so, he would be alive, and I'd be very happy."

Sam scratched his head. "Sam thought Gus and Lightfoot were your brothers."

Lucy smiled broadly. "I have many brothers. Where is this Ore-gone City?"

Lightfoot and Sourdough Sam on the gold

Chapter 5 – All That Glitters

Gold

Why God created gold, only He would know. Why men searched for it only they could say. Why gold invokes fear in an honest man and greed in others, no one knows. Gold is the El Dorado of riches for some, but the fruit of damnation for most.

Like three scruffy sad seagulls, the compadres stood at the stern rail of the steam wheeler ship *Pacific* watching the Arago Lighthouse and Coos Bay slip away in the glistening wake. Deflated and defeated, Gus and Lightfoot had sullen faces and surly moods, while, Lucy stood between them with her auburn hair twisting in the wind and with a bright smile. She had won the day: they were finally on their way to Ore-gone City to see if her brother Leon was still alive.

"No more riding mules," Clint lamented. "I want to wear my buckskins again with a good nag under my butt."

"No more grubbing for gold or coal," Gus added with disdain. "We will need to find new jobs better suited for our talents."

Lightfoot chuckled, "What talents would that be Captain? Killing Indians."

"No," Gus said firmly. "That we will not do."

They had entered Elk Valley poor, came out rich and were now leaving Coos Bay poor again!

≈

Six weeks before, they had departed Elk Valley with a pair of mason jars almost full of gold nuggets and a leather poke filled with dust. Sourdough Sam had estimated the value of their take at near $7,500.00! Wow... they were rich, a dream come true! Although, Sam had warned them that the true value of their poke wouldn't be determined until the Assayer certified its value and purity. The walk-out from the wilderness to meet up with Sam's wife had been a joyful journey. They had plans of returning to the valley in the next few months with more supplies and wood boards to build a proper sleuth that would increase their daily gold output. They had found their El Dorado, now all they had to do was to file a claim and put their money in the bank for safe keeping.

On the last day of their journey to the bay, they waited in the sea grass for the boat *Marianne*. It was here that Sam had given the trio a stern warning. "Sam says we tell no one of our discovery. He fears if news gets out about our valley we will be overrun with swindlers and scoundrels. "We be quiet like an owl."

"Do we tell your wife?" Gus had asked.

Sam had shrugged his shoulders, "She will know, without asking. She knows Sam well."

All agreed that no one would say anything, to anybody, about their valley or their discovery. Sam called this agreement an Indian 'blood oath' and vowed a slow death for anyone violating it.

That was all well and good, until two days later when they took their gold into the Marshfield Assayer office. That's when the wheels started coming off the wagon. The Assayer, a tall rawboned fella named Pete Johnson, required by Federal Mining Laws certain information about the location of the goldfields and the identities of all who had found the deposit. This string bean of a man assured the partners that all this information would remain confidential and that this paperwork was just a normal routine.

Gus didn't like the Assayers many questions and turned to Sam, "Is what this fellow telling us the truth?"

"Sam says yes," he had answered removing a dog-eared Bible from his pouch. "Sam use his Good Book, with all the dates and names, to prove who he is. He do this many times."

Reluctantly, Gus and Lightfoot used their separation papers

from the Cavalry to prove their identities, while Sam used his Bible. But they had no such papers for Lucy, so her name was not registered with the claim.

She didn't like being excluded and let her brothers know it, "Why not me? I work hard just like you."

The Assayer had turned up his bony nose and replied with contempt, "Mining ain't for little girl's missy. Your place be around the campfire."

Lucy fumed with her green eyes on fire. If looks could kill, the Assayer would be without a scalp.

As instructed, two days later they returned to Marshfield for the Assayers final report. When they got to his office they found it all locked up with a note on the door that simply read:

'Gone fishing. Elk Valley claim impounded by Sheriff Moody pending a hearing by Federal Magistrate. Inquire at County Courthouse.'

Like deflated balloons, none of the partners could believe the message on the door. Gus had to read it aloud three times before they recovered enough for the long mule ride to the Coos Bay Courthouse. Once there, they cooled their heels for almost an hour before Sheriff Moody finally showed them into his office. The Sheriff had a strange look on his face, a defiant expression of pending bad news. On top of his desk was all their gold and what appeared to be the Assayers final report. All the partners found chairs, except Gus, who remained standing next to his office door.

"You folks have been busy like beavers," he said from behind his desk with that defiant glare. "The gold assayed out at high quality. The Brewster Brothers should be happy with their payout."

"Who the hell are the Brewster Brothers?" Gus demand loudly from the doorway."

Sheriff Moody glared back at him. "Well Captain Savage, I knew all long your name Client Roe was just an alias. Why you lied to me, I have no idea. Although, I'll bet somewhere there's papers on you. But I don't much care about that because I still owe you for Boston Charley."

The Sheriff picked up a jar of gold nuggets and continued, "But I do care about this. The place you found this gold is not called Elk Valley. According to the land office, it's called Brewster Valley. The Brothers purchased the land and the mineral rights fifteen years ago. Looks like you folks are gold poachers or claim jumpers. This gold doesn't belong to you; it belongs to the Brewster Brothers."

The room fell silent with only a ticking clock. All the partners had surprised looks on their long faces and were lost in thought. How could this be? All their gold, sweat and toil lost over a valley name they knew nothing about?

"Well Sam," Lightfoot finally demanded with fire in his brown eyes. "You're the one that told us about Elk Valley. What do you say now?"

Sourdough Sam shook his head with a bewildered face. "Sam says, not true. He found no monuments in the valley. No signs of any claim. This be open land. He discovered this valley twenty years ago."

"What the hell is a monument? Gus asked.

"It's a man-made pile of rocks that denotes a claim has been filed for the mineral rights," Sheriff Moody answered.

"I saw no such monument," Gus replied quickly.

"No did I," Lightfoot add.

Lucy shook her head, "I didn't either."

"Well Sheriff," Sourdough said glaring at Moody. "We don't much care for each other, but I give you my word, there are no monuments up in Sam's valley."

Sheriff Moody looked disappointed with what he had learned. "I'll take sworn affidavits from you all. Then we'll let the Federal Magistrate sort it out the next time he comes to Coos Bay."

"When will that be?" Gus asked.

The Sheriff shrugged his shoulders, "Don't know for sure. He comes up from San Francisco a few times a year."

Gus fumed from the doorway. "We'll need some of that gold to cover our expenses while we wait."

Moody shook his head. "The gold gets locked up in the county safe until the Magistrate's decision. Your money problems are not my affair Captain Savage."

"Sheriff," Lucy asked looking at him with her deep set eyes. "What be a Mag-u-stright?"

Moody chuckled. "He is a wise man that talks for big chief

in Washington. He's the Federal Law around here."

Lucy's eyes blinked a few times and she nodded her head. "Good, I need to talk to such a wise man to know why big chief steal our gold."

Moody melted with her sweet innocent look and wrote something out on a piece of paper and handed it Lightfoot. "If you guys need to make some money, try the Willow Creek Coal Mine, ten miles south of Marshfield. They are always looking for strong backs and weak minds."

"Thought you didn't care," Gus said from the doorway.

The Sheriff frowned, "Don't much like liars Captain, but for the girl's sake, I'll trust you just one more time."

As they waited for the Magistrate, the partners split up. Sam went back to work aboard the *Marianne*, while Gus and Lightfoot got jobs at the Willow Creek Mine. Lucy moved to the small mining community with the men and helped them set-up a camp site close to the mine. Here each evening she cooked their meals and helped them clean off the coal dust with hot water and soap. It was a never ending task as each day her brothers turned from fair skinned to black skinned inside the dark and dingy pit of the mine.

The men hated the work: coal mining for four-dollars a day was back breaking manual labor as hard as laying track on the Iron Highway. The long dangerous tunnels, inside the mountain were dark, damp and dirty with constant fears of cave-ins challenging their courage. Coal mining wasn't what they expected. They lived underground like prairie dogs, and time in the mines dragged on likes the sands of an hour-glass.

Finally, in the waning days of September, Sheriff Moody summoned them back to his office. That's when the last wheel fell off the wagon. The Magistrate, they had been waiting for, had been arrested for bribery and terminated from his government post. It would be many months before a new Magistrate would be appointed for the district. That was it. Their dreams of gold were over! Neither Gus, nor Lightfoot, wanted to return to the coal mines and Lucy only talked about Ore-gone City and her long lost brother. It was time to move on.

"I do have some good news," Sheriff Moody had told them at their final meeting. "The reward money for the stolen guns and Boston Charley has been paid."

"How much?" Lightfoot had asked quickly.

Sheriff Moody had smiled back at him with benevolent look. "Two hundred for the guns and two hundred for Charley," he replied reaching into desk drawer. Bringing out a stack of coins he placed them on top of his desk.

Gus glared at the Sheriff, "Doesn't look like four hundred dollars to me. What the hell goes on here?"

The short stack of coins had three Gold Double Eagles, three Silver Dollars and a shiny new half dollar piece. Moody pushed the stack of coins and a piece of paper across his desk towards Gus. "This is your share with a complete accounting of the expenses."

Gus read the paper twisting his head sadly, "You screwed us again Sheriff." Then he turned to Lucy and Lightfoot and continued. "After the county and the Sheriff get their share, and after the trial judge got his expenses and even a fee for transporting Charley to the State Prison we get $63.50!"

"That's how reward money works Gus, everyone gets their share," Moody replied. "Look at it this way, your share is a week's worth of time in the coal mine."

Gus's face was red with anger as he handed Lightfoot and Lucy $21.00 each. "I'll keep the Franklin as *my fee* for the distribution. This is all bull-shit Sheriff and you know it."

Moody got fire in his eyes. "Look fellows, if you boys want to make some real money I've got a job right up your alley."

"And what would that be?" Lightfoot asked.

"The State Militia is looking for some Indian fighters and I understand you guys are two of the best. The pay is good and the work light."

"Why would you say that about us?" Gus asked. "We're just gold-hounds looking to strike it rich."

Sheriff Moody grinned, "That's not what your separation papers say. While you were out chasing golden rainbows, I made a few inquiries to the Cavalry. From what I learned you guys are notorious Indian fighters."

"Why do you need Indian fighters?" Gus asked.

"The Modoc Reservation just south of here is up in arms. We

think there is going to be an Indian war," the Sheriff answered.

Gus and Lightfoot looked at each other with angry faces, "What would be the pay?" Lightfoot asked.

Gus shook his head, "Hold on Sheriff! You've got a lot of brass. You confiscate our gold and rob our reward money. Now you want us to fight your battles. No! Our trail of Indian sorrows are long gone."

"Good!" Lucy blurted. "You promised me we go to Ore-gone City."

Lightfoot stood to leave, "She is right, we did promise."

≈

With loud screams of seagulls chasing after the boat, Lucy turned her back to the wake of the ship and looked up at her two brothers still staring sadly at the remains of Coos Bay.

"Sheriff Moody promise to contact us when new wise-man come."

"Lucy, don't trust Moody, he's just a lying politician," Gus answered glaring down at her sweet innocent face.

"All politicians are liars," Lightfoot added with anger in his voice.

Lucy quickly changed the subject. "My brothers need hot baths to rub-off the last of the coal dust. Then I give you haircuts and shaves. You feel better."

Gus nodded, "This is an important day. I should look my best."

Lightfoot frowned, "What makes this day so important."

"September 26th is my birthday," Gus replied. "After my clean-up, I'll play some poker. Maybe the cards will be good to me tonight."

The Good Book

The steamship *Pacific* was a steel boat with both sails and mid-ship paddle wheels. It was much the same size of the *Enterprise* only fancier and faster. The ship was due into Astoria early the next morning.

When the trio had boarded the ship, earlier that morning, they had considered a $10 steerage cabin, but when they saw the cramped quarters below decks with no windows or fresh air, they had changed accommodations to a two room cabin on the Promenade deck for $25.00. It was an extravagance, but after many weeks of working the coal mines, it was worth their meager poke.

Lucy had a steady hand with the straight razor and used her scissors with great skills in giving her brothers haircuts every few months. With the Captains golden brown locks flying and her scissors snipping she asked of him, "What is a birthday?"

"It's just another white-man's holiday." Clint answered waiting his turn at the cabins small table. "They have many fiestas for no reason at all."

"It's an important day," Gus said. "Birthdays remind us how old we are."

Lucy stopped for a moment and looked at Gus with that inquisitive face, "How old are you?"

Gus smiled at her, "You tell me. You can figure it out."

"How?" she asked.

Gus turned to Lightfoot with a grin, "Give Lucy her tablet and a pencil."

He did and Lucy put down her scissors with a bewildered look.

"First write down what year it is." Gus asked nodding at a calendar hanging on the compartment wall.

She looked confused and Clint added, "Remember where we told you to look for the days, weeks and years?"

Like a match to a candle, a light came on in her eyes. "Yes, the calendar," she said glancing over to the one on the wall.

"Use your numbers and write down the year," Gus answered with encouragement.

Lucy wrote down 1869 on her tablet and then glanced at Gus. "What's next?"

"Below that number write the year I was born, 1-8-4-0. She did.

"Now subtract the bottom number from the top number, just like we taught you, and you will find that I'm now twenty-nine years old."

That bewildered look returned to her face. "How do you know

you were born in 1840?"

"The day I was born, my mother wrote the date of my birth in our family Bible. She wrote all the important dates in our Good Book."

Lucy turned to Lightfoot, "How old are you brother?"

Clint shook his head sadly and then coldly answered, "Don't know for sure. Our Bible was lost when the Comanche's slaughtered my family and burnt down our cabin. They took me when I was about eight, so I don't know the date or the year I was born. I think I'm about thirty-eight years old."

Lucy glared at him, his words were so cold and matter of fact. Then she turned back to Gus, "What year was I born and how old am I?"

"We don't know for sure, we think you are thirteen." Gus answered.

"Even old Sourdough Sam has Bible," Lucy said with a frown. "With that Good Book, Sam can prove who he is, while Lightfoot and I are nobodies. We are just orphans in God's eyes."

"We ain't no damn orphans," Clint replied sharply.

Lucy picked up her scissors and went back to cutting the Captain's hair. Lost in thought, she said nothing for the longest time. Finally with a determined voice she announced, "Today is all of our birthdays, I'm fourteen and Lightfoot is thirty-nine. We write this down in my San Francisco Bible for all to see. We are just as good as everyone else."

Gus glanced over to Clint who shrugged his shoulders with a grin as he poured himself a glass of Tequila. He held the water glass high and made a toast, "Here's to all of our birthdays. We will forever be bound together in Butterflies Bible."

She smiled from ear to ear and removed the towel from around Gus's neck. "Tonight we all have a fiesta."

As the Captain got up from his chair he thought about telling his friends of his lost Bible back in Kansas, but he didn't. Lucy looked so proud to have a way of proving she had her own family.

"Why do you want to be fourteen," Gus asked.

"Because I am big girl now. We find my brother and put his name in my family Bible."

As Lucy gave Clint his haircut and shave, Gus sat at the table with an ink pen in hand writing out on paper what the Bible inscription would say. Everyone commented and made suggestions. The wording had to be just right, with the Captain's penmanship just perfect. Finally all agreed on the text and where they would sign their names on the inside cover of Lucy's Bible. She was the first to sign with the date of her rescue from the Cheyenne Indians and her birthday as September 26, 1855. The Captain was next with his birthday listed as of 1840. Clint was last with his listed as 1831.

This signing of the Bible was when Lightfoot surprised Gus with the best birthday gift of all. He signed his name, not with his mark, but with a legible written scroll. Gus was astounded and dumbfounded. "When the hell did you learn to write?" He asked his friend with a grin.

Beaming with pride Lightfoot answered, "Lucy taught me when you were playing poker. I teach her Spanish in return. We are school chums."

Gus picked-up the Bible and showed the finished page to his friends. "I could not be more proud of you two then I am right now. Tonight we celebrate not only birthdays, but learning as well. God Bless you both."

Clint had a sheepish look on his face, "It's no big thing Captain. Let's stay away from any Bible thumping. It gives me the creeps."

The *Pacific* had a dining room just behind the third deck wheelhouse. It was a large plush compartment with square tables, bolted down to the deck, with white tablecloths, candles in old wine bottles and uniformed Stewards. In many ways, it was as fancy as a San Francisco Bistro.

That night when the trio walked into the crowded room, Gus felt the eyes from the other passengers staring his way. This was not uncommon, because of his eye patch, but at times it made him feel like he lived in a glass bowl. One of the Stewards showed them a table set-up for four and gave them each a small hand printed menu. Gus glanced at the listing for the three entrees available. No more buffets of soups, this ship offered fresh fish, beef steaks or a fish stew for six-bits a plate. On the back of the menu he found the listing for the beverages: wine, beer, whiskey or California champagne. The cost per bottle of champagne was $2.25. Gus couldn't resist and ordered a bottle of champagne from their waiter.

"What this champagne?" Lucy asked.

Gus smiled, "I only drank it once in my life, on the day that the Civil War ended. It tickled my nose and made me laugh... why not now for our fiesta."

"Is it a wine? Lightfoot asked. "I don't like wine."

"It's a bubbling wine. You'll like it," Gus answered. "We will drink to our new family and our new adventure."

When the bottle came it was in a small wooden bucket with something you rarely saw on a ship: ice to keep the champagne cold. The friends were wide eyed when the waiter uncorked the bottle, with a loud pop, that made the other diners turn their way. Then they sampled the cold bubbly with smiles and laughter. It was just as Gus had remembered: a sweet nectar with the flavor of grapes and a kick like a mule. They toasted each other's decadence: a word that Gus had to explain to his friends. They ordered their fancy dinners and basked in the glow of being together for this special occasion. It was a time of discovery, reflections with hopes and dreams for a bright future.

They were having such fun, that they didn't even notice the man moving their way in the shadows. In the blink of an eye, he stood before them in the flickering light of their table candle. "Sorry to disturb you folks," he said in a friendly voice staring down at them. "Your table has room for one more, my I join you? I am but a lone diner this evening."

Gus glanced up at the man and his face melted from gaiety to somber in a flash. There was something sinister about this tall man with a long face. He wore a black coat with a dark ruffled shirt and a patch covering his left eye just like the Captains. He was older with a weathered face, neatly trimmed white goatee, and had a curled-up bull whip hanging from his belt. In the dim light he was an imposing figure standing there looking down on the friends.

"I'm Reverend Hathaway, returning to my congregation in Astoria. I hate to impose but all the other tables seem to be filled."

Lucy glanced up at the man with a smile and a glass of champagne in hand. "Please do sir... we are just having a birthday party."

The Reverend bowed at Lucy, "Thank you young lady, I thought you were celebrating something."

Lightfoot frowned as the stranger took the last chair.

Lucy quickly stood and curtsied back to him. "May I introduce my family," she said. "This is my brother Clint and Captain Savage. I am called Lucy."

Hathaway smiled at the trio flashing his bone white teeth, "You be a breath of fresh air little lady." Then turning to Gus he continued, "Can't help but noticing we both have the same eye afflictions Captain. How did you lose yours?"

"In the War Reverend and you?"

"Sadly the same: This affliction is *my* retribution from God for at the time I wore a gray uniform. Now I'm a Christian Soldier for the Lord." He pointed to his dead eye, "This patch brought me to Jesus Christ." Dramatically he made a fist with his right hand and held it up in the candle light. Slowly opening it he said, "First God gave me love." On the palm of his hand was the blue tattooed word *love*. He turned his hand slowly so all could see and then did the same with left hand, opening his palm slowly to reveal the word *hate*. "And He gave me *hate* for all the sinners in the world."

Lucy seemed mesmerized with his theatrics, but then she was trusting of almost everyone. While Lightfoot trusted no one, so he just shook his head with droopy lips and glaring eyes.

Gus nodded sadly remembering all the hypocritical preachers he had seen over the years. But this one was different; he was a real showman that thumped his Bible much like any good thespian.

"I march now in the Legions of the Lord, with one hand on my Good Book and my other hand on my whip. Vengeance is mine saith the Lord."

Thankfully, just then their waiter reappeared with their dinners. As he placed the plates of food on the table the Reverend demanded of him, "I'll have the fish. Only the fish: with a glass of water. I'm fasting until I'm back in the bosom of my con-gregation."

Lightfoot and Gus had the beef steaks and potatoes and started devouring their dinners. Lucy had the fresh halibut and tasted a small piece before pouring more bubbly for her brothers.

"Would you like some champagne?" She asked innocently of

the Reverend.

"No," he answered firmly. "And neither should you young lady." Then he launched into a loud soliloquy by holding up his left palm again, "I hate all sinners: those who don't say grace before their meals, those who drink the devil's brew and those who play cards and lust for the flesh. Take heed little girl, your mortal soul is at risk. God will have His retribution. "

"Enough... poppycock!" Lightfoot finally shouted in an angry voice with a piece of meat stuck on the tip of his hunting knife. "That's all rubbish Reverend. God is not revengeful or fearful. It's only charlatans like you that preach such lies."

Hathaway's face turned resentful, "You know not what you say lad. The devil has your tongue."

"My brother is right Reverend," Gus said, also cutting his meat with his hunting knife. "Your right palm is correct, love is the answer. Your left palm is not. Hate is never the answer. The word on your left palm should be hope."

Lucy looked confused with the conversation; she didn't understand the true character of the man she had invited to their table.

"Move on Reverend, you are not welcome here." Lightfoot said taking a bite from the tip of his knife.

Hathaway quickly stood-up tipping over his chair, "Breed, no one talks to me like that," he shouted glaring down at the table. "I will not break bread with such heathens." His right hand moved to his curled-up whip on his hip.

Lightfoot flipped his knife into the air and grabbed the buffalo-boned handle in mid-air with his right arm cocked and ready to throw. "Don't even think about it Reverend. You touch that whip and I'll be feeding you to the fish."

Like two bulls, the men stared at each other for the longest moment. Finally, the Reverend turned into the shadows yelling, "God will have His retribution."

Gus glanced around the table to the other diners and shrugged his shoulders. "Guess the good Reverend didn't want any champagne," he said loudly to the curious onlookers. Hathaway had been like a wet blanket on a campfire. Could they recapture their gaiety?

Lucy cut into her fish, "This Hal-abut fish better than the

blood red fish. What is word lust?"

Gus and Clint looked at each other sheepishly. "We'll explain that tomorrow," Gus said winking at Lightfoot. "For now, just remember that ladies never invite strangers to their table."

Astoria

Gus woke slowly to the distant muffled sounds of a bell ringing. At first he thought he was dreaming. Then he opened his good eye and glanced around the cabin. It was early dawn with just enough light to make out the shadows in his compartment. There was something desperately wrong. That's when he first felt his head throbbing and his mouth cotton dry. That second bottle of champagne had done the brothers in. Lucy had helped them back to their cabin before a card was played or a dollar bet. Now all that bubbly wine tasted like dirty socks. But what was wrong here and now? Why was he awake so early? He shook his pounding head trying to clear it. That damn bell, why is it ringing? He had to think clearly, something was out of place, what was it? That's when he realized the ship wasn't moving. It seemed dead in the water! There were no sounds of the paddlewheels cutting through the sea, no sounds of the boilers spouting off steam and no sounds of sailors in the shrouds. The ship's only movement was up and down with the sea swells and that damn ringing bell.

Gus tried to get out of bed. He slid out of his blanket and put his bare feet on the cold steel of the deck. But before he could stand he stopped. His hangover was killing him and the cabin was spinning in his head. He sat on his birth for a moment, looking around the room. Lightfoot was still sleeping, as was Lucy in her adjoining compartment. He reached for his pocket watch and snapped it open. It was just after five in the morning but the cabin seemed so dark. Could it be five in the afternoon? No, he needed his head to stop pounding and glass of water to wet his desert mouth.

Before he stood, Gus slipped on his socks and slowly got up holding onto his berth. With one leg at a time, he quietly put on his trousers and tucked in his nightshirt. Then, sitting on the bed again, he gingerly he put on his boots. What was happening? He wouldn't wake his friends until he knew for sure.

After a quick gulp of water, Gus opened the cabin door to a

thick haze that floated through the doorway. The ship was in a fog bank so thick that he couldn't even see across to the passageway to the promenade deck railing. It was a cold and damp gray fog that hung silently in the air distorting all the shapes and sizes of the ship. Gus heard the muffled bell ring again and reached for the outside handrail only a few feet in front of him. Using the rail he moved carefully towards the bow of the boat. His feet on the deck were almost invisible in the gloomy stillness of the fog. It was as if he was strolling surreally within a dream.

Soon he found the gangway to the lower deck and used the handrail down. The sea was like a lake, he could hear it lapping against the hull of the ship. Turning, he felt his way along the main rail towards the bow. It was so quiet he thought he could hear his own heart pounding. Then, out of nowhere, he bumped into another person standing in the gloom.

"Pardon me mate," a voice whispered back with a very British accent. "Didn't hear ye coming. This pea soup reminds me of London."

The bell rang out again, only louder and from above. "What the hell is that bell all about?" Gus asked trying to make out the figure just inches in front of him.

The man leaned forward into the fog putting his face closer to Gus. "The bell tells other ships that we are dead in the water here."

Gus tried to stare back at him through the fog.

"Hell, man you only have one eye," the British voice said. "Are you a passenger? How did you make it all the way down here?"

"I heard that damn bell and felt my way along. What's happening… did the crew abandon the ship? It's so quiet."

The man chuckled, "I hope not mate, me being the Skipper and all."

From above and through the fog another voice rang out. "Captain the lookouts are reporting scattering blue skies moving up from the south. Should we start building-up steam?"

"Aye," he shouted back. "It be an hour before the tide turns. Let's prepare to get underway."

Gus tried swatting away the fog with one of his hands. "Why did we stop out here?"

"The fog rolled in just after midnight. We are about five miles south of the Columbia River but I wouldn't cross that devils Bar in the fog or at night. So we dropped anchor and posted fog watch. We should be underway again within the hour."

Gus could almost make-out the shadow of the Captain a few feet away. "Why do you call it the 'devils Bar?'

"You ever cross it before?" He answered.

"No sir," Gus replied. "This is my first trip to Astoria."

Gus could see him shaking his head. "The next ten miles of water are the nastiest in the world. The Columbia River Bar is called the graveyard of the Pacific for a reason. There's been hundreds of ships sunk crossing this devils Bar"

"When we get underway, can I watch the crossing with two of my friends from your wheelhouse?"

With steam building up in the boilers the boat started to vibrate to life again. The Captain didn't say anything for long moment and then replied with sympathy. "Why not? Bet you gave your eye for your country. We're going to have a smooth crossing this morning. Just don't get underfoot."

Within the hour the fog had lifted revealing a beautiful warm Fall morning with calm green seas, blue skies and a narrow band of rich green land to the east.

With great anticipation the trio stood just inside the wheelhouse watching Captain Ralf Buchman navigate what he called the nastiest Bar in the world. His Mate Mr. Bryan was at the helm with two sailors on the wings of the wheelhouse calling out sea depths, tide currents and the boats speed. The Captain had a chart in his hand that showed all of the surrounding landmarks, shoals, sandbars and shallow waters of the mouth of the Columbia River. This crossing was seven miles wide and ten miles deep and here the river drained into the vast Pacific Ocean. Where these two mighty forces of waters met, given the tide, winds, and sea conditions is where the devil's Bar boiled over with long and tall curling white waves with undertows so strong that it could doom any vessel big or small. "The secret," the Captain said, "was finding a safe path between the all these obstacles to gain access to the calm waters of the river."

As the Captain gazed out the windows of the wheelhouse, he told his guests that Captain Robert Gray had made the first crossing of the Bar in 1792. "He did it with no maps and only using the wind and his sails. Now *he* was a great sea captain."

The Skipper pointed out the tall rocky mountain that stood guard of the north shore. "That lighthouse on top of the mountain is Cape Disappointment. It is the first lighthouse built on the Pacific Coast. It has saved many a Mariner." Then he pointed inland to another monolith and said, "That steep camelback sloop is called Saddle Mountain. When you know where the lighthouse is and where Saddle Mountain is, you know where your ship is. It's called triangulation."

They learned that the Columbia River had many names like: Big River, the River of the West and River Oregon. He told them how the Chinook and Clatsop Indians used the river as a highway to travel to the inland tribes to make trade and wars. "The river has two parts: the upper and lower," he told the trio. "The headwaters of the river start way up in Canada, while the lower river starts at Great Falls at The Dalles. The Columbia, at over twelve hundred miles in length, is the seconded longest river in America and makes Astoria right at the doorstep to the Pacific. This seaport is destined to become the next New Orleans of the west."

The Captain and crew were a fountain of information that morning. They answered all the trio's many questions and gave them advice on how to get up river to Oregon City from Astoria. They also warned them that the town was a rough and tumble seaport filled with opium dens and hucksters. "Astoria may look like a smaller San Francisco, but it is not," the Mate Bryan said. "It's much more like the western town of Deadwood. It's full of rattlesnakes and charlatans, so stay alert and keep your weapons close."

"It's also one of the wettest places on earth," one of the sailors shouted out from the wings. "It might not look like it now, but it is."

Their Bar crossing that morning was as smooth as a washtub full of bathwater. The tide was slick, the wind but a breeze and the sunshine warm. As the ship approached the town, the compadres stood at the outside rails filling their eyes with the rich colors of the river, town and trees. Astoria in the morning light looked like a shiny jewel in a crown.

It was still early by the time the trio disembarked the *Pacific* giving Captain Buckman and his crew many thanks for their hospitality and safe passage. It was a crossing they would not soon forget.

As they descended the gangway Lucy abruptly stopped while pointing to a group of Chinamen on the dock. They were dressed in black, with straw hats and carrying wicker baskets of food.

"Who are they?" She asked wide-eyed

"Don't point," Gus answered. "They are from China a far-away land. Chinamen like them helped build the Iron Highway."

"They are a funny looking tribe," Lucy answered still staring at them. "Why is their skin yellow?"

The west end marina where the *Pacific* docked was filled with tall ships of sail and steam, with fishing boats and small paddle wheelers moving up and down the river. They had been told it was a two mile walk, up the river, to where they would find the moorage for the paddle wheeler *Willamette Express* that could take them to Portland and then onto Oregon City.

As the friends walked towards downtown, carrying their bedrolls and bags, they got their first good look at Astoria. It was much like San Francisco, with wood framed homes and buildings built on hillsides, overlooking the glistening river waters that seemed rich with life. It was quaint, but lacked the architecture and the beauty of the real City by the Bay. Yes, San Francisco was a lot more cosmopolitan then Astoria, but there was a rawness of character here. The waterfront was built upon piers and pilings with a wide timbered road where the planking cantilevered out and over the river shore. On each side of this road was another raised boardwalk fronting wood framed buildings such as saloons, shops and stores mixed in with factories, stables and warehouses. The street was filled with horses, wagons and carriages. Astoria looked to be a thriving little port filled with tradesmen, fishermen, loggers and seafarers. Both Gus and Lightfoot where impressed with the many possibilities in such a booming little town, while Lucy's only thoughts were getting to Oregon City to find her brother.

"Let's get a room and spend the night." Gus said as they walked. "I'd like to see more of this town before we go upriver."

"Why," Lucy protested. "We can get rooms in Ore-gone

City."

"I agree with Gus. Let's spend the night," Lightfoot answered. "We may never come this way again."

Lucy frowned for a moment and then smiled. "Alright, but promise me we'll go to Ore-gone City tomorrow. Today you buy me new shoes. My old ones pinch."

The men chuckled and nodded. Lucy loved to negotiate to get her way. Gus looked down at her old shoes from the 'hell-on-wheels' town. They were well worn and she was growing out of them. Gus reminded himself, that Lucy was only seven months out of the teepee and still new to the white-man's ways.

"Keep an eye out for a cobblers shop," Gus said to no one in particular. "We'll get you some new moccasins." That's when he noticed the sign: Uptown Pub. It was attached to a tall narrow building on the shore side of the street.

"Let's stop at this Pub." Gus said. "I played cards with the owner back on the *Enterprise*. She's a nice lady with a sharp tongue and a foghorn voice. She told me she ran a boarding house in Astoria. Maybe we can get a room for the night here."

"If nothing else, we can get a drink." Lightfoot replied. "My hangover is almost gone from that damn champagne. I hate wine."

The Pub looked like an old house, three stories tall. They climbed the front stoop and entered the saloon through two swinging glass doors. A long fancy wooden bar with stools filled the wall on the right with small round tables and chairs in the middle of the room. On the left wall was a large ornate staircase, that lead to the upper floors. The Pub smelt of tobacco and cheap perfume. In some ways it reminded Gus of the many saloons back at the railhead.

At the far end of the room, Gus recognized Lilly standing behind the counter talking with two other women on bar stools. When he approached her she looked up from her conversation and glared at him with blank expression. Then she recognized his face with a big smile.

"I'll be damned, look who just walked into my gin joint," she yelled in her foghorn voice.

Gus moved towards her, "You didn't forget me?"

Lilly moved from behind the bar with her arms outstretched and gave Gus a bear hug. "Who could forget a one-eyed handsome poker-player like you Captain? Welcome to my Uptown Pub."

Gus introduced Lightfoot and Lucy to Lilly as his sister and brother. "We are on our way to Oregon City and need to get a room for the night. Could you help us out?"

Lilly put her hand on Lucy's face, "Isn't she a sweet little thing. Look at that honey colored skin and those green eyes. A little young yet, but she's going to be a beautiful woman." Lucy reached out and grabbed Gus's hand and squeezed it. She looked little frightened, but who wouldn't be with all that war paint on Lilly's face.

She moved back behind the bar, "Let's have a drink before business. The first round is on me."

As Lilly poured the drinks, Gus and Lightfoot looked around the empty bar. Then they noticed the two women on the bar stools again. They were nice looking gals also with painted faces and all dressed up for such an early morning hour. Maybe Astoria was a little more cosmopolitan then Gus had thought.

As Lilly put the drinks on the bar Gus said, "We were told rooms were hard to come by in Astoria. That's when I remembered you ran a boarding house. Can you help us out?"

Lilly smiled from across the bar taking a big swig from her whiskey glass. She wore colorful outfit way too small for her big physique. "Yes I do run a boarding house Captain. But I don't rent my rooms by the day or week; I rent them by the hour. If you know what I mean."

Her answer went right over Gus's head, but not Lightfoot's. His head immediately twisted to the two girls at the end of the bar with a big grin on his face.

"Why by the hour?" Gus asked still not understanding what she was saying.

Lightfoot kept his eyes on the girls with a smile and answered. "It's all about your proclivities brother. Remember?"

It took about three heartbeats before Gus fully understood what Lilly and Lightfoot were trying to say. When he did, his head also twisted to the two ladies at the end of the bar.

"Oh yes, I remember that now." He finally said with his face turning flush. "We should probably look for a hotel."

Lucy had a confused face. "Why can't we stay here?"

"Seems they don't have any rooms available," Gus replied.

"That's right honey," Lilly added with a warm smile. "But I can help you find a room."

Lilly continued and gave them directions to the Yankee Schooner Hotel. "You can't miss it, two more blocks upriver and just across the street from the County Courthouse. It's the tallest building in town. Tell Mr. Cromwell, he owns the place that I sent you. If he has a room, he'll rent it to you. He's one of my best customers."

Gus drained his glass. "Thanks for the drink and the hotel tip Lilly. We better get moving, I've got some business at the Courthouse."

"What business?" Lightfoot asked twisting his head back to Gus with an inquisitive face.

"I promised Sheriff Moody that I would deliver an envelope to the Clatsop County Sheriff when we got into town."

"That would be Sheriff Bill Chance." Lilly said. "He's alright, but tough as nails. Just don't cross him."

"Why would you promise that prick Moody anything?" Lightfoot said. "He impounded our gold and drove us into the coal mines. I wouldn't give him the right time of day."

Just then they heard some shouting from upstairs and a door slam. Turning to the staircase they found Reverend Hathaway descending it.

Lightfoot smiled and yelled across the room, "Good morning Reverend. You been tending to your flock?"

Hathaway glared at him, but didn't say a word. At the bottom of the stairs he stopped and adjusted his eye patch and then hurried for the front door.

"You folks must know the good Reverend?" Lilly chuckled. "My girls don't care for him much. They tell me that he takes off his eye patch when he gets upstairs. There's nothing wrong with his eye. He uses it as a ruse."

"We know him," Lightfoot answered. "But we don't much like Bible thumpers."

Lilly turned to Gus, "What is it with you guys and the eye patch? You looking for sympathy from the ladies?"

Gus put his empty glass on the bar. "Not all of us," he said lifting the patch off his dead eye. "Sometimes it's for real."

Lilly stared at his mangled eye shaking her head with a sad

face. "Sorry Captain, that was uncalled for. Please forgive me."

As Gus stood to leave, Lightfoot said, "I'm going to stay here Captain and talk with Lilly. I'll catch up with you at the hotel."

Gus turned to his friend, glaring at him and shaking his head. "You think that's a smart idea?"

"It's been a long time sir."

Lucy and Gus were soon back outside in the sunshine and walking upriver towards the hotel. Lucy hadn't said much in the Pub, but now she had a head full of questions.

"What did brother mean: It's been a long time?"

"We should keep an eye out for a shoe shop. Lightfoot is just lonely to talk with people his own age. It's been a long time."

"Why his own age? He no talk with us anymore?"

"He will still talk to us. It's just that older people talk about older things, while younger people talk about younger things."

"Last night Reverend said word lust. What this mean?"

Gus hated theses personal chats about the facts of life. He had no idea how much to tell her, or when to tell it. Her innocence may be blissful, but there might come time when Lucy needs more than that to survive. She trusted too easily and had no since of danger. Gus needed to help prepare for that time. But how and when?

When the Captain looked up again, they were standing in front of a cobblers shop and Lucy was looking at a shoe display in the window. "You buy me big-girl shoes please."

Gus stood next to Lucy looking at the display. "You want big-girl shoes? Good, big girls buy their own. You have your own money now. It's time for you to buy your first pair of shoes. In the white man's world boys buy boots and girls buy their own shoes."

Inside the shop they talked to the cobbler, an older man named Mr. Gibson who had a friendly smile and the rough hands of a shoemaker. He talked with a slight Norwegian accent with a corn cob pipe between his teeth. His shop smelt of leather and soap. He showed Lucy a few different designs of women shoes: walking, dancing and riding. Proudly he showed her how he made the shoes and talked with great pride about his work. She finally selected a pair of black high-tops with buttons and hooks.

The old man sat her down in a chair and knelt in front of her. He removed her old shoes and tried on a pair of high-tops. They were too big. She squirmed and giggled in the chair with his touch for the right shoe size. The old man looked at the bottom of her feet. "Her feet are full of calluses sir," he said with a surprised look to Gus. "She's been walking bare foot too long."

Gus took a knee next to him and also looked at the bottom of her feet. "They are better than when I found her. She was a captive of the Cheyenne Indians for many years. They never gave her any moccasins."

Gibson shook his head sadly, "I have lotion you can use for the bottom of her feet. It's made from whale oil. Have her rub it in every morning and night. It will help heal the calluses."

As the cobbler worked Gus explained how they had found her and where they were going.

He measured the thickness of her ankles and the length and width of her feet. Then he drew a paper outline of each foot. "How old is she?" the cobbler asked.

Quickly Lucy replied, "I'm fourteen."

The old man smiled at her, "I'll make your shoes a little bigger. That way you can grow into them."

"Can I have my shoes today?" Lucy asked with a big smile.

"Yes miss, by the end of the day," he replied standing and looking down on her.

"And the cost?" Gus asked also standing.

"She is a sweet girl sir. For her a discount: four dollars for the shoes and the whale lotion and a pair of socks are free."

Lucy jumped up from her chair with a big smile and curtsied to the cobbler. "Thank you sir, I have big-girl shoes now."

Gus had Lucy pay the four dollars from a rawhide pouch she kept in one of her pockets. She looked at her coins not really sure what to do next. The cobbler carefully removed the Gold Eagle from her hand and gave her back change, counting out the coins from his pocket. "Thank you missy you brightened my day."

Mr. Cromwell, at the Yankee Schooner, did have one last room. It was just a small nook with two beds and a divan that fronted the dock where the Paddle Wheeler *Willamette Express* would depart early the next morning. At a dollar a head per night, the accommodations were expensive, but surprisingly clean with good views of the local fishing fleet. After registering at the hotel they dropped off their bedrolls and bags and walked across the dirt street towards the Courthouse.

The building wasn't much, just a white two story wood frame structure lacking any style or architecture. The courtroom was on the top floor, with the county offices on the street level. Next to the Courthouse was the tall white washed county jail built of stone and bricks. Behind this structure was a stable and corral. The entire compound looked as bland as a rainy day.

After making some inquiries at the Courthouse Gus and Lucy found Sheriff Bill Chance in his office within the jailhouse walls. His office was small and austere with stone walls and iron bars covering the only window. The Sheriff was middle aged with black hair and arms as thick as his thighs. He worked at an old oak roll up desk that backed upon one of the white washed stone walls. Across from this desk was canvas army cot with a small coal fired stove for heat.

When Gus and Lucy entered his office he asked in a demanding way, "What can I do for you?"

"I've got some papers for you Sheriff," Gus replied holding a thick envelope.

Finally he looked up from his desk and eyed his visitors. "More paperwork, just what I needed. And who the hell are you?"

His face was weathered with wrinkles and he had piercing blue eyes. The Sheriff looked like an all business kind of man.

Gus introduced himself and Lucy, handing the Sheriff the envelope. "Sheriff Moody of Coos Bay asked me to deliver this to you when we got to Astoria."

The Sheriff took the envelope and looked at it. Then he eyed Gus and Lucy again. "What's in it?"

"Don't rightly know," Gus answered. "He only asked me to deliver it." Gus felt the Sheriff's blue eyes staring at him. "You a lawman, you look like one?"

"No sir," Gus smiled back. "We are just passing through on our way to Oregon City."

The Sheriff opened the envelope with a knife from his desk. "And who's the girl again?"

"She's our ward." Gus answered watching Chance reading one

of the papers. "We found Lucy a few months back. She was a captive of the Cheyenne Indians living in the Wyoming wilderness. We are taking her to Oregon City so she might find her lost brother."

The Sheriff read another paper, this one yellow and looking like a telegram. Finally he looked up with an inquisitive face. "Where's your sidekick Captain? The man called Lightfoot."

How the hell would he know that? Gus thought. *Did Moody send a dossier on them?* "That would be my friend Clint Roe. He's stopped off at Uptown Pub for drink"

The Sheriff put the papers down on his desk with a broad smile. "Oh, Lilly's place: a lot of the locals want me to close her down. Is he going on to Oregon City with you?"

"Yes," Lucy answered. "Then we find my brother."

Chance picked up the top yellow sheet of his papers. "Sheriff Moody tells me you guys are Indian fighters. He sent me a telegram from your old Commanding Officer, Colonel Rawlins that says you commanded a Cavalry unit for the railroad while your friend Lightfoot was Chief Scout for them. The Colonel calls you heroic Indian fighters. Is that true Captain?"

Gus glared at Sheriff Chance wondering what else he might know. He wanted to read the Colonel's telegram but he didn't ask. "There was nothing heroic in what we did. We just protected the railroad from the Indians. We don't do that anymore."

"What do you do now? Are you guys looking for work?"

Gus shook his head sadly, "As I told Sheriff Moody our trail of Indian sorrow is long gone. We don't kill Indians anymore."

"Good," Sheriff Chance said. "I'm looking for Deputy Sheriff's not Indian killers. Are you interested?"

"Maybe, what would it pay?"

Lucy twisted to Gus with angry eyes, "No, no brother you promised. We go to Ore-gone City tomorrow."

Interview 2: Roots

Astoria, Oregon - October 1899

A gust of wind swirled around the tall Victorian home on the hillside and rain danced on the window panes. Lucy shook her head and looked up at the two reporters seated across from her.

"Hope this storm passes and they don't close down the Bar." She said to no one in particular.

Just then Pong slid the parlor doors open and entered the room with an armful of firewood. As he walked stone faced across the parlor, all conversation stopped and the reporters glared at this giant of a man with a bald head full of tattoos. At over six feet tall, he was one frightening reminder of bygone times of the local Indians. He moved to the fireplace and deposited the wood in the bin and placed two new logs on the fire. Stoking the hot coals, red fire sparks flew up the chimney.

"It was at the McLaughlin house in Oregon City that I first saw Pong," Lucy said noticing the inquisitive faces of the reporters. "He's one of the sweetest men I've ever met. Pong is a Puyallup Indian. Dr. McLaughlin saved his life from the fever when he was just a boy. And now, after he saved me from Reverend Hathaway, we've become very good friends. So he lives here with me as my friend and protector."

"Who is this Reverend Hathaway?" The young reporter

Jimmy Adams asked consulting his written notes.

"I'm sorry," She answered. "I'm getting ahead of myself."

Pong didn't say a word, or look at anyone, as he turned from the fireplace and exited the room. At the sliding double doors he stopped and looked back into the room. "I'll be right out here if you need me Miss Lucy," he said in a firm loud voice.

The older reporter Hank Hawks asked, "Could we interview Pong?"

Lucy smiled at him, "That would be up to him."

"You never did say much about your life with the Indians," Jimmy said. "Did they treat you fairly?"

Lucy shook her head with a frown, "No. They enslaved me. So don't romanticize their culture. The Cheyennes were protecting their lands from the white invaders and could be as deadly as a rattlesnake. But who could blame them, we were taking their land. Had it not been for Gus and Lightfoot, I would have died out there in the wilderness. My brothers saved me, taught me and loved me."

"So after your gold was confiscated by Sheriff Moody what did your so-called brothers do next?" Hank asked, with a scowl on his pug face.

"They are my brothers," Lucy snapped back. "They wanted to winter in Coos Bay, waiting for the Magistrate. So I worked awhile on the boat *Marianne*, with Sam and his wife, while my brothers took jobs working in a coal mine. We all hated what we were doing, and I kept nagging them about Oregon City. Finally, after I'd made a thorough pest of myself, they agreed, and we boarded another packet ship heading north for the Columbia River on September 26, 1869. I remember that date well, because it was my fourteenth birthday."

As the reporters wrote out their notes, Lucy heard the house phone ring, out in the front foyer. She stood and paced the floor while staring at the fire. Soon, the door slid open again and Norma appeared. "That was the Sheriff on the phone. The phone line to the Tillamook Lighthouse is working again. They will keep an eye out for the troopship and keep us informed."

"Good," Lucy replied. "Have the cook make some of her deviled-egg-and-cucumber sandwiches and bring us some fresh coffee." Then she turned to the reporters. "Gentlemen, do you want to take a break or do you want me to go on?"

The men looked at each other and shrugged their shoulders. "Let's go on," Jimmy said.

Hank Hawks pulled a pipe out of his suit pocket and asked for permission to light it. Lucy nodded and sat back down in her chair.

"Was this your first visit to Astoria?" Jimmy asked.

"Yes, we crossed the Bar on a beautiful fall morning when the sea was flat as a lake. Our first impressions of Astoria were outstanding. It reminded us so much of San Francisco with all the hillside homes glittering off the waters of the Columbia River." She answered.

"I don't care about that!" Hank snapped back. "Was your Mexican brother a Confederate Rebel who incited the Indians against the Union during the war?"

"Yes," Missy answered, her eyes flashing, "Just like the blue-coats incited the Negros to fight for the Union during the war. But when we came to the river, the war was long gone and forgotten."

"How did you come up with the idea for Butterfly Seafood?" Jimmy asked.

"If you mean the name," Lucy answered. "Butterfly was what my brothers called me. They said I flew around like a butterfly always asking questions."

Not the name: the idea of canned salmon. Was that yours?" Hank asked.

"No," She said quickly. "I think Robert Hume and his brothers had that idea first."

"Did you use their recipe?" Jimmy asked.

"No, that was all my idea. Before my brothers went off on their first patrol as Deputy Sheriffs, they stocked my panty aboard the boat *Louise* with food. Some of which were cans of salmon from upriver at Westport. I had never tasted that brand before. So one night, I opened a can of fish to have with dinner. It was alright, but there was something missing in the flavor. That bright pink salmon looked so pale and unappetizing in the can, and it left a funny taste in my mouth. The next day I went for a walk up behind the Courthouse thinking about how an old Cheyenne squaw had taken me hunting for wild roots and herbs when I was a captive. She used these ground-up herbs to spice up the evening meals. If she could do it, why couldn't I? Anyhow, I soon found myself walking past some gardens where a young Chinese girl was working. She was a pretty gal but spoke no English and was very shy. So using sign language, I convinced her to sell me a small basket of her garden spices for six-bits. She was delighted with the money and I was curious about her herbs.

I learned later that she had sold me some horseradish, ginger and ginseng. So that night I grounded up these spices in the boat's coffee mill and opened another can of fish. I broke the salmon into three pieces and sprinkled my spices on top. The taste was better, but not right. But that started my search for the secret recipe that made Butterfly Seafood so famous."

Hank looked up from his notes with a frown. "So for seventy-five cents you made millions from a naive Chinese girl.

"It's not quite as simple as that," Lucy replied. "It took years to perfect the recipe. And at that time, I couldn't even make a can of salmon on my own."

The local reporter Jimmy glared at her like a courtroom inquisitor. "Did you ever share your wealth with that girl?"

She took a sip of her coffee holding back her anger. She started regretting the interview. These reporters were out for blood, her blood.

"To this very day," Lucy answered glaring back at the reporters. "My canneries are the largest employers of the Chinese up and down the coast. There are some employees that have been with us for over twenty years. They make their living, and raise their families, because of the Butterfly brands."

"So why did you sell out to National Foods?" The older reporter demanded.

"That's not your affair," She answered loudly still holding back her temper. "You were invited here to learn the news about the return of the Oregon Brigade and the return of Major Savage. This is not going to be an inquisition based on gossip and half-truths. I will not allow that!"

At that very moment the parlor door slid open again and Pong filled the doorway holding a tray of sandwiches. He moved towards the two reporters with a stone face and offered them the tiny sandwiches on small white porcelain plates. He said not a word but glared down on them wearing buckskins trousers, a brown morning coat and his bald copper crown dotted with blue and red star tattoos. Both reporters took a plate and a cloth napkin without making eye contact with his deep set black eyes. He then turned and placed his tray next to the coffee service. With the room quiet as a graveyard he turned again and walked back through the open doors.

"I'm still out here Miss Lucy." He said loudly again exiting the room.

Both reporters seemed dumbfounded with Pongs reappearance. Finally Hank Hawks said turning to a blank page in his notebook, "Maybe we should get back on track. You were telling us about Dr. McLaughlin in Oregon City."

Lucy glared at the reporters. She had two options. She decided to continue.

Chapter 6 – Leon

Ore-gone City

When Lucy and Gus returned to the hotel, they found Clint waiting for them in their room. Lucy rushed to him, pulling up the pant legs of her baggy overalls. "See my new high tops? Cobbler man make just for me. He say I have pretty ankles."

Clint smiled broadly. "You do. How much did those moccasins cost?"

"I buy, four dollars. You have long talk with fat squaw?"

Lightfoot frowned with a surprised look.

Gus smiled and winked back at him. "I told her it had been a long time since you had talked with a lady like Lilly."

Lightfoot nodded with a grin, getting the drift, "Yes, we did have a good talk."

"What did you talk about?" Lucy asked.

Clint thought a moment. "The virtue of honesty, I'll tell you more later."

Lightfoot was pleasant and upbeat, and continued chattering like a bird. "I saw a steam bath down the street, next to the Norwegian Tavern. We should go there and get cleaned up for tomorrow."

"What is steam bath?" Lucy asked.

Clint explained to her how the Indians used their teepees with hot rocks and water to make steam to cleanse their souls. "It's big medicine. Did you ever see the Cheyenne Warriors rush naked into the cold river waters?"

She nodded. "Yes. They say cold river water make them strong like iron horse. We should do same and be clean for McLaughlin."

Lightfoot must have been feeling guilty about his time at the Uptown Pub because he reached into his pocket and gave Lucy a gift. "I saw this medallion in a store window. It reminded me of you. You can wear it with your Oregon Trail Medal."

Lucy showed it to Gus. It was round and pewter, with a fishing boat engraved on one side and the word 'Astoria' engraved on the other side. She loved it and put it on the rawhide thread around her neck. "Thank you, brother. Is painted lady your woman?"

Lightfoot frowned, shaking his head. "No, we are only ships passing in the night."

They spent that afternoon exploring the city, shopping for clothes, and ending up at the Norwegian Tavern, where they rented a family sized steam bath. The tiny room had cedar walls that smelt like the outdoors, and wooden benches with hot rocks to generate the steam. In separate baths, the trio disrobed to nothing except white sheets. But Lucy insisted on wearing her new shoes, even in the steam room.

There in the hot fog, Gus told Lightfoot about his meeting with Sheriff Chance. "He offered us a job as Deputy Sheriffs. Our first mission would be to go to a place called Fort Yamhill, pick up two prisoners being held in the stockade, and bring them back here for trial. The Sheriff said we'd be gone about a week. "

"Why would he offer us such jobs? We're total strangers to him."

"Not really. Seems Sheriff Chance and Sheriff Moody are old chums. Moody sent him a letter about us being Indian fighters. He even included a telegram from Colonel Rawlins about us."

"Thought we were out of the killing business." Lightfoot said, pouring more water over the hot stones.

"That's what I told him," Gus replied over the sizzling sounds of cold water on the hot rocks. "That's when he told me he was only looking for Deputy Sheriffs, not killers."

Lightfoot wiped his sweaty face with a wet washcloth. "What's the job pay, Captain?"

"Three dollars a day: We provide our own mounts, firearms, and ammunition. The county provides us with an extra dollar a day for food and feed while we are out of town. Deputy Sheriffs also get twenty-five percent of any reward money."

"Yeah, sure, Captain." Clint chuckled. "You trust this Sheriff any more than Moody?"

"Yes, I think I do. He told me he wasn't running for re-election next year. I think he's an honest man."

"What happened to his last two Deputies? They get killed?"

"Nope. One took a job working up in the woods and the other one ran off with one of Lilly's girls."

Clint shook his head in the hot mist and poured water over it. "I made more money being Chief Scout for the railroad. But it's better work than coal mining. When would we start?"

When we get back from Oregon City. How's your purse? We'll need to buy a couple nags."

"I've still got a few Double Eagles," Lightfoot answered, with sweat dripping off the point of his nose. "What about Lucy?"

"Yes. What about me?" Lucy asked through the wet fog.

"The Sheriff said he knows a woman that might take you in while we're gone."

Lucy ran her fingers through her wet hair. "I no need woman while you gone. We find Leon first."

At first light the next morning, the trio stood at the rail of the paddle wheeler *Willamette Express,* watching the ship carefully back out from its moorage. They were all dressed in their finest clothes: Gus in his gambling threads, Lightfoot in his best buckskins with a colorful serape, and Lucy wearing an ankle-length new dress to show off her new shoes. The two-deck paddle wheeler was like a cigar, long and narrow. The top deck was for passengers with day cabins to get out of the weather and the lower deck for livestock and freight. The morning sky in the east was crimson red, with the sun just peeking up over the distant horizon and glistening on the river waters. It was a breathtaking vista, so beautiful that the trio stood speechless, watching the sea birds fill the sky. With the lonely steam whistle howling, the *Express* backed into deep water and slowly turned with the rivers flow. The paddle wheels engaged in forward gear and the water churned white as the ship lunged forward, up the Columbia River.

Willamette Express

They had learned much about Astoria, the day before. The locals had told them that the warm bright sunshine they enjoyed was not uncommon in September and October. After that, however, the next ten months would be soggy and cold. "We don't grow old out here," one person had told them. "We just rust and die."

The town itself had a gritty past, filled with stories of opium dens, smugglers, shanghaied sailors, and bootleggers. Clatsop County was a small place with only about twelve hundred people spread out in a wilderness area of over a thousand square miles. Half of the county residents lived in Astoria, which was growing quickly because of all its natural resources. The other half were spread out in dense forests, tributary rivers, and rich bottom farmlands. These hardy folks were few and far between.

The night before, one of the barkeeps at the Norwegian Tavern had called Astoria just a 'Hoot and Holler' kind of place because it had no railroad, no newspaper, and no telegraph yet.

"Gossip blows around here like a winter storm. Believe what

you see, not what you hear."

Astoria reminded Gus of the many early Mississippi river towns he had known: full of hopes, dreams, and opportunities.

One crusty old fisherman, repairing his nets down on the docks, had lamented the plight of the local Indians. He told them that he had come to Astoria forty years before, when thousands of Indians still lived on the river. "There were Chinooks on the north shore, Clatsops on the south, and hundreds of other tribes upriver. Now, for the most part, those native people are all gone, stuck on reservations or dead from all the white-man diseases. I tell you, Astoria without Indians is like the night sky without stars. These people were the rightful owners to all we have now."

As the *Willamette Express* paddled up-river, Gus watched the ships Purser punching tickets for the long line of passengers at the second-deck rail. He seemed like a friendly guy, chatting with the folks in the bright, early morning sun. When he approached the trio, Gus handed him the tickets they had purchased the night before at the hotel.

"Going through to Oregon City? Stay aboard when we arrive in Portland," he said punching the tickets. "We only have a half-hour layover in Stump Town."

"What's Stump Town" Gus asked.

The Purser chuckled. "It's what we Astorians affectionately call Portland— or sometimes Mud Town."

"Why?" Lightfoot asked.

The Purser handed back their tickets. "The town's full of tree stumps, and on rainy days the streets fill with mud. But don't tell the Portlanders that. They'll take offense." He smiled and tipped his hat to Lucy. "Have a nice morning, young lady."

"Where can we get coffee, sir?" she asked.

He gave them directions to the galley. "Try our sweet rolls and honey. They're still warm from our ovens."

Just then, one of the other passengers shouted, pointing north across the river, "See that steam tugboat driving log pilings out there? That's Knappton, where the ships quarantine hospital is, and next to it is Portuguese Point. The rumor is that some brothers from San Francisco are building a salmon cannery over there."

The trio all turned to where the passenger was pointing. The estuary was wide, calm, and cobalt blue. "Do you know the name of the brothers?" Gus asked the stranger.

He nodded. "I think they're called the Hume Brothers."

Lucy turned to the man with a smile. "We know young Robert Hume. He is sweet on me. They make good fish in can."

The man frowned. "Well, I wish them luck, young lady. Portuguese Point is a long way away from the fishing grounds. Astoria would have been better place for their cannery."

Lucy smiled at the man and pulled up the hem of her dress. "See my new shoes?"

The *Express* rounded the tip of a large peninsula, and the south shore soon opened up into a large estuary with many islands of scrub brush and trees. The bay looked like a natural harbor stretching upriver for many miles. The shoreline was dotted with tall green trees, with mountain backdrops full of forests for as far as one could see.

The ship passed a few smaller fishing boats with long nets in the water tied to colorful buoys made of cork. As these nets were pulled in, the fishermen grabbed large, gill-netted fish that looked to be thirty or forty pounds each. These bright, strong, shiny silver fish fought their capture and reflected on the waters with a halo as rich as gold. It was as if the fishermen were pulling up silver bars from the depths.

Clint turned to Gus with excitement. "Look at the size of those damn fish! That's silver gold, Captain. Never seen anything like that before."

A few more miles upriver, a small enclave came into view. The buildings looked to be a sawmill built upon the top of tall pilings, with a thick timber decking. In the water next to the mill were rafts of enormous raw logs waiting their turn for the saw blades. Behind the mill, nestled on the shoreline, was a small hamlet of buildings overlooking the river.

"What is this place?" Lightfoot asked a stranger standing next to him.

"This is Westport," the stranger answered. "It's one of the busiest sawmills around. They also have a salmon cannery here. Old Captain John West, the founder of the place, knows how to make money."

The *Express* was one of many paddlewheelers that plied the waters from Astoria to Portland and then on to Oregon City. The voyage was six hours one way and six hours back. At nearly fifteen miles per hour, the *Willamette Express* was one of the fastest boats on the water. Without a rail line or an improved road, the only way in or out of Astoria was by steamboat or trail.

With such inviting river views, the trio stood glued to the rail, drinking coffee and eating sweet rolls, as their journey unfolded. They passed many islands, wetlands, and tributary rivers. They saw opport-unity around every bend in the river: rich bottom lands for farming, elk and deer the size of horses, silver-gold fish as fat as prairie dogs, skies of birds from seagulls to eagles, and trees as tall as mountains, with crystal waters as clear as glass. This was a place where a man could plant roots, wake up the next morning and harvest gardens as rich as gold. The Columbia River was a majestic land that stretched from horizon to horizon, the true El Dorado of the west. God had blessed this place with such abundance that Lightfoot called it a river of no return.

A few hours later, the ship turned south at the confluence to the Willamette River. Here the land opened up to large valleys that sprawled east to distant mountains, one of which was still crowned with snow. They learned that this dominant peak was called Mount Hood, and that there were many more sisters just like it, collectively called the Cascade Range.

On the western shore of the Willamette, rolling hills and tall cliffs were covered with dense forests of many kinds of trees: Douglas Fir, alder, maple and pine, to name but a few. On this smaller river, they encountered many tall ships, barges, tugs, and fishing boats plying the waters. They passed boatyards, warehouses, saw mills, and other factories. With nearly nine thousand residents, Portland was a hub of commerce, three times the size of Clatsop County.

After a short stop in Portland, the *Express* completed its voyage by turning around at the base of a large waterfall near the town of Oregon City. The spectacular forty-foot-tall torrent separated the upper and lower Willamette Rivers. As the boat turned in the water, the trio could feel the mist of the falls on their faces, and they watched huge salmon jumping out of the water, intent on swimming up the falls to their spawning grounds. It was an astounding example of the pure strength and agility of these mighty fish.

McLoughlin

Twelve miles upriver from Portland was the thriving little community of Oregon City. This wilderness settlement had become the first incorporated town west of the Rocky Mountains and was the provisional capital of the Oregon Territory before statehood in 1859. Originally, the town was known as Willamette Falls.

In 1823, Canadian Dr. John McLoughlin was appointed Chief Factor of the Hudson's Bay Company at Fort Vancouver. Six years later, he was granted two square miles of the Willamette Falls property and began the construction of warehouses, factories, and homes for Hudson's Bay employees who worked at the site. John was an honest, God-fearing man who treated all people equally and would later become known as the Father of Oregon. McLaughlin was the first person to harness the power of the Willamette Falls, and he built the first gristmill in the Oregon Territory. Soon, other mills and factories did the same, and Oregon City grew into an important hub of supplies for arriving pioneers fresh off the Oregon Trail. In 1869, Oregon City had a population of roughly fifteen hundred people.

In the early afternoon, the trio stood on the front porch of a stately home that perched on a cliff overlooking downtown Oregon City and the Willamette Falls. The locals who had given them directions to the home had called it the McLoughlin House.

Gus looked at his friends, brushing off his coat. "Don't be nervous. He's just an ordinary man. Are you ready?"

They nodded, with serious faces, and he knocked on the red-painted front door.

Nothing happened.

He knocked again, more loudly.

Still nothing.

But then, just as he was about to try again, the door opened a few inches, revealing a big, tall Indian with chiseled facial features and a bald head covered with blue and red tattooed stars. The man wore a gray morning coat with buckskin trousers and a white ruffled shirt, with silver rings dangling from both ears and his nose. He was a frightening looking fellow with black eyes and skin the color and texture of rawhide.

For a moment, his horrific face stunned the trio. Then Gus said with authority, "We would like to see Dr. McLoughlin."

In the doorway, the big man frowned, staring at Gus's black eye patch. Then he waved an enormous hand and said, "Go away. He not here."

"We've come a long way to see the doctor. We need his help," Gus answered back.

"No more wagons. You go away."

"Who are you?" Lightfoot demanded, putting his boot inside the door threshold.

The Indian looked down at his foot and then glared at Clint. "I am Pong, his manservant. He is dead. Go away."

They were shocked to hear such news. "We come in peace," Lucy pleaded. "Please, sir, I am looking for my brother Leon."

From inside the house, a female voice called out, "What's going on, Pong?"

The door opened further, and the trio saw a lady standing behind Pong, holding a vase of flowers. She was a pretty young girl, dressed in a colorful skirt and yellow silk blouse. She moved to the door and opened it further. "Please forgive Pong. He means well but lacks English manners. Please, come in."

Reluctantly, the Indian stepped away from the door, and the friends entered the house.

Once inside the spacious foyer, the young lady introduced herself as Mary Ann McLoughlin, the daughter-in-law of Dr. McLoughlin. She had a honey complexion, brown eyes, and shiny black hair. It was obvious she was of mixed blood. "Unfortunately, Pong told you the truth. My father-in-law died twelve years ago, this month. I was the wife of his only son, John Junior. He died in Alaska ten years ago."

Gus introduced himself, Lightfoot, and then Lucy, telling Mary Ann of her capture, life with, and rescue from the Cheyenne Indians. When he was done telling her story, Lucy curtsied and said, "We were told that Dr. McLoughlin has a book with all the names of the pioneers that came through here. Can we see this book?"

Mary Ann returned her curtsy. "We do have his old log books from the Oregon Trail. Who are you seeking?" she asked.

"We rescued Lucy and now she is our ward," Lightfoot answered, eyeing the grand staircase to the second floor. "We are looking for her only remaining blood relative, a brother named Leon Fisher. He may have come through Oregon City around 1856."

"He would have been nine or ten years old at the time," Gus added.

"Do you know what season of year he came through town, or the name of his Wagon Master?" Mary Ann asked.

Lucy's face turned sad. "No, I can't remember." She started to sob. "We were somewhere in Wyoming. It was hot. Mother and father were killed by the Indians, and then scalped and laid dead by our wagon. But I don't remember seeing Leon. I called out to him, and then the Indians took me away."

Mary Ann approached Lucy and put her hand on her face "That's all right. Don't worry. I'm jealous of your auburn hair. You're such a beautiful young girl. If Leon came through here, we will find him."

Through all of this, Pong had stood with a stoic expression. Finally, he uttered a few Indian words. Mary Ann smiled at him and translated. "The Chief says the Cheyenne are dogs. His mother was also held captive by them. He will help you find your brother."

Mary Ann said something back to Pong with Indian words, then walked to one side of the foyer, where she slid open two massive wooden pocket doors. "My father-in-law's ledgers are in his parlor. Please join me."

The parlor was big, with tall windows and a huge stone fireplace in front of a massive mahogany desk. All of the interior walls were filled, from floor to ceiling, with bookcases stuffed with leather-bound books. It was the most books in one room that Gus had ever seen. "Your home is beautiful," he said to Mary Ann as she pulled back the drapes covering the windows, revealing an impressive view of Willamette Falls. In the flood of window light, the trio stared around the room at all of the nautical knickknacks and memorabilia that filled the parlor.

"Dr. McLaughlin had it built over twenty years ago. He hired some Swedish carpenters who came across on the Oregon Trail. When they got here, they had nothing, so he hired them to build this house for his wife. But she died before they could move in."

Mary Ann moved to one of the bookcases that held two full shelves of gray ledger books. She looked closely at the markings on the spine of each book. "You said 1856. There were four wagon trains that year. But perhaps we should start with 1855. There were only three that year. And we can finish with the four wagon trains of 1857." Mary Ann pulled out eleven books from the shelves and brought them to the desk. "We will start with 1855. I'll go through every page, looking for any mention of an orphaned young boy or anyone called Leon Fisher. You had better pull up some chairs. This is going to take some time."

"You've done this before," Lightfoot said, moving a chair in front of the desk.

"Yes," Mary Ann answered, moving to the seat behind the desk. "You'd be surprised how many stragglers and relatives come through here, looking for their kinfolk. My father-in-law's books have reunited many an Oregon family."

And what ledgers they turned out to be! Each book represented a wagon train that had crossed the continent on the Oregon Trail. On the front cover was the name of the train's Wagon Master and the date and place of arrival. On the inside of the logbook, each page was dedicated to a crossing pioneer family with their names, ages, and place of birth for each family member. Below these entries were the names, ages, and place of birth of any family members that had died on the trail. These death lists were often long and detailed, with graphic comments. The next entries were where the ultimate destination for the pioneer family might be. Most went south to the Willamette Valley to take up farming. Some went west to the Pacific Ocean to fish and build boats. Others just planted roots in the Portland area. Their ultimate destination was often as vague and as big as Oregon itself.

At the bottom of the page was an accounting of what every family had brought, borrowed or purchased from Dr. McLaughlin in Oregon City or at the Hudson's Bay Company trading post at

Fort Vancouver. If the family was poor, Dr. McLaughlin would often lend them some money until they were better established in their new life. If money had been lent, there would be a signed IOU included within the pages of the ledger. McLaughlin and his logbooks were a treasure trove of information, dating back to the early1840's, and ending when the Transcontinental Railroad replaced the need for wagon trains.

As Gus and Mary Ann read through the ledgers, Pong returned to the parlor with a tray of hot tea and cakes. He made a point of pouring tea for Lucy first and then selecting her a special sweet treat. "I was good servant to doctor," he said. "I will be the same for you."

Pong's stoic face had melted away and somehow now he had a smile on his face. "My name means fire maker. I will make one now."

Lucy looked up at him with a nod and a smile, more concerned about finding her brother than about his unusual remarks. But both Gus and Lightfoot found his advances quite curious. He moved to the fireplace and soon had a fire warming the room.

"What's the story behind Pong?" Gus asked Mary Ann after he left.

She looked up from the book she was reading and replied, "The Chief is one of the last Puyallup Indians. Long ago Dr. McLaughlin saved his life from the yellow fever. But when he finally recovered, most of his tribe had been wiped out from the fever. So my father-in-law took him in as his manservant. Now he watches over me."

"What's with the red and blue stars tattooed on his head?" Gus asked.

"He and his tribe worshiped a mythical god they call Thunderbird. The dots represent the stars in the sky so Thunderbird can find him when it is his time to join his ancestors."

"The Cheyenne have such a god, but I can't remember its name," Lucy said.

"How old is he?" Lightfoot asked.

Mary Ann shook her head. "We don't rightly know. I guess somewhere in his thirties. He has a big heart and little fear, but no desire to live with other Indians on their reservations. I call him Chief because he is so protective of me."

As they worked at the desk, Mary Ann proudly told them more of the life and times of Dr. McLaughlin.

"My father-in-law was a big man, six foot four inches tall, with wavy white hair and a voice that demanded respect. His wife, Marguerite, was a beautiful Metis Indian maiden. They had three children, but only one survived childbirth, my husband, John Jr."

"Where did you meet him?" Gus asked scanning pages of a ledger.

"At school in Ottawa. He was a handsome young man and just like his father, he worked for the Hudson's Bay Company. After I finished school, we were married and moved to a company trading post up in Alaska. It was a miserable place, but we were happy for a few months. Then John was killed by a drunken Indian. So I returned home, only to learn that my parents had died of the fever. When Dr. McLaughlin heard of my tragedies, he took me in as his ward. He was a man of great virtue."

"There was a lot of death on your doorstep," Lightfoot frowned.

"Yes, and I was an orphan, just like Lucy," she answered with sad eyes.

"How old were you when you came here?" Lucy asked.

Mary Ann gazed at her with a friendly smile, "Just a little older then you. I was twenty when Pong and I arrived here in Oregon City. That was eighteen years ago."

"Those years have been good to you," Gus said with a surprised look. "You still look so young."

Mary Ann opened another book. "Thank you, Captain. When Pong and I arrived here, Dr. McLaughlin was like the Emperor of Oregon. He was in charge of over six hundred HBC employees spread across the entire Oregon territory. He kept the peace and grew the business by treating everyone fairly. That's what I hope I can do here, be fair to everyone."

Gus was taken with Mary Ann. She was not only beautiful, but also witty and intelligent, a very rare commodity for anyone living on the edge of a civilized world in 1869.

They got lucky with the fourth ledger in the stack. In 1857, a wagon train called Dunthorpe had arrived in Oregon City with fifty-six families. They had departed Independence, Missouri, six months before with sixty families. In the listing of the four missing families, they found the Fisher family, with the names of Eric, Bernice, and Lucy Fisher listed as dead by Indians. There was no mention of their son Leon. That was encouraging. Then, in the separate pages of the book, they found the listing for the Walter Larson family. There, under the listing of the family children, they found Leon Fisher's name. At age ten, he was alive! He had made it across the Oregon Trail and the Larson family had taken him in. But the only destination listed for the family was the Willamette Valley.

Lucy was overwhelmed to learn that her brother might still be alive. She thanked Mary Ann with tears of joy. After some hugging and happiness, Lucy asked, "Where is this Willamette Valley?"

Mary Ann took her to the windows and pointed outside. "See the top of the waterfalls? That's where the Willamette Valley starts and it stretches one hundred and fifty miles south and is fifty miles wide. That's big country out there. You could spend a month of Sundays searching for your brother and never find him."

"So what do I do?" Lucy asked, staring out the window.

Mary Ann smiled at her. "The power of the printing press. Come sit down with me. We are girlfriends now and I'll show you how to make Leon come to you."

Mary Ann had done this many times before. There were five weekly newspapers published in the towns and hamlets of the Willamette Valley. By placing small ads in these papers Mary Ann hoped to hear from the Walter Larson family, or from Leon Fisher himself. "This will take some time, a week or two at least," she said, writing out the short ad. "When I hear anything back, I'll send Pong to you with the news."

She showed Gus the handwritten ad: Walter Larson family/Leon Fisher: rich relatives found. Dr. McLaughlin.

"Why rich relatives?" Gus asked.

Mary Ann smiled, "It gets everyone that might see the ad talking. Everybody wishes they had rich relatives and the gossip might help us find Leon."

Lightfoot nodded with a grin. "Good bait."

"Ten little words," Mary Ann replied. "I sure hope someone in that family reads newspapers. Pong will take you to the Western Union office here in town. It will cost two dollars a word, per newspaper. One dollar is for the ad cost and the other dollar for the cost of the telegram. It's an expensive way to start the search, but it usually works. Where will you be staying in the next few weeks?"

Gus showed the ad to Lucy and Clint. "Lightfoot and I have jobs as Deputy Sheriffs waiting back in Astoria. Is there a place where Lucy might stay while we wait?"

"Yes," She answered. "There is a girls Catholic School called Trails End in Portland. It's a boarding school for wayward girls and orphaned children off the Oregon Trail. I can write you a letter of introduction. I'm sure they would take her in."

Lucy's face went from smiles to a frown in the blink of eye. "No! I no go with those penguins. I wait in Astoria with my brothers. Maybe I stay at Lilly's place."

Lightfoot's jaw dropped, "You can't stay there. It is no place for young girls."

"Why not?" Lucy answered with defiant eyes. "The Sheriff say there is woman in Astoria to watch after me. NO penguins."

"All right, let's not argue about this now," Gus said, looking at his pocket watch. "What time is the last boat back to Astoria?"

Mary Ann closed up the books they had been looking at. "The last boat from Portland leaves at five. But you won't get into Astoria until around midnight."

"That's fine with me," Gus replied. "If you get any news, contact us through Clatsop County Sheriff Bill Chance. He'll know where we are."

Mary Ann rang a little bell and Pong reappeared in the room. "Take our friends to the telegraph office and then help them get a water taxi for Portland. Their steamboat leaves at five, so don't dilly-dally."

He bowed to her. "Yes, ma'am."

After Mary Ann wrote out the letter of introduction there were hugs and handshakes all round. They had been fortunate to find such a well-informed young lady as Mary Ann McLoughlin.

"Thank you for your help and hospitality," Gus said to her, his face flushed.

"You're welcome anytime Captain. Let me walk you out."

As they moved onto the front porch, Mary Ann gave Gus the letter and said, "If we can't find her brother, and anything bad happens to you or Lightfoot, I'll watch over Lucy as my ward. You take care of my new girlfriend."

Gus took her soft hand and thanked her for her loving kindness. "Dr. McLaughlin would be proud of you."

Lucy was the last to say goodbye. She hugged Mary Ann and asked, "What is a girlfriend?"

Mary Ann stepped back with a big grin. "It's all about you and me. We are like blood brothers now. We are girlfriends." Then she kissed Lucy on the cheek.

Lucy smiled with her eyes dancing, "I never have a girlfriend before."

Nesting

With a short sprint and a long leap, the friends landed on the main deck of the sternwheeler *Mascot* just as it was pulling away from its dock. Waiting on the deck was the Purser, with a long face and a sharp tongue. "That's about as close as it gets. We don't like leapers jumping on our ship. Next time, be on time!

"Yes, sir," Gus answered. "We had a hard time finding a water taxi in Oregon City."

"That's your problem," he snarled. "It's seven hours to Astoria, and walk-on fare is a dollar a head."

Lightfoot paid the man. "Is there a bar on this tub?"

The man growled back, "Second deck lounge, food and drink."

"Do they play any poker on this boat?" Gus asked, glaring at the man with his one eye.

Lucy interrupted, "Mr. Purser man, I ask question about ship? How it see at night?"

"That's a good question young lady," the grumpy old man answered, smiling down on her. "When it gets dark, the Captain steers the boat from one little river lighthouse to the next. These kerosene smudge pots are maintained by people called lamplighters, up and down the river. You will see them on the shore as we pass them by."

"What about the poker?" Gus asked again, smiling at Lucy.

"Yes, sir, there's poker in the lounge. What a sweet girl you have here."

That was typical Lucy: she could melt an iceberg with just a few kind words and a couple blinks of her green eyes. It was one of her many God-given gifts.

With the *Mascot* underway, the trio moved to the second deck in search of food. The lounge was a long, narrow room with windows on both sides of the cabin. At one end of the compartment was the stand-up bar, with a few round tables and chairs scattered on the deck. At the other end was the café, with a limited bar menu offering a few sandwiches, beef jerky, and fried potatoes. But their specialty was bratwurst and sauerkraut. That's what the men had, while Lucy selected a hardboiled egg and a sweet roll.

Lightfoot grinned at Gus as he slathered mustard on his sausage. "I think Mary Ann lives up to your proclivities Captain. You seemed smitten by her."

Lucy looked at Clint. "What is that word again?"

He chuckled. "First time I've ever seen the Captain blush. I think he likes your new girlfriend."

Lucy turned to Gus. "Is that right, brother?"

He shook his head. "No, she's a little old for me, and way too young for Lightfoot. He's just stirring the pot."

"See, he *is* sweet on her," Clint answered jokingly. "Next thing you know, he'll be moving to Oregon City."

Gus frowned. "Why would she care a hoot for me? I have nothing and she has so much."

"She is a pretty squaw," Lucy said. "And Pong would be your manservant."

Gus ate the last morsel of his bratwurst and stood up. "I'm going to play some poker. You two enjoy your gossiping. Come and get me when we're close to Astoria."

With the help of a favorable tide, the *Mascot* arrived at Astoria half an hour early. The boat was secured at the very dock they had departed that morning. As they came ashore, the skyline of the city looked like a coal pit, with only a few spots of light blending into an overcast sky. Even their hotel was as black as a cat. Walking up the dock ramp, their eyes slowly adjusted, and they were soon standing in front of the Yankee Schooner's front door, which was locked. Lightfoot knocked and rattled the door shouting. "Mr. Cromwell, let us in."

"He's not going like this," Gus said, peering through window.

Clint knocked and shouted again. "It's the way of being an innkeeper."

"I see a light coming down the stairs." Gus said, still gazing through the glass door.

When Cromwell unlocked the door and opened it, he held his oil lantern high above his head so that his sleepy, angry eyes could see the reason for the commotion. "What the hell do you want? We have no rooms. Go away."

"Sorry, sir. We left this morning on the *Express,*" Gus said. "You sold us our tickets and put our pokes in your storage room."

He grumbled and opened the door wider. "Come in, get your gear, and go away."

With a little sweet talk from Lucy, Mr. Cromwell allowed them to sleep on the chairs in the lobby for two-bits a head. It wasn't very comfortable, but better than sleeping on the cold, damp beach or the hard wooden planks of the dock.

As the three friends settled in the dark to find sleep, Lightfoot asked, "How did you do at poker, Captain?"

Gus tried to curl up his lanky body in his chair, but he wasn't having much luck. "Walked away with a little over thirty dollars. With any luck, it will be enough to buy a decent horse and outfit."

"One horse isn't good enough to buy Mary Ann." Lucy said in the night. "You'll need a long string of horses for my girlfriend."

Gus chuckled. "Yes, you are right. I don't have enough nags."

"Not sure it's nags that the Captain wants," Clint answered. "He's thinking about something a little more tempting."

"What is tempting?" she asked.

At first light the next morning, the friends were rousted out of their chairs by Mr. Cromwell as he opened up the hotel. "There's a café across the street from the Courthouse. It opens at seven. They make a delicious omelet with crab. Next to the restaurant is a bathhouse, if you need to clean up before you see the Sheriff."

"How did you know we were seeing Sheriff Chance this morning?" Lightfoot asked rolling up his bedroll.

Cromwell smiled at his lobby guests. "Small town, big mouths."

Once outside the front door, the friends were greeted with overcast gray skies and a rain much like a drizzle or heavy dew. As they slowly started moving across the wet timbers of the pier, both Gus and Lightfoot had slight limps. "I feel like a pretzel," Clint complained. "Sleeping on that damn chair was worse than riding a mule."

"Maybe we'll camp out, tonight. Anything would be better than that lobby." Gus added, finally getting his legs to move right.

Lucy smiled. "I slept good."

"Yes, I'm sure you did," Lightfoot grumbled. "You slept on the only settee."

They enjoyed a hardy breakfast and cleaned up at the bathhouse as best they could. It was near eight o'clock by the time they walked over to the Sheriff's office. They soon found him out back of the jailhouse in the stable, looking over livestock with an older man.

The Sheriff greeted the friends warmly. "Good you're here nice and early. I was just checking out the horseflesh we had to offer you."

Gus made the introductions, after which Sheriff Chance shook hands with Lightfoot. "Nice meeting you. I've heard good things about you from Colonel Rawlins. I'm assuming you guys are taking up my offer to become my Deputies."

Both Gus and Lightfoot nodded their agreement and shook hands with Chance again.

The older man with the Sheriff was called Chester. He was the County Livestock Agent and had over a dozen horses and mules in his corral, some of which he and the Sheriff had already selected for the Deputies consideration.

That was when the horse trading started. Gus and Lightfoot inspected each horse from their teeth to their hooves and from their legs to their shoulders. They checked their eyes, their ears, and the touch of their hair. They both had been around horseflesh all of their lives, and knew exactly what to look for.

One horse was too small, another too old. But Lightfoot liked an Appaloosa mare called Whirlwind. She was bright-eyed and strong with muscular legs. And she was surefooted. "She won't give me speed," he said. "But she'll stay the course."

Sheriff Chance chuckled, "There's not much open country out here, so stamina is better than speed."

"What's her cost?" Clint asked Chester.

"Seventy-five dollars," he answered, and they started haggling.

As they bargained, Gus and Lucy moved to the corral and walked around the other horses. Soon, they returned to the barn, leading a tall gelding with a chestnut coat.

"How about this guy?" Gus asked Chester.

"I thought about Rocky," he answered. "He's got a lot of spunk. But he's also got a mind of his own. He'd be a handful."

"Good. I like a horse with spirit," Gus answered. "How did the county get all these animals?"

"Most of them were confiscated from their owners," the Sheriff answered. "They went to jail, skipped town or were shanghaied. Many were payment of debts or fines. Some bad deed happened and the county ended up with these animals. Hell, out on the county farm, we even have cattle, pigs, chickens, and one animal called a llama."

"Is this all legal and on the up and up?" Clint asked.

Chance smiled. "Yep. Judge Bill Bean presiding. He's the law in Astoria. As my new Deputies, you'll get to know him well."

In the end, both men bought their horses and outfits for forty dollars each, and Sheriff Chance loaned them a county pack mule named Gracie to carry their trail burdens.

They paid for their horses at the Courthouse and received a very legal looking bill of sale for Whirlwind and Rocky. After that, they filled out more paperwork, using mostly the information from their Military Separation papers. Their last stop was at the chambers of Judge Bill Bean next to his courtroom. It was an impressive office with shelves of legal books; walls decorated with dead animal heads, and overstuffed furniture made of red leather. Even his desk was inlaid with leather. It was impressive, yes, but his office did not compare with the elegance of John McLoughlin's parlor.

Sheriff Chance made the introductions and right on cue, Lucy curtsied to the Judge. He was a small, older man with a wrinkled face, white hair, and deep blue eyes. He stood up from his desk and shook hands with Gus and Lightfoot, and nodded a bow back to Lucy with a smile. "Guess you boys are our new Deputies," he said in a squeaky, high-pitched voice. "I'll get my robes on and we'll swear you in."

Gus and Clint glanced at each other with grins. If Judge Bean was the law in Astoria, he sure didn't look or sound the part. His voice was like fingers scratching a blackboard, and his demeanor was that of grandfatherly old man. How could this man be strong enough to be a wilderness Judge?

With Gus and Lightfoot holding back snickers, the ceremony didn't take long. The Judge read a few words from the Bible and the men held up their right hands with a pledge to uphold the Constitution of the United States and the Constitution of Oregon. It was solemn but, because of his voice, it was a little distracting, as well.

When the Judge finished, he handed the two new Deputies their badges while saying with a stone face, "You are my eyes and ears in this vast county we govern. You are my law, for our citizens to trust and our criminals to fear. You shall always be fair, firm, and forthright with my laws. Bring no shame to this court and I will bring no shame to you. Be wary of the trail ahead and always return safely."

For all of his funny quirks, Judge Bill Bean turned out to be a brilliant jurist, with one hand on his Bible and the other hand on his law books.

After the swearing-in ceremony, Sheriff Chance took his new Deputies and Lucy to the jailhouse and gave them a tour. The white-washed stone jail stood two stories tall, with a steep hip roof and medieval turrets on both sides of the entry. It was a cold, menacing-looking structure, built in 1865.

"How many prisoners do you have?" Lightfoot asked as they walked into the jail.

"Right now, only three— one horse thief, one wife beater, and our town drunk. We've had as many as fourteen, but average only five or six. The Judge hands out a lot of thirty-day sentences."

On the top floor, there were eight two-man cells and a guard station for one fulltime jailer. On the lower floor was a large drunk tank, with two more cells across the aisle. At the very front of the building were two corner cells, one of which was the Sheriff's office while the other cell was used as a storeroom. The jail had a dampness and stench to it, pungent and depressive. The lock-up in Astoria was not a place to be.

The tour ended in the Sheriff's office, where he had a map spread out on his desk. "Let's talk about your first assignment and I'll give you a few pointers about traveling around the county."

The men huddled at the desk while Lucy walked around the office looking at wanted posters hanging from his walls. The pictures of the wanted criminals were mostly line art, with a few blurry photographs. The men depicted in the flyers were a motley bunch of scary faces wanted for all kinds of crimes: murder to burglary, horse thieves to cattle rustlers. Lucy seemed to be fascinated looking at the leftovers of society.

"Fort Yamhill is only about a hundred and ten miles from here, as the crow flies," the Sheriff said, pointing to the fort on the map. "But you guys can't fly. So you'll board a supply barge tomorrow morning and steam down the coast to the town of Tillamook. That's not always an easy task. The Bar crossing into Tillamook Bay can be one treacherous journey. When you get there, check in with the local Sheriff, a man named Rigby. Give him this envelope of wanted posters," Chance told Gus, giving him an envelope. "Then ride south-south-east for Fort Yamhill. It will be about sixty miles. Two days on the trail."

"We can usually make that in a day," Lightfoot answered, studying the map.

"Not out here," the Sheriff replied. "This isn't the flat lands of the Wyoming wilderness. This country will gobble you up. There are only two ways of getting around Clatsop County, up and down her mountains or across her boggy wetlands of streams, rivers and bays. You'll be riding in a rainforest where moss grows on all sides of the trees and the canopy is so dense and tall that you'll never see the sun. Blink your eyes and you'll be lost. With that in mind, I've hired a local guide, Whiskey Joe, for your first trip south. He'll show you the ropes of traveling this land and help with the prisoners you'll pick-up at the fort."

"We don't need no local guide," Lightfoot grumbled. "I've never been lost in my life."

The Sheriff smiled. "Trust me, son, I know what I'm doing."

"Who is this Whiskey Joe?" Gus asked.

"He's a breed. His mother was a Tillamook Indian and his father a French trapper. He knows this land like the back of his hand. Listen and learn. He'll meet you at the supply barge on Pier 1 tomorrow morning at seven."

"What are you paying him?" Lightfoot asked.

"A dollar a day, but no pay until you are back here with your prisoners. And keep Joe away from the whiskey while you're on the trail. He's a guzzler."

Gus scratched his head. "Why all this trouble for two prisoners?"

Sheriff Chance's face flushed with anger. "The Parker Brothers. They are the worst of the worst. Two months ago, they and two other riders rode into a small town south of here called Timber. The brothers asked at the local General Store for directions to the Anderson Homestead. They told the storekeeper they were long lost uncle's to Will Anderson. He gladly gave them directions to the farm and they rode out of town. Late that afternoon the strangers rode into the homestead and killed the entire Anderson family. Then they burned down the place with the all the dead family, including their four children, inside the farmhouse. It was a massacre with no rhyme, or reason. Like snakes in grass, they just did it!

When I first heard about the Anderson tragedy it got my blood boiling. But it was of no concern of ours. Timber is in the next county over. Anyhow, that's what I thought. But then I learned the Anderson Homestead was just inside the Clatsop Boundaries. Now this hot-potato is ours."

"How were they captured?" Gus asked.

"It was a fluke," Chance said. "An Army Patrol found them drunk in a little town bar bragging about burning down a farmhouse."

"What is hot-potato?" Lucy asked with a curious face.

"This kind of massacre stirs up the vigilantes. They will come out in droves looking for revenge. That's why Judge Bean is looking forward to their short visit in his courtroom."

"Dead or alive?" Lightfoot asked.

"Yep, alive if you can, dead if you must. Just bring them back with all the paperwork the Army has on them. Judge Bean will do the rest." the Sheriff answered.

The men talked and planned their assignment for over an hour. When they finished, Lucy asked, "What about me? Am I a hot-potato staying at Lilly's place?"

Sheriff Chance shook his head with a frown. "Lillys is no place for you. My lady friend, Mrs. Thayer, is out of town, visiting relatives. But she'll be back early next week. So I came up with a plan. The county owns a river scow. It's all set up like a floating home. The boat is moored down on the public dock in front of the hotel. Lucy can stay aboard while you guys are on the trail. I'll keep an eye on her."

Lucy liked the idea of the boat, but she had her own ideas, as well. "I'll just go with you Brothers. I can help out on the trail."

"No," the Sheriff answered quickly. "These prisoners are way too dangerous."

Lucy hated being told what to do, and that stubborn look filled her face. "If I can survive living with the Cheyenne, I can survive this trail."

"What about Leon?" Gus asked her. "Mary Ann might get some news about him while we're gone."

The mention of her brother was enough. Gus was right. "Alright," she answered reluctantly. "Can we see this floating teepee?"

As they walked to the public dock, that wet dew was still in the air. "What is it with this dew?" Gus asked Sheriff Chance.

He chuckled. "Ain't no dew. It's sticky rain. It's a blessing for Astoria. It's the rain in our rainforests. If you don't own a good slicker, you better buy one today."

They walked along wet planks and rails down to the public pier and were soon standing in front of Slip #6 gazing at the row, pole and sail blunt-end riverboat *Louise*. She was a thick planked boat about forty feet long, with a twenty-foot beam amidships. Both the bow and stern were blunted and about six foot wide with fishing net rollers attached. There were two cabins, fore and aft, with a snapped-off sailing mast dead center of the boat. Gus had seen riverboats like the *Louise* many times on the Mississippi River, although this one seemed bigger and better designed.

"Don't get big-eyed with this boat," the Sheriff said stepping aboard. "It's up for public auction at the end of next month." He used a key to open the paddle lock on the cabin door. As he slid back the hatch cover and opened the door, a seagull flew out, crying loudly.

"Shit," the startled Sheriff yelled, and stepped down into the cabin. "He's not supposed to be in here."

Everyone came below, and Chance pulled back the window curtains. As light flooded the compartment, the trio was surprised by the size and condition of the interior. Hanging from the bulkheads were brass weather and sailing instruments and foul-weather gear. On one side of the cabin, there were bunk beds with bedding, and clothes hanging from hooks. On the other side of the compartment was a booth, with a table and settee, next to a small galley with a sink and coal-fired stove. The cabin looked lived in, as if the owner would soon appear to get underway. The only thing missing was hot coffee on the stove.

"What's the story behind this boat?" Gus asked of the Sheriff.

He took a seat on edge of the settee with a long face. "It's a tragic tale. Ray Cooper and his wife Louise were from Hannibal, Missouri, where Ray learned the shipwright trade. They survived the Oregon Trail and moved to Astoria about fifteen years ago. Ray was a gifted carpenter and started building fishing boats. Working only with his wife, they built two or three boats a year. In their spare time, they worked on this boat from the keel up. They were a wonderful couple and a great team. A few years later, they finished the *Louise* and moved into it, right here at Slip #6. They grew old together, sailing and fishing up and down the river. Many a time, I saw this boat filled with fish up to her gunnels. Those were good days. Last December, they went out sturgeon fishing just as big weather was brewing in the south. The storm was long and violent. The next morning, the *Louise* wasn't in her boat slip. Three days later, a search party found it on a sandbar, upriver. There was nobody aboard. Ray and Louise must have been swept out to sea. Their bodies were never found and the Judge declared their deaths to be accidental. The river giveth and the river taketh. They had no kin, no bodies to bury, and no mourners to weep. That's the sad story of the *Louise*," he finished with a stone face and damp eyes.

Lightfoot pulled a bottle of whiskey from his bedroll and took a swig. Handing the bottle to the Sheriff, he asked, "How in the hell did the county get their hooks on this boat?"

"Because there was no family that I could find, the Judge made the county the executor. All the money from the sale of the boat will be held by the county as their estate, so you can stay aboard until the auction date. "

"No rent?" Gus asked.

"No, and I can keep eye on Lucy until you return," the Sheriff answered, taking a swig from the bottle.

"I'm curious," Gus said, taking the bottle from Sheriff. "How much will this boat sell for?"

Chance stood and looked around the compartment. "My guess? A thousand dollars or a little more."

"Wow, that's too rich for us." Gus answered. "But we'll be pleased to stay here."

The friends spent the afternoon exploring the boat and stocking the pantry with food for both the trail and Lucys time aboard. It was a time of discovery, reflection, and talk of the future.

"You like this boat?" Lucy asked her Brothers, cleaning up the galley.

"I do," Lightfoot answered, snooping through some cupboards. "The forward cabin is big enough for another berth, and there's even a working sea toilet. We could live aboard this boat."

Unrolling his bedroll on the lower bunk, Gus replied, "It's nice, but too expensive."

"We could make lots of money fishing from it," Lightfoot answered. "All we would need is a new sailing mast. The boat's built like a fortress."

"We could add steam to it, like old Sam do with his *Marianne,*" Lucy added.

Gus chuckled. "The *Marianne* is a scow, held together with nails and hope. This boat is a masterpiece of oak planks and dowels. The *Louise* will still be afloat long after we're gone."

"So you think we should buy it?" Clint asked.

"Let's not get ahead of ourselves," Gus answered. "We're Deputy Sheriffs, not bankers."

This conversation went on long into the evening. The friends were excited about what the future might hold.

Just before first light the next morning, Gus and Lightfoot walked to the stables, carrying their gear. It was a beautiful, clear dawn with stars still in the sky and the morning birds singing their calls. Within the half hour, they had their animals packed and saddled, waiting for their riders just inside the barn doors. That was when Sheriff Chance appeared, carrying a double-barrel shotgun.

"Take this with you," he said, handing the rifle to Lightfoot. "There's a lot of water fowl where you're going, and fresh duck is tasty around the campfire."

The men packed away the gun on the mule, Gracie, and then shook hands with the Sheriff.

"Don't worry," he said. "I'll keep an eye on Lucy. See you in a week or ten days, boys. Stay safe out there."

Gus and Clint moved to their horses just as Lucy came through the barn doors. She was still in her sleeping clothes and her hair looked like a birds nest. "Why didn't you wake me?" she demanded with her eyes on fire. "I wanted to say goodbye."

"You looked so peaceful, sleeping," Gus answered.

Lucy moved to Lightfoot and put her arms around him, something she seldom did, and gave him a hug. "We are a family now, so don't forsake me."

Clint kissed on her cheek. "Not to worry, sister. We'll be back soon." Then he mounted Whirlwind, with his face sad and his eyes moist.

Lucy moved to Gus and gave him a hug, with a kiss on his cheek. "I love you, brother," she whispered. "You saved my life."

Gus nodded and returned her kiss on the cheek. "Don't trust anybody but the Sheriff, and keep the cabin door locked." He mounted Rocky and tipped his hat to her. "If anything bad happens, Mary Ann will take you in. See you in a week."

She stood frozen, watching her brothers ride out of the stable and turn down the street. That's when she noticed she had tears in her eyes. Lucy was crying for her family, something she hadn't done since the death of her parents. She wiped the tears out of her eyes and looked away. Could she lose this new family as well?

Chapter 7 – Horse Sailors

Many Waters

Under gray morning skies, Gus and Lightfoot sat in their saddles for the longest time, looking down at the supply scow moored at Pier One. The timbered ship was about sixty feet long, with a twenty foot beam, a tapered bow, and a squared stern. A roof covered the main deck, with a wheelhouse perched on the forward part of the awning. It was an awkward-looking vessel, with one steam boiler driving double paddle wheels amidships.

"Funniest damn looking boat I've ever seen," Lightfoot said in the early morning mist.

"I've seen boats like this on the Mississippi," Gus answered. "They're called Kentucky flat boats because they have shallow drafts and can maneuver up tributary rivers and bays. A boat like this can move an entire troop of Calvary downstream to get behind the enemy."

Clint chuckled, "We ain't got no troop, Captain. It's just like the old days – only you and me. Should we go aboard, sir?"

They walked their animals down the ramp and up to the ship tied to the floating dock. The timbers were still wet from the dew as the morning sun broke through the haze, casting long shadows on the shimmering waters. It was about to be another spectacular day on the Columbia River.

"You boys must be the new Deputies," a man with a clipboard said from the deck of the ship. "Welcome aboard the *Morning Star II*. We'll get underway once the boats finished loading." He stepped from the deck onto the dock with a friendly face. "Horse and rider fare is two dollars, so you owe me six dollars to get you to Tillamook."

"How did you know we were the Deputies?" Gus asked.

"Simple enough. Whiskey Joe told me when he came aboard. That six dollar fare includes his walk-on fee."

Gus paid the man, who wrote out a receipt which he gave to the Captain. "This is to get your money back from the county. But don't hold your breath. They're slow to pay."

Where's this Whiskey Joe?" Lightfoot asked.

"The main deck is split into two halves," came the answer. "The forward gangway is for loading freight and commodities. The aft ramp is for the livestock. You'll find Joe back there with the animals. Hobble your horses and lighten their burdens once they're inside their stalls. It's five or six hours to Tillamook."

"How often do you make this trip down the coast?" Gus asked.

"In good weather like this, two or three times a month. In normal bad weather, once a month, maybe. I'll check on you and your horses after we get underway. Better get aboard."

Lightfoot grinned at him. "Is there a bar on this tub?"

The Purser stepped back to the deck of the ship. "Nope. The *Morning Star* is a working boat. But there's always hot coffee in the wheelhouse."

As the gurgling sounds of the steam boiler coming to life, they walked their animals across the aft ramp and under the roof, where they found a deck filled with wooden stalls waiting for livestock. The horses, and the mule Gracie, each got a separate stall. Then the men unloaded each animals load and hobbled their front legs.

As they settled their animals, they were startled to find a man crouched in the shadows watching them. Once noticed, he slowly stood and said, "You'll be the new Deputies."

"And you must be Whiskey Joe," Gus replied. "Lurking around a dark deck is not a good idea."

Lightfoot glared at the stranger. "A man could get killed, sneaking up on me."

"No mean sneak-up," the man answered, moving into the light.

He was short and stocky, with bowed legs and copper-colored skin. He had a round face with flat black hair, and a fleshy nose with full lips. He wore a pair of buckskins and an old red flannel shirt, and carried a bedroll wrapped around a rifle, with a knife on his belt and a leather shoulder pouch for his sundries. He looked neither old nor young.

"You a breed?" Lightfoot asked, still staring at him.

He moved towards the men standing next to a stall. That's when Gus noticed the color of his eyes. They were deep set and a light gray, almost white. His peepers seemed to glow, subtle but striking.

"That's what I hear," Joe answered Lightfoot. "I'm mostly Tillamook Indian, but with some French blood from my father. Just like you, Deputy. Guess we are both half-breeds."

Calling Clint a half-breed was like waving a red cape in a bull fight. In an instant, his pocked face turned crimson and his brown eyes were on fire. Luckily, just then, more livestock came aboard, and the men had to get out of the way.

Moving next to the stern rail, Joe stared at Gus's eye patch. "People say you are the Night-Eye Indian fighter. Where eye go?"

Gus frowned and replied, "I lost it in a fight."

"You fight Indians?" Joe asked.

"No. gray coats, during big war. Where's your horse?" Gus replied.

"Don't need horse," Joe answered.

"You're full of shit," Lightfoot said. "No horse? What a lie. How could you get around out here?"

Whiskey Joe glared back at Clint. "I hear of you, Lightfoot. People say you too some big Indian fighter. Why? What Indians do to you?"

Clint put his hand on the pommel of his knife, as did Whiskey Joe. They faced off against each other, like two bulls pawing the ground.

"Wait a minute," Gus said, holding up a hand and glaring at Joe. "If you must know, Lightfoot's family was wiped out by Indians and he was raised by the Comanches. But that score was settled long ago. Now we're just Deputy Sheriffs doing a job for the county. Just like you. If you're going to make trouble, get the hell off the boat."

Joe frowned at Lightfoot for a long moment, and Gus noticed his eyes now looked normal and brown in the bright sunlight. "You right, Captain. We do job. No need to call people breeds."

"So, without a horse, how do you get around out here?" Gus

asked him, still trying to diffuse the anger in the air.

"I run or paddle," Joe answered, moving his hand away from his knife grip. "The Tillamooks are fast runners."

Lightfoot chuckled sarcastically. "You run faster than my horse?"

Joe shook his head. "Not in open country, but yes, in forest," Joe answered defiantly.

"Do you live here in Astoria?" Gus asked.

"Now I do," Joe answered. "We have a shack east of town on log pond. Old-man Swenson '*allows*' us to stay on land that belongs to all Indians."

"Who's we?" Lightfoot asked. "Do you have a squaw?"

Joe forced a smile, his gaze still locked on Clint. "I no say."

That was their first impression of Whiskey Joe. He wasn't a literate man; he only knew the time of day by the position of the sun, and he couldn't write or read a word. But somehow, magically, he had instincts about finding trails, the direction of travel, the weather and the tides that were almost always correct. It was hard for Joe to recall what happened the day before, but his glowing gray eyes always seemed to know what was going to happen next.

Within the hour, the *Morning Star II* was fully loaded and out on the water, heading west for the Columbia River Bar. The weather looked peaceful and calm, and Whiskey Joe predicted a lake-like crossing at the Bar. "Many times," he said, "this Bar blocked by big curling waves with riptides so strong that crossing closed for many days. When the Indians still lived here, they cross Bar in bad seas to guide tall ships to safety. The Chinooks almost as good as the Tillamooks with sea canoes. That's all gone now, replaced with steam machines that row."

Whiskey Joe was like that, always lamenting the lost heritage of his ancestors. His many stories were always bitter sweet, stirred up with contempt and hatred for all of the white invaders who had robbed the Indians of their lands. But who could blame him for telling the truth?

Once across the Bar, the ship turned south, with both paddle wheels digging deep into the sea. After the turn, the men climbed the ladder to the wheelhouse and helped themselves to some hot, fresh coffee. Talking with the Captain and his Mate, they learned more about their final destination.

Captain Robert Gray had been the first white man to discover the scant opening to the Tillamook Bay in 1788. He sailed his sloop *Lady Washington* into the bay and traded trinkets for sea otter pelts with the local Indians. At first, the trading was peaceful, brisk, and profitable with the Indians he called Tillamooks. On the second day, however, the trading turned violent and the sloop made a hasty retreat back into the sea. That visit was the first occasion, but not the last, of white men trading trinkets with the Tillamooks.

The first white settler came to the Tillamook Valley in 1851. This opened the flood gates for many other pioneers in the coming years. The first town on the bay was called Lincoln, and it was built at the confluence of four rivers. Then, in 1853, Tillamook County was created by the Territorial Government, and the town was renamed Tillamook. Nestled between the coastal surf and the foothills of the coastal mountains, there was a large, rich, green valley suitable for farming commodities such as wheat and corn. The grass of this valley was also suitable for the production of cattle and dairy products. Tillamook, the land of many waters, was as rich as any gold mine, and ready for the taking.

"We bring in freight, construction materials, mail, and commodities such as sacks of coal, barrels of beer, flower, sugar and kerosene," the Captain said, "while taking out the mail and other commodities, such as cans of milk, wheels of cheese, and bins of potatoes and turnips. The trade is brisk from livestock to farm animals, bolts of cloth to wagon wheels. We've even delivered some oxen to help them plow the fields and pull out the tree trunks. Tillamook is fast becoming the bread basket of the north coast."

"How many people live in this town?" Lightfoot asked.

"Right now, just a few hundred," the Mate answered. "But rumors are that a new wagon road is being built to connect with the Willamette Valley. When that happens, Tillamook will become a big city."

With all the talk about Tillamook, Gus and Lightfoot were

surprised when they noticed Whiskey Joe was gone.

"Did anyone see him leave? Gus asked.

The Captain chuckled. "That's just Joe. He's as moody as the weather. He hates us talking about his beloved Tillamook. He calls it his home and thinks we robbed it from him."

A few hours later, the Mate turned from the wheel and said, "Twin Rocks coming up, Skipper."

"We are about half an hour out from crossing the Bar," the Captain said. "You should see to your mounts. If it gets choppy, they might get spooked."

Thanking the Captain and Mate for their hospitality, Gus and Lightfoot departed the wheelhouse. Soon, they found Whiskey Joe sleeping on some hay in the sunshine on the stern deck. They checked their horses and gave each some fresh water and a quick brush down, while murmuring soothing reassurances. Their animals looked as peaceful as a spring morning.

Lightfoot removed a whiskey bottle from his bedroll and took a swig from it. Then he moved to Joe and nudged him with his boot. "Wake up, White Eyes. Do you want some whiskey?"

Gus frowned at his friend. "The Sheriff said no booze."

Joe stirred and opened his eyes. Clint handed him the bottle. "Most drunk breeds are as stupid as a stump. Let's see what kind of brass he's made of."

Joe took a long gulp and got to his feet, handing back the bottle to Lightfoot. "You surprise me, Mexican man. Maybe we be friends."

Looking astern, Joe pointed to a tall, craggy monolith in the wake of the barge. "We close to home now. That mountain is Neahkahnie. It is a holy place to my people. Some say Spanish gold buried up there, but I no go. Thunderbird say mountain for ancestors only."

"When were you last here?" Gus asked.

"Two seasons ago. Come with Deputy to take back prisoner for Judge Bean. Man bad hombre, kill wife. He jumped off boat and drown before we get him to Astoria. Judge not happy."

The boat slowed as it started its approach to a scant opening obscured by the backdrop of the rocky coastline. The men moved to the port rail to watch the crossing. All they could see before them were the long, white lines of curling breakers. Their progress looked blocked by the lines of heavy surf. Like threading a needle, the Captain used both paddle wheels in forward and reverse to position the ship for the crossing. Finally, it lunged forward with both paddlewheels digging deep in the water and moving between the rows of the curling, roaring waves. With the deck twisting and shifting up and down, their horses started to whinny, and the men rushed to their stalls to calm them down. A few minutes later, they were able to stand back at the rail, watching as the *Morning Star II* entered the estuary of Tillamook Bay. It was a short but threatening crossing that got the mens adrenaline going.

"Bully for you." Whiskey Joe said. "You survived a calm day crossing. The Tillamooks did it every day, in all kinds of weather, with just sea canoes and paddles."

"Yes, but they weren't carrying livestock and freight. It took a white man to figure that out," Lightfoot answered.

As the *Morning Star* paddled into the northern reaches of the bay, it approached a small fishing village next to a river. The hamlet was only a few shacks with three fishing trawlers tied up to a floating dock.

"Is this Tillamook?" Lightfoot asked.

"No." Joe answered over the shore sounds of barking dogs. "It's just a white man's fishing village, right where my family lodge used to be. Now, like all my people, it is gone. The river next to it is called *Mi-me Chuck*. It is where I learned to fish."

"So you were born here?" Gus asked, watching the dreary village slip by.

"Yes. Mother had a bad luck delivery with me and almost died. She survived because my father intervened with the chief who wanted to kill her."

"Why did he want to kill her? Lightfoot asked.

Joe frowned, "It not worth telling. I'll help with the animals. We will be at Tillamook soon."

Within the half hour, the *Morning Star* was moored at a floating dock at the confluence of the Tillamook, Wilson, Trask and Kilchis Rivers. Here the men walked their animals off the boat and up a ramp to a rocky point Joe called Kilchis. Waiting on this mesa were wagon loads of commodities, freight and mail for the return trip to Astoria.

"It short ride to town. I show you way," Joe said, pointing east.

Gus and Lightfoot saddled up. "Do you want to ride double with me?" Gus offered, with an outstretched hand.

"No, I stretch my legs," Joe answered, taking off his boots and slipping on a pair of moccasins. "You find the Courthouse behind Still-well General Store. I see you there."

With that said Whiskey Joe tied his boots around his neck, crouched down with bended knees, bedroll in hand, and took off running like a young buck in rutting season. Gus and Lightfoot smiled at each other. "This should be fun," Lightfoot said, digging his knees into Whirlwind. Gus did the same with Rocky, while leading the mule Gracie with a short rope. Damn, it was good to be back in the saddle again.

Gus found Lightfoot and Joe waiting for him at the hitching post in front of the General Store. They both had smiles on their faces.

"I beat him," Lightfoot said. "But not by much. He can run like the wind."

The men dismounted and tied their animals to the post. The town of Tillamook was just a handful of two-story buildings on either side of a dusty road. There was a sawmill, storehouses and churches, dry goods, and a blacksmith shop mixed in with a saloon and the General Store. Everywhere you looked, there were still stumps in the ground from clearing out the trees to build the town. Tillamook was just another dusty pioneer village, looking to make its mark in the west.

The men went into the store. When Gus asked the clerk where he might find Sheriff Rigby, the man pointed to the rear of the building and told him that the county rented Stillwell's storeroom as the Courthouse. "You'll find the Sheriff back there, or out back at his jailhouse."

Rigby was an older man with graying temples, a weathered face, and hands the size of a beavertail. He shared the storeroom with three other county employees: the clerk, the surveyor and the assessor. They all worked together next to a small open space that was used as a courtroom when the Circuit Court Judge rode over from McMinnville for his monthly visits. Tillamook was a young county still planting roots and finding its way.

Gus did the introductions of himself and Lightfoot as the new Deputies for Sheriff Chance and gave him the envelope of the wanted posters. Sheriff Rigby stared fixated at Gus' face, and he knew there were questions coming.

"What happened to your eye?" the Sheriff finally asked.

"Lost it in the war," Gus answered, noticing that everyone in the storeroom was looking his way.

"What did you do in the war?"

"Cavalry Captain," Lightfoot answered. "We served together."

"You were together in the war?" the County Clerk asked from his desk.

"Yep," Lightfoot said proudly.

Gus shook his head with a grin on his face, "On opposite sides."

The room snickered and Gus introduced Whiskey Joe to Sheriff Rigby as their hired guide.

The Sheriff eyed the breed for a long moment with a stern expression. "Joe and I go way back. He's been to town many times. And he always seems to bring trouble with him."

Now all the eyes seemed to stare at Joe. He had been reluctant to come into the store, and now Gus knew why. "You didn't tell me you had bad blood here. What's going on, Joe?"

Joe shook his head, with a long face and sad glowing eyes. "I like Kickapoo, wander around with no place to go. Me just young buck from reservation that get into trouble. But no more. I have squaw now. She is good woman and we have lodge. Sheriff Chance hire me as guide."

"I only remember you as a thief and a liar," Sheriff Rigby said to him. "I don't want any trouble with you."

Joe's face flushed with anger as he moved his hand to the pommel of his knife. Gus, standing next to him, bumped Joe with his shoulder. "We are on our way to Fort Yamhill to pick up some prisoners," Gus said. "So Joe will be with us, all the way over and back. There will be no trouble, Sheriff."

Rigby nodded his approval. "Joe should know the way to Fort Yamhill. I think he spent some time in their stockade." He handed Lightfoot a county map. "It's a hard two-day ride to the fort, so take this map in case your 'hired' guide runs off."

Sheriff Rigby had dressed down Joe in front of everyone in the room, which was something Gus would never do. Scolding subordinates in public was like pouring salt on an open wound. It just wasn't done.

Gus shook hands with the Sheriff, "We are burning daylight, so we better get going."

When they stepped back into the storefront, Gus said, "If you need anything for the trail, buy it now."

Joe's face was still red with anger and he had not said a word about being humiliated. "Lightfoot," he finally asked. "Loan me a dollar until we get back to Astoria."

Clint did, and he bought a bottle of whiskey on the way out of the shop. Gus didn't like it but he wasn't about to add insults to his miseries. Once outside, Joe took off running while Gus and Lightfoot mounted their horses and followed him heading east-southeast.

That evening, they made their first camp next to a stream down inside a shallow gully, to be out of the wind. After a pot of coffee and some bacon and beans, Joe cracked his whiskey bottle and started drinking from it. Still, he hadn't said a word about what Sheriff Rigby had said. He just squatted by the fire, staring at the flames.

Lightfoot pulled on his own bottle and finally said, "I was a hell-raiser when I was a young buck, as well. One time, I poured molasses all over a Sheriff's saddle. Then I lit firecrackers under his window and yelled the Indians were attacking. He couldn't get off that damn saddle for days! Yes, I got in a lot of trouble and spent a few nights in jail. But I grew out of it."

Gus was surprised by Lightfoot's empathy. He seldom if ever talked about his past.

With firelight on Joe's face, he finally looked up from the flames and replied, "I don't understand you two. Mexican man wear gray coat, white man wear blue coat. You are enemies and kill each other. Now you are friends?"

"The war is over," Gus answered. "Now the blue and gray coats are Brothers."

Joe shook his head. "Why white man always win?"

"There are more of them than stars in the sky," Lightfoot answered. "Make your enemy your friend and you'll will be happy again."

"I not know how to do that," Joe said, taking a drink of his whiskey.

"Don't lie and don't steal. It's as simple as that," Gus answered, putting more logs on the fire. "It's the white man's golden rule."

Joe frowned, shaking his head. "The white man gets the gold and the Indians get ruled."

Friendly Flirt

Like the butterfly she was, Lucy soon made friends with almost everyone who came and went from the public pier where the *Louise* was moored. She relished living aboard and liked to sit on the forward deck of the boat, coffee in hand, watching the skiffs leaving empty and returning in the afternoon full of fish.

Lucy got to know all the fishermen by name and would help them unload their catch and clean their fish for the local markets. Most of the salmon catch would be sold for export and placed in a salted brine that could preserve the fish for a year or more. The salted fish had a bitter taste, but was a food staple and a commodity for many of the merchant ships. Some of the catch was sold fresh to local markets, and some to the two canneries on the river. It was there at the fish tables of the dock that Lucy perfected her filleting skills, dressing and cutting all the different species of fish. She was fast and accurate, with little waste and no complaints. The seasoned fishermen were soon leaving her a few coins as 'tips' and few slabs of fresh fish for helping them out. These crusty old anglers soon became part of her extended family and they watched over her like mother hens.

In the evenings, Lucy roamed the hills around Astoria in search of herbs, spices and plant roots that she could dry on her cook stove, to be ground-up and sampled for her secret fish-spice recipe. It was a search she enjoyed, and she kept detailed notes on each mixture she tried with the canned salmon she purchased or the filets she was given.

A few days after her Brothers departed for Tillamook, Lucy noticed an unfamiliar skiff rowing up to the pier with a load of wooden crates. After the rower stepped onto the dock and secured his boat, Lucy recognized him as young Robert Hume from San Francisco. She didn't say a word to him until he was walking past the *Louise,* carrying a heavy box. "Hello, Bob. Looks like our trails cross again. Do you remember me?" she asked, sitting on the forward deck of her boat with coffee in hand.

Robert turned to her with big eyes and a surprised look. Then he recognized her. "Lucy! What are you doing out here?" he asked, sounding dumbfounded.

She smiled. "Having my morning coffee. Would you like some?"

"Sure. Why not? That sounds great," he said, putting the crate down on the dock next to her boat.

Lucy moved through the forward cabin and into the rear compartment to get him a cup of coffee. "Do you use cream or sugar?" she yelled.

"Black is fine," he yelled back. "Where's your brothers?"

Lucy reappeared on the forward deck and handed him a porcelain mug. "It's hot. Gus and Lightfoot are Deputy Sheriffs now, out on patrol. Where did you come from?"

He pointed across the river. "Portuguese Point, on the Washington side. That's where we're building our new cannery. It's a long row, so this coffee tastes great."

They chatted for a good long time and caught up on all the news. Lucy told him about gold mining, coming to Astoria, McLoughlin, and her brother Leon. She even showed him her new high-top shoes. She liked Bob. He was fun, handsome, and young.

He told her about leaving San Francisco, and how his brothers had come to Astoria to build a modern, steam-powered cannery. "It's amazing," he said. "It's so automated now. Flip a few levers and you can produce more cans of fish in one day than we used to do in a week."

Bob spoke with his blue eyes dancing, clearly proud of his brothers and their scheme to build a new cannery on the river.

"Do you have a girl friend?" Lucy flirted.

He blushed and chuckled. "Not a lot of girls out here. You're the first pretty one I've met in Astoria."

"What's in all your crates?"

"My brothers sent me to town to sell our old hand-cranked canner. We won't need it anymore."

"Is that the machine you showed us at Turner's Cove?"

"Yes," he answered. "I remember you cranked out a few cans of fish. That was fun. Do you want to buy the old machine?"

Lucy smiled, her imagination running wild. By having such a contraption, she could can her own fish. It was tempting. "How much?" she heard herself ask.

"My brothers paid fifty dollars for it, a few years back. They think it's worth thirty-five dollars today."

"If I bought it, would you set it up for me?" Lucy asked with a pleading smile.

Robert stood and peered down into the forward cabin. "There's a fish table down there and room for the steamer. Yes I'll set it up for you."

"Good. You do it and I'll get my purse."

Bob was overjoyed. "Wow! I didn't think I'd sell it this fast. I'll get the rest of the crates and go to work."

Within the hour, Bob had all the pieces bolted together and set up, next to the fish table in the forward compartment. He even gave her a crate of flat empty cans, ready for rolling and soldering into containers. The last thing he did was refresh her memory about how the machinery worked and give her the printed instruction booklet that had come with the machine.

When they were finished, Lucy invited Bob into her cabin and filled his mug with more coffee. Then she brought out her leather purse and dumped its contents out on the table. She had no idea how to count money. All she knew was to let the other person do the counting.

At first, Bob wasn't sure what to do next, and they just gazed at each other. Then it dawned on him. "You want me to count it out?"

She nodded and smiled as Bob started stacking up the coins. Once they were sorted out, he counted them. Lucy had $19.55.

"I'm sorry," he said. "You're short $15.45."

Lucy was puzzled, with no idea what to do. Finally, she removed another porcelain mug from the cupboard and poured its contents out on the table. It held $1.85 in small coins. "My tips," she said proudly.

Robert hesitated. He liked this girl, but he couldn't go back to his brothers with just $21.40. They would give him the devil.

Then a voice rang out from the dock, "Hello on the boat. Sheriff Chance out here, Lucy. Can I come aboard?"

Lucy knew something was wrong, and Gus had told her only to trust the Sheriff. "Yes, please do, Sheriff."

When he stepped down into the cabin and saw all the money on the table, and a young man with Lucy, his demeanor turned serious. "What goes on here, Lucy?"

"It's not what you think, Sheriff," Robert said. "Lucy and I are old friends."

"How in hell do you know what I was thinking, boy?" Chance replied, looking around the compartment. "It's not proper for a young woman and a man to be alone together."

"She bought a canning machine from me, and we were just counting out my money."

"Yes, I buy machine," Lucy added. "What is word *proper*?"

"What canning machine?" the Sheriff asked.

Robert gestured to the forward cabin. "It's up front. Let me show you. I'm Robert Hume. My brothers and I are building a new cannery across the river, at Portuguese Point."

"Yes, I know," Chance answered gruffly as they moved to the forward compartment.

Robert showed him the canning device and how it operated. The Sheriff asked a lot of questions about the machine and listened closely to the boy's answers.

"Why do you need such a contraption Lucy?" the Sheriff asked as they returned to the aft cabin.

"I will make canned salmon for my brothers, for when they are on patrol. But I don't understand money," Lucy said with a sad face. "Seems I no have enough."

Sheriff Chance, still angry faced, turned to Robert. "Your

brothers want thirty-five dollars for an old, used machine. Lucy will pay you twenty from her purse," he said, separating twenty dollars in coins on the table and reaching into his pocket. "And I'll loan her ten dollars from my pocket. You'll go home with thirty dollars. Is that satisfactory, boy?"

Robert nodded with a frown, "That works for me, Sheriff." Then he turned to Lucy. "When the cannery is done, I'll row over and take you out there for a tour."

She smiled back at him. "Yes, I would like to come over."

"Swell," the Sheriff said with a grin. "Your work is done here, Robert. Have a good, long row back to Portuguese Point."

At the time, no one knew that young Robert Hume and Sheriff Chance had just helped Lucy take root as the seafood queen. It would take a few more years of learning about money and growing up, but Lucy now held her own destiny in the palm of her hand.

Unfortunately, that 'growing up' part started just a few days later.

It was all innocent enough. She happened to bump into Reverend Hathaway while taking one of her evening walks. He couldn't have been more friendly, as he crossed the street just to say good evening to her.

"Hello, Miss Lucy," he said, and tipped his hat. "Your auburn hair looks radiant in this late-afternoon light. You are such a picture of virtue. Do you remember me? I'm Reverend Hathaway."

She stopped and nodded at the preacher, with a quick curtsy and a smile. "I remember you, Reverend. You're the man with the tattooed hands."

"Where are your brothers? They didn't like me much, and I wanted to apologize to them. We just got off on the wrong foot."

Hathaway flashed Lucy his bone-white teeth and a pleasant smile. "Forgiveness is so divine."

"They are Deputy Sheriffs now, out on patrol. I'll tell them of your apologies when they return."

Lucy turned to start walking again, but the Reverend put his hand on her shoulder. "Are you here in town alone?" he asked with a benevolent smile.

She smiled back at him. "No. Sheriff Chance is watching out for me. Good evening, Reverend."

That's how it started, so simple and friendly. Lucy had been taken in by his dramatic gestures and sweet-talking tongue. She had been fascinated with his Love/Hate tattoos and his raspy voice. She saw no reason to fear him, and still didn't understand why Gus and Lightfoot despised him so.

The next day, they bumped into each other again at the General Store. Hathaway was buying cigars, while Lucy purchased some fresh bread. They talked for a few minutes about the weather, the high store prices, and what the Reverend called the Great Day that was coming soon. "The next time we talk, I'll tell you a story about it. It's going to change our lives forever."

He lit one of his cigars as they stepped outside. "I always enjoy talking with you, Lucy. You are so pretty, and such a breath of fresh air."

Lucy blushed and said good-day.

The very next day, as Lucy was gutting and filleting fish on the dock, she looked up and saw Reverend Hathaway standing next to the hotel, looking down at her. But once he noticed that she had seen him, he disappeared

That Sunday evening, Lucy stayed aboard the *Louise,* working on her spice recipes. Earlier, in the forward cabin, she had cranked out ten cans of fresh salmon, using four different herb recipes. Now, with the oil lamps burning, she sat at the table in her cramped cabin, using a scratching awl to mark the tin cans with information about the date canned and the spices used, something she did with all her new cans of seafood.

"Hello in the boat," a deep male voice rang out from the dock. "Reverend Hathaway out here, Lucy. I'm with someone you need to meet. May we come aboard?

Lucy frowned. She wanted no visitors. The apron she wore over her coveralls was stained with fish guts and blood. Her hair was a mess and she was tired. She glanced up at the entry to her cabin. The hatch cover was slid open but the door was latched from the inside.

"I have good news about the Great Day that's coming. May we come aboard, Lucy?" He shouted again.

"Yes," Lucy yelled back reluctantly. "The door is latched from the inside. You'll have to reach down and unlatch it."

The boat twisted in the water with the weight of Reverend Hathaway and his guest as they came aboard. They moved to the hatch door, and the Reverend unlatched it from the inside. A young lad, with peach fuzz and freckles on his face, was the first to be step down into her compartment. The Reverend was next, but not before re-latching the doors as he stepped into her cabin.

Hathaway gazed around the room with an air of curiosity. "Your brothers are still gone?"

"Yes," she answered. "Who is this young man that I should meet?"

The preacher nodded. "Forgive me. This young man is Walt Johnson. He is part of the Great Day that's coming."

Walt looked at Lucy with a shy, frightened face. "Nice to meet you, ma'am," he said in a quiet, polite voice.

"Where did you get this boat?" Hathaway asked as he moved around the cabin. His waistcoat was open and his bull whip hung from his belt.

"The county owns it. They are letting us stay on it. Why are you here, Reverend?"

A sinister smile transformed his face, "I can see you're excited to hear about the Great Day." He turned and put a hand on Walt's shoulder. "This young man is a virgin. Just like you, I hope. Have you laid down with a man yet?"

Lucy didn't understand. "Yes, many times, with my brothers, and my Indian family, and with the Cheyenne braves. Why?"

The Reverend's face turned red with anger. "You fornicated with all those men?"

Lucy shook her head. "What is *fornicate*?"

"You don't know the story of the Immaculate Conception and Jesus Christ?" he asked, looking askance. "Are you some kind of a heathen?"

"My brothers and I read the Bible, but I don't recall fornicate. Why are you so mad?"

"I want you and Walt to breed like animals. To have a baby without sin, because you and Walt are without the sin of the flesh. Your baby will become the second coming of Jesus Christ."

It took a moment before Lucy understood his 'breed like animals' comment. When she did, her green eyes came alive. "You are crazy-man. No baby for me. Why you come here with loco idea?"

"I'm not asking," Hathaway said with a manic smile, removing his bull whip from his belt. He moved to Lucy, still seated at the table by the galley. "You will do as I say. And *never* call me crazy." He stopped short of the table and cracked his whip across her face.

The cattail stung her cheekbone and she screamed with pain.

The preacher turned to Walt. "Take your clothes off, boy, or you'll get the same."

When he turned back to Lucy, she threw a can of salmon at his face.

The can bloodied his forehead.

"Get off my boat!" She yelled, holding the side of her face.

The thrown can stunned the preacher for a moment, and Lucy yelled again for help, trying to crawl out from behind the table, clutching the sharp awl in hand.

He raised his whip again and snapped it across the booth, just missing Lucy as she bolted out, screaming for help and raced for the cabin door.

But it was latched, and the Reverend dragged her back into the cabin, slapping her in the face. "You little hellcat, you'll do as I say!" They struggled, rolling around the floor, with blood flying from the preacher's forehead. Lucy pricked him twice with the awl, but he outweighed her by over a hundred pounds, and overpowered her.

The next thing Lucy heard was the sound of cracking wood as someone broke through the latched doorway and landed on top of the Reverend with a thud. It took several heartbeats before Lucy realized that the massive man was Pong, Mary Ann's manservant.

He peeled Hathaway off of Lucy and threw him hard against the bulkhead between the two compartments. "You no hurt Lucy. I kill you!" he threatened, and smacked the preacher hard with his open hand.

Hathaway pushed him away and raised his whip hand.

Pong caught the cattails in mid-air and pulled him close, trapping him against his giant body. Then Pong picked him up and threw him out through the broken door like a sack of potatoes. Scrambling up the steps after him, the Indian picked up the

Reverend again, and lifted him high over his head.

With her adrenaline pumping, Lucy ran up to the deck and screamed, "Don't kill him. He is loco in the head."

Pong looked down at her and hesitated. "Let's see if he swim," he said, and threw Hathaway overboard.

They heard a big splash.

Weak with relief, Lucy turned to him. "Pong, where did you come from?"

"Mary Ann send me with news of Leon."

In the dark, they couldn't tell what might have happened to Reverend Hathaway. So with her face marked bright from the whip, Lucy ran to the Sheriff's Office for help.

The preacher was never seen again around Astoria. Sheriff Chance and the Judge Bean surmised that the man just couldn't swim.

As for Walt, after a short investigation, he went home to his parents.

Pong, on the other hand, vowed to stay with Lucy until her brothers returned. He set up a hammock in the forward compartment and soon became her shadow around town.

As for Leon, Lucy sadly learned that he had signed on with a merchant ship, several years earlier, and no one knew his current whereabouts.

Who to trust was one of the many hard lessons Lucy had to set herself to learn.

Fort Yamhill

At first light the next morning, the men found the gully they had camped in shrouded in a dense, damp fog. Visibility was less than a half-mile and the country side was quiet as a tomb. As Lightfoot tended the animals, Gus broke camp and packed away their gear. Only Whiskey Joe sat on a log snag, drinking the remains of the previous nights coffee.

"Just keep riding south-southeast. You'll have open country until midday. When the fog lifts, you'll see three tall, forested peaks. Head for the timberline of the middle mountain. I'll meet you there in a grove of Alder trees," Joe said, with his tin cup in hand.

"Where the hell are you going?" Lightfoot asked, saddling up

Whirlwind.

"Got an old friend I want to see," Joe answered.

"You're getting paid to guide us," Gus said, rolling up the tent. "Not just to tell us where to go."

Joe tossed out the remains of his cup. "That's what I'll do, Deputy, it's an easy ride to the tree line. But it will be a hard afternoon's ride over those mountains. See you at midday."

They watched as Joe snatched up his bedroll and rifle, crouched down, and disappeared running into the fog.

Lightfoot chuckled as he also saddled up Rocky. "He's like the wind, blowing any old way he can."

Just as the men mounted up for their journey, they heard horses galloping their way. As they waited in their saddles, both men adjusted their holsters. They had no idea who the riders might be.

Within a few moments, like ghosts, the galloping riders came slowly into view: Sheriff Rigby with two other men.

"Whoa! Glad we found you boys," Rigby said in the swirling fog as the riders pulled alongside Gus and Lightfoot. "Where's your guide?"

"He took off running half an hour ago. Why?" Gus answered.

"Someone broke into the General Store last night. They took a pair of pearl-handled Colt revolvers that came in on the barge yesterday. A witness said they saw an Indian riding out of town last night, about two a.m. Was Whiskey Joe with you all last night?"

The other riders with the Sheriff had long, angry faces. They looked to be out for blood.

"He was with us in camp all night," Lightfoot said firmly.

"Lightfoot is right," Gus added. "Joe was here all night, and our horses were hobbled and tethered. None of us went back to town, last night."

One of the other riders turned to Lightfoot with a frown. "Anybody can unhobble a horse and sneak out of camp."

"Not with my hobbled horses," Lightfoot snapped back. "I use a special Comanchero slip knot that no one can untie but me."

"That's bull shit," the other rider said with contempt.

"No it's not," Gus said, glaring at Sheriff Rigby. "I've never figured out his knots. When you fight Indians, you learn to respect Indians."

Rigby shook his head with a frown. "I was sure it was Whiskey Joe. Trouble follows that man like his shadow."

"Not this time," Lightfoot said, glaring at the other two riders.

The fog did lift and Joe was right; it was an easy ride over open country all the way to the forest. There they found their guide waiting for them in a small grove of Alder trees. From there, he took the point in leading the Deputies into the tall, dark rainforest.

He called the trek the Three Rivers Trail. Most of the journey was up, down, and across numerous creeks and rills. These streams were the only roads through a forest so tall and dense that the canopy often blocked out the sun and sky, leaving only an overhead blanket of glittering green. When the rivers and streams petered out, Joe would find hidden game trails that meandered in and around open gullies. Everywhere they looked, there were long strands of moss dangling from the tree limbs, and the forest floor was littered with vegetation and wild mushrooms. It was slow going, and mostly on foot, leading the horses up and over the fallen log snags and through the thick underbrush.

"This trail of yours is like a coal tunnel to hell," Lightfoot groused many times.

Late in the afternoon, they came to a large meadow next to a stand of burnt-out trees. These dead, charred, black sentinels stood tall in a sea of new green covering the forest floor. It was a haunting place, large and undisturbed, struggling to gain life again.

They stopped there for the day, to bask in the late sunshine of the clearing and set up camp. Each man had a job: Lightfoot cared for the animals, Gus established the camp and built a fire pit, and Whiskey Joe went on the hunt for any game that might fill their cook pot.

When Joe returned, he had four fish for the fry pan. When Lightfoot came into camp he had an armload of fire wood that included some charred logs.

While Gus did the cooking, the men sat around the fire, drinking coffee and watching the evening stars come alive.

"How was your friend?" Lightfoot asked. With gloves on, he

hacked at a charred log with his hunting knife.

"He was gone," Joe answered. "No signs of life around his shack."

"How long since you last saw him?" Gus asked, turning over the fish in the pan.

"Two years." Joe frowned. "He was old then. Probably dead now."

"Who was he?" Lightfoot asked, still hacking at the charred log.

"My father. He and his squaw ran trap lines around here. There was a day when these mountains were full of beaver."

Gus glared at Lightfoot in the fire light. "Why are you hacking at that piece of soot?"

"I want to see what's under the bark," Lightfoot answered.

"Why?" Gus chuckled removing the frying pan from the fire.

Lightfoot flipped the short log around to show the end cut. "I sawed this off from one of the burnt trees. See how white the wood is? And the log is as light as a feather."

"So what," Joe said looking at the log.

"There's no moisture in the wood. The fire must have sucked all the water out. All those dead trees out there are as dry as a bone."

"I'm with Joe – so what? Let's eat, before it gets cold." Gus replied.

After their meal, Lightfoot continued hacking at his log. He couldn't say why. Something fascinated him about the charred wood; it was as if it was calling his name.

As they drank their evening whiskeys, Gus told Joe about their morning visit from Sheriff Rigby, and about the stolen pistols.

Joe didn't seem surprised. "White men always think red man is a thief. They cast the first stone without looking for truth."

"Do you even own a pistol?" Lightfoot asked.

He shook his head. "No. I no need white man's guns, only rifle for hunting."

"You should have a side arm for your protection," Gus said. "The prisoners we are picking up are bad hombres."

"I'm only guide. I not fight your fight."

Lightfoot chuckled, still hacking at his log. "Well, Captain, at least we know where we stand with Joe. He likes our money, but not us."

The next day was as long and difficult as the first day, only this time with gray skies and rain. It was late in the afternoon before they got out of the forest and into open country, with gentle rolling hills. Sheriff Chase had been right: the rainforests of the Pacific Northwest would eat you up and spit you out. This was no place for tenderfoots.

They found, and approached, Fort Yamhill with the sun low in a dark sky as rain showers rolled in from the southwest. The entry to the fort wasn't much, just two large log block houses straddling a muddy wagon road. There wasn't a front gate or guards, and no bastions or log walls. They rode right into a parade ground with wood-framed buildings scattered around the perimeter.

The men were wet, cold, and hungry, and they looked forward to hot meals and soft beds. Gazing around the muddy grounds, Gus spotted a two-story white clapboard building with a flag that blew in the wind. Gus and Lightfoot turned for this command post with their hat straps under their chins and their seal-skin slickers dripping wet. Joe, on the other hand, had no such protection. He looked like a drowned rat as he ran alongside of them. Out front of the post, they slid off their wet saddles and tied their horses to the hitching post. Entering the building from the front porch, with their slickers dripping, they found a lone one-stripe soldier stoking a pot-belly stove.

He looked their way with a frown as they came through the door. "You're getting water all over my floor," he said returning to his desk. "What do you want?"

"We're Deputy Sheriffs from Astoria. Here to pick up some prisoners," Gus answered. "I need to see your Commanding Officer."

The soldier shook his head, "He ain't here right now. Come back Monday."

"Soldier, get the hell off your ass and onto your feet when you talk to an officer. This is Cavalry Captain Gus Savage," Lightfoot shouted.

The man jumped to his feet. "Thought you said you were Deputy Sheriffs."

"We are both," Lightfoot said, glaring at the trooper. "With your CO gone, who is in charge of this shit hole?"

"That would be O'Keefe, sir. He's out back, taking care of business."

"Would that be Sergeant O'Keefe?" Gus asked, with a surprised look.

"Yes, sir. Sergeant Major O'Keefe."

Just then, they heard the back porch door open, and in walked a pudgy middle-aged, cheery-faced man, Sergeant Major O'Keefe. He glanced at the visitors, then did a double take when he recognized Gus.

"I'll be damned," he said loudly, coming to attention and saluting. "We have a real officer in our midst. Pleased to see you again, Captain Savage." O'Keefe and Gus had served together at Fort Laramie in Wyoming a few years before. He had been a Buck Sergeant at the time.

"Pleased to see you made Sergeant Major, O'Keefe," Gus replied, returning his salute with a friendly grin. "Who and where is your Commanding Officer?"

"That would be First Lieutenant Lovejoy, sir. He's up the trail at McMinnville on military business. He should be back on post Sunday night," O'Keefe reported. "What can I do for you, sir?"

"We've come over from Tillamook, two miserable days on the trail. We're here to pick up the Parker Brothers. We need some hot grub and a place to bivouac until Sunday morning," Gus said, looking around the empty room with its half-dozen desks. "I've got all the paper work and warrants for the prisoners but Lieutenant Lovejoy will have to sign the release."

"Yes, sir," O'Keefe replied, then glared at whiskey Joe. "What's with the breed, sir?"

"He's Tillamook and our hired guide, over and back. None of your concern. Can you help us out?"

The Sergeant Major smiled broadly. "Yes, sir. Private Carson here will take you to the mess hall and get you fed. Then you can sleep here. Upstairs, you'll find two rooms with cots, and I'll get some troopers to take care of your mounts. After your meal, sir, let's have a nightcap and I'll fill you in about the Parker Brothers. They're real assassins and not worth spit."

Later that evening, with Lightfoot and Joe upstairs in their cots, the Sergeant Major opened a bottle of bonded whiskey and told Gus all the particulars about Fort Yamhill. The post was one of five military forts built close to coastal Indian reservations in the early 1850's. Now, only fifteen years later, most of the forts were being phased out and abandoned. At one time, Fort Yamhill had held a company of hundreds of soldiers; now it was a post of less than fifty officers and men. "The Indians police themselves and fortunately, they're not much trouble anymore." O'Keefe said.

He talked about Lieutenant Lovejoy with great disdain. "He's a graduate of West Point and is as arrogant as a preacher on a Sunday morning. He's got a chippy up in McMinnville where he spends his weekends, leaving the dirty work for me."

"How did the Parker Brothers come into your custody?" Gus asked, standing next to the stove as he sipped his whiskey.

"We didn't know a thing about the massacre up in Timber, at the time. Our troop was just out on patrol, up in the Gaston area, when we stopped in town for some supplies. That's when the town Constable told us about four drunken men in a local tavern, bragging about burning down a farmhouse. He asked for our help and of course, Lieutenant Lovejoy agreed. So, using us as back-up, the Constable went back into the saloon to talk to the strangers. They shot him dead right there in the barroom. That's when all hell broke loose. When the smoke cleared, we had two wounded troopers and they had one dead, one in the wind, and two in custody. It was a bloody mess, sir, and all because Lieutenant Lovejoy opened fire before his troops were in position. Now he thinks of himself as a great warrior, but there's nothing to love about Lieutenant Lovejoy, and no joy in my heart about the man. I wouldn't follow him across a bridge."

"When did you learn about the massacre?" Gus asked, moving back to the Sergeant Majors desk.

"Two days later, sir."

"How did you learn they were the Parker Brothers? Did the local folks know them or did you take them back to the town of Timber for identification?"

"No, sir. We found a family Bible in the saddle bags of the older brother. He fessed up to being Robert Parker and told us that the other man was his younger brother, William. It's all right there, written in their family Bible sir."

Gus poured himself another shot of whiskey. In the lamp light, he could see that his friend had gotten older. "Tell me about their dead comrade."

"Not much to tell, sir," O'Keefe replied. "The brothers wouldn't tell us his name. Said they didn't know him, just a saddle tramp that came into the bar for a beer. We buried him here at the fort as an unknown. But we do have a sketch of his dead face, and we have all his traps."

"And the man that got away?"

"He slipped out the back door just before the gunfight. He looked to be the youngest in the bunch. I saw him ride away on a tall dark mustang with white stockings. He's in the wind now, sir."

Gus took a big gulp of his whiskey. "I'll want to see the prisoners in the morning. After that, we'll do an inventory of their livestock and traps. Until then, I'm off to bed. Thanks for the nightcap, O'Keefe. It's nice seeing you again."

The next morning Gus, Lightfoot, and O'Keefe walked over to the east blockhouse that guarded the entry to the fort. The log bulwark was two stories tall and served as the stockade for the post. The lower floor was for the guards, while the upper floor was the guardhouse, with four iron cells.

One of the guards welcomed them and showed them up the stairs to the cells. The jail room was dark and smelly, with only small gun ports cut into the logs for light and fresh air. It was a primitive jail with only two prisoners behind the bars.

The guard shouted at his prisoners, "On your feet. You have visitors."

The two men stood up from their cots, with blankets around their shoulders, and looked through the bars at the newcomers, with their faces long and gaunt. One prisoner was a tall, big-boned, older man with white hair and a beard, both of which were long and straggly. His face and clothes were filthy and he wore only a pair of dirty wool underwear, without any shoes. The other prisoner was younger and shorter, with unkempt sandy hair and sad brown eyes. He, too, wore only tattered underwear. Both men reeked of urine and sweat.

"Get us out of here," the older man demanded, with a slight southern accent.

"My brother needs a doctor and we need food," the younger man added.

Gus stared at the two men and the squalor of their cells. The men wore iron shackles on their ankles which had caused red sores to form on their lower legs. His Quaker upbringing could not believe what he was seeing.

"How long have they been in here, Sergeant Major?" Gus asked, turning away from the bars.

He shrugged. "Couple months, more or less sir."

"I've seen enough," Gus said, turning for the stairs.

"So have I," Lightfoot replied, shaking his head.

Under a clear sky and a warming sun, Gus and Lightfoot were quiet as they walked back to the command post. Both knew that military justice was often cruel and inhumane, but the squalor they had just witnessed set them back on their heels. Finally, Gus stopped and turned angrily to the Sergeant Major. "What the hell goes on here, O'Keefe? I've never seen white men treated like that. Who ordered such treatment?"

The Sergeant Major shook his head sadly. "I tried to tell you, last night, Captain. Lieutenant Lovejoy thinks of himself as a great warrior now, so he laid out strict orders for the care and feeding of *his* prisoners."

Gus glared at O'Keefe. "I'm the ranking officer at this post, here and now, so I'm rescinding his orders. I want those prisoners fed, bathed, trimmed, clothed and shoed right now. I'll take them out of here tomorrow morning, with or without Lieutenant Lovejoy signature on the release forms. Do you understand?"

The Sergeant Major smiled. "Yes sir, Captain."

When they got to the command building, they found the Sergeant Major's desk stacked with saddle bags, bedrolls and pouches. "These are the personal effects of the brothers and their dead comrade."

The Captain thanked him and sent him off to supervise the

clean-up of the prisoners. Once he was gone, Gus asked Lightfoot to go over to the stables and check-out the horseflesh and weapons of the three men. "Select the best horse of the lot and find us a sturdy saddle bag harness. And bring back a gun belt for Joe. The Parker Brothers will ride double all the way back to Astoria."

"You think that's wise?" Lightfoot asked with a questioning face.

"Yes, as long as we have them ride butt-to-butt, like those Sioux warriors back on the trail," he answered with a smile.

Lightfoot nodded. "I remember. Those warriors didn't know what the hell to do."

With the room to himself, Gus sat down and started an inventory list of all the personal effects of the prisoners and the dead man. There wasn't much: dirty clothes, tobacco, some snus cans, and a few coin pouches. All totaled, he found just $4.22 in the pouches. These men had been traveling light.

In the saddle bags of the dead man, Gus found an old, wrinkled letter address to a Johnny Johnson, General Delivery, Wichita, Kansas. It was postmarked April 18, 1865, just at the end of the Civil War. It was from his mother in Alabama, begging him to come home as the war was over. She needed him on the farm, and his family missed him dearly. She offered to send him money if he was broke, and said she had cried all night when Robert E. Lee surrendered.

Now Gus knew for sure who the dead man was: Johnny Johnson was not only a killer but a Rebel, as well. Not that it meant a hill of beans anymore.

One of the last items Gus picked up was the Parker Brother's family Bible. It was an old book, with scratches and scars on the black leather binding. The pages were dog-eared and water-stained. The Bible had seen better days, and the inside front cover went back three generations of the Parker family. Gus read the entries, with their dates and places of birth, all of which were in Missouri.

At the bottom of the second inside page, he found the entries for William and Robert. They were brothers, separated by five years according to the dates of birth. Gus scratched his head, recalling his jail visit. The old man looked a lot more than just five years older than his younger brother, maybe because it was hard to see them very well in the darkened block house, or maybe because the dates were wrong.

At any rate, he had seen enough. He closed the Bible and reached to put it back in the saddle bags. Then he noticed a small folded paper sticking out from the spine.

Plucking it free, he unfolded the paper.

It held just five handwritten words. ~~Parker~~ (crossed out) ~~Murphy~~ (crossed out) ~~Anderson~~ (crossed out) Cummings (not crossed out) and Prescott (not crossed out).

Gus held the slip of paper in his hands and reread it a number of times. It made no sense to him, but he put the note in his pocket.

Gus stood and walked around the empty office. He felt as if he was missing something but he didn't know what. Why had the Parker Brothers killed the Anderson family in Timber? Were the brothers really who they said they were? And, if not, why had they lied? What the hell was going on here?

Fort Yamhill

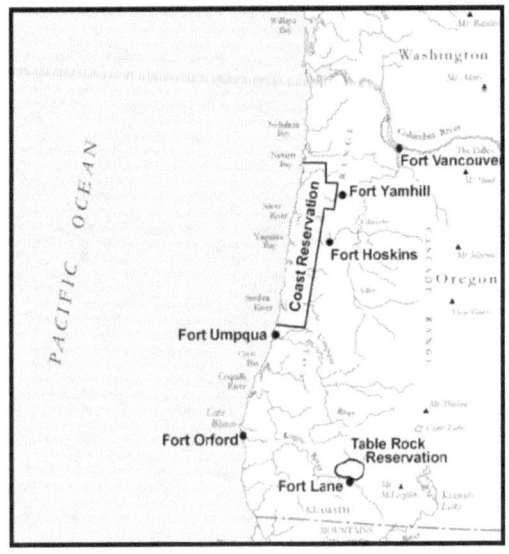

Chapter 8 - Mountain Trails

Timber

That last evening at Fort Yamhill, Gus and Lightfoot returned to the stockade to inspect their cleaned-up prisoners. They found the Parker Brothers still shackled in leg irons but bathed, trimmed, and clothed in Army dungarees, with new ankle-high work boots. Without their beards and straggly hair in the way, Gus got a much better look at the two men as they ate their meal with tin plates in hand. The bigger, older brother, William, looked to be middle-aged, while the other brother appeared to be ten or fifteen years younger. That just didn't add up with the dates in their Bible.

Gus talked to them through the cell bars. "We are Deputy Sheriffs. Tomorrow, we're taking you out of here to Tillamook, then up the coast on a ship. When we get to Astoria, you'll be tried in a court of law by Judge Bill Bean for the Anderson massacre. Our warrant is to take you to Astoria, dead or alive. It makes no difference to us which way it will be."

"Never heard of any Anderson massacre," William answered. "Sounds like a crock of Yankee shit."

The younger brother Robert, got up from his cot, empty plate in hand, and moved closer to Gus and Lightfoot. "My brother is telling you the truth, Deputies. We were just riding through that cow town when the bluecoats jumped us. We weren't doing nothing to nobody. Could you get us more food? We're near starved in here."

Both men spoke with a hint of a southern accent, but then many people in the west did. "Save your excuses for the trial," Gus answered turning to leave. "I'll see about more grub."

On their way out of the stockade, Gus talked to the guards, "Take their leg shackles off in the morning and handcuff them. We'll take the leg irons with us for the trail. Get them some more food for tonight; I want them trail-ready at first light tomorrow."

Long shadows lay across the parade field as Gus and Lightfoot left the stockade and walked slowly back toward the Command Post.

"Why so quiet, Captain?" Lightfoot finally asked.

They stopped, and Gus sighed. "Look, this is just between us... but I don't think the Parker Brothers are the Parker Brothers. That's just an alias they're using. No one knows for sure who they really are, and I don't want their escaped comrade dogging us all the way to Astoria. He could be big trouble for us."

"That's all true," Lightfoot replied. "But we know for sure they killed the Constable up in Gaston, and the Anderson family before that."

"Do we? They claim they never heard of the Anderson massacre. The only person who could identify the real killers is the shopkeeper at the Timber General Store. That's where I think we should go, to Timber. He can give us a positive identification."

"That's fine with me, Captain, but it'll add more days to the trail. And how the hell do we get there from here?"

"The Sergeant Major can help us, and maybe Whiskey Joe knows the way. But don't say anything about my suspicions until we can prove it."

Lightfoot nodded. "Might turn out to be a wild goose chase, but why not? We're getting paid by the day. Are you going to tell O'Keefe that you're no longer in the Calvary?"

"Nope. But I'll sign all the papers just as a Deputy Sheriff. It's like bluffing at poker. Let them think what they want to think."

Lightfoot grinned. "Gee, a little white-lie. Whatever happened to that Quaker lad?"

"He grew up in a war," Gus answered with a sullen grin.

Later that evening, Gus and the Sergeant Major exchanged

paperwork. The government got the warrants for the two prisoners, and the Captain got a release for both brothers, signed by Sergeant Major O'Keefe. He also gave Gus the affidavits regarding the capture of the Parker Brothers.

"After your judge is finished with the brothers, up in Astoria, Yamhill County wants them to stand trial for the Constable's murder."

"Good luck with that," Gus replied. "I think Judge Bean has a rope in mind for them."

When they were done with the papers, Lightfoot and Whiskey Joe joined them, and they talked at length about traveling to Timber. None of their maps had any notations for such a place. It was only Whiskey Joe who had a vague recollection of where the town might be. "Long ago, my father and I trapped up in those mountains. During one trip, we stumbled onto a logging camp that was called Timber. Maybe today it be a village."

With the help of Joe and the Sergeant Major, their plans were made. They would ride open country to the town of Gaston, then turn north-northwest, looking for a river called Nehalem. Once on the river, they would follow it upstream, hoping to find Timber.

"Then where do we go?" Lightfoot asked.

"Over more mountains to a place called Saddle Mountain. Then down to the beach on a good Indian trading trail, two more days." Joe answered.

"Good," Gus said, reaching for a curled-up gun belt on top of one of the desks. "That's six days to Astoria." He gave the belt to Joe. "You'll wear this and ride a horse for this part of the trip."

"I tell you, I no fight white man's fight," Whiskey Joe replied defiantly faced. "I run and scout with rifle, that all I do."

"Then you can run back to Sheriff Rigby in Tillamook," Gus said. "Arm yourself, and ride a horse or you're no longer our hired guide."

Lightfoot turned to Joe. "The Captains right. These brothers and their escaped friend could ambush us anywhere along this trail. We need an extra gun and horse."

"I get paid what you get paid, if I help fight white man's fight?"

Gus removed the brothers coin purse from his saddlebags and

gave Joe two silver dollars. "That's all I have. I'll give you two more dollars when we get to Astoria."

Reluctantly, Joe agreed, and Lightfoot took him over to the stables to pick out a mount. Once they were gone, the Sergeant Major brought out the bottle of bonded whisky from the night before and poured Gus a drink. Then he offered to send some troops to escort them as far as Gaston. "Lieutenant Lovejoy won't agree with my offer, sir, but it's the right thing to do."

But Gus turned him down, "Thanks, but that won't be necessary, O'Keefe. Let's keep your stripes on your sleeve. If you get in hot water with the Lieutenant, just use me as your excuse."

At first light the next morning, the four horses and the mule were made ready for the trail. The last horse to be mounted was a tall, grey sorrel that had once belonged to the older Parker Brother. On this horse, the prisoners rode in what the Cavalry called a restraint mount. It was an odd-looking way to ride, with one rider looking forward and the other rider facing backwards. The two men were leather-strapped together, back-to-back, riding atop a wood and canvas pack saddle, with their hands handcuffed in front of their bodies, and their legs harnessed to the pack saddle. During the Civil War, the Cavalry used this type of horse mount to transfer Rebel prisoners to the rear echelons. It was an uncomfortable ride that severely limited the movement of the riders.

As Lightfoot secured the brothers on the pack saddle, Gus checked their straps, harness and handcuffs. As he did, the older brother, who was riding up front, squirmed. "This is my horse, you son of a bitch. How dare you steal it," he shouted. "You're just a damn Yankee horse thief."

Then the young brother shouted from the rear, "And some damn Indian is riding my horse."

Finished with his inspection, Gus looked up at the two riders. "Here's the rules, boys. If you cause any trouble on the trail, my Scout will hobble your two necks together like a horses legs. You don't want that. Dead or alive, it makes no difference to us."

"Hey, Night-Eye, what if I got to piss?" the older brother asked.

Gus moved to Rocky and mounted him. "You'll piss when I piss, or piss on yourself. That's what assassins do."

With amber skies and a fresh breeze, the detail rode across the parade ground, with a few troopers watching from their barracks. Some of the soldiers shouted obscenities at the brothers, and one added, "Hang them both, back to back." While other troopers saluted and shouted encouragement to the Deputies. Gus returned their salutes and called out to the Sergeant Major, thanking him for his hospitality. The riders exited Fort Yamhill with Gus tethered to the double mounted grey sorrel, while Gracie the mule, Lightfoot, and Joe rode just behind the brothers. As the bugler blew reveille and Old Glory was run up the flagpole, the column turned north and was soon out of sight.

It was a pleasant ride on good roads that ran up and over rolling hills and across shallow valleys all the way to Gaston. About midday, on the outskirts of town, the column stopped next to a creek to relieve themselves and eat some jerky and corndodgers. The prisoners did the same, one at a time, wearing leg irons and guarded by Lightfoot. During this stop over, Gus got his first really good look at the brothers in the bright sunshine, and he soon noticed two things about the older man that he had missed before: he had a scar on one cheek that had previously been hidden by his beard, and he favored his right leg. Gus made mental notes of these identifying marks, worrying about what else he might have missed about his prisoners.

"We're not going into town?" Lightfoot asked, remounting Whirlpool.

Gus remounted Rocky. "No. From what O'Keefe told me, the town folks might want to lynch our prisoners. You take the point and turn north-northwest for those tall mountains in the far distance. Keep an eye out for anyone dogging us and find us a good campsite."

"Hey, Night-Eye," William shouted from the grey sorrel, "you told us Tillamook. This is the wrong way."

Gus frowned at him. "Thanks. I'll check my compass."

That afternoon, along the trail, Gus mulled over what he knew about the Parker Brothers again and again: their southern accents, their age disparity, and how opposite they were in their personalities and looks. What was he missing? He pulled out the piece of paper that had dropped out of the Bible and read the words again. That's when the last word, *Prescott*, hit him like a bear claw to a bee hive: Killing Joe Prescott, the General he had met aboard the side-wheeler *Chrysopolis*. He'd told Gus about the McKay Brothers, William and Jasper, who were wanted by the Government for war crimes.

Gus shook his head not believing his own thoughts. That just couldn't be. The war had ended four years ago. Besides, the older Parker Brother wasn't a redhead, and his younger brother didn't stutter. Gus was grasping at straws. He shook off his thoughts, not wanting to relive those dark days when his own family had been massacred by the bushwhacker McKay, back in Kansas, during the war. When in the hell would that pain stop?

A few hours later, with the landscape changing to a more rugged terrain, Gus spotted Lightfoot returning. He soon pulled up alongside and gave him his report.

"There's a big fresh-water lake coming up. The far west end of it has a good place to camp. There's a grove of trees where we can chain up the prisoners."

"How far from here?" Gus asked.

"Maybe three miles. We should be there before sundown."

"Good. And I want you to do me a favor. Tonight, around the campfire, see if you can befriend the older Parker Brother. Let it slip out that you rode with Quantrill during the war. See what he has to say, if anything, about the war."

"Why? The war is old news, Captain."

"Just humor me," Gus said with a smile. "I've got a notion in my head that won't let go."

That night in camp, Gus and Lightfoot secured the brothers by using the handcuffs and leg irons wrapped around trees. Just in front of them, they built a fire pit where Gus cooked up a concoction of beans and canned salmon, with more hardtack and coffee. It wasn't fancy, but it was filling, and the pot was emptied almost immediately.

"Night-Eye," the older brother asked, with his back against a tree, "why don't you let us ride double the way it should be? We give you our word that we won't be any trouble."

Gus glared at the older man over the fire. "Yep, that sounds reasonable. Why not trust an assassin?"

"I ain't no assassin," the younger brother insisted. "I've never killed nobody."

Lightfoot brought out his bottle of Tequila and took a gulp. Then he handed it to Joe, who hadn't said a word all evening. Joe, too, took a swig, then handed the bottle back to Lightfoot.

"How about me?" the younger brother asked, watching them across the flames.

Lightfoot tossed out the remains of his coffee and poured some mescal into his tin cup. Then, moving around the fire, he handed the cup to the older brother while saying to the younger, "Age has its privileges."

Gus gathered up the pots and pans from the meal and moved towards the lake to clean up. "A waste of good Tequila," he said, glaring down at the two shackled brothers.

With the moon shimmering on the lake, Gus crouched on the shoreline, washing up while he eavesdropped, as best he could, on the conversation between Lightfoot and William. His Scout could be a real sweet talker when he put his mind to it.

When Gus returned to the camp, he told Joe to take the first watch and wake up Lightfoot around midnight. Then he stretched out next to the fire, with his back resting against a tree. On one side of him he placed his rifle, on the other side the shotgun. Then he removed his hat and the patch covering his mangled eye. In the firelight, he could see both brothers watching his every move.

"Hey, Night-Eye, you lose your eye in the war?" William asked.

"Yep," Gus answered, getting comfortable under a blanket.

"Why do you take the patch off at night?" the younger brother inquired.

Gus shook his head, "My bad eye stays up all night, watching while my good eye sleeps."

The brothers looked at each other. "No shit. It can see in the dark?" Robert asked.

"Yep," Gus answered, looking over at Lightfoot, who had a grin on his face. "The bad eye sleeps under the patch during the day." The brothers weren't very bright!

With Whiskey Joe riding point, it was a long, grey day before they found what he called the Nehalem River. On the shores of this shallow but swift waterway, they found their second campsite. That night, with all the booze gone, Lightfoot and the older brother continued their conversations with coffee cups in hand. William expressed his innocence by disavowing any knowledge of the Anderson massacre and blaming the Pony Soldiers for the gun fight in Gaston. Lightfoot did his best, trying to seem sympathetic, but he still hadn't learned anything new.

In the afternoon of the third day, they found the small town of Timber nestled on the shores of the river. The town was just a handful of wood-framed buildings, a few log cabins, and a post office.

When they rode up to the General Store and stopped, William started squirming in the pack saddle. "What are we doing in this shit hole?" he demanded.

Gus dismounted and tied Rocky to the hitching post. "Need to get some supplies. Be right back."

Inside the store, he found the proprietor, Axel Pearson, a beefy fellow with a handlebar mustache. Gus introduced himself as a Deputy Sheriff and showed him his badge. "Are you the man that gave some riders directions to the Anderson homestead, a few months back?"

Pearson nodded, with a long face and angry eyes. "God forgive me, yeah sure, I did. I was a fool. Why you ask?" he replied with a Scandinavian accent.

"I've got some men outside. We think they were the killers that massacred the Andersons. Would you take a look, sir?"

"Yeah sure," he answered. Walking behind a glass counter, he removed a pistol from a holster and checked that the gun was loaded.

"You won't need that, sir. We've got our own."

Axel glared at Gus. "I pledged to kill that SOB if I ever saw him again."

Gus shook his head. "You don't have any blood on your hands, sir. You were just being neighborly when you gave them directions."

"And what did that get me?" Axel answered: "Sleepless nights and long days of hate."

"There's an old Bible saying my father taught me. 'Dark hearts cannot drive out the darkness, only light can. Hate cannot drive out the hate, only love can. Your faith will always show you the way.'"

The storekeeper frowned. "He also said, 'an eye for an eye,'"

"I've already given one eye for hate and I won't give another. Now my only trust is in justice and the laws of our land."

Axel scowled at Gus, staring at his eye patch. "I come to America to build things, not to destroy good people like Will Anderson and his family." He hesitated a moment. Then, shaking his head, he slid the pistol back into its holster. "All right. I will trust your laws."

Once outside, Axel took a good long look at the brothers, still atop their horse riding butt-to-butt. Then, without hesitation, he said, "The older man here is the liar who told me he was a long-lost uncle to Will Anderson. He rode into town with two other men, both so drunk they could hardly stay in the saddle. One was younger and stuttered but it wasn't this young lad. I've never seen this kid before."

"The guy is lying," William yelled, still squirming in the pack saddle. "I've never been in this shit hole before."

Gus asked Axel if he'd sign an affidavit affirming the identification. He agreed, but gave Gus a warning as they walked back inside the store. "I wouldn't go parading that man around town. The Andersons were well liked, up here in the mountains, and some folk might get the idea of lynching him."

As Gus wrote out the affidavit, Axel rummaged around and found an empty gunny sack. He took it outside and gave it to Lightfoot. "Put this over the older mans head. We don't need more trouble here."

Gus had one last question and a favor to ask before they rode out of Timber. Had Will Anderson fought in the war, and if so, which side had he been on?

Axel told him yes, and that Anderson had been a bluecoat. "He never talked much about the war. Will was a quiet man who hated the killings."

As for the favor, Gus asked Axel for directions to the burnt-out Anderson homestead. He was determined to see where the massacre had taken place.

"There's not much out there," Axel told him. "The bodies burned up in the fire so we had no burials. We just put a cross out front of what had been their home."

After purchasing a few supplies, the troop rode out of town on a good wagon road heading north-northwest. A few hours later, they came to the Anderson homestead, where about twenty acres of farmland had been carved out of the forest. The only building still standing was an old barn with empty stalls. In the corral, next to the barn, they set-up camp. The prisoners were soon tethered with their leg irons wrapped around fence posts. They had been as quiet as thieves on the ride from town.

After stabling their horses in the barn, Joe watched the brothers while Gus and Lightfoot walked around the property in the late-afternoon sun. There didn't seem to be a bird in the sky, or even the sound of wind in the trees. The homestead was as quiet as a graveyard, and felt as if it was holy ground.

Their final stop was in front of the twenty-foot wooden cross the neighbors had erected. Behind it stood the charred rubble that had once been the Anderson home. For Gus and Lightfoot, the burnt-out farmhouse was a cruel reminder of the many Native lodges they had used to burn up Indian families while crossing the continent. Those were bitter thoughts, as both men had come to despise their own brutality, disguised under the name of progress for the iron highway.

May God have mercy on their souls... and on ours, Gus thought.

Finally, he asked Lightfoot, "Did you learn anything new about William?"

"Not much. He says he fought in Texas, and he talks fondly of Quantrill, but that only proves he was a Rebel."

"I want to talk to the younger brother. Maybe he can shed more light on William."

In the setting sun, Lightfoot turned to his friend. "I know what you're thinking, Captain. But this burnt out rubble is not of our making. We only did this to the Indians only when we had no alternatives sir."

Sadly, Gus replied, "Oh my God, I pray we find redemption for our evil deeds."

In the coming twilight, Gus removed the leg shackles from the younger brother and un-cuffed his hands. They walked together over to the cross and stood before the charred ruins of the farmhouse.

"You're lucky the shopkeeper couldn't identify you. I believe you had nothing to do with this massacre. But how in the hell did you fall in with this wild bunch?"

His question started their conversation, as the younger man finally opened up with the truth. His real name was Rob Mathews. He was a twenty-year-old unemployed carpenter from Portland. He had met the Parker Brothers and another man on the road to Gaston. They shared some whiskey and grub, then rode into town for more whiskey. He claimed it was all good-natured drinking... until William Parker shot and killed the Constable.

"I have no idea why he did that. Then all hell broke out! I didn't know it was Federal Troops shooting at me. I just defended myself."

"Why did you agree to be the fake younger brother?" Gus asked.

"Before we surrendered, William told me his real brother had escaped and would soon be back with more men to rescue us. So I just played along. I swear, I had nothing to do with this."

"What's brothers name that escaped?" Gus asked, with fingers crossed.

"Jasper," Rob said. "He's older than me."

That name was like a thunderbolt to Gus. "Now tell me something I don't know, to prove you're telling me the truth."

"That's easy, Deputy," Rob answered. "William has a Derringer hidden in his right boot. Jasper smuggled it in through the gun ports of the jailhouse, the night before we left."

"Why hasn't he used the gun?"

"He's been waiting for Jasper to make the first move."

With all this information, Gus had the proof he needed. He now had, in his custody, the Rebel Colonel William McKay, the man who had killed his entire family. What an ironic situation! Gus's body filled with rage; now he would have to kill the bastard, right here and right now!

"Will you stand up for me in front of a Judge?" Rob asked with pleading eyes.

Instead of answering, Gus turned abruptly and marched to the corral, where he confronted the older man with his pistol in hand.

"William," he said, looking down at the man tethered to the fence post, "take off your right boot."

"Why should I?"

With hands that trembled with anger, Gus cocked his pistol and aimed. "Do it now, or I'll blow your damn head off."

Lightfoot rushed over to Gus. "What's going on, Captain?"

"Pull his right boot off," Gus demanded.

Lightfoot knelt down and pulled the boot off and turned it upside down.

The small Derringer fell to the ground.

"Assassins, that's what's going on here," Gus said with a red angry face. "I'm going to kill this son of a bitch, right here and right now."

Lightfoot picked up the Derringer and stepped in front of Gus's cocked pistol. "Why Captain, we ain't killers anymore, remember? We got out of that business."

Gus flashed Lightfoot an icy cold stare. "You don't know what I know. Get out of my way. This man is dead."

"I know one thing, Captain," Lightfoot replied. "We aren't the judge and jury. We're just Deputy Sheriffs doing a job."

There was a long silence while Gus and his friend glared at each other like mortal enemies.

Then Whiskey Joe shouted, pointing down the farm road. "Riders coming in!"

That broke the moment. Gus, with sweat rolling down his

forehead, pointed the gun away from Lightfoot and gently lowered the hammer. Both men pivoted to the road and saw four riders coming their way. One had a gunny sack over his head, and his horse was being led by another.

They rode into camp with dust flying and pulled up next to Gus. Axel Pearson was leading the pack, accompanied by two other men and the rider without a face.

"Good evening, Deputies. I was hoping you'd still be here." The storekeeper smiled down at them from his mount.

Gus looked up at him in the fading light. "And here I was, hoping you might be vigilantes, come to hang old man Parker. He certainly needs to be dead."

Axel made a begrudging face. "Whatever happened to all that *Justice* talk you gave me this afternoon?"

Lightfoot stepped forward. "We've been moved by this place and the memory of the Anderson family. It gets a man's anger boiling." Lightfoot said, and turned a pleading gaze on his friend. "Ain't that right, Captain?"

Gus knew he had to turn down the rage inside of him. "Reckon he's right. What brings you out here, Axel?"

"We are the bearer of gifts. These two men, Hank and Keith, are my friends, and neighbors to this farm. I told them about your visit this afternoon. They wanted to thank you for bringing the Anderson killers to justice."

One of the mounted men said, "I got a slab of fresh venison for your trip to Astoria," and the other added, "Got some mountain whiskey to keep you warm at night."

Then Axel reached out and pulled the gunny sack off the head of the fourth rider. "And I brought you the younger man you were asking about, this afternoon."

Lightfoot looked up at the man, who had a frightened face and red hair. "Who the hell is this guy?"

Gus was startled to see the young man, whom he guessed had to be Jasper, the real brother of Colonel McKay. Now he had both McKay Brothers! "This fellow has to be the one that got away. The actual brother to old man Parker," Gus finally answered, not wanting to share their real identities. "How did you get a hold of him?"

Axel dismounted and helped Hank and Keith get their prisoner off his horse with his hands tied behind his back. "He just walked into my store, big as life. The last time I saw him, he was drunk, so he didn't recognize me. But I recognized him right off. He told me his name was Bobby Smith, on his way up to the mountains to do some trapping. But his horse had no traps and his lips only moved when he was lying. So I figured I'd bring him to you and sign another one of those legal papers you need."

Gus finally smiled, breathing a sigh of relief. All his peas were in the right pod.

He and Lightfoot helped secure the new prisoner in shackles and cuffs. Then, with the campfire glowing, Gus invited the riders to stay the night. They agreed, and shared the whiskey and venison while telling heartwarming stories about the Anderson family. After the tributes, each man took a turn guarding the brothers through the night.

It was during this time that Gus apologized to Lightfoot for his behavior and told him the truth about the McKay Brothers. They agreed to keep this identity secret until they were back in Astoria. For now, their prisoners were just the Parker Brothers.

The next three days were long and arduous, with Whiskey Joe breaking trail on the point and the column of riders not far behind. The weather was so miserable that even the birds went walking, with rain and winds that swirled around the forest of the high chaparral, drenching the riders from all directions. They traveled up and down, in and around the game trails, creeks, streams, and rivers that connected one mountain to the next. Much of their time was spent on foot, with the prisoners in leg irons, while the others led their mounts through deep valleys and rocky gorges with thick brushwood and giant trees that blocked off the light to darkness much like twilight. It was damn slow going, but somehow, to the amazement of even Lightfoot, Whiskey Joe kept the riders always moving in the right direction.

Finally, with improving weather, they arrived at one last saddle-like mountain to conquer. When they reached its summit, they could see and hear the pounding surf of the ocean just a few miles away from where they stood. Whiskey Joe pointed north and said, "Clatsop sand spit over there. Good trading trails, easy ride to big river." Then he turned and started his descent without looking back. "We sleep in soft dry beds tonight."

Caesar Returns

Late in the afternoon, with gray skies overhead, the open deck ferry boat from Skipanon crossed Young's Bay and docked at Pier 1, exactly eleven days from the Deputy's departure for Tillamook. With the brothers strapped back to back, Gus took the lead of their horse and turned Rocky down the main street of Astoria, with the other riders taking up the rear. They were a rag-tag-looking bunch of trail weary men dressed in soiled clothes, with dirty faces and straggly beards. With sunlight breaking through the clouds, the local Astorians turned their heads to gawk in disbelief at the sad-faced, humiliated brothers.

"Hey, Night-Eye, what are you doing with those two back-ward men?" one man shouted.

"Where have you guys been?" another inquired.

Out of curiosity, and ever so slowly, some of the locals started following the column. Soon, like the Pied Piper, the small crowd grew larger. As Gus was about to turn the corner for the Courthouse, he looked to the rear and found twenty or thirty Astorians marching along with his riders. All these people had smiles on their faces and waved at other onlookers, shouting, "Our new Deputies are back from Tillamook."

When Gus came around the corner, he found more people milling in front of the Courthouse. How did they know he'd just returned to town? Like Julius Caesar, for a fleeting moment, he felt like a conquering hero. Then he reminded himself that he looked more like a saddle tramp.

In the Courthouse crowd, he saw Lucy waving at him from where she stood next to Sheriff Chase. Gus headed Rocky in their direction. When he pulled up in front of the onlookers, he looked down at the Sheriff with a grin and calmly said, "Deputy Sheriffs Savage and Roe reporting with two brothers in custody."

Hearing those words, the spectators started applauding, and Gus flushed. Lightfoot pulled up next to him and removed his hat, bowing from Whirlwind's saddle to the crowd. Gus did the same from his horse. With smiles all around, Sheriff Chase said a few words of thanks and offered his posse a welcome home. Gus and Lightfoot dismounted, shook hands with the Sheriff, and hugged Lucy.

It was then that Gus noticed the red welt on her cheek. "What the hell happened to your face?" he whispered to her.

"Not now. I tell you story when you come home tonight," she whispered back, with tears of joy in her eyes. "I have special lady friend for you to meet."

There was more applauding and cheering as the other riders dismounted. Through all this hoopla, the prisoners sat quietly on their horse with long faces and nervous glances; as if they feared that the crowd might try to lynch them at any moment.

Gus handed the lead of the brothers horse to Sheriff Chase and they started walking their mounts towards the corral.

"How did you know we'd made it to town?" Gus asked the Sheriff.

"I've had a runner down on the pier for the last two, days watching for you. We were getting worried."

"Gosh, I didn't know you cared, Sheriff," Gus answered sarcastically.

"Good Deputies are hard to find. But stay upwind of me. You smell like skunk."

"Is there a photographer in this town?" Gus asked as they walked together.

"Yes. Why?"

"Send for him. Tell him to bring some flash powder."

"Why?" Sheriff Chase asked.

"I'll tell you after we get the prisoners safely locked up."

It took five armed men to get the brothers off their horse, still in leg irons and handcuffed with their arms behind their backs. Then they were moved into the jailhouse and up the stairs to the second floor cells. In one cell, Gus placed two wooden stools next to each other and had the prisoners take a seat, with their hands handcuffed again through the adjoining cell bars. They squirmed on their stools spouting obscenities and threatening mayhem.

With the brothers secured in the cell, Sheriff Chase turned to Gus. "Alright, why the need for a photographer?"

With the guards watching, Gus walked over to the two restrained prisoners, his expression doleful. "I should have killed these two bastards on the trail. Why I didn't, I don't know. These aren't the Parker Brothers. These are the McKay Brothers, William and Jasper. They're bushwhackers that rode with Quantrill during the war. The old man here killed, mutilated, and torched my family, back in Kansas just as the war was ending. His younger brother, Jasper here, committed the same type of war crimes. These men are evil through and through. They're wanted for these dastardly deeds by the Federal Government."

Now the two prisoners really started squirming, shouting out more threatening remarks.

Gus reached into his saddle bag, brought out two empty gunny sacks, and handed them to one of the jailers. "Put these over their heads when they start mouthing off. That's what we did on the trail. It keeps them quiet."

"Why the need for a picture?" the stunned Sheriff asked.

"We'll send it off to the government, with copies to General Prescott in San Francisco. He knows what the Colonel looks like, and he was on their hit list. That's why they killed that family in Timber. Will Anderson must have known what Colonel McKay looked like. He had to die, like all the men on the death list."

Everyone seemed stunned by Gus's revelations. He finished with a dire warning. "These men are real bad killers. If news of who they really are gets out, I fear the vigilantes might try to have their way. So, for now, let's just continue calling them the Parker Brothers."

Sheriff Chase shook his head, scowling. "Judge Bean won't like this. The government will get all the glory."

"No they won't," Lightfoot said. "The glory belongs to Gus. He figured it out."

The photographer came and using flash powder, took his picture of the two men side by side. As he packed up his equipment to leave, he promised three prints of the prisoners on the desk of Sheriff Chase by early the next morning. "What name should I use for the print?"

"Parker Brothers," the Sheriff answered.

The sun was low in the sky by the time Gus and Lightfoot, with bedrolls and saddle bags in hand, stepped aboard the *Louise*. In the aft cabin they found Lucy and another woman drinking coffee in the galley. The lady was strikingly handsome, and Lucy introduced her as Mrs. Thomas Thayer, a friend of Sheriff Chase and the proprietor of the Astoria Academy. "After my visit from Reverend Hathaway, I started staying with her," Lucy said nonchalantly.

"What damn visit?" Lightfoot demanded angrily.

"Yes, what the hell are you talking about?" Gus added.

Lucy looked at her brothers sadly and told them the story of the Reverend's visit, the welt on her cheek, and her rescue by Pong. When she finished, Mrs. Thayer added, "Sheriff Chase asked me to take Lucy in, after the incident. Now we've become good friends. Lucy is a very smart young lady."

"She teaches me to cook like white woman. I make special grub for tonight just for you. It is called losscana and come from far off Italia. It is very tasty."

Mrs. Thayer smiled and corrected her. "Please call me Roxanne that is my given name. It is called lasagna and comes from Italy. She cooked it on my stove, this afternoon. It's still warm and ready to eat, if you're hungry."

After a trail of corndodgers, both men smiled broadly licking their lips. Then Gus said apologetically, "If we'd known about this dinner, we would have stopped off at the bathhouse. Please forgive our ripeness."

"No apologies necessary, Deputy," Roxanne said with a friendly soft voice. "The smell of a working man is always encouraging. It proves they are not lazy."

With full plates, a special bottle of wine called Chianti, and flavors neither man had tasted before, they enjoyed a marvelous 'welcome home' dinner. During the meal, Gus and Lightfoot learned more of Lucy's time alone, her new canning machine, and her sad news about her brother Leon. "No one knows when he might be back in town... he famous sailor boy now."

Roxy spoke proudly of her Astoria Academy. It was a boarding school for girls ages twelve to eighteen; currently she had six students, seven if Lucy stayed on. Mrs. Thayer was a widow. Her husband Thomas had been a sea captain, lost in a horrific storm. She had immigrated to Astoria at the age of thirty, after her husband died. Roxy was a delightful and well-educated lady who taught her girls the special skills needed to survive in a male-dominated world where woman were mostly relegated to domestic chores. "I teach my girls to think for themselves and dream the impossible dreams. Someday, they will get the right to vote, and my girls we will be ready for any new tomorrow."

"Those are fresh ideas," Gus said with a condescending smile, "but I'm not sure that's going to happen anytime soon."

"Yes, they will," Lucy said. "Someday, women will own their own businesses and make their own money. Why should we work for little or no pay?"

Gus was taken with Roxanne, right off. She had a nice figure, wore stylish clothes, had spunk, intelligence, and a sweet way about herself. She was the kind of woman a man could set his compass by. But could he afford her? "What is the cost for your Academy?"

She poured more wine into his glass with a smile. "Only four dollars a week for live-in, like the county is paying me for Lucy, or three dollars a week for walk-in."

"Can I stay on in school?" Lucy asked, her smile pleading.

Gus and Lightfoot looked at each and shrugged their shoulders. "Why not?" Lightfoot answered. "But you'll be a live-in. We don't want you staying alone on this boat ever again."

"That reminds me," Gus said. "Where is Pong now? We need to thank him for your rescue."

"He returned to Oregon City when I moved in with Mrs. Thayer. But he will be back after Mary Ann gets married. He told me he no longer be her manservant."

Gus was surprised by that news. Deep down, he had thought about Mary Ann many times. He shook his head with a frown. "Did Pong say who she was marring?"

"Yes, someone called attorney," Lucy said with a confused expression. "But what is attorney?"

Roxanne explained to her, in great detail, who and what an attorney was, and the conversation continued with a second bottle of wine.

Early the next morning, after a visit to the bathhouse and fresh clothes, Gus and Lightfoot returned to the Courthouse to make their reports. They found Sheriff Chase in his jailhouse office in good spirits, drinking coffee. Chase handed them the three photographic prints the photographer had delivered. "It's a good picture of the brothers," he said. "They both have their eyes open."

Gus agreed and said he would write their report and include it with the pictures he would mail to General Prescott and Colonel Rollins. "I wish we had a telegraph line in town. It could take weeks before these pictures get there by mail."

"Well, there's a line over in Rainier. It's a small town fifty miles east of here," Sheriff Chase told them. "The stagecoach roads are good, but it's still a long ride over and back."

"We just might do that, later in the week," Gus remarked, with paper and pencil in hand. "At least I can alert them that the pictures are coming."

Gus wrote out his report and two short letters to Prescott and Rollins, detailing the events of their mission at Fort Yamhill and the suspected capture of the brothers. In his letter, he asked them for their confirmation that the picture was indeed that of the McKay Brothers. After making copies of his report and letters, he sealed and addressed two manila envelopes containing the documents and a picture, and walked the mail to the local post office. The clerk behind the counter assured him that both envelopes would be delivered within a week. There weren't any other options. Astoria was totally isolated, and everything came or went via ship.

As Gus turned to leave, the clerk stopped him. "I have some mail for you, Deputy. It just got off the boat." He handed him a fat white envelope. "It's from Sheriff Moody in Coos Bay. I thought it might be important."

Gus looked at the envelope. It was addressed to Captain Savage c/o Sheriff Chase, Astoria, Oregon. "How did you know I was Captain Savage?" he asked the clerk.

"You're the talk of the town, sir. Everyone is calling you Night-Eye. I saw you first on the *Willamette Express,* and your friends called you Captain."

Gus turned to leave again and thought: *In small towns, gossip travels faster than the mail.*

When Gus returned to the jailhouse he opened the envelope from Sheriff Moody and found official-looking papers headed Magistrate's Order & Disposition, with two paper bank drafts payable to Gus and Lightfoot. Also included was a short written note from the Sheriff:

Gus, here's the final ruling of the Magistrate. Full payment, after expenses and fees, are enclosed. Your draft is $20.00 more than Lightfoot's, as Sourdough Sam is repaying you a debt. Give my regards to Sheriff Chase.

Gus looked at the drafts and read the ruling with a grimace. The $7500.00 in gold they thought they prospected had sold for just under $5200.00. Then the Magistrate deducted his fees and expenses, and Coos Bay County did the same. The remaining balance of $1855.00 was then awarded to the four plaintiffs in the case and made payable to the legal claim owners, Captain Savage, Clint Roe, and Sourdough Sam. There was no mention of Lucy in any of the documents. She wouldn't like that. Lightfoot's draft was for $453.75, and Gus's was for $473.75. Gus looked at the checks again shaking his head. It was a lot of money, but not as much as he had hoped for. Then again, it was gold money, which was always disappointing.

Deciding to keep their windfall confidential, Gus folded up the papers and put them and the checks back inside the envelope. He'd have to talk to Lightfoot and see what he thought about handling Lucy. She'd be mad as a hornet over not getting paid for her work.

Just as Gus was about to leaving the office, Chase came through the door with a big smile. He had in hand paychecks for their first week on the job. Lightfoot's was $28.00 and his was $41.12 including all his expenses for their trip to Fort Yamhill. "Thank you, Sheriff. I'll find Lightfoot and give him his paycheck. Did you settle up with Whiskey Joe?"

"Yes, and he says you still owe him two dollars from the trail."

"He's right, I do. Did you find any wanted poster for the McKays"

He shook his head. "I went back four years but there was

nothing. Are you sure these are the right McKays, and that they're wanted for war crimes?"

"We'll know for sure when General Prescott gets the picture. He had them in custody once before and then they got away. Is there a safe bank in this town?"

"Yes, Astoria Merchants Bank, just down Commercial Street on the right. Tell old man Hanson, the head teller, that you work for me and that I sent you."

Gus found Lightfoot in the barn, cleaning and repacking their trail gear. He was pleased to get his first paycheck and joked about how small the amount was. "Being a Chief Scout for the railroad is looking better and better to me. Four bucks a day just doesn't cut it." Then Gus handed him his second check from Sheriff Moody and read him the Magistrate's ruling. His brown eyes got as large as silver dollars as he examined and re-examined the amount printed on the bank draft. He listened to every word of the ruling and had but one comment: "Wow, I'd forgotten all about that damn gold."

They talked for a while about Lucy and what her reaction might be. Then they decided to give Lucy her share of the gold money in a separate bank account in her own name. This money would be more than enough for her to stay in school until she finished up at the Astoria Academy.

That afternoon, at the Merchants Bank, they had no problem setting up accounts in their own names. But, when they tried to do the same for Lucy, old man Hanson refused. "Woman are not allowed to have accounts in our bank. Their place is in the kitchen, not in the smoky parlors of commerce."

Gus couldn't believe his ears. While he'd known that some non-whites couldn't have bank accounts, Lucy was a white woman. He fumed over the old man's comments, but Hanson had the personality of a mosquito. After some heated words, the banker came up with a compromise. Lucy's share would be deposited into their accounts, and she would be named the beneficiary of the accounts if anything happened to the men. It wasn't a perfect solution, but it was better than nothing.

Late that afternoon, aboard the *Louise,* Gus and Lightfoot did the right thing. They told Lucy the unvarnished truth about the gold money, the Magistrate's ruling, and the banks policy against woman having accounts. She listened carefully, her eyes dancing with anger as the story unfolded. She said not a word until they explained, in great detail, what the word 'beneficiary' meant. "So your name is on our accounts," Gus told her. "If anything bad happens to us, those accounts become yours."

She nodded, thinking about the words they had told her. Finally she asked, "So if you die, I get your money and your horse?"

"Yes," Lightfoot said. "What we have is yours."

Her anger turned to smiles. "We are good family. I do the same for you. If I die, you get my recipes and my canning machine."

The next morning, Gus and Lightfoot found Sheriff Chase in his jailhouse office, reading a newspaper, his expression doleful. He waved them in and told them to take a seat while he continued to read the paper, shaking his head from time to time in disbelief. When he finished, he handed the paper to Gus. "This is yesterday mornings Oregonian from Portland. There's a story about you in it. Seems like you're famous now. What do you think?"

For Lightfoot's benefit, Gus read the story out loud.

Night-Eye Deputy's Triumphal Return

Yesterday, this reporter witnessed the exciting return of the new Clatsop County Deputy Sheriff that the local Astorians call Night-Eye (real name Gus Savage). This tall, handsome Deputy, with a black patch over one eye, had in custody two notorious desperados wanted for the Anderson massacre of three months ago. Night-Eye single-handedly arrested these villains and brought them to justice, riding an old gray mule back-to-back, on an eleven-day odyssey across the high mountains. Congratulations to Night-Eye, our newest crime fighter on the Oregon Coast.

Gus's face flushed as he put the newspaper down. "This is embarrassing and it's none of my doing."

"It's more than embarrassing," the Sheriff answered. "It reads like a dime-store novel, and is humiliating for all of us who helped."

Lightfoot chuckled. "Night-Eye... I like it. Eleven-day odyssey... I like that, too. All reporters are jackals and liars."

"These are none of my words. So what can we do?" Gus said angrily.

The Sheriff nodded. "You can get out of town for a few days. Next year is the census, and you guys are going to be our County Enumerators, so I want you to become familiar with Clatsop County."

"What the hell is an Enumerator?" Lightfoot asked.

"Yeah, I'd like to know that myself," Gus said.

Sheriff Chase got out his county map and explained in great detail the job of an Enumerator. He suggested that they start with the down-river towns of Westport, Knappa, and Stevenson. "Stop at all the little hamlets in between, as well as the logging camps, sawmills, and fishing villages. Get to know the people. Tell them about the upcoming census. Ask about where everyone lives. Next year, every person has to be counted."

On the map Gus saw how close they would come to Rainier. "Can we stop off and use the telegraph in Rainier?"

"Yes, but remember that Rainier is in Columbia County. Your first eastern Clatsop town is Westport, so start your Enumerating work there."

"Who pays us for this nose-counting job?" Lightfoot asked.

"The Federal Government pays the County, and we pay the Enumerators three dollars a day, as set by Government regulations." Sheriff Chase answered.

"How long do you want us gone?" Gus asked.

"Three or four days," the Sheriff answered. "By then, this newspaper will just be a fish wrapper."

Black Gold

Forest fires were not an uncommon occurrence in the Coastal Mountain Ranges of Oregon. Most of these fires were started by lightning that transformed tinder-dry trees into a burning inferno that could cover hundreds, if not thousands of acres of timberland. Even the rain forests dried out, during some bad fire seasons. Before the white mans encroachment, the Indians often used forest fires to herd game animals into specific areas where they could be slaughtered to feed the tribe. These hunting fires were then allowed to burn on and out.

When the white man came, he brought civilization, steam-powered machinery, and campfires into the forest, which only increased the devastation of the land. Other than a few logging camps, homesteaders, and volunteer citizens, there was no organized effort to battle these forest fires. They were just allowed to burn themselves out. What remained after the inferno were acres and acres of black, burnt-out trees that stood skeleton tall, guarding what remained of the living forest. These black carcasses were of little value and were considered an eyesore. Even the game animals stayed clear of the charred clearings in the woods. The aftermath of a forest fire was like a no-man's land of a battle field, full of death and destruction.

≈

Gus and Lightfoot stood at the second deck rail of the sternwheeler *Multnomah,* watching the sights go by. They had boarded the boat at seven AM, secured their mounts and Gracie the mule in the stalls of the main deck. Their 'call-out 'destination was Rainier, one of a half dozen stops the *Multnomah* would make on her twelve-hour round trip to Portland and back to Astoria.

"I'm not sure I want to be an Enumerator," Lightfoot said. "Spending weeks out there in the rain forests, counting noses for three dollars a day, doesn't sound very appealing."

"Are you getting too old for the wilderness trail?" Gus asked with a grin. "Maybe I should get you a rocking chair."

"I'm a warm-blooded man, Captain. These damp forests are too damn cold for me. Anyhow, I have to find a way to make some real money out here."

Gus chuckled, "You're just getting old and impatient. I thought you wanted to go fishing."

"That's not real money, it's just making a living. I want something bigger and better."

The boat arrived at Rainier just after eleven. The town was small and young, with a log-timbered dock, with a working sawmill on top and a few homes and buildings perched on the shores of the river. Above the town were mountains of forest land, as far as one could see, waiting to be harvested.

Gathering up their animals, the men walked them up the ramp and into the town. After asking for directions, they found the telegraph office, and Gus went inside while Lightfoot stayed with the horses. Gus wrote out two identical messages and addressed one to Joseph Prescott, Vice President, c/o of Wells Fargo & Company, San Francisco, California and the other to Colonel Rollins c/o the State Militia, Fort Leavenworth, Kansas. The message was simple, alerting both men that a photograph of Colonel William McKay and his brother, Jasper, was on its way via the US Mail. The last line of the telegraph summed it up: 'Awaiting your confirmed identification and further instructions.' Gus breathed a sigh of relief, knowing that both men had now been given a warning regarding the brothers. All he had to do was wait for their response.

When Gus got back outside, Lightfoot and the animals had disappeared.

Their plan had been to send the telegram and start riding west for Westport, some twenty-five miles away. Scanning the area, Gus spotted their horses tied up to a hitching post in front of the sawmill, so he walked in that direction. Just as he got to the mill, Lightfoot came out the door carrying a scrap of wood.

"Where the hell have you been?" Gus asked his friend.

"Watching the mill make lumber. It's quite a task." He handed Gus the scrap of wood. "This type of milled lumber is called ship-lap. It comes in long boards that are six inches wide and an inch thick. Shipwrights must use it to build ships. But feel how heavy it is, it's so full of moisture. Not like the burnt-out wood of the forest-fire trees. That wood would be much better for building ships."

"How do you know that?" Gus grinned, handing him back the scrap of wood.

"I'm thinking on it," Lightfoot replied with a smile. "You want to come in and watch them making this ship-lap?"

Gus mounted Rocky. "Not today. Let's talk about it later."

Lightfoot nodded and put the piece of wood in his saddle bag. "It's going to rain," he said, looking up at the sky. "Better get your slicker on."

And rain it did, most of the way to Westport. The stagecoach-freight road was in good repair but soon became muddy. In between rain showers, the sun darted in and out of the clouds, illuminating their way beneath a forest so tall and underbrush so thick that steam floated into the air with the stench of rotting vegetation.

"One of the millwrights told me nobody harvests the burnt-out trees. They just rot where they stand. I think there's gold under their black bark," Lightfoot said as they traveled down the road.

"Who'd want that kind of wood?" Gus asked.

"Shipwrights, furniture makers; or so I reckon. But I'm not sure."

"When we get to Westport, we'll ask around and see what others have to say."

"You think I'm loco, don't you, Captain?"

"No," Gus answered. "You're just tired of living on crumbs."

With the sky clearing, they rode into Westport late in the afternoon. The little town seemed quiet, with few people moving about. The Deputies introduced themselves to the General Store keeper and he told them that the town was mostly deserted because it was a Saturday afternoon, which was payday for most folks working at the local sawmill. "There's still two more hours on their shift. When the pay whistle blows, the town will fill up."

The Deputies walked over to the mill and introduced themselves to the shop Foreman. He told them that the owners were in Astoria for the weekend, so Gus told him about the upcoming census, and the Foreman filled them in about the town. "Everyone around here lives nearby, with the exception of the

Erickson log camp. There are thirty or forty people up there." The Foreman gave them directions to the logging camp and told them about Eric Erickson, who owned the camp and much of the timberland up in the mountains. "He's a big Swede who loves his lumberjacks. Every Saturday night, he throws a big party for them. If he invites you to stay, don't say no. It's the best grub in the woods you'll ever eat."

Lightfoot brought out his sample board of wood and asked the Foreman a few questions. The man replied that the Westport mill also made ship-lap, and agreed to mill up a few burnt-out trees and ship the finished lumber COD to Lightfoot in Astoria. "The milling will cost eight cents a lineal foot and the shipping is three cents a foot. Don't know why anyone would want that lumber. It's black, sooty stock to work with."

But Lightfoot was delighted with the deal. Now all he had to do was hire one of Erickson's lumberjacks to cut down a few trees. He'd soon find out whether becoming a lumberman would be worthwhile or foolhardy.

They rode into the logging camp with the sun low and the wind kicking up from the southwest. It had been a miserable day, with foul weather and muddy roads ever since their departure from Rainier. The camp itself was cut out of the tall forest, with a dozen log bunkhouses and a large cookhouse connected to the main office in the center of the sprawling complex. Around the perimeter of the grounds were stables for the work horses and rusting steam-powered machinery on log skids.

The men dismounted at the office and tied their animals to the front-porch railing. Then, using a scraping iron mounted to the porch, they cleaned off the bottoms of their boots and went in through the front door.

Inside the office, they found Erik Erikson and his wife, Martha, huddled around a cluttered desk stacked with papers and pay drafts. They introduced themselves as Deputy Sheriffs and explained the reason for their visit. "How many people usually live up here?" Gus asked them politely.

"What is this word 'census,' Martha?" Erikson asked his wife, speaking with a heavy Swedish accent.

"It be like nose count?" she replied, looking a little uncertain.

Gus nodded and explained in detail the idea of a National Census, explaining how the government paid people to count everyone, every ten years. They were soon joking about Uncle Sam wasting all that good money to count the noses of all the Immigrants. "This could happen only in America," Eric said with a bright smile.

"Think of this," Martha replied chuckling. "President Grant wants to know where our noses are right now!"

The Eriksons turned out to be wonderful people with a great sense of humor. They soon invited the men to stay for dinner and sleep in their guest bunkhouse. "With the government wasting all that good money on noses, we will feed you and sleep you," Martha said proudly.

And what a meal it was! At six o'clock, the dinner gong rang and everyone in camp filed into the dining hall next to the cookhouse. Soon there were nearly forty lumberjacks waiting at the tables. These were big, burly working men, with arms the size of thighs and hands as big as pancakes. As the men waited for their food, a half-dozen women moved through the tables with mugs and pitchers of beer. The room was loud and full of gaiety as the lumberjacks drank their suds and flirted with the wenches. It was all in good fun and went on for a bit before Eric stood from his table, held up his mug of beer, and called for quiet.

As he talked about the past week's work and the good safety of his men, Martha walked along the tables, passing out the pay drafts. When Eric finished, he introduced Gus and Lightfoot as his guests. "They are Deputy Sheriffs here for a visit," he told his men.

Then a voice rang out from one of his lumberjacks. "I know who that man is!" one logger said loudly. "You're Night-Eye, the avenger of the Anderson massacre."

Applause rang out from some of the audience, and a few men stood with their mugs held high. Gus's face flushed and he turned to gesture at Lightfoot. "My partner here was with me all the way," Gus shouted back to the audience, with his own beer mug held high. He was surprised by how many of the people had read the newspaper story, and he didn't relish being the center of attention.

Then the women appeared again, this time with the food: one-inch-thick beef steaks with all the trimmings, fresh bread, and all the beer anyone could drink. It was by far the best damn meal Gus ever had on the trail. These lumberjacks knew how to live hard, work hard, and drink hard.

The next morning, with hangovers all around, Eric and Lightfoot came to an agreement on having the crew cut down four burnt-out trees from a nearby charred forest. The trees were to be limbed and the logs transported to Westport. The cost: five dollars a tree, which Lightfoot paid with a double eagle. With another hearty meal in their stomachs, and the business at hand behind them, the Deputies bid farewell and moved down the trail.

Over the next two days, Gus and Lightfoot stopped and introduced themselves to five more small hamlets and towns. It was an enlightening excursion into the underbelly of the sea of trees that dominated every mile they traveled. Clatsop County, with its endless forests and deep river fish, was a land of opportunities waiting to be harvested.

As they approached Astoria, they heard in the wind, the distant sounds of boat horns and ferryboat whistles. When they reached the top of a hill, the town came into view. Out on the river, they could see a large ship making for port, with ferryboats and fishing trawlers saluting it with whistles and horns.

Using his spyglass, Gus focused on the ship as she maneuvered for the transit pier. "I'll be damned," he said to Lightfoot. "Why would the Navy send a gunboat to Astoria?"

"Don't rightly know," Lightfoot answered, with his own binoculars in hand. "But we better get moving. The Sheriff might need us down there."

Within the half-hour, they were at the Courthouse, where they found a few people milling around. No one seemed to know why the gunboat was in port. Securing their animals, Gus and Lightfoot walked to the jailhouse, where they found the Sheriff in his office with another man. He waved them in. "Perfect timing," he said. "We were just talking about boys."

When Gus got a good look at the other man, he was dumbstruck. It was General Prescott from San Francisco. He stood and shook hands warmly with Gus and Lightfoot. "Pleased you're here. We have a lot of business to cover."

Prescott was tall and stocky, a distinguished-looking gentleman with his expensive suit and salt-and-pepper black hair. His handshake was firm, and his piercing blue eyes clear. General Prescott was not a man to trifle with.

"Gus, I got your telegram the very day your photograph arrived in the mail. Yes, that is Colonel William McKay and his younger brother, Jasper. I can give you my positive identification."

"That's great," Sheriff Chase said. "But I can't find any papers on Colonel William McKay."

The General looked at Gus, then answered the Sheriff. "The papers are out there. They are four years old, but still in effect. The Army has posted a reward of five thousand dollars for the Colonel and three thousand for Jasper. That's eight thousand dollars, Gus, and the reward money is all yours. I've already put in for it on your behalf."

Sheriff Chase had a big smile on his face as he calculated the Countys share of the reward. "Wow, that's just amazing."

Lightfoot slapped his friend on his back. "Not bad, Night-Eye. You're going places."

Gus just stood there, with his one good eye the size of the moon. He had no idea what to say or do next.

"Unfortunately, there's bad news to go with the good," Prescott continued sternly. "I'm taking the McKay Brothers back with me on the gunboat. They will go on trial at the Presidio. And, sadly Gus, I've come for you as well. The Army has decided to Court Martial you for the murder of Martín Brown at the Ogden rail yards."

Timber Cruisers 1869

Chapter 9 - Court Martial

Rewards

It took a moment for Gus to gather his thoughts. When he had, he glared at General Prescott with anger on his face.

"Let's see if I have this right. On one hand, the government wants to give me eight thousand dollars as a reward for capturing the McKay Brothers. On the other hand, that same government wants to court martial me for a crime I didn't commit?"

Prescott nodded sadly. "That's about right, Captain. And they've asked me to be your Defense Counsel, if you'll have me."

"Absolutely, General," Gus answered. "I'll be pleased to have you as my attorney."

"Military Justice? What a crock of shit," Lightfoot blurted. "The brass always wins."

Gus shook his head with a frown and turned to Sheriff Chase. "Sorry you have to hear about this – this way. I never meant to deceive you."

The Sheriff smiled at him, opened a desk drawer, and removed a Wanted Poster of Gus. "Sheriff Moody sent me this poster in the envelope you brought up from Coos Bay. Neither of us believed you were guilty of such a crime. Now you have a chance to prove it."

"That's right," General Prescott added. "General Rollins told me he has more than enough evidence to prove you're not guilty."

More surprises for Gus to digest. "When did the Colonel make Brigadier?"

"Three months ago," Prescott answered. "He's making all the arrangements for these proceedings."

With that said; the General opened his haversack and covered the desktop with papers as he explained, in detail, about the trial of the McKay Brothers and about Gus's court martial. "The McKay Brothers will be tried for the Anderson Massacre by a Federal Judge. I'll be prosecuting the brothers. They will stand trial at the Presidio on Tuesday November 23rd." He reached for a few blank Federal Subpoenas and handed them to Sheriff Chase. "Subpoena everyone who helped transport the brothers from Fort Yamhill to Astoria. They may be used as witnesses, appearing at the trial if needed."

Then he turned to Gus. "Your Court Martial will start the next day, on Wednesday November 24th, with an Article 32 hearing before a three-officer panel. I want you, Lightfoot, and the girl Lucy, to write out an affidavit of what you witnessed at the Ogden rail yards on the evening of May 10, 1869. I'll need your affidavits before I leave here with the McKay Brothers, tomorrow morning."

"Am I going with you on the gunboat?" Gus asked.

"No," Prescott answered. "You're not officially under arrest. You and Lightfoot will remain here until the Presidio Provost Marshal summons you, which should be in a few weeks."

Sheriff Chase gave General Prescott the affidavits Gus had secured on the trail from the Timber storekeeper and the two Anderson family neighbors. He was pleased that Gus had the foresight to secure such documents.

"What is an Article 32 investigation?" Lightfoot asked.

Prescott finally smiled. "It's our ace in the hole, boys. Three high-ranking military officers act like a grand jury to determine whether the prosecution has validity to move forward with a formal court martial. Their decision has to be unanimous, either to move forward or to deny such a Court Martial.

"That's still confusing," Lightfoot inserted. "But then I'm just a dumb Comanchero, trusting the white man's justice."

"Who are the plaintiff and prosecutor?" Gus asked.

"Sheriff Bill Brown of Ogden County is both," Prescott answered, lighting a cigar. "He's the one out to get you, Gus. I objected to him also serving as the prosecutor, but General Rollins turned me down. He wants the Sheriff to have his day in court."

Sheriff Chase handed Gus three blank affidavit forms. "You boys and Lucy need to write out your stories. I met Sheriff Brown a few years back. He's a real tyrant, full of himself and hate."

With papers and bedrolls in hand, Gus and Lightfoot walked to the public pier and down the ramp to the *Louise*. Once dockside, they found Mrs. Thayer having coffee on the forward deck of the boat while watching Lucy filleting salmon at a fish rack with some of her fishing friends. She greeted the men warmly. "Welcome home from your enumerating duties. Lucy will be pleased."

"What brings you to the docks?" Gus asked with a broad smile.

"Lucy likes to come here after class, a few times a week, to help her friends with their catch. I occasionally stop by to keep an eye on her. She has a magical touch with her filleting knife."

Gus and Lightfoot stepped aboard the boat. "How is she doing with her schooling?" Lightfoot asked.

Roxie's face brightened, "She's like a sponge, absorbing everything she reads and sees. Are you boys back in town for good?"

"For a few weeks," Gus answered. Then he told her the reason for the gunboat, which was all the gossip on the dock. He also told her about General Prescott and the trial he was facing at the Presidio at the end of the month. He asked her for help writing out their affidavits. She was clearly surprised to learn about the killing at the rail yards and about Gus's upcoming Court Martial, she agreed to help with the written statements.

With a rain squall starting, they moved to the aft cabin, calling Lucy in from the fish stands. When she got inside the cabin, Gus explained to her the reasons for a written affidavit. "Just tell your story as you remember it. Tell it slowly, so Mrs. Thayer can write it out."

Lucy did just that, adding a few details that Gus had already forgotten. She neither embellished nor told half-truths about what she had witnessed that evening. When Lucy finished, Roxie showed Gus the document she had written. Her penmanship was beautiful and looked much like calligraphy, so neatly spelled-out.

Lightfoot was next, and he told the story from his perspective. His recollections were more colorful than Lucy's, both in detail and verbiage, and he called out Martín Brown as the scoundrel he was. Lightfoot also mentioned the large crowd that had witnessed the fight. He finished his affidavit by quoting the Captains own words to the crowd: "Bear no false witness here, tonight. If you do, the wrath of God will be upon you."

When Lightfoot finished he got up from the galley booth and poured himself a glass of Tequila. "Now it's your turn in the hot seat, Captain."

Gus poured himself the last of the cold coffee. He had been nervous during both of his friends stories. Why? He had no idea. There was just something about Roxanne he couldn't quite understand. She had a quality about her that he didn't want to disappoint. And talking about killing a man didn't seem like a very gentlemanly thing to do.

"It's getting dark," Gus answered. "I'll walk Lucy and Mrs. Thayer back to the academy and write out my own affidavit later."

Lightfoot shrugged and smiled. "That's BS, Captain. I think your proclivities are showing."

Gus frowned at his Scout, and got him and Lucy to sign their affidavits. "I'll drop these papers off at the Courthouse," Gus said.

"You don't have to walk us back, Gus. We can take care of ourselves," Roxie said gathering up her things.

"There's a dark underside to Astoria," Gus replied. "I'll sleep better, knowing you two girls are safely home."

After dropping off the papers at the Sheriff's office, Gus and the girls walked the few blocks in the twilight under improving weather. With Lucy a few paces ahead, window shopping, Roxie remarked, "I'm disappointed that I didn't get to hear your affidavit, Gus. I learned so much about you from Lucy and Lightfoot's stories that I wanted hear more from you."

"Killing a man, for good cause or not, is not something a gentleman should talk about in polite company."

Roxanne smiled at him and chuckled. "Chivalry is not dead in Astoria! What a sweet thought from a sweet man. I'm not a demure woman, Gus. I grew up around boats and my brothers. I was wed at sixteen, widowed at twenty-seven, and I have no children. There isn't much I haven't seen or heard. So no white gloves around me."

Gus felt his cheeks flush and his heart race. Was she laughing at him or just being honest? "Sorry. It's just the way I was brought up. Quakers put their womenfolk on pedestals."

She stopped and turned to him with an alluring look. "Am I your woman, Captain? If you're interested, so am I." Then she kissed him on his cheek. "People say you're a local hero now and call you Night-Eye. If we're going to be special friends, tell me more about your proclivities."

Roxie was one gutsy lady! Embarrassed by the conversation, Gus hemmed and hawed all the way to her three-story home overlooking the river. Later, he could not recall one word that he had said after her question about his inclinations. Gus was smitten.

Later that night, with Lightfoot sleeping, Gus wrote out and signed his own affidavit. It was a document hard to write, his mind swirling with thoughts of the reward money, his upcoming Court Martial, and day dreams about Roxie. How could so much happen in just one day?

Early the next morning, Gus and Lightfoot helped Sheriff Chase and the two jailers march the McKay Brothers, in leg irons and handcuffs, down the streets to the gunboat. General Prescott also provided a detail of six sailors in full Navy uniform, rifles in hand, to accompany the prisoners. The only thing missing was a brass band! It was another street spectacle that would keep Astoria humming with gossip for days to come.

Gus and Lightfoot said their farewells to General Prescott on the deck of the gunboat. "I'll see you men in San Francisco in a few weeks," Prescott said. "I'll take care of all the details. All you have to do now is some Army time: hurry up and wait."

They shook hands at the railing and departed down a gangway, with coal smoke floating high over the transit dock. As the ship pulled away from the pier, Gus saluted the boat out of respect for the ship and General Prescott. Gus's future was in the General's hands.

When Gus had made his triumphal march down the streets with the McKay Brothers butt-to-butt, he had introduced Rob Mathews, the unemployed carpenter from Portland, as only an innocent witness to the gun fight in Gaston. Sheriff Chase had taken his written affidavit and released him without a second thought. But then Judge Bean got wind of Rob Mathews and his story of the gun fight, and demanded that the young man appear before him in his court. Rob was nervous about this appearance and asked Gus to stand up for him. Since Rob had been a big help getting the prisoners across the coastal mountains, Gus agreed to speak for him.

On the morning of the hearing, Gus gave the Judge the affidavit that Sheriff Chase had written, and Judge Bean read it aloud in open court. Immediately afterward, he started peppering Rob with questions about the truthfulness of the document. The way he worded his questions made it seem as if Rob was just a drifter looking for trouble. Gus objected to some of the Judges questions, which earned him a few angry rebukes from the bench.

"This young man needs ninety days in jail to think about his wasted life," Judge Bean finally ruled.

Gus objected. "I don't think you can do that, your Honor. Mr. Mathews has been served a Federal Subpoena to appear at the trial of the McKay Brothers in San Francisco by the end of the month. That subpoena protects him from local misdemeanors."

Judge Bean glared at Gus and said, his squeaky voice full of anger, "Who are you, Deputy, to question my authority? What law school did you graduate from?"

"I learned about subpoena power during the war, sir. I could be wrong, but I don't believe I am."

Judge Bean stood up from his bench, fuming, then hammered his gavel down and proclaimed in an angry voice, "Case dismissed!" Then he turned and disappeared into his office.

Lightfoot had witnessed this little trial drama from the Courtroom benches. After the Judges departure, he approached Gus and Rob to congratulate them on the dismissal.

"My advice is for you guys is to stay clear of Judge Bean for a while. You made no friends here, this morning."

With the departure of the gunboat and the prisoners, Gus and Lightfoot walked back to the public pier with Sheriff Chase. They wanted to look over the *Louise,* one more time, in preparation for the upcoming public auction.

When they got to the pier, they found Rob Mathews and the County Supervisor, Big Eric Nelson, waiting for them. Rob told Lightfoot that his lumber had arrived from Westport and was being unloaded in the stables. Lightfoot beamed at the news, and excused himself with Rob, to help with the lumber. But Big Eric didn't look so happy. He was the penny pincher of the county, always demanding receipts for all expenditures paid. Eric was short and skinny, with thin lips and a dark brown pencil mustache. How he got the nickname 'Big,' no one seemed to know. "We need to talk about the reward money coming our way."

The men moved to the aft cabin and went below. "Do we know when the reward will be paid?" Eric asked.

"I didn't even know there was a reward until yesterday," Gus answered.

"Eight thousand dollars is a lot of money," Big Eric said. "Money that the county desperately needs. Of course, there will be some expenses deducted from your share, Deputy Savage. And I know the Judge has some expenses, as well."

Gus shook his head with a frown. "I've played this game before. Everyone wants part of the winning pot without paying any ante. Well, that's just fine with me, if the reward is paid directly to the county."

"What do you mean by that?" the supervisor asked.

"If the money is paid directly to me, I'll give the county its share of twenty five percent. That's the identical amount the county has agreed to pay the arresting officers if the reward is made payable to the county. It's only fair."

Big Eric didn't like that answer and turned angrily to Sheriff Chase. "What the hell is going on here?"

"He's right," Chase said. "We agreed to pay the arresting officers twenty five percent of any reward paid to the county. If Gus is paid directly, he's under no obligation to us. It's a fair offer, Eric."

Big Eric fumed. "Is he going to be paid directly?"

"I can't say for sure, but that's what General Prescott implied," Sheriff Chase answered. "It's best to make a deal now, so we're not squabbling over the money when it comes."

That started the negotiations, with the county making its plea for seventy five percent of the reward, while Gus was only offered twenty five percent. The bargaining went back and forth, with heated words from both sides. In the end, they reached an agreement, a compromise of sorts. It wasn't perfect, but compromises never are. If the county received the reward money, Gus would be paid twenty five percent of it without any expenses deducted. If Gus was paid directly, he would keep twenty five percent each for himself and Lightfoot, while giving the county fifty percent of the reward money. In any event, the county would agree to sign over the title of the boat *Louise* to Gus and Lightfoot as a bonus for capturing the McKay Brothers.

"Let's keep our agreement under our hats until the money comes in," Gus said as the three men shook hands. "Around here, gossip travels faster than the wind."

With the help of Rob Mathews, Lightfoot cut up some sample boards from his stack of lumber from Westport. Then he and Rob walked around town, showing off their new light-weight wood. They visited furniture makers, shipwrights, and carpenters, anyone who worked with wood. And surprisingly, even though the lumber cost more per board foot, the wood was well received and orders were taken for more lumber in different milling sizes.

"We need to have a name for this new wood," Rob said to Lightfoot as they walked back to the Courthouse stable. "Something interesting."

Lightfoot agreed. "How about Thunder Timber?"

Rob smiled. "I like it. Can I help you get your new venture underway?"

"Sure. Why not?" Lightfoot replied. "We'll need to order more wood. And, if you're not called to San Francisco for the trial, you can take care of business while Gus and I are at the Presidio."

A few days later, an official-looking document arrived from the Provost Marshal of the Presidio. It commanded that Gus and Lightfoot make themselves available on or before 0900 on Monday November the 22nd, to the Commanding Officer of the Presidio. Included with the document were two one-way tickets for the steamship *Pacific,* departing Astoria on the morning of Friday, November 19th. Gus read the summons aloud in Sheriff Chase's office.

"Looks like we'll be spending the holidays in the stockade," Lightfoot scoffed, looking at the one-way tickets.

"What holiday?" Gus asked.

"Thanksgiving," the Sheriff answered. "President Grant just signed the new Holidays Act into the law."

Gus shook his head. "I forgot all about Thanksgiving."

"Are you guys the only ones being summoned?" Chase asked.

"Yes, it looks like that to me," Gus answered. "We're the only names in the document."

"Jail time for the Deputies," Lightfoot said sarcastically.

That evening, with Lightfoot out and about, Gus sat in the galley booth of the *Louise,* reading a book in lamp light. The events of the last few weeks had set him back on his heels, and he worried about the outcome of his Court Martial.

"Ahoy on the *Louise,*" a voice called out from the dock. Gus scooted out of the booth and opened the hatch cover to raindrops falling from the sky. Standing on the dock stood Roxanne, under the cover of an opened umbrella.

"Please come aboard and get out of the weather," he yelled over the sounds of the dancing raindrops. She did, closing her umbrella before stepping down into the compartment.

She wore a blue raincoat with a fishermen's yellow hat. "Sorry. I'm dripping all over your deck."

Gus helped her with her wet coat and hung it on a hook. "Don't worry about it. What brings you out on such a stormy evening?"

Roxanne looked around the cabin, her eyes dancing, "Is Lightfoot here?"

"No, he's in town with a friend, celebrating his new wood venture. Is there anything I can do for you?" Gus asked, admiring her radiant face.

"I wanted to talk to you about Thanksgiving. Would you fellows like to have dinner with us girls at the Academy?" As she spoke, she moved to the booth and picked up the book Gus had been reading.

"Sorry, we can't," Gus answered. "We've been summoned to San Francisco for the holidays. Could you watch out for Lucy?"

"Sure," Roxanne answered giving Gus an alluring smile. "I love that city. Wish we were coming with you."

"So do I, but not this time. It's all official business."

Roxie held up his book. "Is this what you've been reading? *Military Law: Court Martial Procedures.* How exciting is this, Gus?" she asked sarcastically, with a grin on her pretty face.

"General Prescott sent it to me. He wants me to be prepared."

"So do I. How about you preparing me a glass of wine? It will warm us up inside."

With wine flowing and the rain dancing on the roof, Roxie and Gus sat and talked like old friends for the better part of the next hour. She was a brash young woman with high opinions about herself and the students she taught. "Many people run away from life, while I would rather run into life," she said at one point. A bit later, she remarked, "The problem with religion today is that if it looks good, tastes good, or feels good, it has to be bad or sinful." Roxanne, in her own sweet way, was truly a free-spirited woman. She was open like a book, truthful as the gospel, and as strikingly beautiful as a Harvest Moon.

Finally, under a damp, dark sky, Gus walked her home and said goodbye at her door. With the wines fortification, he mustered his courage and kissed her on the lips. She whispered back in his ear. "Don't' fret about your Court Martial. This too will pass. Wish I could be with you in the Golden City by the Bay. Oh, what fun we could have."

As Gus walked back to the boat, his head was spinning. Had he finally found love or was she just a mirage?

Dime Novels

When Gus and Lightfoot boarded the steamship *Pacific* on Friday, November 19th, they found the boats First Mate, Bryan standing under a canvas awning with the Purser.

"Welcome aboard again," the Purser said, finding their names on the passenger list. "We should be underway within the hour."

"When will we arrive in Frisco?" Lightfoot asked him.

He frowned. "We should be in *San Francisco* before noon on Sunday."

Gus turned to the First Mate. "What's the weather look like for the Bar crossing?"

"Not lake-smooth like your last trip," he answered with a smile. "This one is going to be a sloppy Bar. Where's that cute sister of yours?"

"She's staying at school over the holiday," Lightfoot replied.

"Can we watch the crossing from the wheelhouse?"

The First Mate shook his head, "I don't think so. The Captain is going to be busy crossing this Bar. You should just hunker down in your cabin until we get out to sea."

"What about the hot towel brigade?" Gus asked with a smile.

The Purser raised his eyebrow with a sad face, "Yep, right after we turn south. We'll have half the passengers at the rail."

Their one-room compartments were side by side on the main deck. Each had two berths and a tiny white-tiled water closet with a toilet and a sink. The cabins were small and compact but clean and warm from a coal-fired heater. They stowed their traps and dressed in rain gear to watch the crossing of the Bar.

"You sure you're up for this?" Gus asked Lightfoot with a grin. "Last time, you didn't bring your sea legs."

"That was just a fluke. I have my iron stomach with me this morning."

Gus smiled at his friend, "Alright, Captain Bligh. Let's get this voyage underway."

Under gray and rainy skies, they walked to the bow of the main deck and searched out a covered vantage point where they could watch the crossing of the Bar. They found a short passageway under the wheelhouse that opened on the port and starboard sides of the double paddle-wheeled ship. There they watched the last of the loading of the passengers and freight. Soon, with her boilers bursting with steam, the *Pacific* was free of her moorage, sailing across the wind chop of the estuary and towards the Columbia River Bar. They saw few boats on the water and few birds in the sky. The entire landscape looked bleak and gray.

Approaching Baker Bay, on the north side of the river, the ship turned due west for the Bar, with Cape Disappointment and her lighthouse standing guard over a seascape of white curling waves as far as they could see. Soon, the bow of the ship was digging deep into the breakers, with green water spraying as high as the wheelhouse. Amid the heavy surf, the boat rolled and pitched like a wild Mustang, and the bow came crashing down again and again with a loud slap of the roaring seas.

At times, the ship got lost in the bottom of a trough of curling white water, losing all sight of land. At any given moment, they feared the ship might break apart. Then came the sneaker waves that twisted the hull like a corkscrew. With frightened eyes and white knuckles, three times Gus and Lightfoot lost their footing on the wet deck as the ship rolled, plunging one paddlewheel deep into the sea, while the other wheel reared totally out of the water. Each time, the 850-ton ship stopped just short of capsizing, with riptides swirling around her. With great effort, the ship and the men managed to right themselves and prepare for the next set of curling waves. This dance of the violent seas was not what they had expected.

Their journey across the Bar came and went in just under a half hour, but it was the most disconcerting half hour either man could have imagined. Once past Point Adams, on the south shore, the ship turned south-southwest, to the blue, wind-chopped swells of the Pacific Ocean. With water dripping off their raingear, Gus and Lightfoot found that their ordeal left them with a new admiration for all the ships and crews that had survived the crossing of the Columbia River Bar.

"Now we know why this place is called a boneyard," Gus said as they staggered back toward their cabin.

"Why would anyone want to be a sailor?" Lightfoot grumbled.

"If this was just a sloppy Bar, I'd hate to see a stormy one," Gus answered.

By the time they returned to their cabin to dry off, the wet towel brigade was working the rails, tending to the sea sick passengers. It was a spectacle that Lightfoot, ignored not wanting to conjure up his bout of seasickness aboard the *Enterprise*. Surprisingly, despite a few bruises, both men still had their sea-legs after their journey across the Bar.

That evening, with the seas still choppy and half the passengers still sick, the dining hall and barroom were nearly deserted of fellow travelers. When the men entered the chow hall Lightfoot saw two women at a table by themselves and like a hound dog in heat, made a beeline for a table next to them. With a pleasant smile, he tipped his hat as the men took their seats. "Good evening, ladies. Pleased to see you survived the Bar crossing."

They just smiled back at him with a nod and went on with their conversation. The ladies were pretty and both were all painted up for their first evening on the ship. Gus paid them no heed, and they kept giving Lightfoot the cold shoulder all through their meal. Finally, after they had departed the hall, Lightfoot gave up. "The hell with those girls. They don't know what they're missing. Let's play some poker."

Finding five for a game took some doing, but soon Gus and Lightfoot were playing cards with three other men, all of whom were traveling to San Francisco for Thanksgiving. The game was two-bit ante and slow going. The table talk was all about the crossing of the Bar and how frightened the other passengers had been. One of the players kept eyeing Gus; the man had introduced himself as Raymond Ramsey of the San Francisco Morning Call newspaper. He was young, dressed in a blue tweed suit with a high-collared white shirt and a waxed goatee. He didn't say much, but he kept staring at Gus and his eye patch. This was not uncommon, but Raymond kept smiling at him, as well, as if they were old friends.

"Are you a reporter?" Gus finally asked him.

"Yes," he replied. "I write feature stories for my paper. I just finished a story about the proposed new lighthouse for Point Adams." He folded his poker hand with a frown. "I know who you are, Deputy. Read about you in the Portland paper, a few weeks ago. You're called Night-Eye, the avenger of Colonel William McKay."

Lightfoot's face brightened. "Yep, you got the right man. We've ridden together for the past three years."

Gus frowned at Lightfoot. "I don't like that nickname. And I had lots of help taking the brothers into custody."

"Bet you boys have plenty of great trail stories," Ray replied.

"No, we don't," Gus said firmly, remembering that embarrassing story in the paper. "Let's play the game."

The cards started out good, but Lady Luck said an early farewell. But then, Gus wasn't really concentrating on his cards. His head was still filled with doubts about his Court Martial, Roxanne, and the trial of the McKay Brothers. His stack of gold and silver coins soon went from tall to short, and Gus finally threw in the towel. Enough was enough.

He excused himself and went to the bar, where he took a seat for a night cap. Lightfoot stayed at the table, as one of the pretty ladies from the dining room took Gus's warm seat. Lightfoot was on a winning streak, enjoying himself as he flirted with the lady and regaled her with old stories of the Iron Highway. Gus was in no mood for such trivialities. Finishing his drink, he stood to go to his cabin, and found the newspaper man standing next to him.

"From what Lightfoot tells us, you guys have some great stories," Ramsey said in a matter-of-fact voice. "What if I told you I could make you a rich man?"

Gus glared at him. "Had gold fever once, it didn't take. Reckon I'll never be rich."

"Yes, you will," Ray answered with confidence. "Ever hear of dime novels?"

Gus nodded with a smile. "I've seen them but never read them."

"Well, I write them. Give me five minutes and I'll explain how I can make you rich."

Gus chuckled. "How can anyone get rich, one dime at a time?"

"Let me buy you a drink and I'll tell you how."

"Why not?" Gus answered, and sat down again.

Over the drink, Raymond told Gus the ins and outs of dime novels. Long before the Civil War, dime novels of sensational stories filled with romance and adventure were wildly popular back east. After the war, these cheap little booklets of fictionalized stories became all the more popular, sold in dime stores, at newsstands, and in dry goods stores all around the world.

"Last year," Ray told him. "One publisher in New York produced a series of stories about an Indian maiden who married a white trapper. The first book sold 65,000 copies in the first six months of its publication. That's how a man can become rich a dime at a time."

"How big are these books?" Gus asked.

"Small enough to fit in the overall pockets of the hayseeds that read the stories. Each book is thirty to forty thousand words long. They sell for tens cents a book, of which the authors, that's you and me, get a three cent royalty."

"What's that in real money?"

"If you sell 65,000 books, just under two thousand dollars. And that's just for your first book."

"Why do you need me? I'm no writer."

"The publishers want real stories from real people. That's

where Night-Eye and your sidekick Lightfoot come in. You tell me your stories and I ghost-write your books, using your pen name."

"And what do you get paid for all of this?"

"I do all the work and you pay me a penny for each book sold. Tomorrow, tell me your story of capturing the McKay Brothers. I'll write out a short treatment and send it to a publisher I know in Chicago. If he likes it, you'll be on the gravy train."

Gus shook his head with a frown. "What the hell is a pen name? What's a treatment? And what's a ghost writer?"

Over more drinks, Raymond answered his many questions, and they talked more of Rays idea. In the end, Gus still wasn't sure he wanted anything to do with dime novels. The whole thing sounded too good to be true. Was he being hustled? In any event, he wanted to wait and see what Lightfoot had to say, so he agreed to sleep on Rays proposition.

The next morning, over a breakfast of hash and eggs, Lightfoot was all smiles, full of stories about his evening of playing poker with one of the ladies. "Her name is Bernice. She's married to a ship's Captain in the Navy. He's been out to sea for over six months. She's lonely and loves to play poker. The other lady is her sister, Nancy. They're going home for the holidays. Maybe we could have dinner with them tonight."

Gus shook his head with a harsh frown. "She's married, Clint! So don't go poking around where you're not wanted."

"She's sweet on me, Captain. I can tell by the way she looks at me. Anyhow, my fantasy has always been about conquering sisters."

Gus shook his head again. "Do what you want. But don't get me involved. While you were playing cards with Bernice, I was making us money. Remember that newspaper man from last night? He's wants to make us rich. Do you want to hear his story or lust over your fantasies?"

Lightfoot smiled at his friend. "Money always trumps love."

With fresh coffee in their mugs, Gus outlined Rays proposition. Both men were cautious of the reporter and his motives. Trusting any newspaper man was like stalking a mountain lion that could turn on you at any time. In the end, however, they both agreed that they had nothing to lose by telling Ray the story of the capture of the McKay Brothers. If the publisher liked it, they could revisit the deal.

Late that morning, Raymond sat down with Gus and Lightfoot, and they told him the story of the McKay Brothers capture. As they talked, Ray made notes on paper, using a funny-looking alphabet. He asked many questions, pressing them for descriptions of people, places, and things. He was thorough and professional, and it seemed clear to them that he knew what he was doing. In the end, he had over a dozen pages of what he called 'shorthand' notes, a hodgepodge of abbreviated words and symbols that only he could read. The men were impressed by his written secret code.

"I'll longhand my treatment after lunch and let you guys read it before dinner. It's a good story and a good start."

"We are having dinner with some ladies tonight. Please join us," Lightfoot said.

"What ladies?" Gus asked, startled.

"Is one of them Bernice, the one who played poker with us last night?" Ray asked.

"Yes, and her sister Nancy. Do you know these girls?" Lightfoot answered.

Ray gave Lightfoot a sheepish smile. "Unfortunately, yes. I've seen them many times on different sternwheelers. Underneath Bernice's dress and her makeup, you'll find the body of a man called Lucky Jake Collins. He's a cheat and a pimp, and he works the boats as a poker shill. Nancy is his wife and a prostitute. One way or the other, Jack always gets his money."

Lightfoot was bewildered. "Why the need for a woman's costume?"

"His face became too recognizable. The ship owners started blackballing him. So he came up with 'Bernice' as a disguise."

Gus laughed out loud, almost choking on his coffee. "Well Lightfoot, you always wanted to conquer sisters!"

"But I beat her, last night, playing poker." He answered in disbelief.

"No, you didn't," Gus said, still chuckling. "He was just setting you up for tonight."

Lightfoot replied sheepishly. "What's this world coming to?"

The three men had dinner together that night, but without the ladies. Over the meal, Ray read aloud his two-page treatment. His story seemed factual enough and his characters sounded believable, although he did overstate the gun fight in Gaston, and Whiskey Joe's help finding the right trail over the mountains. But, all and all, it was a good outline of the story.

"I'll post this tonight in the ship's mail. It should be on my publisher's desk by Tuesday of next week. There are just two more things we have to do. I'll need a list of your top ten adventures and a picture of each of you for the cover of your books."

"We can take care of that in San Francisco," Lightfoot said with a frown. "That is, *if* we aren't in the stockade."

Ray smiled and poured more wine. "Don't worry about your Court Martial."

"You know about that?" Gus asked.

"Yep. I'm covering the McKay trial for my paper. Your Court Martial is right after it. Don't worry about it. It's not going very far."

"How the hell do you know that?" Lightfoot asked.

"Let's just say a little birdy told me so," Ray answered with a charming smile.

The name 'Lucky Jake Collins' had struck a chord with Gus. General Prescott had pointed the man out many months before. He had warned Gus that the man was a cheat and a shill, and it was his girlfriend who had humiliated Gus by calling him a saddle tramp. Now, according to Ray, Jake was dressed up as a woman and pimping out his wife. Was that wife the girlfriend called Nancy? Gus had to know. He remembered her as one of the most beautiful women he had ever seen. Now she was a prostitute! How could that be?"

Gus bathed and shaved, polished his boots, and dressed up in his finest poker outfit. He was curious and nervous about confronting her again, but he had to know how such a beautiful goddess had fallen from grace.

Later that evening, when he walked into the barroom, there were three tables playing poker. One of those tables included Bernice and Lightfoot, with three other men. Gus glanced around their table and surveyed the action. Bernice seemed to have the edge, but Lightfoot seemed to be holding his own. Gus eyed Jake's disguise, it was near perfect; he did look like a woman with bold features.

Gus whispered in Lightfoot's ear, "Why are you playing cards with a drag queen and a cheat?"

Lightfoot smiled at him and said aloud, "Join us. Bernice is new to poker and we are giving her lessons."

"Sure you are," Gus said, looking around the room. "I'm going to get a drink. Do you want one?"

"No, thanks," Lightfoot answered. "I need to keep my wits about me."

At the bar, Gus took a seat and ordered a whiskey. He nursed his drink, watching the action at the other tables. One thing was for sure, he wasn't playing poker with Lucky Jake Collins. He wasn't that stupid.

Soon, the other woman entered the bar, dressed in a revealing red taffeta gown. She walked around the tables, flirting with the other players. In the dim light, Gus couldn't quite make her out. She was a redhead, not a blond. She was pretty, but not the queen that he remembered. She moved to Bernice and gave her a hug. All the men at the table laughed at what she said. Then she came to the bar and ordered three drinks. As she waited, Gus got a good look at her. She wore high-heeled shoes and white linen gloves, with a choker around her slender neck. She had deep-set hazel eyes, high cheekbones, and overdone makeup. This was indeed the girl that Gus had spoken with, so many months before. She even had on the same perfume.

"Do you remember me, Nancy?" Gus asked her.

"Yes, from last night at dinner," she answered, looking over at Gus. "Your friend was quite rude."

"No, I mean six months ago, aboard the paddlewheeler *Chrysopolis*. You had a sharp tongue for me. You called me a saddle tramp, among other things."

She chuckled. "Sorry if I hurt your feelings, honey." She gave him an alluring look. "I do vaguely remember you and your patch. You were the soldier boy who came on to me. You look much improved. You must have prospered. You might be worth my time now, for the right price." She winked at him. "If you know what I mean."

She looked tired, and older then Gus remembered her. She was no goddess, but still tempting. "Unfortunately, I think I do. Where's your boyfriend, Lucky Jake Collins now?"

Her expression turned testy and she gathered the three drinks into her gloved hands. "Never heard of him. I need to get these drinks to my sisters table."

With that said, she turned and walked away without another word.

Gus just sat at the bar for the longest time. He hadn't gotten much satisfaction from confronting her again. Deflated and dejected, he felt the same as six months before. He just wasn't confident around women; no, he was conflicted around them! He wished he could be as smooth and savvy as Lightfoot. Confronting Nancy had been a bad idea.

Justice

The *Pacific* reached the San Francisco pier late Sunday morning. Waiting on the dock to welcome Gus and Lightfoot was General Prescott dressed in a cashmere morning coat with his personal carriage, which had two pure-black Hanoverians in harness. The carriage itself was an impressive-looking outfit, with brass headlights and polished leather, driven by a uniformed footman. It was as if President Grant himself was waiting on shore.

As the Generals man helped load the rig, the men talked on the dock.

"Henry will take you out to the Presidio and help you get squared away. I'll come out later this evening and we'll have dinner together. Did you bring your uniform, Gus?"

"Yes, sir, what's left of it. Never thought I'd need it again."

"Have Henry take you by the PX. You can buy what you need there. It will look better if you're all dressed up in military garb."

"I don't have a uniform, General," Lightfoot said. "Why do we need to be dressed up for the stockade?"

Prescott chuckled. "Dress up the best you can, Scout. I think you'll like our stockade."

With the carriage loaded, the men shook hands and moved to mount the rig. Just then Bernice and Nancy walked by. They both glared at the men, and Nancy said to Gus, "You are prospering, soldier boy. Hope to see you again. We have some unfinished business to tend to."

The General and Lightfoot smiled at Gus, who was red faced. "What happens on the bay stays on the bay," General Prescott remarked with a grin.

The carriage ride through the city, despite the cobblestone streets, was as smooth as floating on a cloud. They were impressed with the quality and construction of the buggy. It seemed to be brand new, and they wished Lucy was with them to experience such a luxurious ride. As they moved through the city Lightfoot confided about playing cards with 'Bernice' the night before and losing over a hundred dollars to him.

"I told you he was a cheat," Gus scolded.

"I watched him like hawk," Lightfoot replied. "I never saw no cheating."

Gus chuckled, "Lucky Jake Collins always gets his money."

"What about you and Nancy? I saw you talking to her. Your two looked thick as thieves."

Gus told him the story of having met Nancy six months earlier, and his encounter with her the night before. He felt relieved to clear his mind of her.

When they arrived at the front gate to the Presidio, the sentry braced himself with a salute and waved the carriage inside the compound. Obviously, the buggy was well known to the guards.

The Presidio was a sprawling reservation, with tall brick and stone buildings that surrounded a large parade ground where uniformed soldiers drilled, with display cannons and statues everywhere.

Henry pulled up to a building and told them they were in front of the Post Exchange. The store looked bigger than the downtown Emporium. Both men went inside and did some necessary shopping.

Their next stop was at the Presidio Headquarters, where they checked in with the Provost Marshal. Being Sunday, the Colonel himself was off the base, but one of his clerks signed the men in.

Their last stop was at the BOQ (Bachelor Officer Quarters), where they were assigned quarters for the next few days. Their room was on the third floor of a red-brick building overlooking

San Francisco Bay. As they stood at the window, looking out at the view, Gus asked Lightfoot, "Is this the stockade you fussed about?"

"I was part right," he replied sheepishly. "We can see Alcatraz Island from here."

At each of the stops, their driver Henry had helped them with directions by pointing out other facilities they might need. As he prepared to return to the city, he made one final suggestion.

"If you have the time, walk down to the bay and towards the Golden Gate. There you can watch the ships come and go, and see some of the most spectacular views God has ever created."

Henry proved to be a big help in getting the men squared away. His last remark was the time and place where they would meet up for dinner with General Prescott.

They dined that night in a private room at the Officers Club. Gus was dressed in his new blue uniform, right down to his boots and a fancy tooled-leather patch that covered his mangled eye. Lightfoot was dressed up in a new blue utility jacket, with his old leather trousers and a new blue forage cap. They looked as fresh as recruits. The meal was outstanding, with fresh seafood and two bottles of local wine to fortify them as they engaged in a lengthy conversation about the trial and the upcoming Court Martial.

"The proceedings are being held in the Transit Barracks, just a few blocks from your quarters. The courtroom is on the lower floor. Be there at 0900 on Tuesday," the General told them. "This will most likely be the last war-crime trial of the Civil War, so there will be a lot of reporters there. Stay away from them. They only want to sensationalize the story. You will sit with the other witnesses, at the rear of the courtroom. When you're called, come forward to be sworn in." Prescott glared at Gus. "Your new uniform is fine, Captain, but you're only wearing your Civil War ribbons. According to my records, you're missing five Union Pacific Railroad medals. Buy them tomorrow at the PX and wear them at the trial. I want Judge Harper to see you as the decorated veteran you are. And your new ribbons will help you at your Court Martial, as well."

"I don't have any ribbons," Lightfoot scoffed. "Just lots of scars and lumps."

"You're entitled to the Railroad medals," Prescott said. "Buy them if you wish."

"He can have mine after the trial," Gus said. "Can we go to town tomorrow?"

The General shook his head. "Sorry, boys. You are restricted to the post until after the proceedings."

At 0830 on the foggy, dreary morning of Tuesday, November 23rd, Gus and Lightfoot took a seat in the last row, on wooden folding chairs, of the Transit Barracks. It was a row reserved for witnesses only. The barracks itself was devoid of any beds or lockers, just a large, narrow room with roughly fifty seats for the gallery. At the front of the room was a large table with a witness box next to it, and a dark cloth backdrop with flags standing upright in holders. In front of this table and the flags were two more tables, one for the prosecutor and one for the defense attorney. The room was crowded with Army brass, reporters, witnesses, and interested parties, and it was well guarded, with armed soldiers stationed at all of the entries and exits.

As the men watched the room fill up, they heard Raymond Ramsey call out to them from across the floor. They gave him a nod. Then Gus noticed Axel Pearson, the Swedish shopkeeper from Timber, enter the room, with an older woman at his side. He waved at them as they moved through the crowd to sit down next to the Deputies.

"What brings you all the way here?" Lightfoot asked.

Axel introduced his wife, Helga, then replied proudly, "A subpoena from the government. I want to see what kind of justice is given to these killers. Why are you in Army uniform, Gus?"

"I was a Cavalry Captain during the war. Now I'm just a Deputy Sheriff."

Helga looked at Gus, her brown eyes widening. "Look at all his ribbons, Axel! He was hero in big war."

"No," Gus quickly replied. "The real heroes never returned from the battles of that damn war."

At precisely 0900, the clerk came out from behind the backdrop and yelled, "All rise for Federal Judge Roy Harper."

Instantly, the room went silent and everyone stood as the

Judge made his appearance. He was an older gentleman with a neatly trimmed beard and wavy gray hair. Judge Harper had a reputation of being a firm but fair jurist.

Then the clerk called out General Prescott as the prosecutor, and the General came out from behind the cloth and moved to his desk. Next Colonel 'Bull' Williams name was called out as the defense attorney. He looked to be a Southern gentleman, dressed all in white, with a gray beard and bushy sideburns. He pranced around the Courtroom with a silver-tipped cane. Rumor had it that he was the former Attorney General for the Confederacy. Finally, he took his seat at the defense desk. Judge Harper then read aloud the particulars of the Government vs. William and Jasper McKay and gaveled open the trial.

Everyone in the gallery took their seats.

The clerk called out for the prisoners to make their appearance. Under heavy guard, they came out from behind the cloth, their feet and hands shackled. Both were dressed in gray inmate overalls with stony expressions and their eyes downcast. They took their seats at the defense table.

Then the arguments started. With a heavy Southern accent, Bull Williams asked the Judge to have the shackles removed from the brothers during the trial. General Prescott objected to the request, and the men argued for a while. In the end, the Judge ordered that the shackles would remain on the brothers.

Next, General Prescott gave his opening statement. It was full of violence and death, with grisly details about the Anderson Massacre and how the McKay Brothers killed and butchered the family.

Then the Southern Colonel made his opening statement. It was full of sorrow and forgiveness, with many reminders that the war was long over. The McKay Brothers only defense was that they had been wrongly arrested.

When the trial got underway, General Prescott read into the record all of the written affidavits he had collected. Then he called his witnesses. Axel Pearson was first to take the stand. Lightfoot came next, and then Gus. They all told the same story and were supported by the affidavits.

After each witness, the Colonel cross-examined them. He did his best to belittle and humiliate the witnesses, harping to the court that the war was over and that the country needed to heal its wounds.

The only real surprise question came from General Prescott when he asked Gus why he had arrested the McKay Brothers. "Did you arrest them as a former Calvary Captain or as a Deputy Sheriff?"

Gus thought for a moment, then answered truthfully, "Neither, sir. I arrested them to kill them. In the closing days of the war, the McKay Brothers killed and butchered my family back in Kansas, just like they did to the Andersons. I wanted revenge, plain and simple. But I couldn't bring myself to do it. If I'd killed them, it would make me just another assassin as bad as they are."

His answer brought a gasp from the gallery.

Prescott handed Gus the slip of paper that had dropped out of the Parker Brothers family bible. "Have you ever seen this slip of paper before?"

"Yes, sir," Gus answered, and he told the court the story of finding the list of words.

The last witness the General called was a professor from a local college who was a handwriting expert. He testified that the slip of paper with the words had been written by William McKay.

Bull Williams challenged the professor as an expert, but the Judge overruled his objection.

General Prescott then gave the slip of paper to the Judge and told the court that the words on the paper were really the names of different people who knew the true identity of the McKay Brothers. "They rode with Quantrill's Bushwhackers during the war, and were vicious partisan guerrillas long after the Confederate surrender. I call this slip of paper a 'killing list,' as all the crossed-out names were killed by the brothers over the last four years. But," Prescott said loudly to the court, "we aren't indicting them for those crimes. We are only charging them with the Anderson Massacre, which happened only a few months ago."

General Prescott rested his prosecution just before noon.

After the lunch break, Bull Williams called only two witnesses for the defense. Both were former officers in the Confederate Army, and they testified to the good character of the brothers. Neither of the McKay's took the stand in their own defense and when Colonel Williams made his closing statement, he could only plead for mercy without the gallows. "If there must be retribution, let it be merciful. The younger brother, Jasper, still has a full life ahead of him, while his older brother, William, could serve out his time in prison. Give them a chance at redemption."

Judge Harper took the case under consideration in the early afternoon. During the recess, General Prescott invited Gus and Lightfoot to sit with him at the prosecution table. When they joined him, he was mad as a hornet as he whispered to them, "That crafty old Colonel wouldn't allow the brothers to take the stand. He knew my name was on their killing list. I wanted to nail them in cross examination. But no, that son-of-a–bitch wouldn't allow it."

"Don't think you're going to need it, sir," Gus whispered back.

With an angry grimace, Prescott reached into his coat pocket and brought out a silver flask, opened it, and took a swig. Then he handed the flask to Gus, saying, "If you boys hadn't caught the brothers, they would be coming after my family. I owe you much."

"No you don't, sir," Gus answered, looking over at the defense table. "Those men deserve this retribution."

Within the hour, Judge Harper returned to the courtroom.

The prisoners and their attorney stood as the stone-faced Judge read his verdict aloud.

"Wars bring out the worst in mankind, but what I witnessed here today is the worst of the worst. You brothers are nothing more than mad dogs. There can be no redemption for your eradicating and no mercy for your motives. Therefore, I find you guilty of the murder of the Anderson family. You will be removed from this courtroom and returned to Alcatraz today. There, at high noon on Thanksgiving Day, you will be hung by the neck until dead. May God have mercy on your souls." With that, Judge Harper gaveled the proceedings to a close and retired behind the cloth.

The prisoners and their attorney stood, stunned and silent, for the longest moment. Then the guards approached the brothers to remove them from the courtroom. Jasper had tears in his eyes and fear on his face, while William resisted the guards with all of his might. During the scuffle, he turned his head and yelled to the gallery, "Long live the Confederacy! We are soldiers and demand a firing squad."

General Prescott jumped to his feet and yelled back, "You're not soldiers! You're assassins of women and children. Now die like assassins."

It took a few moments, and half a dozen guards, to get them out of the room. No one in the gallery seemed surprised by the verdict, and they all watched in silence as the McKay Brothers were escorted out of the courtroom. Would this damnable Civil War never end?

In the crowd leaving the barracks, Gus was stopped by a stocky man with a beer belly, a crooked frog nose, and sad eyes. Angrily, he shouted, "What happened to William McKay today is going to happen to you tomorrow. You're dead, Night-Eye!"

Alcatraz Thanksgiving Day 1869

Chapter 10 – Time

Court Martial

With a sparse room of onlookers, at 0900 the next day, Gus and Lightfoot sat down at the defense table next to General Prescott. Across the aisle from them, at the prosecutor's table, was the man who had accosted Gus the day before, Sheriff Bill Brown from Ogden County, Utah. He was a big man with a sinister face and beady, hateful eyes.

In front of them were three Military Officers whose uniforms bore rows and rows of battle ribbons on their chests. There was a Major, a Captain, and a Lieutenant Colonel as the presiding officers. Unbeknownst to Gus or Lightfoot, all three officers on the panel had served under General Prescott during the Civil War.

Sheriff Brown started the proceedings by reading aloud a list of particulars of his allegations against Captain Gus Savage. He told the panel that his brother, Martín Brown, had gone for a stroll in the new rail yards, on the evening in question. During that walk, he was waylaid by Captain Savage who, without cause, killed him in the course of a knife fight wherein Martin Brown was only defending himself. There was no mention of Martín's attempted molestation of a woman, nor of his use of a concealed Derringer that wounded Captain Savage when his back was turned. In Sheriff Brown's twisted thoughts and words, Gus was the sole aggressor and deserved to be Court-Martialed and punished to the full extent of Military Law.

Next the Sheriff presented, to the panel, three sworn affidavits from witnesses, none of whom were in the courtroom, and called to the witness stand two others who were present. All of their sworn testimonies supported the Sheriffs allegations. But, upon cross examination by General Prescott, both courtroom witnesses admitted that they were related, by blood or marriage, to Sheriff Brown.

When it came time for General Prescott to present the defense, he provided the panel with documents from an Army investigation that had taken place immediately after the incident, along with four sworn affidavits from witnesses to the incident. Then Lightfoot took the stand and related his account of the knife fight and explained the use of the Derringer pistol. "The first bullet hit the Captain in his left shoulder, when his back was turned. The second bullet was a misfire. That's when the unarmed Captain used his knife to defend himself. I stitched up his wounds that night, on our way out of town."

Gus testified next, showing the panel his scar from the bullet wound and confirming the details of Lightfoot's testimony. On cross examination, Sheriff Brown was all over Gus's statement, attempting to intimidate him with words like *liar, cheat* and *assassin*. In response, the Captain kept a cool head, stating, "If your brother Martín hadn't been molesting that woman, he'd be alive today."

"There was no woman," the Sheriff shouted angrily, red-faced. "It's all a pack of your skullduggery."

The last defense witness was a brilliant choice by General Prescott. He called out for a lady named Madame X.

She appeared, dressed in all black, with a dark mesh veil covering her face.

"I apologize to the panel," Prescott said. "This lady is formerly from Ogden, Utah, and wishes to keep her true identity a secret. She is the woman in question regarding the alleged molestation by Martín Brown."

Sheriff Brown objected loudly and demanded that the panel not allow her testimony.

The presiding Colonel asked Madame X why she needed such secrecy.

She responded that she feared Sheriff Brown. "I still have family in Ogden. The Sheriff and his many Deputies are the bullies of the county. They will stop at nothing to get what they want."

Madame X was allowed to testify incognito. She confirmed the testimony of Gus and Lightfoot. It was the final nail in the coffin of Sheriff Brown's list of particulars. The panel didn't even adjourn to confer. Shrugging their shoulders in agreement, they found for the defense, dropping all charges of the Court-Martial. Gus was finally able to breathe a sigh of genuine relief.

Both the plaintiff and the defense were shocked by the firm and speedy judgment of the panel, and they stood silently for a moment, gathering their thoughts.

Then General Prescott snapped open his pocket watch. "You have an important lunch within the hour," he said to Gus and Lightfoot. "I want you to shake hands with Sheriff Brown and wish him well, while I obtain a written copy of the panels judgment. I'll see you outside."

Reluctantly, the men approached the Sheriff's table. Gus offered his outstretched hand to Brown. "Sorry about your brother, Sheriff. We wish you well."

Brown glared at Gus. "I'd rather stick my hand in a pile of horse shit than shake your hand. What a kangaroo court this was!" He gathered up his things from the table and turned to leave the room, then stopped and looked back. "On some dark and windy night, we will meet again, and I'll have the pleasure of killing you."

"And I'll do the same for you," Lightfoot replied, offering the Sheriff a mocking salute.

When Gus and Lightfoot walked out of the courtroom, they found Ray Ramsey rushing up the stairs. "Pleased you're still here," he said, out of breath. "Got a telegram from Chicago. The publisher loves your story! He wants fifteen episodes by the end of January. Do we have a deal?"

"What's the royalty he's offering?" Lightfoot asked as they clattered down the stairs together.

"Standard contract with a three-cent royalty, I get a penny and Gus gets two cents. We could be on the gravy train!" Ray exclaimed.

Reaching street level, Gus heard his name called, and turned to see Henry waiting for them next to the General's fancy buggy, waving.

"We've got to go," Gus told Ray. "Let's meet for a drink this evening and we'll give you our decision."

"Fine," Roy agreed. "I'll see you at the party."

"What party?" Lightfoot asked.

Looking startled by the question, Ray fumbled for words. "Any party. There's always a party somewhere. I'll see you tonight." And he hurried off without another word.

At the carriage, Henry urged them to get in, explaining that General Prescott would join them later.

Under a warm, sunny sky, he drove them around the parade ground, past the headquarter buildings, and up the hill to what was called Officers Row, an area of elegant homes for high-ranking Presidio Officers. There the buggy stopped in front of the Commanding Officers house.

It was a beautiful Victorian home with tall white pillars and manicured grounds. As instructed, the men knocked at the front door and were ushered inside by a uniformed butler. Then they were taken into a parlor as elegant as the McLoughlin house. There, to their amazement, they found Brigadier General Rollins waiting at his desk.

General Rollins welcomed the men warmly and Gus saluted him with pride. When the General had waved them to chairs in front of his desk and reseated himself, he said, "Sorry for this round-about way of meeting up, Gus. I didn't think it would look proper if your old Commanding Officer was in the courtroom during your Court-Martial hearing. My staff did the original investigation of the Martin killing, right after it happened. We knew all along that you were innocent. But now its official and your name is cleared."

"Cleared for what?" Lightfoot asked.

"That's what we're here to talk about," General Rollins replied with a smile. "But first, let's have a drink to celebrate your acquittal."

"And your promotion to Brigadier," Gus added.

The General used a small bell to ring for the butler. "Thank you, Gus. With my promotion come many new responsibilities. One of them will be helping to reorganize the Federal Marshal Services, starting in the New Year. Now, with your name cleared, I'd like to ask you to become the Chief U.S. Marshal for the Pacific Northwest, with Lightfoot as one of your Deputies."

The surprising offer triggered a lengthy conversation, over champagne and coffee, about what the future might hold for Gus and Lightfoot. The Northwest Marshal Service worked out of Portland, with a small office in the state Courthouse. The Chief Marshal would have a staff of three Deputies and a clerk, and he'd be paid eighteen hundred dollars year plus expenses, while the Deputies would each receive twelve hundred a year.

"That's better money than being Chief Scout," Lightfoot replied with a smile.

"Yes," General Rollins answered. "And next year, when the new Federal Courthouse is finished, you'll have new offices with room to grow, including a dozen new jail cells."

"What made you decide to offer this to us?" Gus asked.

"Times are changing, Gus. We have rail lines and steamship lines, telegraph lines and soon, telephone lines. We need U.S. Marshals who don't carry the law in their holsters. Men who know the law and how to enforce it without getting blood splattered all over the barroom floors, just like you did with the McKay Brothers."

Over a lunch of sardine sandwiches and coffee, General Rollins detailed the duties and responsibilities of being a Federal Marshal. They protected the federal judiciary, apprehended federal fugitives, and transported federal prisoners to federal prisons, to name but a few of their duties. It was a big step up from being a County Deputy Sheriff. The Marshals had to know the law inside and out, and their territory of jurisdiction would be three wilderness states. But with the new railroads and telegraph lines to help with rapid transportation and communication, General Rollins was confident it was a doable task.

"What about reward money?" Lightfoot asked.

The General searched through some papers on his desk and handed Gus a bank draft. "Here's your reward for the McKay Brothers. I'm pleased to give it to you. *But*, if you join the Marshal Service, all future rewards would be the property of the government."

Gus looked at the draft and showed it to Lightfoot with a big smile.

"There's another problem, sir. We've been approached by a publisher out of Chicago who wants to write dime novels about us. "The Adventures of Night-Eye and His Sidekick, Lightfoot". If I was the Chief Marshal, would that be a problem?"

General Rollins puffed on his cigar, sending up blue smoke to cloud the air over his desk and his fingers dancing on the desktop. Finally, he nodded a smiled. "Not a problem. The government only knows you as Augustus Savage, not 'Night-Eye' or 'Lightfoot.' And stories that reminisce about the old west are always good for recruiting. Just never use your legal names in those books."

Gus looked at his former Commanding Officer, older, wiser, and still a decent, honest man. "You went to a lot of trouble to clear my name, sir, so you can count me in."

"Me too, sir," Lightfoot added, shrugging his shoulders. "I like the money."

With that agreement, they shook hands and had another glass of champagne. Their new jobs would start January 2nd with the publication of the government list of U.S. Marshal Appointees for 1870.

General Rollins walked them to the front door and said, "Henry will take you to the BOQ so you can check out. Then he'll take you to town, where you can meet up with General Prescott again."

"We're not staying on post tonight?" Gus asked.

"No, he has other plans for you."

As the men shook hands with the General on the porch, he said to Gus, "Please tell Lucy that I received her sample cans of salmon and they were delicious. Let her know that I'm sending some cans up to the Quartermaster for his consideration."

Gus and Lightfoot were bewildered by that news. "We had no idea she was sending canned fish to you. Please accept our apologies, sir."

"No apologies necessary, Captain," the General answered with a smile. "I was wrong about her. She's one smart young lady."

With the cadence of eight hooves prancing on the cobble-stones, Henry turned the buggy for town. The men inside the cab watched the sights go by. The day was surprisingly warm, and Henry was as tight-lipped as usual. They asked him several times where they were going and when they might see General Prescott again. His answer was always the same: "Sorry, sirs, I'm not at liberty to say."

Resting back on the leather upholstery Lightfoot finally said, "I smell something fishy."

"It's the sardine sandwich," Gus chuckled. "He might be dropping us off at the wharf to board a steamer for home."

"I hope not. I wanted to see the city again," Lightfoot replied with a disappointed expression.

A few minutes later, the carriage pulled up in front of the Seafarer Inn, the very place they had started out from, just a few months before.

They dismounted the buggy and Henry helped them with their bags. "See Mrs. Brown inside. She has rooms waiting for you. Everything has been taken care of. Be back down to the lobby at 1900 sharp, dressed in your best. The General will be waiting."

That was all that Henry said until he had remounted the buggy. Then he looked down at the men, tipped his hat, and added, "It's been a pleasure to serve two new U.S. Marshals. Have a wonderful evening, gentlemen."

Mrs. Brown and her husband Louis greeted their new guests with open arms and showed the men to their rooms. Lightfoots was on the second floor, while Gus had his own room on the third floor. Both rooms were newly remolded and overlooked the waterfront.

"How's that Lucy girl doing?" Mrs. Brown inquired.

"She's up in Astoria, going to school." Lightfoot answered. "What's the cost of these rooms?"

Louis shook his head with a smile, opening the drapes. "Not to worry. General Prescott is covering all costs."

"Tomorrow, the hotel is serving a Thanksgiving feast for our guests. We hope you will join us," Mrs. Brown added, fussing over the room.

At 1900 sharp, the men came down from their rooms wearing their finest garb. Waiting for them was General Prescott in a black cashmere overcoat, blue tweed frock coat and bowler hat. He greeted them warmly.

"Right on time, fellows. We don't have far to go."

"Where are we headed, General?" Gus asked.

"If I remember right," he replied with a grin, "you men like playing poker. Mrs. Brown tells me there's a nice poker parlor across the street at the Bistro. Thought we should try our luck."

When they walked into the restaurant, the maître d'greeted them like old friends and showed them to the backroom. As they moved through the crowded dining room, General Prescott nodded at many of the guests, and they nodded back. Clearly, the General was no stranger to this Bistro.

When the doors to the rear room slid back, they saw a stand-up bar and half a dozen large, round tables with chairs. But these weren't poker tables, they were dining tables, and the room was packed with people. At their appearance, the crowd started smiling and applauding, and a Mariachi band started to play. For a moment Gus and Lightfoot were baffled by what they saw. Was this some kind of party in their honor? Gus began recognizing faces in the crowd: Judge Harper and his clerk were in the audience, as well as Ray Ramsey and Madame X out of costume. Nearby, two of the three officers from the Court-Martial had drinks in their hands. Then Gus saw Lucy moving through the crowd with open arms.

"What the hell are you doing here?" Lightfoot asked her as she hugged Gus.

"Surprising my brothers," she answered, with a bright smile.

Then Gus noticed Roxanne moving his way in a blue taffeta gown. She looked stunning, with pearls around her neck, and her brunette hair rolled up into a high bun.

Roxie gave him a hug and whispered in his ear, "Told you I wished I was coming with you."

"What's going on here, General?" Gus asked of him.

"It's just my little private celebration of the outcome of the trial and your new appointments as Federal Marshals. Enjoy the weekend, boys. There are steamship tickets waiting for you on Monday morning for your trip back home."

General Prescott only stayed for a couple of drinks. Then, making his apologies, he departed for a house full of family and his Thanks giving holiday.

What remained was a gala affair of food and wine that lasted well into the evening. During the party, Gus and Lightfoot finalized their deal with Ray Ramsey. They also learned from him that General Prescott had made his fortune in kerosene and coal and was now considering running for Governor of California. He had also paid for Lucy and Roxie to make the trip, and had put them up at the hotel. The General was a rich and powerful man with deep connections to President Grant.

The Bistro closed at midnight, and the friends, giggling and laughing, walked back to the hotel in a thick mist to the accompaniment of foghorns blaring. Once in the lobby, Gus learned that the girls had a room next to Lightfoot. They said goodnight to each other in the stair-well, and Gus climbed to his third-floor room.

When he unlocked his door, he saw the glow of an oil lamp burning next to his bed. Turning up the flame, he took off his waistcoat, sat down on the bed, and removed his boots. Rubbing his feet, he noticed an ice bucket on the table next the window. In the bucket was a bottle of champagne with a note that read, *Compliments of the House.* He smiled, guessing it was from Mrs. Brown, who had been so attentive upon their arrival.

Moving to the armoire, he removed his trousers and hung them with his coat. Standing in just his long johns and a ruffled white shirt, he thought about the cold champagne, then decided against it. It had been a long day.

Then he heard a scratch at his door. He moved to the threshold, heard another scratch, and replied, "Yes? Who's there?"

"It's Roxie," she whispered. "Did you get some champagne?"

"Yes," Gus answered back in a whisper. "Why?"

"Let me in for a drink."

"Give me a moment, I'm not decent," Gus replied.

"Neither am I. Let me in!"

Gus unlatched the door and opened it.

Like a whirlwind, Roxie swept into the room, clad only in a blue bathrobe and slippers, and closed the door after herself. "That's better. I was afraid somebody might come down the hall!"

"Is Lucy alright?" Gus asked, his mind reeling.

Roxie looked around the room. "Yes. She's out like a lamp. I sent you the champagne and thought we should talk. We didn't get a dozen words together, all evening."

"Let me get some clothes on," Gus said.

"Don't bother. You look alluring in long johns."

Gus felt embarrassed to be standing in front of her with no pants, but he'd had enough to drink to be able to put his shyness aside. Lighting a second lamp, he uncorked the champagne and poured two glasses full of the wine. "Here's to a wonderful surprise evening," he said, holding his glass high.

Roxie smiled back at him with an alluring look and clinked her glass against his. "And to this evening, which is still young. Let's talk about us."

Roxie took a chair at the table and sat with one of her legs dangling free of her bathrobe. Gus sat down, averting his gaze. They could still hear the foghorns outside the window.

"Did you have many girlfriends while you were in the Cavalry?" Roxanne asked, taking a sip from her glass.

Gus studied her pretty face in the glowing lamp light, "Not really. I went from the warmth of my family to death and destruction in just a few weeks. There was no time for girlfriends. Then I lost my eye, and all the girls started looking away."

"Do you wear your eye patch to bed?"

Gus squirmed in his chair and took a drink of wine. Roxie was one forward, precocious woman. "If I'm alone, I take it off."

"How long has it been since you've made love to a woman?"

"I'm not sure I ever have," Gus answered, embarrassed. "The Army taught me many things, but lovemaking wasn't one of them, so I don't have much experience."

Roxanne stood from her chair with a captivating smile. "Let me show you the first rule of lovemaking. Stand with me."

Gus took another sip of wine, got to his feet, and stood to face her.

"Rule One, when you find a willing woman like me," she whispered, slowly untying her sash and letting the bathrobe drop to the floor, "it is the time to give the lady a kiss."

Roxie was naked from the waist up and Gus felt frozen in place for a moment. Then he kissed her passionately and whispered in her ear, "What's Rule Two?"

She grinned and returned his kiss, then whispered, "No further instructions required."

That night Gus learned about love – not the kind of love for family, friends, or country, but the kind of love between a man and a woman. It was a lesson that had been long in coming, with many surprises along the way. One of which, was that he felt comfortable removing his eye patch in front of Roxie. That night, he gained back some long-lost self-respect. Roxanne was a marvelous teacher, and he was enthralled with every inch of her.

The next morning, over a late breakfast, Gus and Roxie did their best to conceal from the others their new-found affection. They were successful with Lucy but not with Lightfoot. He knew right off that his Captain had a new girlfriend, and no wisecracks were needed. It felt of love and it looked of love.

Changing Times

On Monday morning, after a magical weekend in San Francisco, the friends boarded the steamship for Astoria. Their holiday had been a memorable time for a variety of conflicting reasons. Just before noon on Thanksgiving, Gus had excused himself from his friends and walked soberly to the bay. There in the gloom of an overcast day, he looked out at Alcatraz Island and watched his pocket watch slowly tick towards high noon. As he waited, his eye filled with tears at thoughts of his family. He said a silent prayer for them. Then, at noon, he imagined the gallows swinging open, with the McKay Brothers dangling from the hangman's noose. He could not pray for them. There was still too much hate in his heart. Then he slowly walked back to the hotel and enjoyed a delicious Thanksgiving dinner with his friends.

That holiday weekend, Gus and Lightfoot entertained the girls with shopping, sightseeing, and eating their way across the city at the finest restaurants. Along the way, they rode in their first cable car and watched a demonstration of something called a Magic Lantern. And they experienced new things, like talking to each other over a telephone line and watching people riding high-wheeled unicycles. Oh, the wonderment of the Gilded Age!

Roxie even dragged them to a lecture at the local library, where a man from India told the audience he refused to consume the flesh of any animals, and only ate grasses and greens. He called himself a vegan, and Roxie called him a dietary visionary, but Gus and Lightfoot scoffed at his bizarre ideas and called him a fool. Each day was a new adventure and each night ended with another scratch on Gus's door. It was a weekend like no other. But now, as they prepared to embark, it was time to move on.

They arrived back in Astoria on Wednesday afternoon and walked the girls to their Academy. Then the men walked to the

Courthouse to check in with Sheriff Chance.

"He's not going to like our news," Lightfoot said, approaching his office. "He'll have to find new enumerators and Deputies."

But, as it turned out, the Sheriff had news of his own. While they had been gone, the telegraph had come to town. Western Union had opened an office just down the road and it was connected to a local hotel with the very first phone line in Astoria.

"And just yesterday," the Sheriff continued, "the cornerstone for the new Post Office and Custom House was laid. Rumor has it that, starting in the New Year, we might also have a new daily newspaper to read. Astoria is growing like a weed. I'm pleased you boys are back. We're going to be busy around here."

With that opening, Gus told the Sheriff his news of the trial and showed him the government draft with his name for the reward money. "We'll settle up with the county tomorrow. But, unfortunately, there's more. Lightfoot and I have been appointed Federal Marshals for the Northwest by President Grant. We start our new jobs in Portland after the first of the year. Sorry for the change in plans. We had no idea this was coming our way."

"What about your Court-Martial?" the Sheriff asked.

"Free and clear," Lightfoot answered.

Sheriff Chance sadly shook his head. "Good for you, bad for me. I knew there was something afoot. On Monday, a big package of books came for you, Gus, sent by the government. I put them on your boat. Why the need for books?"

"I have no idea," Gus answered. "Probably just manuals. The government has a handbook for everything."

"Can I tell him about Night-Eye books?" Lightfoot asked enthusiastically.

Gus nodded and grinned. "Why not? Everyone is going to know, sooner or later."

Lightfoot enjoyed telling the story of the dime novels and the potential of the books for making them famous. They all had a good chuckle, talking about Gus as a drugstore cowboy riding off into the sunset.

"I hate to lose you boys," the Sheriff said with a smile. "You're fun to have around."

Their next surprise came at the public dock, where they saw their boat *Louise* pulling at her lines, with a new sailing mast and rigging standing tall. Going aboard, they found Rob Matthews finishing up the woodworking on a new berth in the forward compartment. In his carpenter overalls, he was delighted to see them, and proudly showed them the improvements he had made to the boat. "I traded some Thunder Lumber for the new mast and rigging, and built the new bunk out of some spare wood. Now you can sail the *Louise* out on the river and have an extra berth for a guest – such as me!"

Gus ran a hand across the wood of the bunk. "Your work is beautiful. But who gave you permission?"

"That would be me," Lightfoot said sheepishly. "He asked me before we went to Frisco. Rob's been living on the beach and needed a place to stay. I told him you wouldn't care."

"You're right, I don't," Gus replied with smile. "I look forward to sailing her."

There was more news for Clint. Rob told him that his Thunder Timber business had taken off while he was gone. They looked over new orders for the wood and began talking about buying up timber contracts for the burnt-out forests. Soon, with whiskey glasses in hand, they turned their conversation to dreams of making a fortune with their light-weight wood.

As they continued to talk, a young messenger called out from the dock. Gus went topside and was given a folded telegraph printed on yellow paper, along with a small envelope with Roxie's delicate handwriting. Gus tipped the boy a dime and remained on deck reading his messages.

The telegraph was from General Rollins alerting Gus and Lightfoot that the Federal Courthouse in Portland would be finished by the end of January. They were to report for duty there on the first of February.

The envelope from Roxie had a key inside with a note; Gus, look for a lamp flickering on my back porch. If you see it, use the key to scratch my bedroom door on the right. Be assured that the girls will be fast asleep upstairs. Your sweetie Roxie.

Gus read her message twice, with a smile on his face. He had wondered how they might continue their love affair after the departure from San Francisco. Leave it to Roxie to be a resourceful lover. And yet, deep down, there was something about it he didn't like. Skulking around in the dark just didn't sit well with him.

Early the next morning, Gus and Lightfoot visited the Astoria Merchants Bank with the reward draft in hand. Old man Hanson was impressed with the size of their deposit.

"You boys are doing well," he said, stamping the back of draft.

"And there's going to be more deposits just like this," Lightfoot answered proudly. "Gus has signed a contract with a Chicago publisher. They're going to write books about us."

Hanson's greedy little eyes narrowed as he wrote out the deposit slip. "That's good news for all of us."

"That's why it's a shame we'll have to close our account soon," Gus said nonchalantly.

"Why?" the banker asked with a startled look.

"We're moving to Portland, and we found a new bank that allows women to have bank accounts, so we're going to give them our business," Gus answered.

"Now wait a minute, boys. It's best for you to support your local merchants. I can see myself clear to giving Lucy an account. Just tell me what you need."

Gus handed old man Hanson a slip of paper with it all written out. "Just set it up like this and give me her ledger card. We'll give it to her as a Christmas present."

Reluctantly, Hanson did just that, making Lucy the first female account holder at the Astoria Merchants Bank. Times were changing, and the trio was now sharing their wealth equally: one for all, and all for one.

Footprints

In the days after Thanksgiving, Gus and Lightfoot were just marching in place, waiting for their new jobs to start. But they still were on the county payroll, and every morning they reported to Sheriff Chance and helped out as best they could. Mostly, they saddled up and rode the county, serving summons and warrants, even collecting overdue taxes. It wasn't a job they relished but it kept them busy, traveling to parts of the county they had never seen before. While there had been a few local burglaries and some barroom brawls, for the most part the city Constables patrolled the town, keeping the peace. Astoria was a busy port, with ships of all sizes and shapes, and hundreds of sailors coming and going. Between bootlegging, opium dens, prostitution and corruption, this underbelly of the county was a challenging place for anyone with authority. Judge Bean's laws were always feared, and a lawman's hand was never far from his holster.

On one of their tax collecting trips, they traveled to Warrenton aboard the Skipanon ferry. Standing on the deck, they talked about the upcoming Christmas holiday.

"Roxie has asked us to come to dinner on Christmas Eve. All of her students, but Lucy will be with their families, so it would be just the four of us." Gus told Clint.

"Great. We should bring them something special," Lightfoot answered.

"I was thinking about a few bottles of good champagne," Gus replied.

Lightfoot made a face. "I don't like that stuff. It makes my head spin. You drink the bubbly and I'll stick to my cactus juice."

"We'll need to buy presents for the girls," Gus added. "Let's do some shopping when we get back to town."

"Good idea. How about if we take the girls sailing aboard the *Louise*, weather permitting, on Christmas Day?"

Gus grinned at his friend. "That would be a great idea, too, if either of us knew how to sail."

Lightfoot nodded. "We've got to get that damn boat out on the river. I heard the sturgeon are in. They say some of them are as big as a man."

"Let's see if someone down on the docks can teach us to sail." Gus replied.

They stood in companionable silence for a few minutes. Then Lightfoot asked, "How are you and Roxie getting along? You still creeping around to her back porch?"

Gus frowned but didn't blush. "What are you talking about? Roxie and I are just friends."

Lightfoot chuckled, his brown eyes dancing, "Friends with benefits. Good for you, Captain. Just don't let Lucy find out. She'll get jealous."

Gus shook his head. "There's nothing for her to be jealous about."

On Christmas Eve morning, they reported to the Sheriff, hoping for the day off to complete their shopping. They found him in his jail house, standing in front of the drunk tank, staring at a prisoner sprawled out on a bunk. The mud-covered man was a pitiful sight and smelled like a cesspool.

"What the hell are you looking at?" Gus asked, coming to stand next to the Sheriff.

"See that kid on the bunk? The city Constables brought him in, a couple hours ago. All he owns is that muddy pair of long johns. He is drunk, drugged, or both, and I think he might be dead. He has nothing, no clothes, no boots, no identification."

"He looks dead to me," Lightfoot agreed, peering through the bars.

"Throw a bucket of cold water on him. He'll sober up fast." Gus said.

"The Constables found him face down in a mud pit behind the Uptown Pub. When they got him on his feet, he came alive and started shouting, "Forgive her, she knows not what she has done" over and over. Then he passed out again and they carried him here. I think this kid was drugged and rolled. He hasn't moved a muscle since they brought him in."

"Somebody worked him over, that's for sure." Gus said, glaring at the prisoner. "Is that dried blood on the mud?"

"Yep," Sheriff Chance replied. "Let's try the water and see if he moves. It's Christmas Eve, for God sakes."

The water was cold and wet, and it shocked the young mans system. His eyes popped open and he moved, spitting water. Then he passed out again.

They threw more water on him and he did the same, but this time his eyes remained open. Gus and Lightfoot held his arms while the Sheriff wiped his face with a wet towel. He moaned and resisted, but the towel soon revealed a young face with a fair complexion and auburn hair. He had some small lacerations on his face, along with a few bruises, and he smelled like a skunk, but at least he was moving again.

That was when Gus noticed a mark on his upper right arm, visible through the ragged material. Gus ripped the fabric of the sleeve so they could see that it was the tattooed image of a sailing ship, with the words *Sea-Witch.*

"Surprise, surprise. He's a sailor," Lightfoot said, and chuckled.

"I'll get him some coffee," Sheriff Chance said. "You boys saddle up and go see the Harbor Master. See if he knows anything about a ship called the *Sea-Witch*. Then pay a visit to Lilly at the Uptown Pub and see what she has to say. If this kid is a sailor, where's his damn sea bag and poke?"

At the Harbor Master's office, they learned that the *Sea-Witch* was a British freighter out of Bristol. She had been in port a few days before and had moved on to Portland to pick up a shipload of wheat. The ship was an old windjammer that sailed the world, delivering freight from one port to the next.

When they walked into the Uptown Pub, they noticed a carpenter working on an upstairs doorway. Lilly was surprised to see the Deputies and over the sounds of hammering and sawing, offered them a drink at the bar. They refused her offer and explained their reason for the visit.

Lilly was cordial but claimed no knowledge of a young sailor dressed only in his skivvies. "That might happen upstairs," she chuckled, "but never here in my barroom."

"So you don't know anything about this lad?" Gus asked.

"No," she replied, failing to make eye contact. "I know nothing about him."

Lightfoot wanted to linger at the bar, flirting with some of the working girls, but Gus wanted to move on from their evasive answers.

Back at the Courthouse, they told the Sheriff what they had learned.

He listened patiently and told them the kid had sobered up some. "He told me his name is Larson and he's the Third Mate on the *Sea-Witch*. He claims he was drugged and waylaid last night at the Uptown Pub. He has a real foul mouth and if you get him talking he doesn't stop. Also, while you guys were gone, Judge Bean got wind of him and came over and talked to the lad. He wants him all cleaned up and in his courtroom at 3 o'clock."

"I think Lilly knows a lot more than she's telling us," Gus said. "Let's bring the kid into your office and hear his story. Maybe the mate is telling the truth."

"He stinks and he talks in circles. Shouldn't we get him cleaned up first?" the Sheriff asked.

"No, let's do it now while he's still off guard." Gus answered.

With clouds of drugs or booze still circling in his head, and his hands shaking, Larson told his story with graphic details and a vulgarity in every sentence. He had been shanghaied from Astoria five years before. He'd only been eighteen at the time, fresh off a farm in the Willamette Valley. He and a friend had taken a paddle wheeler from Portland and came to Astoria to see the tall ships and sow some wild oats. While on the waterfront they were befriended by a man who bought them drinks at a local pub. He introduced them to a fat lady with a foghorn voice who owned the bar. She invited them to a party aboard a tall ship anchored out in the river. "There are pretty girls out there, and lots of rum. You'll get to meet the crew and have a good time." The farm boys, mesmerized by the invitation, had accepted immediately.

But when they rowed out to the ship there were no girls or booze, only five sailors waiting for them with ropes and belaying pins in hand. The farm boys were tied up, gagged, and thrown into a rope locker along with two other lads who had fallen for the same dirty trick. They remained in the locker until the *Sea-Witch* was far out to sea.

"When your ass gets shanghaied," the kid said, "you have only two options. You can cry in your fucken beer or go along with the scheme. I went with the fucken scheme and made Third Mate in three years. But I never forgot that fat bitch with the foghorn voice. I vowed retribution if I ever got back to Astoria. And that happened yesterday."

When the *Sea-Witch* tied up at Pier 2, Larson had grabbed his sea bag and jumped ship, searching for the lady with the foghorn voice. He couldn't remember the name of her pub, so he stopped at every gin joint in the west end of town. Late that evening, when he finally found the Uptown Pub, he was drunk as a skunk. When he'd staggered into the bar, Lilly hadn't even recognized him, and by now he was more interested in her girls than his vendetta. Lilly kept buying him drinks, and even stored his sea bag behind her bar.

The next thing he knew, he was on a bed in one of her upstairs rooms, with a fat bitch of a woman removing his clothes. As she pulled off his boots, he came to life and kicked her in the face. Staggering to his feet, he saw all his money and personal effects on top of the nightstand. He shouted and yelled at her, and heaved her head-first through the closed room door. That was when the big burly bouncer barged in and beat the shit out of him. The next thing he remembered was waking up face down in the mud hole and being dragged down the streets by the Constables.

"That bitch got everything. What the hell do I do now? I have nothing!" wailed the Mate, with dried blood and mud still on his face.

Gus looked him over and felt sorry for the lad. "What's your first name?"

"Leonardo," he answered. "Why am I being held in this shit hole of a jail?"

"Disorderly conduct and vagrancy, to start with," the Sheriff said.

"Leonardo? What kind of name is that?" Lightfoot asked. "How much money did you have on you, kid?"

"Sixty dollars, give or take. What's going to happen to me now?"

"We're going to get you cleaned up for Judge Bean and then have another talk with Lilly at the pub, to see if we can get your bag back," the Sheriff answered.

Gus looked at Sheriff Chance, "I've got an idea. Let's fill out a summons for Lilly to show cause before Judge Beans at 3 o'clock. Then we'll go see her again, with me carrying a length of chain and a padlock. Maybe a few white lies might help her find the truth."

While the Sheriff and Gus revisited Lilly, Lightfoot prepared to take the kid to the local bathhouse to get him cleaned up.

"Take him to the barn first, and get some overalls on him,

before he's seen in public," Sheriff Chance had instructed Lightfoot.

At the baths, Larson never stopped talking and swearing. He had an abrasive personality and Lightfoot soon regretted his assignment.

Arriving at the Pub, the Sheriff and Gus found Lilly cleaning up the back bar, but she wasn't nearly as cordial as before.

"What the hell do you want now?" she demanded as they walked up to the counter.

Gus put the length of chain on her bar top and said, "Sorry, Lilly. We're going to have to close you down."

"You can't do that," she protested, a surprised look on her over-painted face. "Christmas Eve is one of the busiest nights of the year? Why all this trouble now?"

"Five years ago, you shanghaied a young man from this pub. Last night, you waylaid that same young man and robbed him of his sea bag and money." Sheriff Chance said and placed the summons on the bar. "You can show cause before Judge Bean at 3 o'clock today."

Lilly smiled. "The Judge is one of my back-door clients. I don't think he'd be happy with me telling the town about his many visits. He won't close me down."

The Sheriff slid the summons across the bar to her. "Have it your way. We'll tell him of your attempt to blackmail him. He hates folks who shanghai sailors from our docks. Be at the Courthouse at 3 o'clock or we'll have your doors padlocked by 5."

Lilly kept glancing at the length of chain on the bar and the angry faces of Gus and the Sheriff. "Wait a minute, boys. Is this all about that lad in his skivvies? He came in last night drunk as a monkey and kept spouting vulgarities that were driving off my patrons, so I had him thrown out. It was as simple as that."

Gus glared at her with his one eye. "Yes, *after* you stole his sea bag and poke."

She shook her head, fear showing on her face. "I had nothing to do with any shanghaiing. Yes, I may have sent some young men out to the ships for parties, but I had nothing to do with what happened to them out there. I swear that's the truth."

"What did you spike his drinks with?" Gus asked, flipping the paddle lock on his index finger.

She looked away, not sure how to answer. "Just some laudanum. Nothing to hurt him."

"Well, if you want us to go away, give us back his possessions," Gus demanded.

She scowled at the men, shaking her head. "You two are just bullies with badges." But she lifted a canvas bag from behind the counter and placed it on the bar.

"And his poke," Gus said. "He told us he had sixty dollars."

"He's lying. There was only forty dollars," she answered, opening her cash drawer.

"Make it fifty and we're gone," Gus said firmly.

"And if you ever shanghai another sailor again, I'll close you down permanently." Sheriff Chance added.

"And a Merry Christmas to you, Sheriff," Lilly replied angrily, counting out the money.

When they returned to the office, Lightfoot was still at the bath house, and the Sheriff was called away soon thereafter. As Gus waited, he emptied the kid's sea bag onto a table and snooped through its contents. There wasn't much: a few wrinkled uniforms, some underwear, boots and his rain gear. But at the bottom of the bag he found a broken, hand-carved wooden flute and a tobacco tin that rattled. Opening the tin, he found different coins and paper money from all around the world. That was when he noticed a pewter medallion attached to a bronze chain. As he looked at both sides of the coin, his mouth dropped open. He examined the coin a second time, with the same results. Then he put the medallion into his pocket and closed up the tin, with a smile on his face. Packing the other contents back into the bag, Gus knew what he had to do next.

When Lightfoot returned with Leonardo, Gus couldn't believe his eye. Still wearing the dirty overalls from the barn, the kid looked human again. His body was free of mud, his face was clean-shaven, and his wavy hair combed and trimmed. The kid was as happy as a clam to see his sea bag waiting for him. Quickly, he changed into one of his uniforms and soon looked like the Merchant Sailor he was.

When Sheriff Chance returned, he had papers in hand. He had talked with Judge Bean and explained to him that Larson had been a guest of Lillys the night before and had taken some medicine before retiring. This medicine had caused him to sleepwalk, and he had fallen off the back porch and into a mud pit. But now, with the return of his bag and poke, he was all cleaned up and wanting to rejoin his ship, which was waiting in Portland. Being Christmas Eve, the Judge had agreed and released him from custody. Leonardo was free to go.

Lightfoot listened to the Sheriff's tale with a smile on his face. Then he chuckled and said sarcastically, "Can't believe Judge Bean fell for that line of crap. It must be a Christmas miracle."

"Yes, it is… a God-given miracle," Gus replied. "And there's more to come. Leonardo, why don't you join us for Christmas dinner tonight?"

Lightfoot's mouth dropped open. "Poppycock," he said. "I'm sure the kid has a better place to be."

"No I don't," Leonardo answered quickly. "Don't know much about this God stuff, but I would love to join you tonight."

At the appointed time that evening, the men climbed the steps of Roxie's home, carrying apple crates filled with Christmas cheer. Before their arrival, Gus had a long talk with Leonardo about his behavior in front of the girls. "These ladies aren't barroom wenches, they are our friends, and we respect them. Watch your tongue tonight. We want no vulgarities. If you'll just do this, you'll have an evening you'll never forget."

Leonardo promised to do so, although Lightfoot doubted he knew how.

On the front porch, they were greeted with a spectacular view of a rising blood-red moon glistening off the river. "Look at the size of that thing," Lightfoot said, with the reddish light dancing off his face. "Never seen such a moon before."

"God works in mysterious ways," Gus said, knocking on the door. "It's a reminder that God gave us his only son, Jesus Christ, as our Savior. Before this night is over, we'll all witness His Christmas miracle again."

Lightfoot frowned, but before he could say 'poppycock' again, the girls filled the doorway. They were all dressed up in their finest outfits, with colorful Christmas chokers around their necks. They were surprised to see the extra face, but gracious as always.

Gus performed the introductions, telling Leonardo that Lucy was their sister and Roxie was her teacher. He explained to the girls that Leonardo was a wayward sailor far from home and alone for the holidays. Lucy and Roxie gave the lad an enthusiastic welcome.

The girls had done a marvelous job brightening the house with Christmas decorations, including a tree festooned with popcorn strings and unlit candles. The entire house smelled like the evergreen and holly that adorned their table. Roxanne had even placed mistletoe above the entry to the dining room. The home was as festive as any of the men could remember, bringing back visions of their childhood pasts.

Being the contrarian that she was, Roxie's dinner was a surprise. While most people on the river would be feasting on seafood or game birds, Roxanne, was fixing a pot roast. As it cooked in her wood stove, the friends sat at the dining room table, drinking champagne and nibbling on nuts and greens.

The conversation was friendly, without any vulgarities, and with many reminiscences of Christmases past. Leonardo told stories of Christmas aboard his ship, while Roxie talked of her family and the great holiday meals they had shared. Only Lucy and Lightfoot were mostly silent to the subject.

As the table talk went on, Gus was about to burst with the miracle he had up his sleeve, so he asked Lucy to name the best Christmas present she had ever received. She thought for a moment and told him it was a stuffed doll her mother had made for her when she was a child. He asked the same question of Lightfoot, who answered that it was his first big-boy knife. Roxie said ballet slippers. Then came Leonardo's turn, and he said it had been a wooden flute his father made for him when he was a boy.

That answer made Lucy's green eyes twinkle. "My brother had a flute, too. I remember him playing it all the time."

"Did he play it on the Oregon Trail?" Gus asked her.

"Yes," she answered with a smile.

Gus turned to Leonardo. "Did you play your flute on the Oregon Trail?"

"Yes. It broke, eventually, but I've kept the pieces all these years."

"I know," Gus replied.

Leonardo looked at him, startled. "How could you know?"

"I looked in your sea bag and saw your broken flute," Gus answered. He reached into his pocket for the pewter medallion and placed it on the table. "That's when I remembered that the Larson family took you in on the Oregon Trail. Your real name is Fisher, Leon Fisher. Here's your trail medallion, and your sister Lucy here has one just like it around her neck."

With eyes big and tongues tied, the table went silent, with everyone staring at Leon. With her mouth open and her eyes dancing Lucy reached into her blouse. Removing her medallion on its rawhide string, she gave it to Leon. "You are my long lost brother and the answers to my prayers. Now *this* is my best Christmas present ever!"

He looked at the coin with tears in his eyes. "I thought you were dead with Mom and Dad. That's why I took the Larson name. This is a wonderment I'll never forget."

They got up from their chairs and went to each other for a hug full of tears. Even Lightfoot raised his glass with moist eyes and mumbled, "The Lord does work in mysterious ways."

Call it a twist of fate or an act of God, Christmas of 69 was a miracle that no one would soon forget. For the first time, Lucy had her entire family together again. And each of them would go on to make their own indelible footprints on shores of this river of redemption.

END

Interview 3: Heroes

Astoria, Oregon - October 1899

"So that's how we started out here on the river," Lucy said fondly. "We were just like thousands of other pilgrims that came here with high hopes and empty pockets. No one gave us a thing, and we didn't ask. We just heard the call of the Columbia and answered her call. My footprints were just a few million cans of Butterfly Seafood, while Lightfoot made his mark with his Thunder Timber business. And Gus became a famous drugstore cowboy and the Chief Federal Marshal for the Pacific Northwest. We each went our own separate ways while staying together as a family."

"Over the years, who made the most money?" The older reporter asked.

"I don't really know and we didn't count," Lucy replied. "In the first few years of his publishing contract Gus sold over three hundred thousand copies of his dime novels. While his books weren't of any great literary value, they sold well to the hayseeds looking for romance and adventure. And now with over thirty different titles in the series, some of his books are still in print today. But Gus didn't keep much of his book money. He shared his wealth as working capital with Lightfoot and me."

"Did being a dime store cowboy ever effect his reputation as a Marshal?" The young reporter Jimmy asked.

"No not at all," Lucy replied glancing at the fireplace clock on the mantel. "Over the years he built the Marshals office up from just a handful of Deputies to fifty Deputies today spread out in three states. He was the first Federal lawman to employ finger-printing techniques, and he pioneered using photography for mug shots and crime scenes. He also helped organize all the State Militias into National Guard units for local emergencies. He even got a mail-order law degree and taught his Deputies the law. Gus was an innovator, who never fired his pistol again in anger during his twenty-nine year career with the United States Marshall Services. "

"Did he ever marry Roxanne?" Hank Hawks asked.

"Thank God no," Lucy replied with a look of confidence. "They just weren't suited for each other. She was older than him and he was always gone. Then Roxie got involved with the Suffragette Movement, which soon included the Temperance Movement, and they just drifted apart."

Lucy heard the phone ring again out in foyer. "But didn't you marry Mr. Mitchel right out of high school," Hank asked with curiosity.

"Yes, Walter was a few years older than me. We had a good marriage and a wonderful son. But then came that tragic train accident and they both were taken away from me."

The parlor door slid open and in walked a young man in a blue jacket. He was handsome with sandy hair, a tall lanky figure and bright hazel eyes. He moved into the room and handed Lucy a slip of paper. "That was the lighthouse on the phone. His ship is crossing the Bar. Here's the name of the ship he's on."

Lucy read the note with a smile and replied, "The Brigade is coming home in style on the Battleship Oregon. Colonel Roosevelt must have had a hand in this."

"The ship should be here in the half hour," the young man said. "I'll get Pong to bring the carriage around. It's still miserable weather out there so bundle up tight."

Lucy stood up from her seat with pride on her face, "Let me introduce my son Gus Junior. He's been attending West Point for the last few years and has traveled out here to welcome his father home."

The reporters stood with bewildered expressions and shook hands with Gus Junior. "I had no idea you had a son," Jimmy Adams said.

"Neither did I," echoed Hank Hawks.

"Gus and I married right after the death of my family. That was almost twenty years ago. While our family and friends knew I had become Mrs. Savage, we tried to keep it private all this time because of the gossip it might stir up. Now with the Majors return and Junior graduating soon from West Point, we are full of pride and have nothing to hide."

"Are you boys coming with us to the reception?" Junior asked.

With a new understanding of the Savage family story, both reporters nodded and started gathering up their notes.

In the early evening gloom, with rain drops dancing on the canvas of the carriage, Pong maneuvered the four-up team of horses down the hill to the city center. Inside the cab, the two reporters sat across from Lucy and Junior, all bundled up in their coats and with umbrellas in hand.

"You didn't say much about Lightfoot," Hank said looking out of the rain swept buggy window. "How did he make out?"

Lucy looked at them with a sad face, and then over the sounds of horse's high-stepping replied, "Clint didn't take to being a lawman like Gus. He hated the paperwork and all the rules. He resigned within a few months of taking the job. Gus was sad to see his backside go, but with his Thunder Timber business booming Gus knew it was the right move for him. After that, Clint started buying up timber contracts and building his own sawmills. Lightfoot innovated using water sleuths and log rafts and helped develop new methods for reseeding the harvested forest. He was a visionary in his own industry.

"Did he ever marry?" Jimmy asked.

Lucy forced a smile. "No, but as he got richer, he counted more ladies around his arm."

"Do you still see him occasionally?" Hank asked.

Jimmy shook his head sadly, "Being from Portland, you wouldn't know Hank. Ironically Lightfoot died in a forest fire about ten years ago. I went to his funeral when I was just a kid. He was quite a character around town."

"Gus and I buried him at the Ocean View Cemetery," Lucy said. "We also bought a family plot alongside of him. He was one of my brothers and we will remain together into eternity."

"What ever happened to Leon?" Jimmy asked.

"My brother Leon and I have remained close. His life is at sea. He has risen through the ranks of the Merchant Marines and now has his own ship."

The carriage turned on Exchange Street and as it approached the Odd Fellows Hall they could see a long line of people waiting in the rain with umbrellas open. It was a gloomy windswept evening and this crowd had come out to welcome their men home from the Philippines.

"We are going to use the rear entrance Mother," Junior said with his pocket watch in hand. "That way you and Father can have some time together. The doors don't open to the public for another fifteen minutes.

With umbrellas up they entered the backdoor of the Odd Fellows Hall and found themselves inside a dark cloakroom. Junior guided his mother to an interior door and opened it a crack. "He's right outside this door Mother. I'll stay here with the reporters. You wave at me when you are ready." They hugged and he opened the door.

Lucy took one hesitant step at a time and walked into the large empty hall with dewy eyes. Once inside she found a bright light focused on a flag draped coffin in front of the hall. On top of which she could see Gus's Army uniform, all pressed and neatly folded, with his forage cap and eye patch on top. She knelt alongside the coffin and put her hands on the flag. That's when she noticed that his gold-leafed Majors insignia, pinned to his hat, had been replaced with a silver-leafed insignia. Colonel Roosevelt had promoted Gus posthumously to Lieutenant Colonel. She nodded and sobbed touching his hat. Then she placed her hands on the silver cremation urn resting next to his uniform and ran her fingers gently across the engraved inscription. She forced a smile with tears on her cheeks. "Welcome home Night-Eye," she mouthed with silent words as she draped her Oregon Trail medallion on his urn. "You were always my first love," she said with a sobbing voice.

Gus Junior held the cloakroom door open a bit, so the reporters could watch Lucy by the coffin. They had been caught off guard with the decorum of the reception.

"When was he killed?" Hank whispered to Junior.

"Three weeks ago in Manila," he whispered back. "He died from malaria and was cremated there because of the tropical heat."

"When did your mother find out?" Jimmy whispered.

"Two weeks ago Colonel Roosevelt called her on the phone. When she learned that Gus died from malaria her reply to the Colonel was classic: 'There isn't a bullet made, a knife sharp enough, or a vial of poison strong enough to kill my Night-Eye. No, he had to die from an invisible stealth virus that no man could see coming.' Roosevelt answered her back with great sympathy: 'Sadly in war, death comes in all seasons for all reasons. So celebrate his life and the courage he had to live it.' That's what the Colonel had engraved on his urn."

"What will Lucy do now with him gone?" Jimmy whispered to Junior.

"Bury his ashes next to Lightfoot, with *her plot* waiting between them."

BOOK END

Acknowledgments

Writing a novel like 'Call of the Columbia' would have been nearly impossible without a gifted supporting cast that helped my storytelling take shape. As with all of my historical novels, I let my characters move the story, while history dictates the direction and substance. COC is generously sprinkled with kernels of historical truths and glimpses into another time and another place, when work was hard and life was cheap.

During the writing of this novel, I am grateful to have had a wonderful team of professionals, friends, and family who helped and supported my efforts.

Judith Myers, my story editor, has collaborated on all my novels. She has a magic touch with language and is a joy to work with. Judy knows my writing weaknesses and somehow, like an anchor, she can reel me back into a safe harbor.

And many thanks to my proofreader Kate Miller who provided a second look at punctuation, and enthusiastic feedback on story development. Her comments and thoughtful observations were invaluable and deeply appreciated.

I also wish to thank the wonderful people at the Coos Bay History Museum and Fort Umpqua for sharing their valued expertise. They helped me plant the seed for this story. And to fellow author Jan Bono for helping me with my opening poem.

My wife, Tess, has always been the first to read my stories and provide non-stop encouragement and unwavering support. Her constructive feedback keeps me focused, and her heartfelt enthusiasm keeps me hopeful.

Having said all this, it's my name on the title page, and I am responsible and accountable for every word. Any errors, mistakes or misinterpretations, are solely mine. With that said, I enjoyed writing this book to the last word!

Colonel Roosevelt and his Rough Riders July 1898

About The Author

Brian D. Ratty is a retired media executive, publisher and graduate of Brooks Institute of Photography. He and his wife, Tess, live on the north Oregon Coast, where he writes and photographs that rugged and majestic region. Over the past thirty five years, he has traveled the vast wilderness of the Pacific Coast in search of images and stories that reflect the spirit and splendor of those spectacular lands. Brian is an award-winning historical fiction author of eight novels and the owner of Sunset Lake Publishing. For more information: www.DutchClarke.com

USS Battleship Oregon (BB3) 1896 - 1956

Other Books by Brian Ratty

Lighthouses and their Keepers have gone the way of the blacksmith and the milkman. Nevertheless, the weathered relic one mile off shore of Oregon's Tillamook Head reminds us of the once-powerful sentinel Tillamook Rock Lighthouse and her seventy-seven years of service, keeping the sea lanes open and seafarers safe. This is the fascinating history and tales of the Tillamook Rock Lighthouse, tall, proud, and strong.

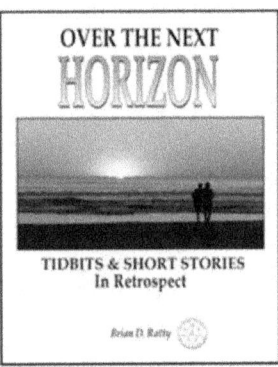

How do we know where we are going, if we don't stop and reflect on where we have been? Over the Next Horizon is such a moment in time. This uniquely different book is an assortment of photos, essays, articles, tidbits and short stories from award winning author Brian Ratty. He offers this gratifying volume as an introduction to his story-telling and as a handshake of appreciation to his readers.

Other Books by Brian Ratty

History and Adventure

WWW.Dutchclarke.com